D0828783

Sweet
Southern
BAD BOY

MICHELE
SUMMERS

sourcebooks
casablanca

Published by Sourcebooks Casablanca, an imprint of Sourcebooks, Inc.
P.O. Box 4410, Naperville, Illinois 60567-4410
(630) 961-3900
Fax: (630) 961-2168
www.sourcebooks.com

Printed and bound in Canada.
MBP 10 9 8 7 6 5 4 3 2 1

Chapter 1

IF IT WEREN'T FOR CRAZY, CRAPPY LUCK, KATIE MCKNIGHT wouldn't have any luck at all.

Until today.

Excitement coursed through her as she put her car in park. Leaning forward to see through the bug-spattered windshield, she stared at the old white farmhouse with a wooden front porch and rusty swing. In the distance stood a picturesque barn with a fading red roof and yellow doors. Katie smiled and started to hum: *Nothing could be finer than to be in Carolina...*

When she'd gone looking for the perfect location for a horror miniseries, she'd had no idea she'd find it in rural North Carolina. Where she was exactly...she wasn't sure. But the fresh, crisp air smelled country. Not salty from an ocean breeze on the coast where her dad had requested she go—*ordered* her to go would be more accurate.

Katie scooped up the manila folder housing the McKnight Studios contract. Her cork wedges hit the packed-dirt driveway, and she straightened her stiff spine. Hours of driving had taken their toll. Her knees gave a loud squeak. At twenty-eight, wasn't she too young for creaky knees? Her limbs loosened as she moved toward the ideal location. Her insurance for her future career at McKnight Studios. Her last shot before Daddy gave her the ol' heave-ho. The late-April midday sun cast a glow over the house as if it were wearing a halo. Blooming daffodils and colorful tulips lined the walkway. Katie sighed with pleasure. Of course, they'd be replaced with something more sinister, like thorny bushes. Minor details. Shouldn't be a problem.

The wood steps gave an eerie moan as she climbed to the shaded porch. The breeze had picked up, and the dark-green swing to her right groaned in the wind, causing a shiver to run down her spine.

This house was perfect.

The gnarled oaks lining the winding driveway would look especially creepy in the autumn after their leaves had fallen. A few trees might need to be cleared out to make room for the equipment and portable trailers, but it shouldn't be too noticeable.

"Here goes nothing." The screen door gave an ominous groan when she pulled it open. Katie rapped the sweet bunny-shaped wrought iron knocker on the pale blue door. "Nothing some bloodred paint and a ghoulish head knocker couldn't fix," she murmured to herself. Easy solution. Faint voices could be heard drifting from the back of the house. A dog barked, and then Katie heard the squeal of a child. She jumped at a loud thump, followed by the sound of breaking glass. Katie wondered if something sinister was already taking place inside.

"Pixie, no!" a strong male voice yelled from behind the door. "Donald, put down Lollipop and go find Danny."

Katie leaned closer to the door, trying to pick up the conversation. More scuttling and dog barking. It didn't seem anyone had heard her knock over the ruckus building inside. Covering the knocker with her hand, Katie rapped harder the second time and listened to the rever-beration through the house.

"Fuh—Hold on a minute," the male voice called. Suddenly the front door flew open, and Katie stumbled back. A small boy wearing only Pull-Ups and a backward baseball cap stood inside the door, with what looked to be blue slime covering one hand, hugging a well-loved stuffed bunny with a missing eye and matted hair.

"You not s'ppose to touch kitty's butt," the little blue-eyed urchin said.

"Uh, okay. That would probably be a bad thing." Katie smiled, hoping the horror she felt on the inside didn't show.

"Danny! Get away from that door." Katie glanced up at the rough, deep voice that almost knocked her flat. The little boy, Danny, scooted away from imminent danger. Wise kid. On the other hand, not-so-wise Katie stood frozen to the spot.

She had lost the ability to speak, or maybe she'd just swallowed her tongue. Because she couldn't have scripted this any better, even in her most fantastical dreams. Before her stood a beast of a man with wild dark hair and piercing black eyes. His worn chambray shirt hung unbuttoned over a well-defined, muscled chest, and his jeans had that lived-in, faded, authentic look that Hollywood spent thousands of dollars trying to copy. *Zing* went Katie's insides. There was nothing phony or surgically enhanced about this scary pirate looming in the doorway. And then her eyes widened at the fluffy black kitten with snow-white throat cradled in his big hand, licking his index finger as if it were made of catnip.

"Thank God you're finally here." Pirate Man moved back, making room for her to enter. Katie glimpsed large, tan bare feet. "Come in, and I'll give you the lay of the land. I'm late for a meeting. The agency said you'd be here an hour ago." His deep, smoky voice held an underlying layer of Southern twang. Totally authentic. Something most Hollywood stars couldn't seem to harness no matter how much they paid their speech coaches. Nothing worse than a cringe-worthy, fake Southern accent on the big screen. Hmmm, maybe she could get her dad to sign this guy. New, raw, *real* talent…her dad would be thrilled.

"Um." Katie stepped onto knotty pine floors into a gracious foyer. Beyond the painted staircase to her left, a white fluffy dog barked and scampered down the hall.

"Come back, Pixie." Danny stretched out a slimy hand and chased the dog as it disappeared into the next room.

"Danny's three. And there's Donald, he's seven, and Dover, who's five," Pirate Man said as he gently dropped the kitten onto a pink, furry kitty bed beneath the stairwell. "The kitchen's this way." He moved easily, stepping over Tonka trucks, police cars, action figures, and various discarded articles of clothing. Mostly kids'. With the exception of the oversized sweatshirt and huge pair of Nike tennis shoes. "The agency said you cook and clean, and I hope that's true, because we've been without help for…er, a while."

Holy freakle! He wasn't kidding. The kitchen looked like a mad scientist lived there. Spilled bowls of cereal covered the scarred farm table. Milk slowly dripped on the black-and-white vinyl tile floor. Beneath her shoes was the undeniable crunch of chips and crumbled cookies. The smell of burnt toast hung in the air. Dirty dishes filled the porcelain farm sink that sat below a large double window. Pirate Man rinsed his hands under the copper faucet and dried them on a red-and-white-checked dish towel looped over the gas oven door. He had a Jack Sparrow vibe going, minus the dirty dreads, gold teeth, and aversion to personal hygiene.

"Sorry it looks so bad. I'd love to stay and help, but I'm seriously late for an important meeting, and I can't seem to find my shoes or my notes," he said, somewhat distracted. "I won't be long, and Donald can tell you where everything is." Again, she was struck by his voice with its relaxed, languid pace. A girl could get silly and lose her head over a voice like that.

"Uh, Mister—"

"Uncle Vance! Danny's shoving a peanut butter sandwich inside the DVD player again." Another half-dressed boy ran into the kitchen, wearing pajama bottoms printed with green and yellow trucks. He stopped, blinking big blue eyes up at her. His dark hair stuck up at odd angles, and peanut butter and jelly covered both cheeks.

"*Shi*—ucks. Donald! Get off the computer and grab Danny," the boy's uncle yelled. "Dover, this is your new nanny."

Katie's head jerked as though she'd been doused with cold water. Nanny? *Hashtag: not-on-your-life*. "Mister–"

"You don't look like a nanny," Dover said, gaping at her with a toothless grin.

"Dover, go find Donald and Danny. Hurry, I need to leave."

"Uncle Vance, Danny wants to go outside," the older boy, Donald, said as he sauntered into the kitchen, playing a hand-held electronic game, not looking up. His long UNC T-shirt hung just above scabby knees.

The white fluffy dog scampered into the kitchen, followed by Danny, who was still wearing the backward Durham Bulls baseball cap, Pull-Ups, and nothing else. "Pixieee!" Danny squealed.

The dog started barking, and suddenly all three children chased it around the kitchen table, screeching at the top of their lungs. The kitten joined the fray, barely escaping death by trampling, and Pirate Man squeezed his eyes shut and rubbed his forehead as if in pain. The noise escalated until Katie couldn't hear herself think. She shoved her thumb and index finger in her mouth and let out a piercing whistle.

Everyone stopped. Dirty little faces stared up at her, and even the pets cowered under the kitchen table, not making a sound. The kids' uncle recovered quickly and displayed a brilliant smile, flashing strong white teeth against his scruffy morning beard.

"Cool. Where'd you learn to do that?" he said in his mesmerizing husky voice. His measured soft speech with the almost nonexistent *r*'s tingled her spine.

"Older brothers. Now about this nanny thing…" Katie tore off several paper towels from a roll tacked up under the upper cabinets. She dampened them at the faucet and motioned for each dumbstruck child to come forward. Scrubbing the breakfast grime from their cherubic faces and the blue goop from the little one's hands, she said to their uncle, "My name is Katie McKnight, and I have a proposition for you."

He was shoving his cell phone in his back pocket when he glanced up with a startled expression.

"Proposition?" He looked interested, but not in the way Katie wanted. She had a feeling he had something more prurient in mind by the way his dark eyes roved over her, stopping at all her very, very hot points. Her spine tingled again. *J. Lo's bootay*. This was not going the way she'd hoped.

"You wanna hold my kitty?" Dover asked, breaking the trance between her and the scary, but mostly sexy pirate/rock-star/badass guy. "Her name is Lollipop."

"Sure." Katie cuddled the chubby kitten in her hands as she gave their uncle a sympathetic look. Clearly this man was in over his head. Time to take charge. "Um, boys? Why don't you get dressed while I talk with your uncle? Okay?"

Pirate Man looked up from the stacks of papers, seemingly pleased with her suggestion, and nodded. "Donald, Dover…do as she says. And help Danny." He indicated the toddler with a jerk of his head.

All three boys scampered off, and the dog followed, nipping at their heels. Katie tucked purring Lollipop into the crook of her left arm and extended her right hand. "Katie McKnight. And you are?"

"Vance Kerner. I'm the kids' uncle." His big hand engulfed her small palm. And for the briefest second, Katie felt connected…to what, she had no idea. The feeling was foreign and even a little frightening. He shook her hand slowly and gave her a piratical grin. Like he could chew her up and spit out her bones in no time flat. Katie was shorter than he was by four or five inches, but she was by no means petite. More on the heavy side, as her willowy size-two mother constantly pointed out.

"Is there a Mrs. Kerner?" she asked, needing all the decision makers to be present and in agreement with her proposal.

"Only my sister-in-law. My mother died fifteen years ago," he said in a matter-of-fact tone, but something flickered behind his dark eyes.

Lollipop stabbed at the tail of her braid, and Katie shook her hair loose, along with the wayward thoughts inside her head. "Oh, well, then I'm sorry, er, about your loss. Mr. Kerner, I'd like to talk to you about using your house to film a miniseries."

"Excuse me?" His dark eyes narrowed, sending a fissure of alarm down her back. This had to be karma or the perfect storm, because not only did he own the ideal house, but he could star in the horror series about disappearing teenagers in love.

"Yes. I'm from Santa Monica, and I'm a location scout for McKnight Studios, and I'd like—"

He gave his thick black watch an irritated glance. "You're not from the agency, and you're not a nanny." He started buttoning his shirt in agitation. Disappointment washed over her; she hated seeing his glorious chest disappear behind clothing. She had no business dreaming about his chest or any other part of his anatomy. But she was female, and at the moment, everything female about her liked everything male about him. *Think business, Katie. Not body.*

"If you could give me five minutes of your time, I'll be happy to explain and—"

"Look, Kat, I don't have five minutes." He slipped a

piece of paper from under a plastic hamburger magnet on the refrigerator and started to dial his cell. Katie listened as he barked at some person at the nanny agency. She set the kitten down on the faded green oval rag rug in front of the kitchen sink. From the gist of the conversation, she gathered no nanny was coming today, and Mr. Kerner was not happy.

"Dammit. I can't believe this bullshit," he muttered, texting as he cursed. "Listen, I hate to cut this visit short, but I need to pack up Larry, Curly, and Moe, who are probably playing in the toilet this very minute, and rush to my meeting," he said, shoving papers and folders into a brown leather satchel sitting on the seat of one of the kitchen chairs.

Katie stood on top of mashed cereal and some sort of sticky substance, watching Pirate Man hunt for his misplaced shoes. Her timing sucked—again. He was in no mood to hear her offer, and once he left, she wasn't sure he'd let her back in again. This called for some quick thinking and a solution he couldn't refuse.

"Uh, excuse me? Mr. Kerner, I understand that you've got somewhere very important to be, and um...I don't. So I'd be happy to babysit your nephews while you attend your meeting," she offered, hoping this would buy her some time and maybe win him over.

He looked up with startled eyes as he shoved his foot into a brown leather loafer he'd located inside the tall wicker basket of assorted balls next to the kitchen door.

"What'd you say you did again?"

"I'm a location scout, but I have experience with children. I majored in elementary education at UC Berkeley."

He hesitated, but Katie could tell by his desperate expression he really wanted to accept her fabulous offer. He warred with needing to go and being a responsible uncle.

"I assure you, I'm normal as baseball, apple pie, and Chevrolet, and the kids will be perfectly safe." She reached inside her handbag and fished for her business cards. "Here. That's all my information and my cell number. You can call the studio if you want to check."

He took the card and read it. "Thanks," he said, slipping it in his back pocket.

"Now, if you'll give me your information, you can get to your meeting, and I'll tend to the kids." She gave a nervous glance toward the back of the house where she heard loud banging and the sounds of a TV. Vance got busy scribbling his information on a piece of scrap paper. "I'm actually pretty good with kids," she said, smiling, hoping to reassure him—and herself—as he handed her the paper. "You, on the other hand, have the handwriting of a psychopath," she murmured, trying to make out his chicken scratch. "Is that a five or an eight?"

He chuckled. "Eight. Sorry. I'm a writer, but I do it all on the computer. Penmanship was never my strong suit. Are you sure you want to do this? I won't be long. Just a couple of hours, and I'll pay you when I get back."

"That won't be necessary. All I want in return is fifteen minutes of your undivided attention." *And the use of your house for the next eight months*. She'd get to that later. Katie picked up his satchel and handed it to him, escorting him to the door, acting as if she owned the place. "Now, make that meeting, and don't forget to come home," she half teased but actually meant it.

"Call me if you need anything. Donald knows where everything is. Oh, and Danny sometimes eats the dog food and drops the kitten in the toilet, so you might want to watch out for that." Katie's face must've registered shock. "Not to worry. No one has gotten sick, and the kitten hasn't drowned…yet. Thanks again. You're a life-saver." And before she could react, Pirate Man cupped the back of her neck and pulled her in for a quick, hard kiss. Katie's knees almost buckled, and her mind went blank. This must be what it felt like to be kissed sense-less before walking the plank.

Chapter 2

SNAP! KATIE JUST GOT SWOOPED. AS IN SWOOPED OFF HER feet by a kissing pirate! She stood rooted to the spot in complete shock where Vance Kerner had laid a big, warm kiss on her. Her. Katie, the runt of the McKnights. Good-looking, albeit slightly scary men didn't go around kissing the black sheep of the McKnight family superstars.

She watched as he drove away in a weathered black pickup truck. Vigorously shaking her head, she wondered if she'd been dropped from the sky into the mystical world of Harry Potter. Nothing seemed real in this place. Wherever *this* was. Especially that lip-tingling kiss that had shocked her from the roots of her hair to the balls of her feet. Not because she'd never been kissed, but because she'd actually *felt* something. From a complete stranger. More than she'd ever felt from Tad, her boyfriend. Oops, slight mental lapse. Technically, she and Tad were *on a break*, going on four months now. He'd wanted the break, testing Katie's ability to stick and make the most of her opportunity at McKnight Studios. He needed to know she could commit to something before he made the ultimate commitment to her. Clearly, her track record had been spotty at best, according to her parents and Tad. Squeezing her eyes closed, Katie had to agree.

In her defense, the right job opportunity hadn't come

along. Over the past two years, Katie had worked with her dad's studio as production runner, production assistant…even boom operator, but nothing seemed to be the right fit. And at the end of each job, she always found her way back to her parents' formal living room, sitting on the uncomfortable straight-back chair with the scratchy mohair cushion, listening to the same lecture over and over again: She needed to get serious and make something of herself. Majoring in elementary education and teaching school had been a "whim," according to her parents, and not a very smart one. No child of Walter McKnight would choose a career with a history of paying such a low salary. Teaching did not spell *success*. All McKnights thrived on monetary success. And Katie would be no exception.

The weight of her handbag suddenly felt like too much, and her shoulders drooped. Katie dropped it onto the old, painted green chest next to the front door. Glancing at her face in the bark-framed mirror, she was shocked at her well-kissed lips. She touched the tip of her tongue to her bottom lip and then jumped a foot in the air. Loud screeching, as if the house was on fire, could be heard through the foyer, followed by splashing noises.

"Snoop Dogg! Not on my watch." Katie whirled around and ran toward the back of the house, expecting the worst but hoping for the best.

———

"You okay?" Mike Clancy asked, sitting in a navy business suit, his clear blue eyes clouded with concern.

Vance nodded, but the inside of his head was

screaming *hell no*. He hesitated, gripping the ceramic coffee mug. He sat in a small restaurant in downtown Raleigh across from Mike, his agent and friend, who appeared sympathetic and confused. Mike was beginning to doubt. The signs were all there. Mike kept checking in three and four times a day, asking if Vance needed anything. Doubting Vance's ability...his talent. Why now? He had been on such a roll. Vance ground his back molars as the answers to his persistent questions eluded him.

"What, man?" Mike asked in a low voice. "You look like you're in pain."

Vance took a fortifying gulp of his strong black coffee, then looked Mike square in the eye and told the lie that kept repeating itself over and over in his mind.

"I'm great. Perfect. Everything's fine. Well, as fine as it can be with my brother's kids underfoot." And his deadline weighing on his shoulders like a Sherman tank.

Mike raised his blond eyebrows. "I understand it's hard taking care of kids and trying to write, but you *are*"—he mimed typing with his fingers—"writing, aren't you? Deadline is in four weeks, and you're meeting it. Right?" Mike dug into his chicken Caesar salad. It was Saturday around one, and Vance had been over an hour late to this meeting because of the kids and the no-show nanny. Vance glanced at his black Victory watch, a gift from his brother and sister-in-law for making the *New York Times* bestsellers list. He hadn't heard from Katie McKnight since he'd bolted, and that had him worried. Yes, he had jumped at her offer because he had needed to make this meeting, and he had needed to get away from the kids. And yes, she had looked reasonable, capable, and…available. Not to mention, cute as hell and totally seductive. A groan of pain escaped his lips.

"Taking care of Eric's kids is stressful. Can't you get some help?" Mike said around a mouthful of salad. "How long are they staying with you?"

What had possessed him to hire a perfect stranger to watch Eric's kids? If word got out—and it would, because he lived in Harmony, North Carolina…home of the gold-medal gossipers—he'd be committed to the loony bin. And to add a whole heap of crazy on top, he'd gone and kissed her. Christ. He'd kissed a complete stranger and then left her at the mercy of his brother's wild, unruly rug rats. Shit. She was probably tied to a tree and being used for target practice at this very moment. No question…he was losing it.

"How long?" Mike asked again, giving Vance a strange look.

"Oh, um, another four weeks." Vance needed to get out of here and save Kat. His phone buzzed with a text message, and he flipped it over to read.

U might want to buy new TV remote. Drowned in toilet. Need more disinfectant wipes. Katie. ;-)

Vance texted back: R u ok??

Fine. U owe me a new pair of shoes.

Damn. Vance didn't want to contemplate what the kids had done this time.

"Shit. That's not good. Not good at all. You need to make this deadline," Mike said, referring to Vance's four more weeks in purgatory. Mike stopped stabbing at his salad. "Who's watching the kids now? You manage to get another nanny?"

Not exactly. "Temporarily. This gal happened to stop by and volunteered when she realized the predicament I was in. Apparently, she's a location scout from California and wants to talk to me about using my house for some movie or show. I don't know. I didn't give her a chance to explain." Vance shoved a French fry in his mouth but tasted only cardboard. "Now you know what a bad uncle I am."

Mike laughed. "I don't think you're a bad uncle. I think you're a brave one. I wouldn't take my sister's kids if you offered me skybox seats at the Super Bowl. No way."

Vance grinned, remembering Mike's niece and nephew he'd met on a few occasions. They definitely made his monsters look like angels.

"How did Gloria break her legs?" Mike asked, referring to Vance's sister-in-law, who was presently laid up in bed with two broken legs and three broken ribs.

"Skiing with Eric. She hit a patch of ice and took a nasty fall. Broke her legs and ribs, sprained her wrist, and bruised some internal organs."

"Man, that has got to suck. I know she's frustrated as hell. And your brother's doing another tour in Afghanistan?"

"Yeah. He's in charge of training and advising Afghan partners. When he asked if I'd take the kids, I had to say yes. Gloria can't exactly chase after three monkeys with her legs in casts and her arm in a sling." Too doped up on painkillers to put up any resistance, Gloria had agreed to the arrangement. But once her head cleared and the painful reality sank in, she realized it was for the best. She needed rest and therapy, and that wouldn't happen with kids crawling all over her.

Mike drained his glass of iced tea. "And who's looking after Gloria?"

"Her girlfriends are taking shifts helping her out. It's too much for her parents. They're getting on in years. Her mom's hands are full with her dad. He has trouble getting around. I drive over on the weekends whenever I can and let Gloria visit with the children." Gloria and Eric lived in a small, three-bedroom house in Greenville, South Carolina, four and a half hours from Harmony. Road trip from hell with three screaming kids, barking dog, and adopted kitten.

Vance had convinced Gloria it'd be best if he took the kids to his much larger home so he'd have a place to sleep and work and the kids could roam and play without bothering her. He had temporarily enrolled them in second grade, kindergarten, and pre-K so they wouldn't get behind in school.

"So, how'd you get lucky with this babysitter?" Mike had finished his salad and waved the waitress over to refill his iced tea. He wasn't from the South, but he'd acquired a taste for the South's addicting elixir: sweet tea made with simple syrup.

"She knocked on my door. I was expecting a nanny from the new agency. But I'm beginning to suspect that Larry, Curly, and Moe have scared away every nanny within a thirty-mile radius. I'm running out of options. This is the third agency I've tried. Anyway, this gal said she'd help out if I agreed to listen to her proposition." Vance could think of only one proposition he'd like to hear from Kat's watermelon-pink lips, and it didn't have anything to do with making a movie set out of his mother's one-hundred-year-old family home.

"That's pretty wild. You can make a shitload of money renting your house to production companies. A friend of mine rented his beach house for a movie and made forty thousand dollars in three days."

Whoa. That *was* a shitload. But Vance wasn't exactly hurting for money. His books had done pretty well. And he still collected rent from neighboring tenant farmers who used his land for their crops. Besides, the idea of strangers roaming through his family home and all over the grounds bothered him. Even though he didn't have much family left these days. Eric hadn't lived in the house since enlisting in the Army right out of high school. And his dad...Vance knew, the way he knew the covers of his own books, his dad would go ape-shit ballistic at the intrusion. His dad didn't own the farmhouse, but he did own some of the property. The farmhouse had belonged to Vance's mom, and she'd left it to her sons. Eric and Gloria had chosen to live closer to Gloria's parents since they had kids and Eric was often deployed. So, that left Vance. And his reclusive dad who remained holed up in his barnlike house on the edge of the property.

"Did the babysitter tell you what studio she was from?" Mike asked, breaking into his musings.

Vance shrugged. "Her name is Katie McKnight." He fished for her business card in his back pocket. "Yeah. She's with McKnight Studios," he said, reading the bold print.

"Let me see that." Mike reached for the card. "Unbelievable. This must be Walter McKnight's daughter." A big smile spread across his face. "Do you know what this means?"

"Not exactly, but I have a feeling you're going to enlighten me." Dollar signs spun around Mike's blue eyes, and Vance sensed he'd be playing a role in whatever scheme his agent was hatching. Mike's boyish good looks deceived a lot of people, coming in handy during negotiations and giving him the advantage. He could swim with the meanest pool of sharks and emerge victorious.

"You have no idea how long I've been trying to get in front of Walter McKnight or anyone at the studios. I'm talking movie rights to *your* series. This could be huge." Mike spoke faster and faster, his excitement escalating.

That would be the series Vance couldn't seem to finish. The one where he'd lost his desire to write and his inspiration to continue the story of the soldier who could. *Honor Bound* and *Without Honor*, his first two books in this series, had been bestsellers, but recently, he'd lost his mojo. He just wasn't feeling it for the last one, titled *Honor Is Dead*. And it scared the living shit out of him. He thought of his contact for research, Adam Reynolds, sitting in the metal folding chair at Helping Comrades, his support group, struggling to overcome his flashbacks of incoming mortars during his deployment, admitting his weakness and how he self-medicated with alcohol to help numb the memories.

Mike's words brought him back to the present. "Look, this could be a huge break, putting you in the big leagues. Skyrocketing your exposure and career." Mike leaned closer. "And the money ain't so bad either."

Again, Vance didn't have money woes, but he knew the exposure could go a long way toward boosting his career. Other authors would give their right arm to sign a movie deal. This opportunity didn't come along every day.

Mike had been talking projections and numbers when he finally said, "Listen, whatever you do, don't let go of that girl. She could be our golden ticket."

"I don't think Katie's planning to hang around to babysit the Three Musketeers." Not that he'd blame her. Those three devils could make a saint weep. "When she finds out I'm not interested in renting my house to a bunch of Hollywood weirdoes, I think she'll pretty much hit the trail."

Mike pulled out his tablet and started tapping. Without looking up, he said, "I understand that you might not want to rent your house, but at least hear her out. You know, stall a little. Let her think you're really interested. Whatever it takes. Use your bad boy charm. Girls love your badass tortured image. Is she attractive?" Mike waved his hand dismissively. "Doesn't matter. Don't scare this gal away. Not before I've done some research and made a few calls." He continued to tap notes onto his tablet as if the world's safety depended on him.

Vance pressed his back into the dark-green vinyl booth and crossed his hands behind his head. Bad boy... not lately. Tortured? Absolutely.

"Okay, I'll stall, but you better dig up whatever you're looking for fast. I don't want to lead her on any longer than necessary." However, he wouldn't mind leading her straight to his bedroom, but he didn't think the offer of sleeping with her was on the table. And how pathetic that he'd consider sleeping with a stranger from Hollyweird. Cute stranger, but still. He needed to do something about his dateless, colorless life. He'd had plenty of opportunities but never took the time. No more. Vance smiled, remembering the dumbstruck faces of the kids when Katie had whistled. Her face had been flushed, and her pretty eyes had sparked to life. He had to hand it to her…Katie had spunk.

—∿—

After his lunch meeting, Vance drove the twenty-minute ride back to Harmony from Raleigh. Deciding he needed to pick up food to feed the growing clan at his house, he hurried into BetterBites on Main Street. His good friend and old high school buddy, Brogan Reese, owned and operated the health food store. The fresh smell of baked bread hit him the minute he stepped onto the repurposed-wood floors. Customers bustled about, shoving fresh, organic foods into their baskets. Business had not always been booming. Brogan had gone through a rough patch, trying to get the small-minded residents of Harmony to accept his healthy way of eating. But he'd found a jewel in Lucy Doolan, who had helped him with marketing and made a success of this location. Brogan and Lucy had a strained history, but they'd overcome it and now shared a sweet baby girl who would one day be breaking hearts like pretzel sticks.

"Hey, Vance. What brings you in?" Brogan asked, coming around the cashier counter and clapping Vance on the back.

"Need some dinner for my ankle-biters. Have any of that homemade mac and cheese?"

"Sure. How 'bout some fresh-baked rosemary chicken and our sautéed green beans?" Brogan suggested as Vance followed him to the cooler with the ready-made meals.

"Sounds good. Add some sourdough bread, chocolate chip cookies, and a coconut cream pie." Vance didn't know anything about Katie McKnight, but he thought homemade desserts might go a long way. With a good bottle of wine.

"Coming right up," Brogan said as he placed the food packages in a green shopping basket.

Vance wandered over to the wine section and selected a dry Chardonnay. "How's that cute baby of yours?"

"Charlotte is cutting teeth again, which means our precious angel has officially left the building."

"Sad to say, but I can relate, and I haven't even fathered any yet," Vance said in sympathy. "Why don't you bring Charlotte over so the kids can play?"

Brogan laughed. "Aren't your hands full enough?"

"Yeah, but it's not like one more kid is going to make a difference. Bring Parker along. He can ride herd." Parker was Brogan's seventeen-year-old nephew. He and Brogan had become very close over the last couple of years.

"Sounds like a great idea. Parker needs community service hours for high school. Babysitting small-children-gone-wild has got to qualify." Brogan chuckled, ringing up Vance's food. Vance placed the wine bottle on the counter and reached for his wallet when the front door blew open.

"There you are. Thought I saw your pickup truck in the lot." Vance and Brogan both looked up at Dottie Duncan, standing by the entrance in Carolina blue cowboy boots, tight jeans, blue vest with pink ruffles, and a scowl on her face. "Did you know your kids are running around bare-assed nekkid, chasing some poor girl with the garden hose?"

"Seriously?" Vance asked, not quite believing Dottie, since she tended to spread a little gossip along with a whole heap of trouble.

Dottie stomped forward, glaring at him as if he were the perfect imbecile. "Vance Kerner, you've got your head so stuck in your books, you don't know what's going on around you," she accused. "I'm tellin' you those wild young'uns of yours were chasing some pretty girl, screaming at the top of their lungs. What's going on over there? Is that your new babysitter?"

A few shoppers stopped to hear what Dottie had to say…not that she ever said anything in a quiet voice. Vance gripped the edge of the cashier counter to keep from clapping his hand over Dottie's big mouth.

Brogan finished bagging his groceries and started to chuckle. "What *is* going on over there, Kerner? New babysitter or new girlfriend?" he asked, being a smart-ass.

"Did you say *girlfriend*?" Dottie boomed loud enough for the entire county to hear.

And that was all it took; the Harmony crazies started babbling out both sides of their mouths.

"Vance, you got yourself a girlfriend?"

"'Bout time…Candy Lou and I wondered if you might be light in the loafers."

"What's wrong with his loafers? They look fine to me."

Vance scowled at Brogan and grabbed two bags of homemade granola and shoved them in the bag. "On the house. Thanks for being a fucker," he said under his breath, and Brogan howled with laughter.

"Girlfriend or not, you need someone to take care of things." Dottie Duncan, the scariest broad in town, shook a long, light-blue nail at his face. She owned the Toot-N-Tell, a drive-up convenience store with sixteen locations across the state, which made her one of the richest women in the state and also one of the nosiest.

"How you feeding those kids? And keeping up with the laundry? That house of yours probably looks like Grant took Richmond." Dottie cocked her platinum-blond head and narrowed her overly made-up blue eyes at him. "Your mama is probably turning over in her grave. God rest her soul."

At the mention of his mom, Vance's heart constricted into a painful knot. She'd died when he was in high school, and things had never been the same. Eric had taken off and joined the Army, and Vance's relationship with his dad had gone from barely tolerable to who could remain silent the longest. But Dottie couldn't be more wrong about his mom. She would've loved Eric's kids running around underfoot and making messes. Then cuddling up next to her at night for homemade sugar cookies and the reading of *Goodnight Moon* for the millionth time.

Vance wrapped his arm around Dottie's plump shoulders and squeezed. "Listen, little mama, if my living conditions distress you, then come on down and lend a hand." He winked, flashing his sexiest grin. Dottie grew flustered, and her monstrous chest heaved.

She swatted at his midsection as a blush crept up her neck and inflamed her rouged cheeks. "You don't need another mama. What you need is a *wife*."

"You took the words right out of my mouth," Brogan

added with a shit-eating grin. Vance discreetly flipped him off with the hand behind Dottie's back. The last thing he needed was all the matchmaking mamas hustling up girls and hauling them out to his place. Until he'd staked his claim on Lucy, Brogan had had his fair share sniffing around his store when he first moved back. And Keith Morgan, the ex-professional tennis player married to Bertie Anderson, had had hordes of them showing up at his house when he first moved to town. It was like a damn singles parade down Main Street. Vance planned to avoid that unwanted attention at all costs.

Which was why he then said the stupidest thing imaginable. "That girl is from Hollywood. She wants to use my house to make a movie. And I need to get home to turn her down—"

Dottie's eyebrows rose, and Brogan's jaw unhinged and hit the countertop.

"A Hollywood movie?"

"With Brad Pitt and George Clooney?"

"I could be the leading lady!"

Putting up his hands, Vance scanned the screwy, yapping shoppers. "No. Look, everyone…there's no movie. You've misunderstood. I'm—"

"Vance Kerner, you think we're buying this baloney you're selling about a movie? Why don't you save those wild stories for your books? I think you're shacking up with some out-of-town filly." Dottie gave him the don't-mess-with-me look. "I'm gonna be watching you," she warned, fists planted on her generous hips.

He was a bonehead. Dottie wouldn't be the only one watching. In about five minutes, half of Harmony would be gossiping, tweeting, texting, Facebooking, and emailing about his *new filly*, and he wouldn't hear the end of it until he'd reserved the Methodist church for the ceremony and booked the community center for the reception. And the other half of Harmony would be spreading rumors about George Clooney coming to town. Vance shuddered, thinking of the lengths this town would go to to catch sight of a movie star.

Dottie picked up one of Brogan's specialty bags of granola and flipped it over. "Humph. Still a rip-off," she said, indicating the $7.95 price tag. She dropped the bag back in the display basket and huffed her way out of the store.

"Damn, Kerner, now you've got her all riled up again. She's gonna run around bashing my granola to anyone with ears," Brogan complained.

Vance scrubbed the back of his neck. Dottie Duncan and her partner in crime, Miss Sue Percy, Harmony's most notorious gossip, would be talking about more than expensive granola. Like movie stars, flowers, and wedding cakes...not necessarily in that order. He needed to warn Kat. Then he needed to stall until he'd heard back from Mike.

"What is wrong with this town and its obsession with marrying everyone off? It's like the worst *Bachelor* show on meth," Vance said, shaking his head.

Brogan nodded. "Shee-it. Don't I know it!"

Chapter 3

"K-k-k-atie...I'm home," Vance called out as he pushed open the front door, carrying his purchases from BetterBites. He hoped Kat hadn't flown the coop, or worse...called the authorities. It had been over four hours since he'd left. She hadn't texted to complain, but still, Vance deserved whatever crap she chucked at him. Just inside the door, he stopped to listen.

Something was off.

Blissful silence filled the air. Vance sniffed, detecting the scent of Pine-Sol. He moved easily through the foyer. No navigating toys or clutter on the clean wood floors. "Donald? Dover? Where is everyone?"

As he approached the kitchen, Danny scampered out. "Uncle Pance. You bring me kitty?"

Vance bent down and scooped up Danny. "No, baby. No kitty." And that was when he noticed the pink shirt, flowered jeans, and baby-blue tennis shoes. "Who dressed you?" he asked, entering the kitchen, where he came to a complete halt, almost dropping the toddler. "What the fuh...funny bone?" The countertops were clear of all food and piles of junk. The old farm table had been wiped clean, and he could actually see the scarred surface. Froot Loops and potato chips no longer littered his tile floor, and his feet didn't stick to its surface when he walked. But even more surprising than a spotless kitchen were the kids. Donald wore yellow rubber gloves up to his elbows, with his hands submerged in soapy water at the sink, and Dover held a Swiffer as he dusted the shelves of the robin's-egg-blue hutch that housed his mother's collection of antique creamware. The more valuable pieces had been moved to the top shelves for safekeeping, but Dover uncharacteristically dusted in slow motion, careful not to break anything.

"Hey, what's going on? What did you do with my nephews?" he asked half-jokingly and half not. Danny squirmed in his arms, and Vance put the toddler down.

"Kay-tee gave Pixie baf," Danny said.

"Really? Donald, where's Katie?" Vance asked, almost afraid to hear the answer.

Donald looked over his shoulder, still soaping up a large pot. "She went to change her clothes."

Vance cringed, remembering Dottie Duncan's tale of naked kids chasing Katie with a garden hose. "Uh, did she happen to get wet today?"

"Soaked."

Vance whirled around. Katie stood in the kitchen doorway. Damp hair slicked back in a smooth braid accentuated her widow's peak. She'd changed into threadbare jeans and an oversized, gray UC Berkeley Golden Bears sweatshirt. Her face shone squeaky clean, with the barest hint of pink gloss across her lips. Lips he remembered tasting with perfect clarity.

Vance swallowed…hard. She'd been pretty before in her skirt and top with designer shoes and handbag, but now…now she looked fresh and bright and lovely. He cleared his throat. "I see you survived, and by the looks of things"—he gave the kitchen another once-over—"you've performed a miracle. Do you walk on water too?"

"No, but I run through garden hoses." She bent down and clapped. "Come here, sweet pea." Danny skipped toward Katie with outstretched hands. "By the way, are you aware Danny is a girl?" she asked, scooping his niece up in her arms and resting Danny on her hip. "I mean, it took me awhile, but after the third and final accident, I gave her a bath, and imagine my surprise at the discovery." Katie gave Vance a droll smile.

"Girl? No way." Confusion colored Katie's pretty brown eyes. Vance bit back a laugh. "Danny? Are you a silly girl?" He chucked his niece under the chin.

"No! Girls are dum-dums," Danny yelled, making Katie stare at them both in shock.

"See? She says she's not a girl."

"You've got to be kid—"

"Where's Pop? I want my kitty, Kay-tee," Danny interrupted.

Katie arched an eyebrow. "Lollipop is sleeping. We need to let her rest. She's had a traumatic day." She examined Danny's face as if looking for signs of mental damage. "Danny, sweetie, I'm a girl, and I don't think girls are dum-dums," Katie said in a soft voice.

Danny shook her head so hard her wispy blond curls flew around her head. "I no girl. I gonna be foo-ball player like Donald and Dovey." Vance grinned, and Katie rolled her eyes.

"Katie, we've finished cleaning. Can we go watch TV now?" Donald asked, removing his rubber gloves.

She redirected her attention to his nephews. "Only after you both take baths."

"Then can we have dinner and go to bed?" Dover

asked with way too much excitement for a kid who hated anything to do with bedtime.

Gobsmacked. Vance shook his fuzzy head. If Michael Jordan, the greatest basketball player to walk this green earth, appeared in his kitchen and asked him to shoot hoops, he wouldn't be more surprised. "Seriously, what have you done with my nephews? These two look like my nephews, but they aren't behaving like them." Vance began to wonder if she held mystical powers and had bewitched the entire household. He was starting to feel funny himself. Like hot under the collar—and a few other places.

"It's called the reward and incentive program," Katie said, padding across the clean floor in tan flats. "Working with a lot of entitled actors, you tend to understand this program quite well." She wiped down the water near the sink with a clean kitchen towel. "The kids and I had an eventful day, and now they will reap their reward, right?" Both Donald and Dover nodded, wearing big smiles. "Okay. You know what to do. Shoo fly. And don't be all day about it."

Before the boys bolted from the kitchen, Vance held out his hand. "Whoa, hold up there. What's this great reward you're getting that you've cleaned house, and now you're willing to clean your bodies without the usual whining and bellyaching?" he asked the aliens inhabiting his nephews' bodies.

"It's a surprise," Dover announced.

"We don't want you to know yet. And don't come upstairs." Donald pulled on Katie's hand. "Make him stay here, okay?"

"I don't know, guys...don't you think she's too small

to take me? Besides, she's only a girl." He winked at Katie's flushed face.

"She's tough, Uncle Vance. She wasn't even afraid of Mr. Cornwaddle's mean dog. She shooed him away with a big stick," Dover said, pride coloring his voice.

A smile started to curl Vance's lips. He wished he'd been here to see Katie take on old man Cornwaddle's half-blind, crippled, toothless golden retriever. Colonel hadn't retrieved anything in years, much less frightened any humans.

"Well, good thing Katie was here to protect you. Okay, I won't peek, but hurry, because I've brought home a good dinner." Both boys bolted from the kitchen, making loud boy noises as they bounded up the stairs. Vance reached for Danny, who was squirming in Katie's arms. "Miss Dana Sue, you have a surprise to show me too?" He kissed her soft hair and breathed in her baby-girl scent. "It's amazing how much better they smell when they're clean." He smiled at Katie, and she started to pull groceries from the green shoppers. "You want to watch a movie?" he asked Danny.

"Can we watch *Fwozen*?" Vance tried to keep his smile in place at the mention of his most hated movie, only because he'd seen it four hundred times in the last two weeks.

"You can watch *Frozen*. Uncle Vance needs to help Katie." Or get blasted by Katie, who appeared to have been holding her tongue. Very patient woman, this Katie. Vance admired her calm demeanor.

After settling Danny in the playroom to watch her movie, Vance returned to the kitchen. The table had been set with mismatched blue and white transferware, all left over from when his mom was alive, and Katie was preheating the oven for the chicken, mac and cheese, and green beans.

Vance hesitated, watching Katie hijack his kitchen. "Sorry I was late and you got dumped on today. I know they're more than a handful."

"Well, I'd be lying if I said those kids weren't a challenge, but once I established who was boss, we were fine, all things considered." She handed him Danny's sippy cup filled with milk, and Vance placed it on the table.

Not sure what to do next, he watched Katie puttering around the kitchen like she'd lived here for years. *Unsettled* didn't begin to describe the feeling crawling inside him. "Well, I'd like to pay you for today and whatever a new pair of shoes cost." Vance went to the desk drawer where he kept his checkbook.

"That won't be necessary. But you did promise to listen to my proposal. I'd like to talk to you after the kids have eaten."

He looked up with checkbook in hand. Katie averted her gaze and bent down to put the food in the oven. He'd promised he would listen to her nutty idea about using his house, but he had no intentions of agreeing. He had a book to finish. Four hundred eighty-five pages weren't going to write themselves. And at this rate, he'd never get it done. Babysitting three kids and two animals, school drop-offs, pick-ups, cooking, cleaning—well, he'd been slack in that department—and helping with homework sucked all his time. Single parenting had to be the hardest job on earth. His appreciation for what Gloria did without any help from Eric grew each minute.

With a deadline looming, he didn't have the time or the patience to monitor a movie crew running roughshod all over his house and grounds. He couldn't get a moment's peace as it was.

Mike didn't understand. He assumed Vance was almost finished and would be turning this book in on time. What Vance had failed to tell Mike was he was suffering from a paralyzing case of writer's block and he really, *really* didn't want to write this book. The subject matter brought back too many bad memories, and Vance didn't have the stomach for it anymore. Adam Reynolds's strained face and tired, blank eyes flashed through his mind. A bead of sweat trickled down his back.

The thought of turning the first two books of this series into movies held serious appeal, but not if it meant losing control over content. Historically, books had been much better than their movie counterparts, and Vance would hate to see Hollyweird turn his into some sappy, tug-at-your-heartstrings, banal war story with no vision, originality, or grace. On the other hand, if he could control and oversee the screenplay, then he could be sure the movie portrayed his intent. And maybe his dad would watch the movie, because he sure as hell never bothered reading Vance's books.

And maybe…maybe he'd finally accept Vance's apology.

He gave his head a vicious shake. Back to Katie. He'd listen to her pitch, and then he'd shoot her down nice and easy without scaring her off until he'd heard back from Mike. Katie had stepped outside the kitchen door and returned with a fistful of white daisies she arranged in an old blue mason jar. Vance remembered his mom doing the same thing for their dinner table, and his heart squeezed into a tight ball.

"Don't you think you're getting a little carried away?" His voice was harsh.

She gave him a startled look. "Hmm? What do you mean?"

"I mean, we don't need flowers on the table or cloth napkins or any other decorative crap. It's just dinner with three runny-nosed brats." Katie flinched as if she'd been stung. Vance immediately felt like an ass, but dammit, his home was turning into a 1950s television show, complete with Ma in her pearls and Pa with his pipe. He couldn't play house in *Leave it to Beaver*'s world and write about death and gore and war at the same time. He should be locked in the barn with a bottle of scotch, his coveted Cuban cigars, and some beef jerky, watching videos of war footage, writing his next thriller. And Katie needed a little shove out his front door and back into her old Mercedes parked in his driveway.

He fished for his chiming phone in his jeans pocket and read the text from Mike. Publisher loves idea. Don't lose that girl. She's our ticket. Do whatever it takes... Vance suppressed a groan. Well, that certainly settled things. Time to convince Katie she wanted to stick around Harmony for its unique small-town charm, because no way in hell was he letting her movie crew anywhere near his house.

Katie started to gather her handbag as if she meant to leave. "Whoa, where you going?" He moved to her side; she smelled of orange blossoms. Drawn to her unique scent, he leaned toward Katie as if sniffing flowers from the tree…light and sweet. Vance gritted his back molars. He was losing his man card, and it had to stop.

She shot him a wary look. "This has been a long day…for both of us. If you'll tell me where the nearest motel is, I'll leave you alone with your family. We can talk in the morning."

"No. You can't leave. We haven't had dinner, and I bought wine…and desserts." *Smooth, Kerner, real smooth.* Vance maneuvered his way around to blocking the exit from the kitchen. "Besides, you haven't told me everything that happened around here. And what about your proposition?" As his voice lowered, Katie's brows rose.

"It's a *business* proposition. Not"—she fluttered her hand—"whatever you're thinking," she said with starch in her voice, lifting her perky, delightful nose.

"And just what am I thinking?" He couldn't stop his suggestive tone, staring at her lush, watermelon lips. They had tasted as juicy as they appeared.

"Something that would no doubt land on the cutting-room floor." She squinted her brown eyes at him. His laughter filled the kitchen, and Katie's lips twitched, trying to suppress a smile.

"Do you kiss your girlfriend like you kissed me?" she asked, surprising him again.

Vance reached for her handbag and heard the inhalation of her breath as his fingers brushed the back of her hand. "Don't have a girlfriend." Yet. *Don't go there, Kerner.* Wayward thoughts of Katie's sumptuous mouth attached to her equally luscious body had no business clogging his already cluttered brain.

"Uncle Vance, is dinner ready?" He pulled back.

His nephews pushed past him with Danny tight on their heels, squeezing the life out of Lollipop with her pudgy hands.

<center>~~~</center>

Phew! Saved by the kids. Katie exhaled, locking her jelly knees. Almost swooped again by a charming, conniving, up-to-no-good pirate. She ducked her head and shoved her trembling hands inside the pouch to her sweatshirt. She would need all her wits to keep up with Vance Kerner, Hunk-o-Mania, who smelled earthy, topped with a tantalizing dollop of pure sin. Enough sin to make California girls fall for his Southern boy charm. Not this California girl. Nailing this location was imperative, and nail it she would as long as Pirate Man focused on some other booty...and not hers. Because when Katie set her mind to something, LA's famous Stack—the four-level interchange full of rush-hour gridlock—couldn't keep her from her task.

"Kay-tee, you sit by me," Danny said, sitting in her red booster seat, patting the chair next to her. Vance had placed the hot food on the brass trivets on the table. He tousled the boys' hair and shot her a risqué wink as he delivered the bread in a basket. *Shizzle!* What had she gotten herself into? This day had hurtled like a loose boulder gaining momentum into utter chaos. She'd been trampled, tripped, and hosed down—literally—with a garden hose. Her favorite pair of wedges was covered in North Carolina red clay. Now she was about to dine with Pirate Captain and his unruly crew. *Arrrgh.*

Through dinner, the kids filled Vance in on the she-nanigans that took place while he'd been away. Starting with the dunking of Lollipop in the toilet just as Vance had warned—thankfully, she'd remembered to remove the dog food bowl from Danny's sight—to "accidentally" falling down and getting covered in clay, which led to the cold dousing from the garden hose.

"Everyone was covered in mud. Even Pixie," Donald informed his uncle.

"I see. That's why Katie had to give Pixie a bath?" Vance asked as he helped Dover cut up his chicken.

"Pixie shaked"—Danny shook her tiny body in her booster seat like a dog—"and got Kay-tee all wet." Danny gave her a mac-and-cheese smile that Katie wiped clean with a napkin.

"And then Katie made us march and take orders like soldiers," Dover said around a mouthful of bread. "Or else," he added with great emphasis.

"Or else what?" Vance asked.

"Or else she'd make us rake the whole backyard all the way to the Cornwaddle fence and pick up sticks and stones," Donald said. "And we'd only get two five-minute breaks for water and stale bread."

"Like a chain gang!" Dover's eyes lit with the idea of working like state prisoners on the side of the road.

Vance stared at Katie in shock or wonder or both. Hard to tell behind his black eyes. "So, we're into corporal punishment?"

"Certainly not." Katie straightened her shoulders. "No pain would've been involved, and those little sneakers added the part about bread and water." She pointed an accusing finger at Dover and Donald. "I merely suggested that if they didn't help clean house, I'd find other more tiring chores for them to do." Vance's lips tipped in a sly smile. "Like raking, picking up sticks…that kind of thing."

"We helped clean house 'cause Katie promised us a really awesome surprise," Donald said, picking at his green beans.

"Sweee! Your belly's gonna smile, Uncle Pance," Danny squealed as she smashed beans into the mac and cheese with her hand. Vance smiled at her over Danny's head, making Katie's heart stutter.

"Eat up and drink your milk. After you've taken your dishes to the sink, you can show your uncle." Donald and Dover shoveled the last bit of food into their full mouths. "Two more bites, sweet pea." Katie held Danny's spoon to her mouth with a small piece of chicken.

Vance stopped with his fork midair as he seemed to be amazed by his nephews' behavior. "Are you some kind of Svengali?" he asked in awe.

"Hardly. My intent is not evil, if that's what you're implying."

"Evil, no. Crafty, definitely yes." Katie smiled at that assessment. She liked being considered crafty. Nothing wrong with being clever and adept at changing your situation. It did come in handy. And she'd actually enjoyed herself today—the ruined shoes notwithstanding. She loved working with kids and putting her teaching degree to use. It felt good. Right.

But her dad had never thought so. He had insisted she ditch her dreams of teaching and focus on a "serious" career. Like working under him, where he could criticize and lecture every step of the way. Katie loved her dad, but, quite frankly, being his only daughter and the youngest child was exhausting. And sometimes degrading.

Don't screw this up, Walter McKnight's voice said in her head. *I'm giving you one last chance. Don't disappoint me.* Katie had spent her entire life trying *not* to be a disappointment to her parents. But for some reason, they hadn't seen it that way.

Chapter 4

"YOU MADE THIS?" VANCE ASKED KATIE, REFERRING TO the layered tent made from quilts and blankets. After the kids had gobbled up chocolate chip cookies and carried their dishes to the sink, they rushed upstairs, pulling on Vance's hand to show him the surprise. And to his credit, he'd been genuinely amazed and pleased by their efforts.

"Well, I had help." Katie beamed at Donald and Dover. Vance set Danny down from his arms, and she scampered onto the pillows piled high beneath the tent.

"Heee! See my pillow." She smacked her pink pillow scattered with fairies before flopping on top.

Dover dug for his hidden flashlight inside his Spider-Man pillowcase. "We can read in the dark," he announced, flicking his flashlight on and blinding Katie with its beam. Vance crawled toward the tent on his hands and knees.

"This is seriously cool. Where'd you get the line?" he asked, referring to the rope holding the tent up.

"From the toolbox in the laundry room, and I helped Katie tie it to the top bunk bed," Donald said. The boys had helped her move the lower bunk so she could erect the tent.

"We have our games and books." Donald showed Vance his stack of books and Danny's LeapFrog game.

"And look, we hung paper stars and planets with dental floss."

Vance nodded in amazement. "You plan on sleeping here tonight? All three of you?"

"Yes-s-s, and Pop, too," Danny said, dancing in circles on top of the covers.

"Oh no. Not a good idea. Lollipop needs to sleep downstairs in the laundry room. You can play with her in the morning."

Danny stopped dancing and stared at Vance; her bottom lip trembled, and tears pooled in her big blue eyes. "N-n-n-o-o-o! I want Pop! I seep with Pop!" she screamed as she threw herself down on the covers and kicked her feet.

"Uh-oh. Dana Sue, do you remember what we talked about?" Katie dropped to her knees in front of the tent. Danny stopped kicking and looked up with a tear-streaked face. "Only stuffed animals are allowed in the tent. Here, take your bunny." Katie handed her the stuffed bunny with the patchy fur and missing eye. "No more crying, or we'll have to go to boot camp." Vance gave her an odd look, and Danny screwed up her face, seeming to measure Katie's words. "Okay, brush your teeth so you guys can hunker down for the night." Donald and Dover crawled out and hurried to the bathroom, but Danny didn't budge.

"I want Pop. No Floppy," she said, hurling the bunny at Katie's face.

"Hey, you know better than that, young lady," Vance said in a stern voice. Danny had worked herself into a fine baby fit and wasn't listening. "Come here—"

"No. Let me." Katie pulled Danny up by her arm.

"Time for boot camp." She picked her up by the waist and plopped her down on the carpeted floor away from the tent. Danny stopped crying and stared at Katie, her mouth hanging open. "You remember the rules?"

"I do jumpy jacks?" she asked in a tiny voice.

"Yep. Okay, here we go." Katie started doing jumping jacks as she counted. "One, two, three…come on, Danny, count with me."

"What the hell?" Vance mumbled as he stood and watched Danny jumping awkwardly, trying to coordinate her arms and legs. Katie slowed to match Danny's pace.

"Danny's in boot camp," Dover announced as he bounded back into the room from brushing his teeth. "Donald had to do ten push-ups, and I had to do fifteen sit-ups."

"Yeah, we were in boot camp after we ruined Katie's favorite shoes and tracked mud in the house." Donald ambled back into the bedroom with dark, damp hair sticking up from pushing his wet fingers through it.

"…nine and ten. Okay, good girl. Now, let's get dressed for bed." Katie bent down to pick up a puffing Danny when Vance intervened.

"Uh, I'll do that." He hauled Danny into his arms. "I'm exhausted just thinking about your day. Why don't you head downstairs and relax…put your feet up. I'll join you in a minute." Vance gave her a wide berth as he left the room to dress Danny for bed, as if she'd been dancing in nothing but her undies and lip-synching to Maroon 5. Katie shrugged; her techniques might be unconventional, but they worked. She tucked the boys in under the tent and said good night.

—◦◦◦—

It was past eight thirty when Vance finally got the kids settled down. They had Skyped Gloria so she could hear about their day and read them a story. Vance reluctantly descended the stairs. He dreaded meeting with Katie and listening to her proposal, because he'd have to act as if he was interested before turning her down. All without scaring her out of town until he'd gotten word from Mike. Even more, he dreaded telling her about the nosy, gossiping, marriage-minded, movie-crazed, good-hearted people of Harmony, who dreamed of stardom and Katie becoming Mrs. Vance Kerner. Not an ounce of reality to either scenario. But the damage had been done. He'd already checked Facebook on his phone and, sure as the sky was Carolina blue, there'd been posts about his new girlfriend and speculation on the wedding date. Along with false sightings of George Clooney and Chris Hemsworth strolling Main Street. Brogan, Lucy, and Bertie had tweeted six times already, stating they couldn't wait to finally meet the gal who'd captured his elusive, bad boy heart. Wanda Pattershaw, another local, outrageous friend, kept texting red hearts and stupid pictures of wedding cakes. His Twitter account was exploding with retweets and speculations from his followers. A marriage pool had started, and some of his vocal female followers bemoaned his almost-married state. If he could kick his own ass, he would for being so freakin' stupid.

Vance glanced at his phone again, reading Mike's most recent text. Got people working on this. May need Katie's influence w dad. Don't lose her! In other words:

lie. *Dammit*. He didn't need to babysit another person, and he certainly didn't need a fiancée. A nice long, sensual lay in his bed for a solid week would be the ticket, but again, he had gotten the distinct feeling Katie wasn't offering. Too bad. Because he liked her unique smell of orange blossoms and the way her eyes danced with laughter when she dealt with the kids, meting out discipline.

At the bottom of the stairs, Vance stopped. The sound of voices carried from the living room on his right.

"…I play tuba, and Opal plays piccolo. The smallest and the largest band instruments. Isn't that a hoot?"

"And we're both learning to twirl batons. I've only poked myself in the eye three times."

Too late. Word had traveled fast. The middle-aged Ardbuckle twins, Emma and Opal, stood in the center of the living room's green braided rug, wearing matching blue-and-gold band uniforms, talking to a stunned Katie.

"Nothing like good band music to liven up a movie, don't you think?" Emma or Opal said. Vance could never tell the identical twins apart, and neither could the rest of Harmony. When he cleared his throat, three sets of eyes swiveled his way.

"Hey there, you handsome devil. Isn't it exciting? Hollywood wanting to make a movie here in Harmony?"

"We've always thought Vance looked like a rock star, but, you know, he'd make a really good villain. Don't you think, Opal?" Emma said, nudging Opal with her elbow.

Opal nodded. "Put a gold hoop in his ear, and he could star in the next *Pirates of the Caribbean*."

"Thanks, but I'll stick to writing. How can I help

you ladies?" Vance would rather have angry fans hurl flaming books at his head. If the Ardbuckle twins had gotten word, then the remainder of Harmony was not far behind.

"Katie said she'd be happy to let us audition—"

"Um, not exactly." An uncomfortable Katie tugged on the bottom of her sweatshirt. The Ardbuckle twins gave her an expectant look. "The thing is, this miniseries has a real dark side about teenagers falling in love and then turning into zombies and going on a killing spree." Alarm washed over Opal and Emma as they clutched hands, and Vance couldn't quite blame them. Teenagers turning into zombies and going on killing sprees? Perfect. Just how he pictured his family home: covered with blood and guts and dead teenage bodies. Uh, hell no.

"You ladies are lovely, but I don't think this is the right show for you." Katie tried to put a positive spin on killing the twins' dreams of fame.

"Emma, Opal, would you like a slice of fresh coconut cream pie?" Vance moved deeper into the room, gesturing for his guests to take a seat. Not that he wanted them to stick around, but he couldn't squelch the years of ingrained Southern hospitality by not offering.

"No thank you, Vancy-Pancy—"

The twins giggled, glancing at Katie. "We used to call him that when we babysat. He'd run and hide. Didn't you, Vance?" Emma said.

He'd like to run and hide right now, but Vance pasted on a grim smile and nodded. And Katie coughed—or more like laughed—behind her hand.

"We were hoping to audition. What a shame," Opal said in a disappointed voice.

"We better get going." The twins hooked arms, wearing identical defeated expressions.

Katie appeared worried and said, "I'd still be happy to hear you play." Their heads popped up. "I've an idea...you can entertain the crew when they get here. You know, during lunch breaks and—"

"That would be marvelous," both twins squealed. "We'll be back to perform. Is tomorrow good?"

"Check with me first," Vance said as he efficiently ushered the excited twins toward the front door. "We need to make sure Eric's kids won't interfere...you know, with the performance." Lame, but his brain was fried, and he was running out of material.

Twin heads bobbed. "Excellent. It was nice to meet you, Katie," they called over their shoulders as Vance closed the door in their faces.

"Seriously?" His tone was incredulous, but before he could grill Katie, he heard a loud knock. Thinking the Ardbuckle twins had forgotten something, he pulled the door open.

"Hey, dude." There, smelling of sweat and grass, stood Clancy Perry, the stupidest tool in town. "I hear Hollywood is gonna make a movie here."

"No, you've heard wrong," Vance said, his teeth clenched.

Clancy pushed his way into the foyer and removed his battered straw cowboy hat. "That ain't what I heard. It's all over town. A movie right here in Harmony."

"It's not really a movie. It's a miniseries." Katie appeared by his side, and Vance wished she hadn't.

Harmony wouldn't distinguish the difference between a movie and a miniseries, because either one presented endless opportunities for fame and star status.

"Hey, there. You ain't from around here, are ya? I'm Clancy Perry." Clancy stuck his hand out, and Vance immediately hated the glint in his eyes.

"Katie McKnight." She shook Clancy's hand.

"You from Hollywood?"

"Santa Monica, technically—"

"Well, Katie McKnight...I'm your man." Clancy ambled closer to Katie, blocking Vance with his back. "And I'd like to audition for any and all love scenes. Especially if I get to make love to Carrie Underwood or Brooklyn Decker."

"Oh, well—" Her unease was visible as she glanced at Vance.

"You don't have to pay me or nothing. I'd do it for free. As long as the actress is smokin' hot." Clancy inched closer to Katie.

"Welcome to Harmony," Vance said to Katie's surprised or alarmed face—either would have been fitting. He clapped Clancy on the shoulder over his worn Skoal T-shirt. "Look, go tell everyone *not* to stop by, because there's not going to be any movie. Got it?"

"That ain't what I heard—"

"You're hearing it now." Clancy got that belligerent look on his face and was about to say something really stupid, when Katie hooked her arm through his and steered him toward the door.

"Mr. Perry, as soon as Mr. Kerner and I have ironed out all the details, I will personally let you know if there are any parts in the miniseries suited for you," she said to a goofy-smiling Clancy. "Thank you for stopping by and informing me of your availability."

Clancy shuffled his dirty cowboy boots on the wood floor. "Sure thang. Maybe you and me can talk over beers." He made a suggestive leer with his tobacco-stained teeth. "You ever ridden on the back of an ATV—"

"She's not available," Vance cut in as he tried shoving Clancy out the door.

"How do you know?" Clancy dug his booted heels in, preventing Vance from slamming the door in his face. "You ain't her boyfriend, you douche bag."

"Yes, I am. Now get the hell out of here," he snarled in Clancy's stupefied face. "And make sure you tell your brother, Clinton, too." Vance slammed the door so hard it rattled the frame.

Katie stood with crossed arms. Pointing a finger at her disapproving face, he said, "Don't give me that look. I did you a huge favor. Clancy and his brother, Clinton, are two characters you want to avoid. They don't run on all four cylinders. They trim trees for a living and have fallen out of more than I can count, which explains the brain damage."

Katie took an aggressive step forward. "I don't care about Clancy. You promised to listen to my proposal with an open mind. And now you're saying no before I've had a chance to explain." A wrinkle creased her brow directly below her widow's peak. "And I'm not your girlfriend, you…you *butthurt!*"

He was unable to form a coherent thought, and his pulse quickened as he stared at Katie's flustered face and heaving chest beneath her oversized sweatshirt. "Did you just call me *butthurt?*"

"Yeah. And I meant it." Katie whirled around and stormed away. "I'm outta here. But I'm coming back tomorrow to present my proposal, and you're gonna listen."

Snapping out of his stupor, Vance followed her to the kitchen. "Where're you going?"

"Hotel, motel, bus station. I don't know. Maybe I'll sleep in my car."

Katie leaving, even for one night, unsettled him. Vance didn't want her going. He didn't want her out of his sight. And he really didn't want to piss off Mike by blowing his chances of getting a movie deal for his books.

"Look, let me make it up to you. Don't go yet." Katie slung her handbag over her shoulder, a distrustful expression marring her pretty face. "Stay and have a glass of wine. I'll listen to your proposal"—she gave him a you're-lower-than-dog-shit look—"I promise. Scout's honor." He held up his fingers, wearing his most dazzling smile.

"I bet my new Nikon camera you were never a scout."

Vance chuckled, because Katie was as wise as she was beautiful. "What gave me away?"

"Only the pirate vibe with a side of badass you've got going." She flicked her hand in his direction.

"A pirate badass? I like it. Might use that in my next book. Thanks."

"I'm sure you have plenty of material to work with."

"Kat, sarcasm doesn't become you." Katie gave a loud snort. "You need to chill. You've had a rough day…believe me, I know. Taking care of my brother's kids is draining."

"The kids were fine. I enjoyed being with them." Her face softened at the mention of the hellions on wheels.

"Good. Good. Let's sit down for wine and dessert. BetterBites coconut cream pie is amazing. Okay?" He eased her handbag from her shoulder and placed it back on the countertop.

Katie checked her watch and gave a curt nod. "Ten minutes. Wine, but no pie. I can't afford the calories."

Relief flooded over him, because he didn't want her leaving angry…or at all. "Grab two glasses, and we'll sit on the porch. It's nice out tonight." He started uncorking the wine. "Wineglasses are in the cabinet above the silverware." Vance poured the Chardonnay in the glasses she provided. "I insist you try this pie. And you *can* afford the calories," he said, appreciating all her curves in all the right places.

A pretty shade of pink flushed her cheeks. "A very small sliver, and according to my mother, you can never be too thin," she mumbled.

Vance stopped, holding two plates of pie. "No offense, but your mother is dead wrong." Katie tugged on her big sweatshirt as if not to draw attention to her shape. And something told Vance she wore baggy clothes for that very reason, which was offensive on too many levels to contemplate. She withdrew as a shadow swept across her face. "Come on, K-K-Katie," he said to cheer her up. "We're gonna sit on the front porch, North Carolina style. And you're gonna eat pie and listen to chirping male crickets trying their darnedest to attract the womenfolk."

Katie raised a delicate brow. "If you write the way you talk, your books are in big trouble."

Vance grinned. She had no idea.

Chapter 5

KATIE SETTLED ON THE PORCH SWING NEXT TO VANCE Kerner, *New York Times* bestselling author. Yes, she knew who he was and what he wrote...thriller stories about war. She'd Googled him earlier. But she didn't feel compelled to fuel his already egoistical head with any more compliments. She'd recognized his book covers immediately, because her brothers had raved about them.

The porch swing groaned under their weight. The quiet April night settled around them like a soft baby blanket. Vance placed the pie next to the swing on an end table designed from a tree stump.

He kept finding ways to make contact, like when his fingers had brushed hers as he reached for the wineglass, or when he'd slipped her handbag from her shoulder. Katie knew his game. She'd been around enough slick Hollywood types to know when someone was pulling a fast one. And Vance Kerner was as slick as a whistle.

"Cheers. To crazy days and lazy nights." Vance clicked his glass against hers and then handed her a piece of pie.

"I'm going to regret this in the morning, but it looks too good to resist." Katie almost groaned in ecstasy over the delicious coconut and cream melting in her mouth. It had been ages since she'd indulged in something so decadent. Her mother's dire warnings of gaining weight played loudly in her head. Being overweight in Hollywood could destroy your career. Not that she had a career in the movies, but since she lived around movie stars, everyone got caught up in the land of human perfection…especially her mother. In the companionable silence, the horny male crickets serenaded with their chainsaw buzzing, and fireflies danced on the front lawn. Katie closed her eyes and simply breathed. The smells of spring hugged the air. Different from California. Here the earthy pungency mixed with honeysuckle, and spring blossoms created a sweet aroma in the simple darkness.

"Better?" Vance's voice mimicked the calm surroundings. But she knew better than to be lulled into a false sense of complacency. His sexy voice be damned. This was war.

"I'll be better when you agree to let me use your house." She met his gaze, catching him off guard; he appeared momentarily startled.

The Prince of Darkness heaved a huge sigh and leaned back, rocking the swing. "Okay. Lay it on me."

"Don't sound so excited. I wouldn't want you to burst anything."

"Now there's a phrase. Just what exactly are you referring to my bursting, oh Kat of mine?"

Katie bristled. His familiarity and sly smile unsettled her. "Don't call me Kat, and I'm certainly not yours." Her voice sounded prim and starchy to her own ears. Vance's sly smile grew wider. She gulped her wine for courage. *Now or never, Katie McKnight. Make your dad proud.*

"Your house and property are the perfect location

for my dad's new miniseries. As soon as you give your permission, I can FedEx the contracts back to California, and the crews can get started on transforming the place."

Vance took a long, slow sip of his wine, never breaking eye contact. Katie was no mind reader, but she sensed his dark look didn't bode well. "And this is the show about teenage vampires on a killing spree?" His silky-smooth voice got even silkier.

"Sorta. It's about this teenage girl named Alexis who discovers she has unusual powers, and she's being chased by the zombies of Squirrel Hollow and"—she gestured to the front yard—"your lawn would make the perfect Squirrel Hollow. Anyway, the zombies want to steal her powers, but she teams up with Evan, the teenage vampire who helps her, and they have to kill the zombies in order to be free." Vance continued to study her as she spoke, giving nothing away. "Uh, we would need access to the house and grounds to create their spooky world." Katie glanced at the dark oaks lining the driveway. "They might have to cut down a tree or two, because we need room for trailers, but they'll replant as soon as they're done filming." She glanced at the closed front door with the bunny knocker. "And we'll have to paint the door bloodred and change the knocker… things like that, but again, all that will be fixed when we finish."

For a solid minute, Vance didn't move a muscle. Katie began to fidget, waiting for his reaction. The longer he took, the more nervous she became.

Finally, he placed his empty wineglass down. "Aw, fuck no."

Okay, not exactly what she wanted to hear. "That's just a quick overview. The rest is spelled out in the contract, along with how much you'll be paid for leasing your property." Vance pushed his long fingers through his thick, wild hair, making it appear even more pirate-like. "Um, it's really a lot of money. McKnight Studios pays well on location," she said, hoping to sweeten the pot and remove the appalled look from his chiseled features.

"You've got to be kidding me. No freakin' way anyone is cutting down one-hundred-year-old oak trees on my property." His voice was gruff and irritated.

Obviously a deal breaker. "Well, there's certainly room for negotiations. Why don't you have your attorney look it over, and you can discuss it with the McKnight team." Spearheaded by her two attorney brothers. Katie was scrambling for ways to make this deal appeal to Vance.

"Kat, you appear to be a nice, sweet girl, and I'd love to do this for you because, well, you've been great, and the kids seem to love you, but holy shit… I can't wrap my head around a team of movie makers tromping all over my grounds, cutting down trees, and painting my door bloodred."

Katie jumped up from the swing and paced the length of the porch. "But there's room for negotiations. I'm sure if you specify no trees are to be touched, they won't touch them." She really had no idea. She was grasping at straws.

Vance rose slowly as if his back ached. "Look, Katie, here's the thing. I've got four weeks to finish three quarters of my next manuscript to meet my deadline, or my agent, not to mention my editor, is going to rip me a new one. And I've got three monkeys posing as kids sleeping upstairs who will be awake"—he glanced at his black watch—"in less than nine hours, which means my day will careen straight to hell from there. Just like every day for the last five weeks. In other words, the creek's rising, and I'm up to my ass in alligators. I don't have time to babysit kids and a movie crew at the same time."

"What will it take for you to agree?" Katie blurted without thinking.

Sparks shone in Vance's inky-dark eyes, and he shoved his fisted hands in his jeans pockets. "Aw, Kat. You don't want to know what it will take. And quite frankly, once I started, I'm not sure I'd be able to stop... with you," he rumbled low.

Smacksy. Katie stopped pacing at what he'd implied, and her pulse skittered for shelter as her heart took a big tumble.

The Dark Knight continued, "You see, as much as I'd like to help you so you'll stick around, I don't see how it's possible. I don't want to keep you from doing your job and finding another appropriate location." His silky drawl sucked all the air from her lungs.

A crazy feeling of doom came over Katie at the prospect of leaving. She barely knew where she was, but she couldn't see herself leaving...yet. And losing this location was not an option. She had to prove to her family she could do this job. Because she craved their approval. Yeah, way pathetic. Gnarly pathetic. Even at the ripe old age of twenty-eight, she hadn't figured a way out from under the pressure. Which was why the next words tumbled from her lips. "I'll make a deal with you." Sudden interest sparked his dark, devil face. "I'll babysit for the next four weeks so you can finish writing your book *if*"—Katie stood mere inches from Vance and poked him in his rock-hard chest—"at the end of those four weeks, you let us have access to your property to film the show."

Vance wrapped his callused palm around her hand. "I don't think you know what you're getting yourself into. There's gonna be crying, begging, and misbehaving—"

"I can handle the kids."

"I was referring to me."

Katie smiled. "I'm a big girl. I can handle you too."

"If only you would," he whispered, tipping his head. Breath unsteady, her lips parted...

His head popped up. "Mother fuh—" Vance pushed Katie aside and bounded down the front steps.

Katie blinked. *Beach bunnies!* He was a pirate with mystical methods of persuasion, and Katie should be tased for falling in lust. *Not smart, Kathryn Ann McKnight.*

She watched as a black SUV wound down the long driveway. Vance stood with hands splayed on his hips, glaring at his unwanted visitors. More eager Harmony citizens wanting to audition? Katie shook her head in disbelief. This small Southern town could be its own reality TV show.

—∿∿—

Vance frowned at the black Porsche Cayenne. It belonged to Keith Morgan, retired professional tennis player. Vance liked Keith. He was sharp, hard-working, and drove a lot of business to Harmony with his Keith

Morgan Tennis Academy and high profile. What he didn't like was Bertie, Brogan, and Lucy sitting in Keith's car, coming to call on him. More like spy, snoop, and give him grief over Katie. Damn small towns and damn social media. Worst combination ever.

"What's up, Kerner?" Keith called, climbing from his car and opening the back door for Lucy.

"Hey, Vance, how's it going?" Lucy Reese asked. "Brogan and I brought you some homemade muffins for the kids." She held a brown pastry bag from BetterBites in her hand. Nice cover. He'd bet his left nut they didn't all pile in a car and drive ten minutes from town to deliver baked goods. Brogan had jumped out from the passenger side and opened the back door for Bertie.

"Hey, handsome," Bertie said, gliding forward wearing a stylish yellow skirt with white top and blue geometric sweater. Bertie had the same flair for fashion as she did for interiors. She stretched up and kissed him on the cheek. "How you holding up?"

Keith shook Vance's hand, and Brogan followed, wearing jeans, a green BetterBites collared shirt, and a cocky-ass grin. Vance narrowed his eyes. He knew Brogan had gossiped like a seventh-grade girl and told everyone Vance had a woman stashed away. *Pinhead*.

"Great. What brings you guys out here?" he barely gritted between his teeth.

"Just a friendly visit…amongst friends. Speaking of friends, why don't you introduce us?" Brogan, the jackass, was enjoying himself at Vance's expense. He ambled toward Katie who, judging by her expression, thought they were all nuttier than a jar of dry roasted Planters.

"Hey. I'm Brogan Reese, and you are?" Brogan

extended his hand, and Keith, Bertie, and Lucy crowded behind him, peering at Katie as if she were the freak exhibit at the state fair.

Katie cleared her throat. "Nice to meet you. Katie McKnight from McKnight Studios out of California."

"My wife, Lucy"—Brogan put his arm around Lucy's waist as he smiled down at her—"and Keith and Bertie Morgan." Lucy and Bertie shook Katie's hand, trying not to gawk and blatantly check her out.

"Keith Morgan? Aren't you the Prince? I didn't realize you lived here now," Katie said, referring to Keith's nickname when he'd been on the pro tour.

"Yeah, I moved here a few years ago," Keith said.

"Not happily, I might add." Bertie gave Keith a cheeky grin. "But we managed to change his mind, and now he loves Harmony and wouldn't trade it for the world. Right, Prince?"

Bertie's expression dared Keith to disagree with her.

Known for his high intellect, Keith responded, "Yes, dear. Anything you say, dear." He kissed the top of her mahogany-colored hair.

Bothered by how severely he wanted to kick his friends off his porch and snatch Katie in his arms, Vance said, "Shouldn't you be home tending your kids? Potty training or telling bedtime stories?" He hoped they'd take the hint and get the hell off his property. Instead, Brogan chuckled and shook his head as if Vance might as well hand his balls over to be smashed with a hammer, because they weren't going anywhere except inside to get settled for a more formal interrogation.

"Maddie's babysitting." Lucy gave him a sly you're-busted look. Maddie was Keith's daughter from his first marriage. "Come on, Katie McKnight." Lucy slipped her arm through Katie's. "Let's enjoy Vance's wine while we get to know each other." Code for *we're going to grill you until you're charred*. Katie shot him a nervous glance over her shoulder.

"Crap," Vance muttered under his breath, climbing the steps.

"Charming, rock star. Now smile and quit scaring Katie with your badass, scowling face." Lucy, who never held her punches, knocked him in the gut with the side of her fist.

"Don't make me give you a noogie like I did in sixth grade. And don't think buffed Brogan can save you. I've kicked his ass too many times to count," Vance warned.

"Bullshit, Kerner. The only time I got whipped is when you didn't block worth a shit on the football field and got me sacked. You sucked, by the way."

Vance held the front door open and gestured for his nosy friends to enter. "You got sacked because you couldn't release the ball worth a damn."

"Enough! You testosterone-loaded morons. None of us cares, nor do we want to relive your glory days," Bertie said while Keith rocked with laughter. "Don't think you're off the hook; you're just as bad," Bertie huffed at her husband.

"Yeah, you're all legends in your own minds. Come on, Katie. We need wine to numb our brains," Lucy said.

Katie slid another nervous glance in Vance's direction and then followed a determined Lucy to the kitchen.

"I'm gonna need something stronger," Vance mumbled under his breath.

"Got your back, bro." Keith lifted a bottle of Mount

Gay rum in his hand. "All we need is ginger ale, and we're good to go." His smile held a hint of sympathy, as if he could relate to Vance's predicament.

Once settled in the large, clutter-free family room, thanks to Katie and her drill sergeant cleaning orders, Vance leaned back on the charcoal plaid sofa with a cool Mount Gay and ginger ale in his hand. He propped his feet up on the large brown leather ottoman and listened to Bertie and Lucy chatter while peppering Katie with questions about California. Katie answered, but in the short span of time he'd known her, he could sense her discomfort, her fear of offending with her answers. She answered questions about her family. Katie was the youngest, with two older brothers. Both her brothers had law degrees from Stanford and headed up the legal team for McKnight Studios. Katie made it sound as if she didn't measure up.

"My dad and brothers really love the studio and making movies. It's all they ever talk about." She chuckled, but Vance didn't hear the humor. "When you grow up around it, I guess you take it for granted." She shrugged.

"I'm sure. But to us, it sounds so glamorous," Bertie said with a genuine smile. "Tell us about this movie in Harmony. We're dying to hear all the details." Bertie sat between Vance and Keith on the sofa, while Lucy squeezed next to Brogan on the oversized, gray lounge chair angled toward the TV. Katie sat perched on the single armchair, facing them, back straight, knees pressed together as if on trial in front of a jury.

Keith controlled the remote for the flat-screen TV mounted on the wall, switching between a tennis match and an NBA game, with the sound muted. Vance wished he could crank up the volume and drown out this next conversation.

"It's a miniseries. Not a movie. Probably something your teenagers would like more than you."

"Does it star Zac Efron? Because Maddie is wild about him," Bertie said.

"Please… I'd like to go a day without hearing about that teenage heartthrob," Keith said in disgust. "Him and One Direction. Maddie has plastered the inside of her closet with posters of that lame band."

Bertie laughed. "Because you wouldn't let her put them on her bedroom walls."

"And you would? I don't think so, Miss Control Freak Designer. You won't even let me display my trophies."

Bertie whirled on Keith, eyes blazing. "That is not true. I'm redesigning your home office, and all your trophies and awards will be on full display when I'm finished. I only packed them away so Harry wouldn't get into them." Harry was Keith and Bertie's very active, three-year-old son. Vance knew firsthand what kind of trouble he got into.

"You're an interior designer?" Katie asked with renewed interest. "I've always found that fascinating."

"Yeah, but we want to hear about this miniseries. Who's starring in it? If you say Ryan Reynolds or Bradley Cooper, I'm gonna faint right here on the spot," Lucy said.

"Or Patrick Dempsey or Hugh Jackman. Lordy!" Bertie fanned her face with her hand.

"Uh, are we invisible?" Brogan gestured to Keith and himself. "Is this your way of telling us we haven't been doing our husbandly duties?" he asked, his tone incredulous.

"I thought you were happy. You acted happy just this morning…multiple times," Keith said, leering at Bertie.

"And what about this afternoon in my office…on top of my desk? Weren't you *happy*?" a grinning, confident Brogan asked Lucy.

Blotches of red bloomed on Katie's perfect cheeks. Vance hurled a Nerf football he'd found under a sofa pillow at Brogan's head. "Shut the frick up. Don't ruin my one evening with adult company, spewing horseshit. No one's interested in your exaggerated sexual prowess, Reese. Morgan I might believe after maybe six more strong drinks, but Reese…hell no." Brogan and Keith both burst into laughter.

"*Shhh*, you'll wake the kids." Bertie pressed a finger to her lips. "Vance is right. Katie, we didn't mean to be rude or embarrassing." Bertie swatted Keith's thigh, glaring at him. "You are in so much trouble. Big. Trouble."

"Katie, excuse Vance. He's not usually this cantankerous. Abstinence will do that to a guy. How long's it been, buddy?" Brogan had the nerve to ask, tossing the orange football with one hand. "What was your last girlfriend's name?"

"Tatiana, the Russian publicist…meh." Lucy made a face. "Not your finest moment, Kerner. No one in town could stand her."

"I liked Tatiana," Brogan said.

"You liked her fake boobs and collagen-filled lips." Lucy gave Brogan a squinty-eyed glare.

"She had fake boobs?" Brogan asked, playing

innocent, and Keith rocked with laughter again. "I didn't notice. Couldn't get past her thick Russian accent."

"She's Ukrainian, you granola-eatin' idiot," Vance growled.

Brogan continued, unfazed by Vance's death glare. "No, seriously, I'm talking about the one with red hair." Brogan snapped his fingers. "What was her name? She was a stripper or an erotic dancer. Not sure which."

Bertie gasped, Keith snickered, and Katie's eyes practically bugged from her head.

"Her name was Bella, and she was an *exotic* dance teacher. She taught belly dancing, you numbnuts," Vance said while silently conjuring up ways to get even with his now ex-best friend.

"That's it. Bella the belly dancer. She was awesome." Brogan chucked the football to Vance, grinning like a jackass fool.

Vance groaned, dropping his head back against the cushions. By bringing up Tatiana and Bella, his so-called friends were doing an excellent job of running Katie straight out of town. Before he'd had a chance—at what? He had no idea. But he'd like her to stay around long enough for him to figure it out. So desperate for them to shut up about his past affairs, he changed the subject back to the dreaded miniseries.

"Kat, why don't you finish telling us about the mini-series? Otherwise, you will be further shocked by the lack of intelligence and decorum of Harmony's finest."

Katie twisted her pretty lips as if to keep from laughing. "You sure? I think your exotic girlfriends are far more entertaining. Great material. I know a top-notch studio that might be interested." She winked, and their gazes met and held. Something warm unfurled deep in his gut. Katie had an invigorating energy. She was quick and funny and forgiving, which would come in handy, because he figured he'd be begging for forgiveness before this was over.

"Like I said, it's geared toward the teenage audience. I'm not sure who's starring in it. My brothers are more privy to that kind of information," Katie explained.

Vance drained his drink, hoping the alcohol would ease the tension building up between his shoulders as Katie described the bloody series and explained why she wanted the use of his property. It didn't sound any better the second time around.

"Wow. I can't wait to see all the action," Lucy said once Katie had finished.

"I hope you get the chance. It all hinges on whether Vance allows McKnight Studios to use his house." She shot Vance a pointed look.

Lucy's curly blond hair whipped around her shoulders as she turned and arched her brow at him, and Bertie nudged him in the side.

"You're not thinking of saying no, are you?" Bertie asked.

"You better not. This will be the most exciting thing to happen to Harmony since bad boy tennis star Keith Morgan moved to town," Lucy added.

"Hey, I resemble that remark," Keith said with a chuckle. "Here, let me refresh your drink, Kerner. You're going to need it." He left the room for the kitchen with Vance's empty glass.

Great. Maybe if he got rip-roaring drunk, he'd forget about this, and tomorrow would be a better day. But then he watched Katie cross her jean-clad leg and wiggle her foot as if nervous or anxious or both, and he didn't want this day to end, and he didn't want to forget her.

"What's your decision, Kerner?" Brogan asked.

Vance rested his forearms on his thighs. Katie's foot stopped jiggling. "It's not that simple. I've got Eric's kids to contend with and a deadline looming over my head." The weight of his responsibilities froze his brain. "My book is not writing itself, especially with all the interruptions around here. Adding movie-making chaos will only make things worse."

"We can help with the kids. Lucy and I have offered numerous times," Bertie said, sounding concerned.

"I know, and I appreciate it. But you both work. Besides, you've got your own kids to deal with."

"We can take—"

"I've offered to babysit the kids for the next four weeks in exchange for using his house," Katie blurted to everyone's surprise.

Keith returned. Taking measured steps, he handed Vance his drink. "You need this more than I thought," he murmured.

"Whoa." Brogan glanced back and forth from Katie to Vance. "That's a very generous offer. I'd say Kerner's a fool not to accept it."

Katie licked her lips. "The crew won't arrive for another two weeks. Contracts still need to be signed. But starting tomorrow, I can be here first thing in the morning and stay until the kids are fast asleep." She crossed her arms over her sweatshirt and studied Vance's face.

Brogan's cocky grinned returned, and Lucy and

Bertie nodded in agreement. Only Keith settled back with an unreadable expression.

Katie glanced at her watch and sighed. "Can you guys recommend a motel or somewhere to stay? It's getting late, and since spotting this perfect location today, I stupidly haven't left the house or made any reservations."

"Well, there's the Lazy Oak Inn on the outskirts of town toward Raleigh. But you don't want to stay there for any length of time. It's infested with cockroaches. Hazel's Boarding House near the center of town will probably be your best bet," Bertie offered. "Does anyone know if she has any vacancies?" she asked the room in general.

"Hazel and Frank Conway are supernice, but Bible study is mandatory on Wednesday nights, and they're fierce about it."

Katie appeared baffled. "Er, well, that sounds okay. I didn't exactly bring my Bible with me. Will that be a problem?"

"Nope. She keeps a fresh supply behind the front desk," Lucy said.

Keith had pulled out his phone and started scrolling. "Here's the number. You can call right now and see if she has a vacancy."

"Thanks. My phone is in my handbag." Katie stood as if to leave the room. "I'll be right back."

"Wait a minute." Brogan shifted forward. "I have a better idea."

Uneasiness crept over Vance. He'd seen that calculated flicker in Brogan's eyes way too many times, and he seldom liked the outcome.

"Vance, what you need is a live-in nanny. Someone who can help with those kids 24-7." Brogan paused, making sure he had everyone's attention. "Katie, how 'bout you stay here? In Vance's house?"

Yep. Brogan had managed to come up with the worst idea ever. Vance pictured his hands circled around Brogan's jock-thick neck...squeezing. How would he survive with Katie under his roof, tying him in sailor knots? And worse, she'd be standing buck-naked in his shower with a *Do Not Touch* sign plastered on her ass, and sitting at his breakfast table wearing only a thin T-shirt covering her plump, braless breasts. Vance shifted, uncomfortably aware of the tightness around his groin.

"Um, I'm not sure that would be wise," Katie said.

Vance caught Katie's guarded look. Exactly. Unwise on so many levels.

"It's the perfect idea. You can stay in the master bedroom." Vance gave an involuntary growl, gaining everyone's attention. "Wait, let me finish. Vance, you sleep in the loft in the barn. That's where you write anyhow. Let Katie have the house with the kids for the nights," Brogan added to the already very bad idea.

Katie lurched forward with hands outstretched. "Oh no. I could never do that. I could never make him sleep in the barn." She appeared horrified at the idea.

Bertie laughed. "It wouldn't be a hardship. That barn is nicer than this house. I should know. I helped him convert it into his office-slash-living space."

"It's actually awesome. You've got to see it," Lucy said.

Brogan hopped up and pulled Lucy with him. "Then it's settled. Katie McKnight, welcome to your home for the next four weeks." He spread his arms wide, grinning

like he'd just won the lottery. Dread followed by a
kernel of excitement coursed through Vance's brain.
Judging by Katie's expression, she appeared paralyzed
with shock.

"Sounds perfect." Bertie stood. "Come on, Luce.
Let's write all our numbers and contact information
down. Vance, where do you keep your clean sheets? We
need to freshen up Katie's room."

"Please. That won't be necessary." Katie came to life
and tried to stop Bertie and Lucy.

Bertie chuckled. "Honey, don't deprive us of practic-
ing our Southern hospitality. Wouldn't be right."

Bertie barked more orders, and before Vance could
blink, his house was bustling with Operation Move
Katie In. Keith went to retrieve her luggage from the
car, and Brogan helped Lucy change sheets and put out
fresh towels.

Standing in the kitchen, Bertie handed a flabbergasted
Katie a sheet of paper with everyone's contact information. "If you need anything, do not hesitate to call."
Katie nodded numbly. "I mean it. Vance is like family
to us. We may tease him mercilessly, but we still love
him, and we're very grateful you're here to help." Bertie
smiled, and Vance squeezed her shoulders in appreciation. His friends were nosy, obnoxious, and annoying,
but they were also the best in a crisis and would give the
shirts off their backs to anyone in need.

"Why didn't I marry you when I had the chance?"
Vance asked, kissing the top of Bertie's head.

She snorted. "You had no interest in me, and you
know it. I couldn't compete with the mysterious women
who came and went around here."

Vance laughed, and it felt good. "Hardly mysterious. Nothing stays a secret around here."

"Well, now you have Katie." Bertie met his gaze with a glimmer in her green eyes. "We feel much better knowing you have help and can finish your book."

Katie suffered a coughing fit. "Excuse me. Just need some water." She ducked her head and made a beeline for the fridge.

Keith stepped into the kitchen with Brogan and Lucy. "When will it be published? I'm looking forward to reading the last one in the series," he said.

"Imagine you'll be tying up all the loose ends in this one," Brogan added.

Right. Loose ends. Thinking about all the loose ends made his stomach tighten and his head pound. "Won't come out for another year." Unless he never finished. Vance rubbed his sweaty palms against his jeans.

Brogan gave him a knowing look. "Stop worrying. You've got this. Especially now that Katie's here." He usually could read Vance's mind. Except on this one.

Vance suppressed a howl of frustration. Now that Katie was here…he'd *never* be able to focus.

Chapter 6

ALONE. AT LAST.

Well, not exactly. Vance breathed down Katie's neck, literally, as she stood inside her bedroom, more commonly known as Vance's master suite. Katie held her breath, wondering how she'd ended up here. And when she meant *here*, she meant inside this beautiful but oh-so-masculine bedroom with Harmony's hottie playboy standing so close she only had to sway a half inch and her back would be touching his well-defined front. Holy cliffhanger.

Vance's friends had left in a flurry, and Katie's head hadn't stopped spinning from the moment they'd arrived. A tropical cyclone created a calmer day than the one she'd had today. She and Vance had gone upstairs to check on the sleeping children and found Dover holding his baby sister tucked into his side with one arm and Donald sprawled at the bottom of the covers beneath their tent. Perfect angels. Katie smiled at the pure sweetness of it all, snapping pictures with her phone, wishing she'd thought to grab her Nikon while Vance made a few adjustments with the blankets.

Katie's gaze now landed on Vance's king-size platform bed with fresh white sheets and fluffy gray down comforter looking lush and inviting. It'd be even more inviting if occupied by the swarthy pirate. Katie's nails dug into her palms. These inappropriate thoughts must cease and desist. Her job: to conduct business and business only. Not play mattress tag with the resident gigolo. Besides, wasn't she practically engaged? Sure, sure, *engaged* might be a huge exaggeration, but being on a break didn't give her freedom to cut loose and hook up with other men…or pirates. That may be the norm for Hollywood, but not Katie. She had a career to build, a reputation to uphold. Parents to impress. A sigh escaped her lips, and her shoulders drooped.

"Is the room okay?" Vance asked in his rich, laid-back voice. Katie could crawl inside that voice and be lulled to sleep, it was that comforting.

"It's beautiful." She touched the mellow wood of the antique dresser. Her suitcases and bags sat on top of a cream-colored, plush leather ottoman at the foot of the bed.

"The master suite is an addition to the original house. I had it built about four years ago. Bertie helped with the interiors."

Katie nodded. The room held a special elegant touch. "I still feel bad commandeering your room. I can sleep in the loft or in one of the kids' rooms." Her insides turned squishy as his eyes burned, holding hers. His look said he desired her. How long had it been since she'd felt desirable? Instead of empty inside, unappreciated, or worse…used?

He moved closer until he stood inches from her UC Berkeley sweatshirt. A shiver prickled her skin. And it felt good, which made Katie feel bad.

"You're my guest, and the house is yours. Please, make yourself at home," he said softly. Oh boy. He was good. His voice could melt cold steel. Next thing you knew, she'd be luxuriating in the copper tub she'd spied in the beautifully appointed master bath…with Vance, the bronzed god. *Oh salty. No more.* He was a womanizer who preferred his women experienced and exotic. No. Make that a schemer. Because somehow she'd agreed to stay in his house, take care of his brother's kids, and he had yet to agree to the use of his property for the miniseries. Cunning devil.

Katie stepped back on watery legs, away from his intoxicating heat. "What time will you be up tomorrow? I'd like to get those contracts signed as quickly as possible."

A smile teased his lips. "The triple D will be screaming at the top of their lungs by six or seven." He reached for her hand and pulled her close again. "You sure you're up for this, oh Kat of mine?" he murmured.

She tried tugging on her hand, but he only squeezed harder. "I'm up for anything as long as you sign those contracts." *That's it. Be firm.*

Something glinted behind his gaze and then he kissed the back of her hand. Her skin tingled from the brief pressure of his lips. "Good night, K-K-Katie. Sleep tight."

He moved to the door. "My phone will be on if you need anything. Or…you can walk out that French door and cross the yard, if you feel so inclined." He waited. The wily manipulator.

"I won't. G'night. See you in the morning."

His smile turned wicked before he closed the door behind him. Katie blew out a huge breath. She was in trouble. Huge. Massive. Trouble. To calm her nerves, she let her gaze roam over the lovely room, taking in the pitched wood-beam ceiling, large windows covered in light gray bamboo blinds, built-in bookcases crammed with books, and the tall antique chest of drawers that probably housed his socks and T-shirts. Katie rushed to the door and flung it open.

"Vance?" He turned, already halfway down the hall. "You forgot your pj's, and, er, your toothbrush…"

White teeth flashed in the darkness of the hallway. "Got everything I need up in the loft. And I don't own any pj's…I sleep in the buff."

Gulp. "Oh. Um, I guess we're all good here. Night." She gave a small wave, ducking back into the bedroom and closing the door. Katie pressed her forehead to the warm wood and whimpered. Gorgeous Pirate Man in the buff. How would she ever sleep? Picturing his tanned skin against snow-white sheets, wearing nothing but a sexy smile. Oh snap.

Katie trudged to where her suitcases sat, opening the one that held her pajamas, because she *did* wear them to bed, unlike the Prince of Darkness. Her cell phone gave a familiar ring, indicating a call from her dad. She stiffened. Yeah, he'd be checking in, expecting a full report, because that's what he did best. That and lecture. Her palms started to sweat; her heart pounded. All of her ingrained insecurities slammed into her at the sound of that ringtone. She'd endured endless lectures her entire life about everything from making A's to making friends to making sacrifices. For a nanosecond, she considered not answering. But years of blind obedience would not allow her.

She hit Answer and put the phone to her ear. "Hi, Dad."

"Kathryn, I hadn't heard from you today and was

getting worried. Have you reached Wilmington yet?"
he asked, referring to the North Carolina coast. "I was
not impressed with those pictures you sent from South
Carolina. Not what I'm looking for." It was eleven
o'clock her time, which made it eight p.m. Pacific time,
and her dad was in full business mode even on a Saturday
night. Never considering she might be exhausted, which
she was. She bit back her sigh of frustration.

"I know, Dad. I'm in North Carolina but not on the
coast. I've found a great location. It's perfect, and I
think you're really going to approve."

"What do you mean you're not on the coast?" Her
dad's temper was building. "I sent you specifically to
the North Carolina coast. It's the terrain I'm looking for,
and Wilmington has authentic old homes perfect for this
series. Kathryn, was I not clear enough for you in this
assignment?" His disappointment rang crystal clear,
never mind the words.

Katie pressed her palm over her spasmodically
twitching left eyebrow. A common occurrence during
discussions with her dad. Or mom. Or brothers.

"Yes, Dad. You were perfectly clear, but this location
is amazing and has all the requirements."

"That's what you said about the last one, and I hated
it." His words stung. He hadn't appreciated the rundown,
abandoned two-story Georgian she'd found in Florence,
South Carolina. Or the old Craftsman with the burned-
out windows she'd discovered somewhere in Kansas.

Katie had a copy of the script and studied the descrip-
tions every day. The houses he'd rejected all had possibilities. But this time, the script and location were in
sync, if only she could convince her dad.

"I'm in a small town called Harmony, kinda near the coast. I'll email you pictures tomorrow. The home fits the description, complete with barn in back that the script calls for. But the best part is, the property is huge. Room for all the equipment and trailers. We won't have to get permits to use city streets for parking." *As long as we cut down a few oak trees* was better left unsaid.

Walter McKnight listened without interrupting, and Katie held her breath. "Have you spoken with the owner?" *Uh, yeah, getting ready to sleep in his bed.* She left that thought unsaid as well…no point in giving her dad a heart attack.

"Yes. I'm in negotiations with him right now. I plan to go over all the details in the morning."

"Who is he?" Tapping on a keyboard could be heard through the phone, which meant her dad was preparing to Google Vance Kerner. No getting around this. Katie wished just once her father had faith in her ability and would allow her to do her job.

"Vance Kerner. He's a bestselling author." And pirate, womanizer, and oh yeah, schemer.

"Did you say Vance Kerner?" Surprise colored Walter's voice.

"Yes. He's written like a dozen war thrillers. Sam and Doug have read them all," she said, referring to her two older brothers.

"Yes, yes. I've read his latest series. *Honor Bound* and *Without Honor*. Third one, *Honor Is Dead* is due out next year. He's very good. And he owns this house you're talking about?"

"Yes."

More key tapping. "He has over fifty thousand

likes on Facebook and twenty thousand followers on
Twitter. High ranking on Amazon." Katie could feel her
dad nodding as he studied his computer screen. "He's
selling some books." From his voice, his admiration
couldn't be ignored. "I want to speak to him. Give me
his number, Kathryn," Walter demanded in his strongest
I'm-in-charge-voice.

Box office bomb. Acid ate the inside of her stomach,
and her twitching eyebrow added a new cadence. "I can
handle this, Dad." She hated it when he dismissed her
and found her incapable or lacking…or incompetent.
"When you gave me this assignment, you promised I'd
have the same chance as anyone else."

"Kathryn, last time I checked, I was head of this
studio. Did you happen to forget that?"

She heaved a sigh of weariness. "Of course not."

"This is too important. I can't afford another…"
Walter's voice trailed off, and even though he didn't
voice the rest of his thought, Katie heard it anyway.
He couldn't afford another one of her screwups. Katie
swallowed hard and blinked back stinging tears. Her dad
cleared his throat. "You've got one more chance. Try
not to blow it."

"Thanks, Dad. I promise," she said in a subdued voice.

"One week. I'm giving you one week to wrap this up,
and I want pictures by tomorrow."

"Yes sir."

"How's your camera holding up?" All location scouts
carried a reliable digital camera, along with camera
phones and iPads. But Katie loved photography and carried several cameras, always prepared to snap pictures
of subjects she liked.

"Great. No problems," she said.

"Where are you staying? Is there a hotel in this town?" Katie didn't think Hazel's Boarding House would be categorized as a hotel. No way was she revealing the babysitting deal she had struck with Captain Skunk or that she'd be staying in his house for the next four weeks. Once she had everything signed, sealed, and delivered, she'd break the upsetting news. For now, keeping her job required lying.

"There's a Comfort Inn just outside of town. I'll be staying there."

Walter grunted, signifying he was already busy working on something else and she'd been dismissed. "Good, good. Your mother wants to speak with you. *Crystal!*" Katie jumped at his bellow. "Your daughter's on the phone," she heard him say to her mother.

Her mom picked up the extension. "Katie?"

"Hi, Mom. How are you?"

"Well, I've been better…" It took all Katie's willpower not to set the phone down and go about her business. Her mom had a talent for taking a simple question like *how are you* and instead of answering *fine,* like any normal human, turning it into a litany of what procedure she'd scheduled next, from gel nails to hair extensions to having her ears pinned back or bladder tucked.

"…and the doctor said he'd never seen such perfectly formed toes. He wants to use them in his brochure. Should I wear hot pink or coral nail polish? What do you think?"

"Are you talking about your pedicure?"

"Yes, for the doctor's brochure. Maybe I'll wear one of those off colors that's all the rage, like lime green. How are your toes, Katie? I haven't looked at them lately. Are you getting pedicures regularly?" Katie curled her toes inside her leather flats and tried to remember what color she'd had them painted last, grateful they were discussing toes and not rhinoplasty, breast augmentations, or collagen injections. "Um…it's pretty late out here, and I need to get going. Tell Sam and Doug I said hi."

"Oh, yes. Right. You're three hours ahead of us. Good night, honey."

"Night, Mom."

Katie rubbed her aching forehead. Every conversation with her parents, mostly her dad, resulted in a game of second-guessing and self-doubt. To distract herself from the latest disappointing conversation, Katie unpacked and hung her clothes in the master closet next to Vance's numerous outerwear jackets and very few dress shirts. His woodsy scent, intensified inside the closet, calmed her. Closing her eyes, she breathed in, touching the soft, worn denim of the sleeve of one of his jackets; she imagined him wearing it. Dropping her hand, she gave herself another silent warning: no dreaming about the South's famous ladies' man. Then she went to bed and did just that…dreamed about Vance.

"Don't want a nose job," Katie mumbled. "No. Stop." She brushed the doctor's furry hand away from her nose. Huh? Furry hand? Why were her legs immobile? A huge weight rested on the lower half of her body. Katie groaned and blinked groggily. Her eyes popped open. Two inches from her face, a twitching black kitty pawed her nose. Blinking sleep from her eyes, she focused on Danny kneeling by her head, squeezing the kitten's middle.

"Pop wants to kiss you, Kay-tee."

Katie pushed slowly up on her elbows. The early morning sun peeked through the slits of the bamboo blinds she'd closed the night before. "Good morning," she croaked. She looked down her torso at Dover sprawled on the blanket, covering her numb legs.

"Katie, why are you sleeping in Uncle Vance's bed? You married to him now?"

Oh no. Another groan slipped from her lips as her head fell back on her pillow. Oh no. There'd been no marriage, but Pirate Man was the reason for her lack of sleep and her pounding headache. "What time is it? How long have you been up?" she asked in a rusty voice.

"Uncle Vance's clock says six one five," Dover said, reading the digital clock sitting on the nightstand.

Six fifteen. Well, she couldn't say Vance hadn't warned her. "Where's Donald?" she asked, clearing her dry throat.

"Outside with Pixie." Oh Lord. Katie struggled to sit up in earnest. She needed to get outside and make sure Donald hadn't wandered off. No sooner had the thought formed than the star of her dreams came strolling through the bedroom door, looking better than a human had a right to at this ungodly hour of the morning. Hair damp from his morning shower, dark stubble from lack of shaving, worn jeans, and black Harley-Davidson T-shirt stretched across his muscled chest.

"Morning, California Sunshine."

Katie scrambled to sit up as Dover rolled off her

legs. Heat crept up her cheeks. "Why are you up so early? Thought you'd still be sleeping." Vance eased down on the side of the bed, causing the mattress to dip. Katie caught his gaze hovering around her chest. She tugged on the sheet to cover her breasts, fully aware the thin T-shirt she'd worn to bed had seen better days.

"Hey, Katie." Donald ambled into the room, followed by Pixie. Climbing up on the bed, he sat next to his sister. "Uncle Vance, are you and Katie getting married?"

Katie had the pleasure of watching Vance's dark complexion redden to match the cherries on Dana Sue's nightgown. "Uh, no—"

"They got married last night," Dover announced as if he had performed the ceremony.

Katie enjoyed watching Harmony's Holy Hotness try to dig his way out of this hole.

Thunder crossed Vance's face. "No marriage. Nobody's getting married."

"Why?" Dana Sue asked, unperturbed by her uncle's harsh answer.

"Because I'm not the marrying type."

Katie's brow arched. No, he was the fooling-around type.

"Katie's going to be staying with us and taking care of you so I can finish my book. Remember I told you I write books for a living?"

"*Goodnight Moon*. You write *Goodnight Moon*," Danny said. "You read *Goodnight Moon*." She started to scramble from the bed as if to fetch her favorite book.

"Whoa. Hold on there." Vance scooped her up before she tumbled to the floor. "It's time for breakfast.

Let's give Katie some privacy, and then she can join us in the kitchen."

"I want Cap'n Crunch!" Donald jumped from the bed and ran for the kitchen.

"Me too!" Dover followed his brother.

"Down. Down." Dana Sue squirmed in Vance's arms, and he placed her gently on the floor so she could chase after the boys.

The bedroom returned to morning quiet without the extra occupants. Vance stood next to the bed, a seductive smile playing around his lips. "Meet you in the kitchen. I'll be the one corralling the three wild mustangs, in case you're wondering."

"Give me two minutes, and I'll help," she said.

"Take your time. Usually takes fifteen minutes before the kitchen is totally trashed."

"I'll be there in one."

Vance laughed, closing the bedroom door behind him.

Katie hadn't taken more than five minutes to dress, and the kitchen already had that just-been-bombed look about it. She stood on the threshold and planted her fists on her hips. Vance sat with Danny in his lap, spilled cereal at his elbow, burnt toast on the floor, and grape jelly handprints on the front of the refrigerator. Donald and Dover crawled on their hands and knees, trying to force-feed Pixie a BetterBites muffin.

"Look at this kitchen. It was spotless when I went to bed last night," she said, shaking her head. This called for coffee. Katie poured a cup from the carafe and added milk from the carton sitting on the countertop, wondering for the millionth time what she'd gotten herself into.

Vance set Danny on her feet. "Everyone outside for a while before you have to wash up and put on your church clothes."

"Aw, man. Do we have to?" asked Donald.

"You heard your mama last night when we Skyped. She made me promise."

Katie eased down in her chair, glad to know she'd have a reprieve, if only for a couple of hours, to get her notes and thoughts together before she met with Vance.

"Hurry…outside. Let's go." Vance held the door open to the backyard while Katie looked around the destroyed kitchen. *Hold up, Johnny Depp. Not so fast.*

"Just a moment," she said as the kids faced her. "This kitchen needs cleaning first."

"But Uncle Vance said—"

"And Uncle Vance is going to help." Her look dared him to disagree. Katie snapped her fingers. Ten minutes later, the kitchen appeared straight, and the kids played outside.

Vance even started the washing machine with yesterday's load of dirty clothes. He stepped back in the kitchen, brushing off his hands.

"What time would you like me to have them ready for Sunday school?" she asked. The big green clock shaped like an apple above the door read seven fifteen. "And how long will you be gone?" Hopefully long enough for her to grab a shower and wash her hair. She wanted to be fresh and alert for the sales pitch of her life.

"Well, here's the thing…" Sirens went off inside her

head. Avoiding eye contact, Vance fiddled with the red rooster pitcher sitting on the table. "I need you to take them so I can get back to work."

"Wait—"

"It's the Methodist church right off Main Street. It's not hard to find. They need to be there by eight thirty."

"You're not going?" Katie hoped she had disguised the panic in her voice. She didn't have anything against attending church. She'd been meaning to get back into the habit. But not in this small town, which made her uncomfortable since everyone seemed to know her name.

"Sorry. Didn't get as much done last night as I would've liked. Noticed you were up kinda late too," he said, jolting her back to her sleepless night.

"How'd you know I was up late?" Images of him lurking outside her bedroom window should've angered her, but kinda didn't. *Hollywood harlots*. She was losing it.

"Light was on. For a long time. Couldn't sleep, could you? What were you doing, K-K-Katie?" he asked, as if he knew she'd been fantasizing about him and his big, bad naked self bathing in the copper tub…with her. Eep.

Mother of Miley Cyrus! Katie wondered when she'd become so transparent. She lived around actors 24-7. You'd have thought she'd have picked up some acting skills by now and could hide her feelings.

"Unpacking. Oh, and talking to my dad. He wanted to know if I'd found a location." All true. No point admitting the whole fantasy thing.

Vance shoved his fists in his jeans pockets. "What did you tell him?"

Placing her dirty mug in the dishwasher, she said, "That I'd found a location. And you were signing the contracts *today*."

"Right." He straightened the chairs around the table. "But first the kids go to Sunday school."

Katie recognized avoidance when she saw it. She tensed at the setback. Between Vance's obvious reluctance and the pressure from her dad, she had a big challenge ahead.

"Okay. Under one condition. When I return, you and I are gonna talk, got it?"

No one was messing with Katie McKnight. Especially big, sexy tomcats up to no good.

Vance crossed the kitchen in two long strides. "Thanks, Kat, you're a lifesaver." Relief flooded his face. He hooked his arm around her waist and pulled her in for a long, hard kiss. Katie resisted by pressing her palms against his rock-hard chest—well, *resist* might be a bit strong. More like, she pressed herself against him and looped her arms around his neck for closer contact. The kiss deepened as he backed her against the kitchen cabinets. His rough hand moved to her throat, making her pulse jump. She savored the flavor of his mouth…coffee and forbidden wickedness. He nibbled on her lips, and the kiss softened. Katie reveled in his warmth and strength. She knew she should stop, but…not yet. As if he could sense her surrender, he crushed her closer and deepened the possession of her mouth.

"We…you…have to…stop," she said in between nips and licks. This time she did push against him, and his head lifted.

"Why?"

Katie blinked, trying to clear her kiss-befuddled head. One hand heated the small of her back; the other rested precariously close to her already excited breast. "B-because. I have a boyfriend."

Vance looked at her as if she'd spoken Swahili. "Boyfriend?" His hold tightened, and he swooped down for another brain-dissolving kiss, as if to wipe thoughts of her boyfriend from her mind. Which he did. Quite nicely, too. Making her knees turn to wet noodles, unable to refuse—okay, *refuse* might be wrong, more like *surrender* to burning desire.

"What's his name?" he murmured, nibbling her lips as if they were made of sugar drops.

"Hmm?" Katie loved the texture of his firm mouth and the way his tongue swirled around hers. "Who?"

"The boyfriend." Vance sucked her bottom lip.

"Er, oh. Hmmm," Katie moaned, weaving her fingers through his long, thick hair. Vance rained nibbling kisses around her jaw, down her neck, and back up to her begging mouth.

"T-Tom." Kiss. Kiss. Nibble. Kiss. *Pop* went the sound as Katie unlatched her lips from his. "I mean, Tad. His name is Tad." She shook her head. Katie made an effort—weak at best—to move from the circle of his arms, but he refused to release her, staring with unreadable dark eyes.

"Tad? That's not a name. I've never heard of it. What's his last name?"

She cast her eyes down and examined their feet entwined on top of the black-and-white-checkered tile floor. She'd never been a big fan of Tad's name. It always sounded juvenile, but when coupled with his last name, ugh…even worse.

"I'm not buying this relationship you have with Tad whoever. You don't even remember his name."

Her head popped up. "Yes…yes, I do. His name is Tad Poole, and he's a wonderful guy," Katie lied. He used to be wonderful when they first started dating, but as soon as he started working at McKnight Studios, he changed. He became obsessed with work, shamelessly sucking up to her dad at every opportunity. When Tad started lecturing her about her career choices, Katie felt betrayed. He'd barely been with the company a month, and he'd already gone over to the dark side.

"I'm sorry, but did you say Tad Poole, or Tad Pole?"

No pulling one over on this guy. He made his living with words. "Poole. He's Tad Poole the Third. He comes from a very prominent family in Los Angeles. And—"

"You mean there's a Tad Pole first and second? Do they come from a prominent family of frogs?"

"Yes. And since I've had the great fortune of kissing him and turning him into a prince, I will soon be a princess when we marry." She gave her head a regal toss.

Vance moved back. Katie missed his closeness and hated herself for it.

Pointing a blunt finger at her face, he said, "Marry? You didn't say anything about getting married. Your tadpole, frog-kissing days are over. Mark my words."

Katie gave a nervous laugh. "This is a ridiculous discussion and has no bearing on why I'm here."

Vance curled his hand around her neck. "I'd like to change that. Maybe we should go back to what we were doing before you brought up tadpoles."

She pushed him away with force this time. "No. No more kissing."

"Never?"

"No. Never. I'm here on business and business only. Well, that and babysitting. Business and babysitting. Kissing and groping are not part of the deal."

He grinned down at her. "Sure I can't change your mind?"

Maybe. Yes. No. No! She had a brief desire to punch him in the stomach, because she wanted to put kissing back on the table. Damn him.

"Vance Kerner, you are a black-hearted pirate with no scruples, and you should be thankful I'm going to church to pray for your soul." Katie pushed past him and stomped out of the kitchen.

"Don't run off. Where are you going?"

Katie wanted to press her palms over her ears to block out his boisterous laughter. "To shower. *You* can get the kids dressed for Sunday school." If he didn't stop laughing, she'd make him take the kids too.

"May I—"

Katie whirled around. "Don't say it. Don't even think it." She shook her finger at him. "*No*. You may not join me."

Chapter 7

"Hey, Miss California. Hold up a minute."

After one and a half hours, church had let out and Katie was in the parking lot wrestling Danny into her booster seat inside the back of Vance's truck. That was right. She was driving a beat-up, black Ford pickup truck to church. A first. Vance had to practically haul her up in it because the running board was missing on the driver's side. He took great pleasure in placing his hand on her bottom while boosting her up and brushing her breasts while reaching for the seat belt. And her traitorous breasts properly saluted him, putting a devilish grin on his face. She had a long four weeks ahead of her, if her body continued to misbehave and act like a Hollywood Boulevard slut.

She pulled her head from inside the cab after buckling Danny's seat belt. "Yes?" A woman with platinum-blond hair, revealing electric-blue knit dress, and silver-studded pumps approached, followed by a much-thinner older woman with gray helmet-head, wearing a matching floral skirt and tucked-in top, along with beige Easy Spirit shoes.

"Dottie Duncan here." The blond extended a hand sporting long orange nails and gold rings on every finger. "And Miss Sue Percy." She indicated Helmet-head.

"Katie McKnight." She shook hands with the women. A crowd was beginning to form in the parking lot as curious onlookers inched closer to hear the conversation.

"You're Vance's new girlfriend, aren't you?" Dottie asked, narrowing her heavily made-up blue eyes.

Surprised at her bluntness, Katie stammered, "Oh, well, um…no. I'm a location scout and—"

"Katie's going to marry Uncle Vance," Donald announced loud enough from inside the truck for the growing crowd to hear. Katie cringed, squeezing her eyes shut. She'd known sleeping in the town gigolo's house would somehow come back to haunt her.

"Yay, Kay-tee marry Uncle Pance," Danny chimed in, clapping her hands.

"She's sleeping in his bed." Beautiful, blue-eyed, dark-haired, innocent Dover, who may not live past today, had sealed her doom.

"I told you Vance was shacking up with some California gal, Sue," Dottie said to her companion.

"Only temporarily. I mean—! Um…we're not shacking up. I'm here on business—"

"Well, if you're not shacking up…it's only a matter of time, dear." Miss Sue Percy wore a pleasant but you-can't-fool-me smile.

"Hey, you the girl from California?"

"You ever been on *Wheel of Fortune*?"

"When do auditions start out at the Kerner place?"

Katie grabbed the open door for support.

"Honey, you'll get used to our ways soon enough." Dottie gestured to the crowd. "Herman, Lois…y'all give our guest here some breathing room. They'll be plenty of time for auditions later."

The church crowd dispersed, waving their good-byes,

leaving Katie alone with Dottie Duncan and Miss Sue Percy.

"You kids hungry?" Dottie asked, peering inside the truck.

"Yeah!" they all three chorused.

"Well, come on over to my place. Geraldine's making hotcakes, with country-fried steak and grits."

"Hotcakes too hot," Danny said, shaking her head.

"Nah, taste just like pancakes. I've got lots of maple syrup."

"Dottie, thank you for the invitation, but I should probably get the kids—"

"Nonsense. My grandkids are coming over, and they'll make good playmates. How old are you?" she asked, pointing to Donald.

"Seven."

"Perfect. You're right between Jason and Bobby. You like to swim?"

"Sure." Donald nodded.

"Go on home and get your swimsuits. Pool's heated, even though it's supposed to climb to the eighties today. Hannah, my granddaughter, is thirteen, and she can help with this little one here." Dottie chucked Danny under the chin and then pulled a card from her bright yellow hand-bag and handed it to Katie. "Here's my address. I'm a few blocks over on Chestnut Street. Vance can tell you."

Katie stared at the card with a glamour shot of Dottie wearing a red boa around her neck; the business name *Toot-N-Tell* was inscribed at the top. She hesitated. "I should check with Vance first."

"Don't worry about that no-good playboy. He'll be glad to have the peace and quiet."

Probably. And not have to face Katie and her contract. One more delay. A nervous jolt kicked her stomach. She dreaded calling her dad with any more disappointing news.

Dottie nudged her friend. "Come on, Sue. I know you can use another cup of coffee and some delicious hotcakes."

"Hurry, Katie. We wanna go swimming," Donald said with the impatience of a seven-year-old.

"Don't be late. Geraldine will have breakfast on the table in thirty minutes," Dottie said in Katie's ear. "You and me have some talking to do."

They did? About what? If Dottie Duncan had some hidden talent she wanted Katie to critique, she might have to shoot herself.

Katie stood on the gray stone pavers outside Dottie Duncan's ornate, three-story Mediterranean mansion, which looked out of place in small-town Harmony, and watched the boys horse around in the pool with Dottie's grandkids. Young Hannah entertained Danny near the swim-out, flanked by two huge gilded dolphin fountains.

Katie sipped her fourth cup of coffee of the morning, wondering if her stomach lining would rebel from the abuse. Geraldine's breakfast had been delicious, and Katie's first taste of homemade grits had been surprisingly…good. A surge of guilt swamped her after consuming her third buttery hotcake with warm maple syrup. If her mother had been present, information on high body fat, bad cholesterol, and weight gain would've been dispensed with a direct, lethal hit. Katie frowned into her coffee. If her mother had been here, Katie would not have eaten at all.

Earlier, Vance had been too eager to shove her and the kids out the door with their swim gear stuffed in bags. He had appeared frazzled and strained around the eyes. Katie gave a resigned shrug, knowing it wasn't the best time to bring out the contract. Preoccupied with his writing and all. Not that she knew him. She'd barely met the guy. But yeah, she kind of knew him, sleeping in his bed aside. This time when he hoisted her back into his truck he didn't even cop a feel. And Katie had never been more relieved. *Ha! Who you fooling, girl?* She'd been flattered by all the attention Vance had paid her.

Especially when they'd locked lips. She'd managed to forget everything, including her judgmental dad, self-absorbed mother, and her now ex-boyfriend, Tad.

Initially, Tad had been charming and kind. But once he'd starting working for her dad, the bloom on their relationship had quickly faded.

Katie released a shaky sigh. Tad loved his job with McKnight Studios and had visions of following in her dad's footsteps, since her brothers worked the legal end of the business. Guilt twisted like a sharp knife in her stomach. Something had to be seriously wrong with her if her family and boyfriend found her so lacking.

Katie's cell chirped, jerking her from her disturbing thoughts. She didn't need to look to know who was calling. It was as if he could read her mind.

"Hello."

"Katie? Where've you been? I've been texting all morning," Tad said, sounding exasperated.

Katie moved away from the pool for privacy, next

to the large stone planters filled with blooming rose bushes. "Sorry. I was in church and had my phone off. Is everything okay? You sound upset."

"You haven't sent the pictures for your latest loca—*church?* What were you doing in church?"

"It's a long story." Something she would tell on a need-to-know basis only. She didn't want her babysitting job getting back to her dad until she'd nailed down this location.

"Kathryn, your dad wasn't happy with the previous places you showed him, and there's been nothing new for the last four days. What have you been doing besides attending church?"

The bossy tone he reserved for her rubbed Katie wrong. She had to take it from her dad. She didn't have to take it from Tad. "Did he tell you to check up on me? I already talked to him last night, and I've found the perfect place. He'll be getting pictures today. What's this all about?"

"Of course I'm checking up on you. Our getting back together hinges on your ability to do this job. Remember? I need you to work at this career and show me that you've got what it takes to stick."

Katie ground her back teeth. How many nagging parents did a girl need? Part of the reason she took this scouting job was to get away. Away from the pressure. And now that she thought about it, away from Tad. Katie took in her surroundings: lush blooming garden, green lawn sprinkled with play equipment, sparkling blue pool filled with laughing, happy kids.

In Harmony, North Carolina.

A small town far, far away from Hollywood,

California. If it weren't for cell phones, she could disconnect completely. She sighed. That dream held merit.

Tad was still rambling on about her responsibilities when Katie interrupted, feeling irritated and cranky. "Last time I looked, you weren't my father. And I have a few conditions of my own. Like stop checking up on me. Our getting back together hinges on *that*."

"Katie, honey, I know you don't mean that. My checking in with you is based on true concern. I only want what's best for both of us. You must be tired from traveling. I'm sure you'll be back to normal as soon—"

"Donald, Dover! Don't!" Katie yelled.

Aaaeeeeeeeeoooooooowwwww! Splash went the pool water, and droplets hit Katie in the face and chest. The boys' cannonballs knocked little Danny with their wake. "Tad, I've gotta go. The boys are drowning Danny…"

"Wait. What boys? Kathryn, what the hell is going—"

Katie pushed the End button and shoved the phone inside the pocket of her khaki shorts. She stood on the edge of the pool. "Don't make me put you in boot camp. Stop trying to drown your sister." She wagged her finger at the rambunctious boys, who all wore sheepish grins before they ducked beneath the water. "Hannah, you doing okay with Dana Sue?" she asked the sweet teenager who seemed to have an unending supply of patience.

"Yeah, we're diving for pennies."

Katie nodded. Good. Maybe they'd all go to bed early and sleep like the dead tonight and give her a chance to pin down the elusive Jack Sparrow—disguised as Vance, the master of evade and avoid.

Dottie emerged from the house with a large glass of

iced tea. "Katie, come sit with me beneath the umbrella." She'd changed into a red maxi dress with blue rhinestones spelling *flirty* across her massive chest. Miss Sue followed, the only one who remained buttoned up in her church clothes.

"Hmm, interesting you don't believe in gilding the lily," Dottie said, turning her nose up at Katie's outfit.

What was wrong with her loose, light pink tank top, matching lightweight cardigan, and khaki shorts? Dottie Duncan had to be the bluntest person she'd ever met. Vance had warned her that she'd be in the company of Harmony's most infamous gossipers, and to beware. Katie sat in one of the Italianate wrought-iron chairs around the umbrella table. The mingled smells of gardenias and roses, mixed with chlorine from the pool, filled the heated air.

Miss Sue sipped a tall, cool glass of lemonade and fanned herself with a red cardboard fan that said: *NC Home of the Toot-N-Tell*.

"You don't do too much to make yourself look good. You got a pretty face"—Dottie wiggled a finger at Katie's chest—"makes me wonder what you're hiding underneath those ill-fittin' clothes."

Just because Katie didn't wear tops three sizes too small, with her breasts spilling out, didn't mean she was hiding anything. She'd learned to cover up at an early age in hopes of deflecting her mother's constant critical barbs.

Katie looked down at her sad tank top. "I'm not trying to hide anything." Maybe. "These clothes are comfortable."

"You might try wearing something that fits, dear. Show a little cleavage. Especially if you expect to keep a lovable rake like Vance interested," Miss Sue said in a prim voice, as if she were discussing scripture and not Katie's assets.

"I'm not interested in keeping Vance interested." Dottie snorted, and Miss Sue pursed her lips. "You have to believe me. I simply need his permission to use his house, and then I'm off." After four weeks of free baby-sitting. She'd agreed to those terms out of determination and desperation.

"He's never gonna allow you to use his house. His mama left that house to him and his brother. Vance isn't likely to let some Hollywood execs get their hands on it and turn it into 'The House of Usher Meets the Playboy Mansion.' He's way too private for that nonsense. Just like his daddy." Dottie leaned back in her chair, crossing her legs. "You can use my house. I think it would look great in the movies."

Katie tried for a polite nod, without giving away what she really thought of all the rows and rows of ruffles Dottie had on every piece of furniture, fabric, and drapery inside her house. Even the oversized dog bed sported ruffles. "That's kind of you, but we need a farmhouse-look for this series. Your house is, um, far too elegant." A smile spread wide across Dottie's face at Katie's use of the word "elegant."

"I have to agree with Dottie. I don't think Vance will let anyone mess with his mama's house."

"Are his parents dead?" Katie asked, wondering about his family. She'd seen framed photos of his parents and his brother scattered around the house. His dad had mostly been pictured in a military uniform, and there were pictures of the grown-up brother.

"His mama died back when Vance was entering high school. An aneurysm, something sudden like that. Purely awful. Those poor boys. The most loving parenting they ever had was from their mama," Miss Sue said.

"Chuck Kerner is a hard man. He was a two-star general in the army. Fought in Vietnam and a bunch of wars after that."

Katie poured herself a glass of lemonade. The day was heating up, along with the conversation.

"But he was never the same after Helen died. And Vance got the brunt of it."

Katie sipped the lemonade but didn't benefit from the cooling liquid. She burned with the thought of Vance being the brunt of anything. "Did he b-beat him?" She pictured a rigid general using his military might on a helpless child.

"Not that I ever heard, and I know most of what goes on around here," Miss Sue added with pride in her voice.

"Nah, Chuck and Vance just didn't see eye to eye, that's all. Eric followed in his daddy's footsteps. He signed up for the Army right out of high school, not long after his mama died," Dottie said, drinking her tea. "Kids, we got lemonade over here," she called to the kids still swimming like fish in the pool.

Dottie swiveled in her chair and pinned Katie with a curious look. "After Eric enlisted, that only left Vance and his daddy with no one to buffer their arguments."

"What would they argue about?"

"Anything and everything. If Chuck said the sky was blue, Vance would argue and say it was green," Dottie said.

"That's not all. They argued about Vance's girlfriends.

One time Chuck caught Vance…you know"—Miss Sue waggled her eyebrows—"in the barn, and you would've thought World War III had broken out."

"So, he had a strict moral code, and Vance rebelled against it," Katie stated. Okay, she got that. Lots of teenage kids rebelled against their parents' edicts. And yeah, sometimes it caused familial wars. Something she'd never done…ever. Her only radical move was majoring in education, which went against her dad's religion, *and* not doing a very good job for McKnight Studios.

Dottie jiggled the ice in her glass. "Yeah, got caught with his chemistry tutor. Eleven years older than Vance." Katie sucked in a hard breath. A sly grin curled Dottie's red-painted lips. "*And* his dad's date for that night."

Fritzschizzle! Katie bolted upright in her chair, eyes wide. Boy, some people really knew how to put the *R* in *rebel*. "Seriously?"

"Served Chuck right," Miss Sue said, fanning her flushed cheeks. "He was making a complete fool of himself. That gal was too young for him."

And too old for Vance. Wow. His playing days started early.

Dottie tipped her head up and sighed. "Chuck was in a bad place back then. He'd lost his wife and was hurting. Too proud to get help, so he took everything out on his son." Then she locked gazes with Katie. "Unfortunately, he still does."

Vance stood on the front porch, watching for his truck to roll down the driveway. Katie had texted, saying they were on their way home. Vance grimaced. Dottie had been up to something when she'd invited Katie and the kids for a swim. Bullshit on claiming she'd only wanted to help him find quiet time to write. Vance didn't have to see her calculating face to know she had an ulterior motive, like interrogating Katie. She and Miss Sue Percy could spread dirt faster than all the social media outlets combined.

His black truck came bumping down the winding driveway. Vance smiled, remembering hoisting Katie up in the driver's seat for church. She'd worn some long, shapeless skirt with a loose top, and then later, some boring khakis and sweater set. For some unexplained reason, Katie covered up, as if ashamed of her body. Vance had already held her in his arms, his hand on her shapely ass, and everything was fine...very fine indeed. Katie didn't appear unkempt or frumpy. Just hidden. Not every item of women's clothing was made for the sole purpose of enticing sexual interest in men. But come on...those floppy, ill-fitting clothes weren't doing Katie's natural blessings any favors.

Vance met the truck as it came to a stop in the driveway. Donald and Dover bounded from the back of the cab, lugging towels and extra clothes, looking wet and worn-out.

"How was it, guys?"

"Awesome. Miz Duncan said we can come back and swim anytime," Donald said.

"We need to get some aloe on your faces," Vance said, noticing Dover's red cheeks. Katie slid from the driver's seat with wet hair, soggy shoes, and a beach towel wrapped around her shoulders.

"What happened to you?" Her squinty-eyed response didn't bode well.

"Katie fell in the pool," Dover said as he trudged up the front steps.

"Yeah, Miz Duncan's big dog, Sweet Tea, came running real fast outta the house and barreled right into Katie. You should've heard her scream, Uncle Vance. It was so funny," Donald said, smiling.

Vance's grin widened as he pulled a sleeping Danny from her car seat and cradled her head on his shoulder. When Katie's glower didn't fade, he bit the inside of his cheek to keep from laughing. "Um, yeah, that doesn't sound good. You okay, K-K-Katie?"

"Go. Away." Katie reached for her handbag inside the truck, and the towel slipped to her waist, exposing her now-see-through wet tank top. Vance's gaze zeroed in on the perfect mounds wrapped in very thin, wet fabric, outlining tight, hard nipples. A surge of pure lust punched him below the belt...

Scrambling to cover herself with the towel, she glared. "Stop staring at my boobs"—she shook her finger at his face—"you scourge of Harmony." Katie spun on her heels and stomped toward the front door.

"Whut? Why am I suddenly the scourge of Harmony?" He caught up with her on the front porch.

"Shhh, you'll wake Dana Sue," she whispered and then practically slammed the front door in his face. With squeaky wet shoes she hurried down the hall toward the master suite, taking her luscious tush with her.

Damn Dottie Duncan and Miss Sue Percy for filling Katie's head with stories of his past. Scourge of Harmony. Jesus. Now any play he made for her, she'd put the wrong spin on it. Yeah, yeah...he'd wanted to seduce Katie. Ever since yesterday, when she stood in his kitchen and whistled. Yep, that probably classified him as the scourge of the South. But for some unexplainable reason, something shifted inside him when his thoughts centered on Katie, who inspired smiles and made him want…things. Things he couldn't name, but rather felt. And dammit, it was weirding him out.

Vance put Danny down for a nap and made sure the boys were clean and dry, slathering their faces and shoulders with cooling aloe before they settled in for an afternoon of gaming. He went down the stairs, intent on returning to the loft. His blank computer screen with the blinking cursor waited, screaming to be filled with words…specific words that told a story. A story he no longer had in him to tell.

On his way out, he glanced in the living room and stopped. Katie stood with her back to him, in dry clothes and damp, braided hair, holding a photo. Vance knew which one without even seeing it. A picture of him and his dad taken on a day they'd spent together fishing. The one happy memory Vance could recall before all the arguments and recriminations tainted and destroyed their relationship. They used to spend hours fishing out on the lake, enjoying each other's company. They'd laugh and tell stories, and Vance would feed the fish his lunch if he didn't like what his mom had packed. The tight knot in his chest made breathing difficult.

Katie glanced up. "Sorry. I didn't…is this a picture of you with your dad?" She held the framed photo out.

Vance gave the doorframe a soft tap with his knuckles, allowing the happy memory to wash over him. "Uh-huh."

"You look so…young and skinny," she said, mouth twitching with a smile. "It's a great photo. Who took it?"

"My mom. It was the biggest largemouth bass I'd ever caught."

"Your mom was a good photographer."

Vance shrugged. "Listen, I'd like to apologize for anything and everything Dottie or Miss Sue said about me today. And I'd really, *really* appreciate it if you'd take all their elaborate stories and dial them down about fifty notches. They can weave and color a story better than Walt Disney."

Katie replaced the photo back on the bookshelf. "You mean like the one where your dad caught you having sex with your chemistry tutor?"

He felt the heat of humiliation warm his cheeks. They actually went that far back in the archives? Super.

"Yeah, well, on that one, they were telling the truth." He wasn't proud of it, and the older woman hadn't been worth the backlash…for sure.

"Or the one where you got caught doing a debutante in the coatroom at the country club dance? Not your date, I might add." She smirked as if all-knowing, which kind of pissed him off.

"Guilty. On both counts." He crossed the room and stood mere inches from a startled Katie with flushed cheeks and rosy lips.

"Turnabout is fair play. Why don't you tell me about a scandalous place you've done it?" He grabbed her arm before she could skirt around him and pulled her against his chest…where she belonged. "Oh no. You're not getting away that easy. You've heard my stories…now it's your turn." Katie struggled for release, but Vance tightened his hold, careful not to hurt her.

"Ever get caught?" he whispered against her ear,

kissing it. Her distinct orange blossom scent made him careless. "Ever been excited about the possibility of getting caught?" He nibbled her earlobe; her fragrance filled his head with seductive desire. Tightened nipples poking his chest almost buckled his knees. Katie trembled, and Vance wrapped her in his arms and feasted on the soft skin over her exposed neck, sucking and licking the areas he nipped with his teeth.

"Tell me," he murmured as he kissed his way down her heated chest. "Tell me…where you'd like to do it… with me," he growled. "In an elevator? On a balcony? Under a blanket of stars?" A moan of pleasure filled the air before Katie appeared to come to her senses and pushed hard, stumbling back, chest heaving, hands shaking, and stark need coloring her face.

For a moment, she didn't move. She stood motionless, as if waiting for something else to happen.

"Kat—"

"You! You don't play fair." The finger she pointed at his face trembled. "I'm…I'm going out. For some fresh air. You…you, go take a cold shower." With her finger still pointing, she edged around him as she if didn't trust him…or herself.

His laugh filled the room. Katie got smarter by the minute.

Chapter 8

KATIE SNATCHED UP HER PHONE AND HER FAVORITE Nikon camera before bolting from the den of iniquity where the wicked pirate exuded dangerous sexuality with his mesmerizing drawl and his talented lips.

"Grrr. What's the matter with me?" One whispered word from Vance, and she turned into a buttery plate of Southern grits. "I never lost control with Tad. Ever," she mumbled as she stomped around the perimeter of his property, snapping pictures she should've taken earlier instead of falling in swimming pools and falling under the sexy pirate's spell. "It must be this country air." Or Tad's disapproving looks and thin lips.

Katie snapped pictures of the side and back view of the barn, wondering how the inside looked. Where Vance worked and ate and…slept. She rolled her eyes in exasperation. The job pressure must be getting to her. And Vance Kerner with his badass look and tough attitude held too much appeal for her frame of mind.

She ventured farther away from the barn, meandering where the grass grew thicker and taller toward a low, crumbling stone wall, snapping more shots of the wildflowers growing among the weeds. Cooler air prevailed under the dense trees' shade, and Katie smelled the damp, earthy moss beneath her feet. Brushing dirt from the stone wall, she dropped down and fished out her phone. Frazzled by her dangerous thoughts, Katie needed talking off the ledge of lust. Going to Favorites, she dialed her best friend, Inslee, in Santa Monica.

"Oh snap! Look who decided to call. Hello, doll, where are you?" Inslee had picked up after only one ring.

"North Carolina. I've found the perfect location but still need to convince the owner…and my dad."

"Are you at the beach?"

"No. I'm in a small town called Harmony." Katie proceeded to describe to Inslee the house and barn and the amazing grounds for the miniseries.

"I wanna see. Send me pics. This job sounds promising for you." Well aware of Katie's dismal track record after quitting as a schoolteacher, Inslee knew the pressure she suffered from, not measuring up in the McKnight School of Overachievers. "Who owns the house?"

Under the shady canopy of trees, heat infused her body, remembering the owner and his smoldering kisses. Katie cleared her throat. "Okay, you ready for this—Vance Kerner, bestselling author."

"Hmm, I've heard of him." Tapping could be heard over the phone. Just like her dad, Inslee got busy Googling Vance on her computer. Inslee made an abundant living developing computer games and had no trouble with research. "Booyah. Have you actually met this guy?"

Katie stood, continuing her exploration of the surrounding fields. "Yeah. I'm trying to negotiate with him, but he keeps changing the subject. He's a schemer, and a womanizer—"

"And a rocket. This guy is gorgeous, doll. I'm starting to envy you and this job."

Katie chuckled, but it lacked humor. "It gets even

better. He's also a serial horn dog..." She proceeded to
fill Inslee in on her zany situation the last two days, with
babysitting the kids, meeting the people of Harmony,
Tad's phone call, and her dilemma with the smokin'
kissing pirate who seemed intent on seducing her.

"And all this kissing is a bad thing? I'm not seeing a
problem. Just say the word, and I'm on the next flight...
ready to replace your lips with mine." Leave it to Inslee
to glom on to the crux of Katie's problem.

"You are dating my brother Sam, remember?"

"Oh. Oh yeah, Sam. How could I forget? Yeah, I
love Sam."

Katie burst out laughing at Inslee's despondent tone.
"I don't think Sam would appreciate your commentary
on the hottie of Harmony."

"No, I don't suppose he would. But, come on. I'd
have to be blind or dead not to notice this slabali-
cious hunk."

"Get over your cyber lust and help me here. What
should I do?"

"About what?"

"About Vance and my dad and trying to make this
work. Everything. I can't tell Dad I'm babysitting to get
Vance to agree to the contract. He already thinks I'm out
of my league. I can already hear the lecture even before
it begins. One more slip-up, and he'll have me pushing
a broom at the studio after hours. And what about Tad?
Every time Vance kisses me, I feel like I'm cheating."
Or like I'm falling in love. Mother of Mariah Carey.
Did she just think the l-word? With someone she'd only
met yesterday? Impossible. She was too practical and
cynical to believe in love at first sight or even after eight

months of dating. But something inside Katie twisted and disagreed.

"First of all, Walter needs to lighten up," Inslee said, referring to Katie's dad. "Personally, I don't know why you keep working for him. Listen, doll, the only way you're going to be your own person is by getting out from underneath Daddy's thumb."

"Easy for you to say. He's a hard man to say no to."

"Only because you've allowed it. You're twenty-eight. A grown woman. Quit acting like the understudy or like you're never going to get the main role in your own life, for chrissakes. Take charge. Be the star of your life."

What life? Katie had been living in her parents' world and listening to their dictates since the day she was born. Their strong will and influences had impacted her life on so many levels that she had no idea who she was anymore. Her past kept crowding her present. She hated being a wimp, and she hated not living life on her terms.

"And second of all, Tad is a class A jerk who has to check his balls at the door every time he goes to work. He's such a kiss-ass. Even Sam calls him a suck-up. I told you to ditch him months ago. Forget him and focus on Vance da bomb, not Tad the butt nugget." Inslee always made it perfectly clear where she stood on any given issue, and she didn't take crap from anyone.

Katie passed a grove of trees and came upon a clearing where an old farm-like house stood about a football field away. The brown weathered boards had been patched, and the tin roof appeared to be rust-red. In its dilapidated state, it had a picturesque quality with the low afternoon sun casting a pink tint. The photographer in Katie couldn't wait to capture it with her camera.

"…besides, what do you have to lose?"

"Excuse me?" Katie hadn't been listening to Inslee's explanation.

"Go for it. You're on the other side of the country, living with a very hot, eligible, extremely hunky-dunky guy. Take advantage of what he's offering. No one knows you there. And no one will find out about it here. My lips are sealed. Even to your adorable brother."

Katie hesitated. What Inslee suggested sounded slutty and tawdry and completely depraved. And Katie had never been more tempted. "I don't know. I'd feel like Hailey the Hussy, remember her?"

"Hailey's a B actor at best, and a ho who slept with the entire cast and crew of *Pretty Little Backstabbers*. She even tried to seduce Sam. You're not trying to sleep with the entire town of Harmony. Are you?"

"No. Only its most famous resident, besides Keith Morgan, the professional tennis player. He's pretty hot, too, but he's married."

"Seducing a married man in a small town probably isn't a great plan. However, seducing a married man in LA is a common occurrence. Think your dad has ever been seduced?"

Katie gave an involuntary shudder. "Stop. That's not something I even want to consider." It didn't seem likely, but maybe that was why her mom tried so hard to turn back the clock.

"Sam doesn't think so either. Anyhow, live a little. You act like an old spinster, and you dress like one too."

"I do not. That's ridiculous—"

"Even Sam agrees. Come on, Katie...now's your chance," Inslee said in a tempting lure-you-to-the-dark-side voice.

"Well...maybe—" *CRACK!* Katie jumped about a mile in the air. Struck with heart-stopping fear, she jerked her head, scanning the surroundings. "Inslee? Somebody's shooting, and looks like I'm the target. I'm outta here! Later."

"Sonofa—Go! Call me back when you're safe."

Katie shoved her phone in her pocket and started to sprint back in the direction she'd come.

"Hold it right there!" She skidded to a halt at the gravelly voice. Her heart thumped like a bass drum, pounding in her ears. Shaking like a pathetic leaf, Katie had only one thought: She'd been to church on the last day of her life. Thank the Lord.

"Who are you, and what're you doing trespassing on my property?" The gravelly voice had drawn nearer. Afraid of whom she'd face, Katie turned slowly and got the second shock of the day. A tall man with thick gray hair and black eyes cradled a shotgun/rifle/machine gun—she had no idea—across his arms. He wore a crisp khaki shirt, belted inside new jeans, and a deep don't-mess-with-me scowl on his face. Katie recognized him from his pictures: General Kerner...Vance's father.

"Speak up. I asked you a question," he barked in an authoritative tone. The sudden urge to straighten her shoulders and salute came over her.

"K-Katie McKnight, sir...General Kerner, sir." His dark eyes narrowed like his son's, but whereas Vance's never frightened her...his dad's were a different story. And the big, scary gun full of bullets didn't help.

"Katie McKnight, why don't you tell me what you're doing trespassing on my land and how you know my name?" he all but growled.

"Yes sir. Um, I'm sorry about the trespassing thing. I didn't know this was your land." Katie gave a nervous glance over her shoulder. Now would be the perfect time for Vance to come sniffing after her, like the horn dog that he was. "I'm working, er, helping with your grandkids"—she motioned with her hand—"over at Vance's house." Something flickered behind his dark eyes. "I, uh, recognized you from the photos."

Moments that felt like hours passed before either spoke. Katie drew a long, unsteady breath. The general's rigid stance relaxed, and he finally broke the silence.

"You like iced tea?" General Kerner lowered the gun in his arms.

"Excuse me?" Katie's mind stuttered. Was this a trick question?

He shrugged and turned. "Come with me."

Katie nervously glanced around. The strumming banjo music from *Deliverance* started to play in her head. Where was Vance when she needed him?

Suddenly General Kerner faced her, making Katie jump in her skin. He held his hand out, palm up. "I'll take your phone and camera. You don't need to contact Vance and tell him where you are."

Katie hesitated. "You do realize you're scaring the bazooka out of me, don't you?"

A small smile curled the corner of his firm lips, and Katie caught a glimpse of Vance in that smile. "You'll be all right. Hand over the phone and camera."

Katie fumbled with the phone in her pocket; with

shaky hands she placed both phone and camera in General Kerner's large, rough palm. "I'll get them back?" Without answering, General Kerner strode toward the dilapidated house Katie had admired earlier. She had to skip to keep up.

"You're not planning to kill me and bury me in the woods, are you? Because I'd like you to consider—"

"Kill you? What gave you that idea?" He stared as if she were the dumbest woman on earth. "I'm simply inviting you inside for something cool to drink. I was hoping you'd be good company."

Katie's mouth dropped open. *Good company?* She lifted her head and leveled her own scary look, maybe not strong enough for the military, but she'd scared her fair share of nine-year-olds when she taught school. "Your gun for starters. And your delivery could use some work. Instead of scaring the poop out of me, you could've introduced yourself and asked nicely."

General Kerner surveyed her for a long moment and then tossed his head and laughed. It sounded rusty, as if he didn't do it very often, and in that moment, he reminded her of Vance. She gave a tentative smile, unsure of his change in tactics.

"You're going to be real good company, I can tell," he said between hoots. He stuck out his hand. "Chuck Kerner."

Katie paused and then shook his hand. "Nice to meet you, Gen—"

"Call me Chuck. I'm retired now. Come on."

Not knowing what to expect, Katie stepped over the front-door threshold and froze. Judging from the outside, you'd think the interior would be rustic, rudimentary, and downright creepy, but not so. Inside, Chuck's home was warm, inviting, and the perfect cozy hideaway.

"Have a seat." Chuck gestured to a black Windsor-back barstool in front of a large kitchen island. He retrieved a pitcher of iced tea from the stainless steel refrigerator and pulled down two glasses from the open shelving. "Tea's sweet. Hope that's okay. I can tell you're not from around these parts."

Katie leaned her elbows on the butcher-block island top. "Sweet tea sounds great."

Chuck handed her a glass and held his up as if to toast. Katie clinked her glass with his. "What are we toasting?"

"Good company and pretty girls," he said, smiling, and then took a long drink.

～ww～

Katie strolled back through the fields and woods to Vance's house with a slight frown playing around her lips. She'd spent almost two hours visiting with Chuck Kerner, and she'd really had a nice time. He'd been the perfect gentleman, after scaring years off her life with the whole sinister/*Texas Chainsaw*/Ted Bundy thing in the beginning. But once inside, over tea and pimento cheese sandwiches—her first ever…not bad—they'd had an interesting conversation. More like she did all the talking, and he did all the asking.

When she told him about his grandkids and baby-sitting for Vance to allow him to finish his third book, Chuck had gotten real quiet. He didn't open up about his relationship with Vance. At. All. And Katie didn't ask why he hadn't visited his grandkids. But when she'd explained about using Vance's house for the miniseries, he'd gotten that over-his-dead-body look, just like his son. Katie sighed as she bent to pick some wildflowers, knowing she hadn't gained an ally for her cause, but left his home feeling as if she'd gained a friend.

As she approached the back of the house, she drew near the beautiful outdoor living space, equipped with fire pit and cushioned sofas. The back door slammed hard, as if someone was trying to break it. She glanced up, and Vance was coming straight for her in an all-black pirate rage. *What the…?* Twice in one day, Kerner men scared her gray. Katie stumbled over a rock, catching herself before falling, when Vance was on top of her in two seconds flat.

"Where the hell have you been? I've been worried sick. Don't you answer your phone?"

"I was taking—*humph*—"

Vance snatched her off her feet and rocked his mouth over hers, kissing the California avocados right out of her. Katie wrapped her arms around his neck and held on for dear life. The kiss was rough and demanding and punishing, and Katie loved it, but then his lips softened and lingered and toyed with hers, and she loved that even more.

"God, I'd thought I'd lost you," he murmured against her mouth. Katie nibbled his lips, enjoying the texture and taste, when he suddenly let go and dropped her back to the ground.

"Where'd you go? What were you doing?" His angry voice flared again. She straightened her shirt, along with the confusion inside her head.

"Taking pictures." She folded her arms across her chest. "What's your problem?"

"For three hours? You've been taking pictures for three hours?"

That and talking with your dad. But Chuck Kerner had made Katie swear she wouldn't tell Vance about meeting him.

"You didn't think to text or call or anything?" Fear, rage, and something Katie couldn't quite identify flashed across Vance's fierce face.

"I'm sorry for leaving you with the kids. I know you need to write. I didn't think—"

"The hell with the kids. I thought you'd left. Run off." He pushed his fingers through his tousled hair, giving him a dark avenging angel appearance.

Katie blinked. "Without my car? Why would you think that?"

"I thought I'd scared you off." She wondered if he knew his entire heart controlled his voice. She'd really shaken him up. In all of her twenty-eight years, she couldn't remember anyone ever being distraught over her whereabouts to this degree. Except for the time when she'd been seven and wandered off at some movie premiere. She remembered her dad's anger at her carelessness more than his fear of losing her.

Chuckling, she tried lightening the mood. "Scare me off? Not a chance, Pirate Man. You still have a contract to sign." Vance brushed the backs of his knuckles down her cheek in a gentle caress. Odd that he could make her feel cherished in such a short period of time.

"Uncle Vance! Mom's on the phone." Donald stood by the kitchen door, holding Vance's cell phone.

"I'm hungry," Dover said, jumping down the back steps. "What's for dinner?"

"Pixie! Pop!" Danny tumbled from the steps, chasing the cat and the barking dog.

"Oh Lord," Katie sighed. "I'll get the kids. You answer the phone."

Vance stood upstairs in the loft, looking out the window onto the backyard. It was almost ten o'clock, and the kids had been fed and put to bed an hour ago. Katie had managed to get dinner on the table, save the kitten from a near-drowning in the toilet, and catch Dover as he slid down the stairs on a cardboard box. Vance had been very quiet during dinner, still reeling from the afternoon he'd spent pacing and cursing and knocking his head against a brick wall for running Katie off like a scared rabbit. Until he discovered she'd been wandering aimlessly, snapping pictures and picking wildflowers. It took every ounce of control in his body not to haul her over his shoulder and lock her away in his loft for safekeeping. This surge of lust, hunger, need, at least on his part, was starting to piss him off. He'd never felt this way about anyone before. Why now? With a woman he'd met less than thirty hours ago?

He stared down at the outdoor fireplace where Katie sat on one of the cushioned sofas, sipping her mug of coffee. Temperatures had dropped, and Vance had lit a few logs for her. The outdoor space had been built at the same time he'd added the master suite, equipped with small bar, flat-screen TV, reading lamps, and ceiling fan. Vance enjoyed the amenities during the fall and winter months.

He wanted nothing more than to share the comfortable

sofa with a soft Katie, holding her close and never letting go. He ached for this woman. Surviving the next four weeks with the sweet, pretty, and enchanting Katie McKnight would be his biggest challenge. She didn't make this shared attraction easy. She kept fighting him and herself. Vance placed his palm against the cool glass, creating a handprint, just as Katie's handprint had touched his heart. He hadn't expected this connection, but it existed in all its tumultuous glory, and he couldn't deny it. Didn't want to. But the speed at which it had happened scared the living crap out of him.

The blank glow from his computer screen caught the corner of his eye, taunting him. Telling him to get his head out of the clouds and back where it belonged, writing the next bestseller. The bottle of Jim Beam sitting on his desk with its amber liquid lured him into believing everything would be fine with one more belt.

His phone buzzed, pulling him away from the window and his thoughts.

"What's up?"

"Vance, my friend, we are onto something big. We've been in touch with McKnight Studios, and the word is Walter's very interested in your series," Mike, his agent, said.

"That's good."

"No, that's great! This could be huge. We're talking film rights, *not* movie-of-the-week or TV rights. Now do I have your attention?"

"Absolutely. Who writes the screenplay?"

"Not sure. Usually they use their people." Vance's grip tightened over the plastic cover to his phone. If his dad wouldn't read his books, maybe he'd be tempted to watch the movie. And for that reason, Vance didn't want his story mucked up by some Hollywood screenplay-writing hack. "We're still in the infant stages. I might know more tomorrow," Mike said.

"Sounds promising. Thanks. I'm very interested."

"How's the book going? And more important, how's Katie McKnight? That wonderful daughter of Walter? You haven't scared her off?"

Not yet. Almost. Remembering this afternoon caused anxiety to ride up and grab him by the throat. "She's here and seems to be content to babysit the monsters."

"I bet that's not the only reason she has agreed to hang around." Mike laughed at his innuendo.

"Considering I haven't signed her damn contract, I'm thinking she isn't going anywhere until I do." He hoped and prayed that was true for completely different reasons.

"Whatever it takes. We want Katie and her daddy real happy, because we want to turn your bestsellers into blockbusters. It's a good day to be alive," Mike said, and Vance could practically hear him rubbing his hands together in anticipation.

Right. Vance needed that reminder.

Chapter 9

THE NEXT MORNING, KATIE DRESSED, FED, AND LOADED the kids in Vance's truck for school. First stop, Harmony Elementary, where she dropped the boys, and then the Methodist Church, where Danny attended preschool. Vance had shown up at the breakfast table looking like he'd slept in his rumpled clothes...or not, with bloodshot eyes and a two-day growth of beard. Instead of speaking, he grunted his hello, poured a huge mug of coffee, and disappeared back to his loft to continue the difficult task of writing his next book. Katie couldn't imagine the stress of being under the gun to produce another bestseller. She experienced stress trying to live up to her parents' expectations, but not the entire book-reading public. That had to be huge.

After delivering Danny to her classroom, Katie ran into Bertie Morgan in the church parking lot. She'd dropped off her three-year-old son as well.

"Hey there. How you holding up?" she asked Katie.

"Fine. It's only been two days, but so far, so good."

"And Harmony's hottie? How's he holding up?"

The heat of embarrassment flamed her cheeks. "Fine. He's been holed up in the barn, writing...at least I think that's what he's doing." When he wasn't railing against her for leaving him. *Leaving* him. How absurd, and yet...Katie had been flattered. Who wouldn't be? The hunk of Harmony went a little loco because he thought floundering Katie was going to leave him.

"Yeah, when he's writing, he can get a little testy."

"Oh, I didn't say he was testy."

"You didn't have to. Having a beautiful woman right under his nose, living under his roof and sleeping in his bed while he wrestles a whopper of a deadline is more than enough to make Vance Kerner testy. Especially when he'd rather be doing the wild thang with you." Bertie winked.

Katie stumbled in her tan leather flats on the black-top parking lot, refusing to believe Bertie's explanation. "Hold on there. Nothing's going on between Vance and me, really." Except a lot of kissing and heavy groping. "I can't even get him to focus long enough to sign my contract."

Bertie smirked. "He will. Don't worry. Anything to keep you around longer."

Doubt and apprehension skittered along Katie's spine. She didn't want Vance to sign the contract because he wanted to keep her around. She wanted him to sign because of her incredible ability of persuasion. She almost snorted out loud. Get real. At this point, she didn't care why he signed it. She wanted the assignment finished. She'd already lowered herself by agreeing to babysit as part of the bargain, and lied about it to her dad. She didn't have much lower to go. She wanted to show her dad she'd done a good job. For once, she wanted to prove him wrong. And then...and then she wanted to quit. Katie stopped just as she reached the truck. *Quit.* Did she have the nerve? Katie's palms began to sweat, and her left eyebrow twitched.

Bertie gave her an odd look. "You look hungry. Come on. Follow me." Bertie waved her hand. "My brother owns the best diner in town."

"The Dog?" Katie asked, tamping down her anxiety.

"Yeah. How'd you know?"

"From Dottie Duncan. She invited the kids swimming at her house yesterday."

Bertie unlocked the door to her green Lexus SUV. "Girlfriend, you have gotten the seal of approval if Dottie extended an invitation. Be thankful Miss Sue Percy wasn't there…you'd be as good as married."

Katie's face must've blanched, because Bertie stopped with her door half-open and arched one brow.

"Bertie? Miss Sue was there," Katie whispered.

She gave a sympathetic nod. "My brother makes a mean Bloody Mary. You're gonna need it."

<center>~~~</center>

Inside the Dog, Katie's gaze darted around, taking in the bright, colorful decor. Bertie explained that she'd redecorated a few years back to breathe new life into her deceased parents' old restaurant, and the customer response had been very positive. Except when Keith had seen it for the first time and insulted Bertie about her design talent.

With a sly smile, she said, "He eventually came around to my way of thinking…in more ways than one."

Katie ordered the special: cheesy eggs with a side of bacon and homemade grits. She was becoming a real Southern girl, with her second helping of grits in two days. The waitress, wearing a lime-green T-shirt with *Get Down at the Dog* in black sequins, delivered Bloody Marys with celery stalks in Mason jars.

"Welcome. May your stay in Harmony be fun and filled with adventure." Bertie held up her glass.

"Thank you." Katie sipped her drink and moaned. "Man, that *is* good. What's your brother's secret?"

"I have no clue. He won't share. Not even with his wife, Liza." Bertie sipped through the straw provided. "How do you like Harmony so far? I know you're used to the big city, and we've got nothing on Hollywood, but—"

"Harmony has something Hollywood doesn't…soul."

Bertie's grin widened. "I like that. We do have soul and lots of character. Or rather, *characters*?"

Speaking of characters, they both spotted Dottie walking with determined purpose in their direction in a patriotic combo that would've made the Founding Fathers proud. Perched on thick, red wedge sandals, with navy ruffled walking shorts and the first few buttons of her red-and-white gingham shirt undone, exposing the tops of her generous breasts.

"Move on over, Bertie." Dottie made a shooing motion with her hands. "I'd like to talk to Miss California here."

"I thought you talked yesterday," Bertie said as she scooted down the booth's bench.

"Yeah, but we didn't get 'round to that miniseries she wants to make over at Vance's place." Dottie shifted her full hips over the yellow-and-green Dalmatian-spotted vinyl seat. "How goes your method of persuasion? Having any luck?" The waitress delivered their meals and Dottie's large iced tea. With a smug expression, Dottie said, "Looks like I've converted someone. You let me know if those grits are as good as Geraldine's."

"Nothing's as good as Geraldine's," Bertie added as

she speared a fresh strawberry from her healthy fruit plate. A pang of guilt stabbed Katie's stomach as her mother's voice on watching her waistline played like a broken record in her head. But the smells of crisp bacon and warm butter convinced her that Crystal McKnight was three thousand miles away and unable to monitor calorie intake.

Katie groaned with pure pleasure as the savory, buttered grits melted in her mouth. "These are truly delicious, but I have to admit"—Dottie leaned in with one arched brow—"Geraldine's are better." Katie smiled, enjoying another bite.

"Damn right." Dottie settled back in the booth. "Now…what tricks you using to get Vance to come on board with this Hollywood series? I like a gal who uses something other than sex to get a man. Shows spunk and imagination."

Katie almost choked on the bite of bacon in her mouth. She hadn't been imaginative in the least. It took all the willpower she possessed last evening not to follow the lure of Pirate Man's heated gaze as he'd watched her from the loft's window. She had warred with herself all night, repeating over and over that he was a player and had her tune memorized. With a dismal shake of her head, she said, "I'm afraid I haven't been very imaginative."

"You mean you've had *sex* already?" Dottie boomed. Color flooded Katie's face. The breakfast crowd all stopped eating and stared.

Bertie mumbled, "Watch out…here it comes."

"W-what?" Katie gripped the edge of the table.

"Told ya, they're filming sex."

"Vance is making porno with that Hollywood gal?"

"He's a porn star. Never did believe he wrote no books."

Katie slumped low in her seat. If…*when* this got back to Vance, it wouldn't be beneath her to use the children as shields to deflect his anger.

"Don't worry. It'll die down, and they'll be onto something else…eventually," Bertie said.

"Colorful people, that's all. If Hollywood had any smarts, they'd make a movie out of Harmony." Dottie leaned over the table and said in a loud whisper, "Unless you're making porn." She waggled her eyebrows.

Katie's ponytail smacked her cheek from shaking her head so hard. "Absolutely not. Strictly a teenage horror show. Lots of killing zombies, but no sex."

"If you say so."

"I do. I do."

"Good. That's settled. Now how you gonna convince Vance, if you say you aren't sleeping with him and you're not very imaginative?" Dottie asked.

Katie gave herself a mental shake. Jumping from topic to topic was making her dizzy. "Patience? I'm waiting him out. I've been blessed with a huge amount of perseverance." Evident from working two years in an industry she hated.

Dottie shook her cobalt-blue nail at Katie. "Vance's smart, and he's tricky."

And soon to be enraged when all this porn talk got back to him.

Bertie nudged Dottie in the ribs, her gaze riveted on the entrance. "Look…can you believe it?" she said in a low voice.

Katie swiveled around and gasped as Dottie murmured, "Well, don't that beat all."

Near the entrance stood an awkward General Chuck Kerner, holding his battered fishing hat and wearing stiff jeans and a tight scowl on his face.

"Miss California, you are in for a treat," Dottie said, waving her hand with flashy gold rings at Chuck. "Morning, Chuck. Come on over here. Got someone I want you to meet."

Katie held her breath. Chuck had been insistent she not inform Vance of their meeting. But Katie knew it was just a matter of time before Vance found out. Chuck's scowl deepened, but he worked his way toward their booth.

"That's Vance's dad, General Kerner," Bertie whispered to Katie. "He doesn't get out in public much. Lives in a really old farmhouse on the back of the Kerner property."

Katie nodded, biting her lower lip when Chuck reached the table.

"Chuck Kerner, what brings you into town on a Monday morning? Run out of squirrel meat for breakfast?" Dottie asked. Katie's mouth dropped open, and Bertie ducked her head and pretended to be fascinated with her fruit plate.

"Good morning, Bertie, Katie…Dorothy," Chuck said with a tense set to his jaw. "Katie, may I join you?" he asked.

"C-certainly." Katie scooted over to make room. Bertie and Dottie exchanged stunned looks.

Never one to beat around the bush, Dottie demanded, "What's going on here? How do you know Chuck?"

"Um, we met yesterday when I was walking the property and taking pictures for the studio."

"Does Vance know about this?" Dottie leaned forward. "Do you know that Chuck is Vance's daddy?"

Katie nodded. "Y-yes and—"

"I asked Katie not to bring Vance into this, and I'd appreciate it for once if you'd keep your mouth shut, Dorothy," Chuck snapped.

"I just bet you would." Dottie gave Chuck the squinty eye. "You still holding that grudge? Over something a young, reckless boy said against you. When you gonna give him another chance?" She shook her head, but her stiff, platinum-blond hair didn't move. "It's time to let it go, Chuck. That boy is your son."

And the plot thickened. Bad blood between a father and son made Katie's heart spasm. "Dorothy, I don't need you telling me how to run my life. I've managed quite nicely without you all these years." The thick tension between Chuck and Dottie hung over their booth like a black thundercloud.

Katie shifted uncomfortably, and Bertie said in an overly bright voice, "General, what would you like for breakfast? It's on the house."

"That won't be necessary—"

"I insist." Bertie gave the waitress a frantic wave.

After Chuck ordered, he smiled at Katie. "Nice to see you again. I was out walking this morning when I saw you drive by with my gran—the kids." He folded his large hands on top of the table.

"I didn't see you, or I would've stopped."

"No, no. That's not necessary. I wouldn't expect—"

"The hell it isn't. When was the last time you visited with your grandkids?" Dottie butted in.

"Don't start with me, Dorothy," he growled low. Bertie gave Dottie a warning nudge with her elbow, but Dottie's focus never left Chuck's stone-like face.

"Somebody's gotta stand up to you. And I'm volunteering, since I'm old enough and mean enough. I don't care how many troops you commanded over the years. This time I'm giving the orders, and you're gonna listen, you stubborn ol' coot."

Chuck eased back, and Katie didn't know him well enough, but it seemed his lips thinned as he repressed a smile. The waitress arrived with his meal and hot coffee. He nodded his thanks and returned his attention to Dottie's mulish face.

"You may be mean, Dorothy, but there's not an old bone in your body." Dottie's brows arched up beneath her stiff bangs. "And you can give all the orders you want…doesn't mean I'm gonna listen."

"Katie, now you know where Vance gets his stubbornness from. Apples don't fall far." Dottie rocked her way out of the booth and stood. "I'm gonna say what's on my mind before I leave—"

"Don't let the door hit you on the behind on your way out," Chuck mumbled into his coffee mug. Bertie choked on her fruit, swallowing a laugh, and Katie sat frozen, watching the exchange.

Dottie planted her palm on top of the table and leaned forward, giving Chuck a ringside view of her generous chest. "Vance's supposed to take *your* grandkids to see their mama this weekend in Greenville, and he don't have time, with his deadline only a few weeks away.

If you were any kind of grandfather at all, *you'd* volunteer to take those wild hooligans and give your son a break." Chuck's gaze sharpened on Dottie's face before it dipped to the tops of her exposed breasts.

"And how is it that you know my family's schedule, you meddling, irksome woman?" Exactly. Even Katie didn't know about these plans. Another conversation she needed to have with the elusive ladies' man.

"I make it a habit to know lots of things about people I care about…you should try it sometime, you battered, old, grumpy recluse." And with that parting shot, Dottie spun on her red sandals and sashayed out of the Dog as Chuck Kerner tracked her every step.

He shook his head. "Interesting woman. But she needs a hobby besides snooping and interfering in everyone else's affairs." Katie had a feeling in this instance, *hobby* meant *man*.

"Dottie can be blunt, but she always means well," Bertie said, trying to soften Dottie's harsh words.

"Ever since Ron died…instead of grieving, she filled her days with everyone else's business." Chuck sounded introspective and not combative, as Katie would've expected after the battle lines had been drawn. Strange for a military man.

"Everyone grieves in their own way. Some would say you're still grieving…is that true, General?" Katie glanced up, surprised at Bertie's daring question.

Chuck chewed for a moment and then said, "In a way, I guess I am. But not just for my wife, Helen. When you've seen as much death and destruction as I have, you're always grieving deep down. It never leaves you." His voice sounded hollow. Katie wrapped her palm over his strong, large hand and gave a squeeze. Chuck squeezed back.

"You two are about the prettiest things a man could ever wish for at his breakfast table. Thank you for sitting with an old man way past his prime," he said, striking a lighter mood.

"Anytime, General. And I'm not buying *past your prime*… If you got out a little more, you'd be turning a lot of heads around here." Bertie waggled her eyebrows, and a slight blush appeared on Chuck's weathered cheeks.

"General, about your grandkids"—Katie could feel Chuck stiffen next to her—"I think it would be a great idea if you drove them to Greenville to see your daughter-in-law, Gloria. Vance could use the break, and Katie will definitely need one by Friday, won't you, Katie?" Bertie said.

"Well, they haven't been bad, but they are…lively." Katie feared her boot camp would pale in comparison to the one the general would put his grandkids through. Probably fit for a marine. *Yikes*.

Chuck nodded. "Let me think about it. I'll give Katie my answer when she comes by for another visit this week. You are coming again?" He speared her with his sharpened gaze, but this time a flicker of hope flashed behind his dark eyes.

"Sure. Only if you promise to teach me to play chess on that beautiful set of yours." Katie had admired an antique chess set with carved figures from the Battle of Gettysburg, sitting on an old pine table. It appeared as though a game was already in progress.

"Be my pleasure." Chuck stood, fishing for his wallet.

"Your money's no good here, General," Bertie

teased, waving away his cash. "But I expect to see you back again real soon."

"Thank you, ladies. Have a nice day." He turned with his back and shoulders military-straight and left the Dog.

"Wow. Very interesting. You want to tell me what's going on with you and General Instill-Fear Kerner?"

Katie fidgeted with her floral tunic top. "You heard it all. Ran into him yesterday. He scared the bejeezus out of me with his shotgun. I thought he was some scary mountain hillbilly and I was a goner, but then he invited me inside for iced tea, and we chatted for over an hour."

"We're a few hours away from any mountains and hillbillies," Bertie said with a wry smile. "But he can be intimidating with or without a shotgun. Why didn't you tell Vance?"

"He asked me not to. And it's not like I owe Vance anything. Right now, that conniving womanizer owes me." Katie clapped her hand over her mouth. "I'm so sorry. I know he's a very good friend of yours." How catty. She didn't know Bertie well enough to bash one of her best friends.

"Don't apologize. He's been known to womanize here and there, but those days are behind him. Especially with those kids. Poor baby." Bertie sounded as if she didn't feel sorry for Vance at all.

"Do you know why Vance and his dad have a strained relationship? Sounds like it's been a long stalemate."

Bertie shook her head, reaching for her drink. "Something they argued about when Vance was barely out of high school. I don't know the exact conversation, because Vance never talks about it. But I do know he's been trying to make amends ever since. That's why he writes books about war. Has something to do with his dad and his career." Bertie shrugged. "Brogan probably knows the whole story but keeps it to himself."

"Nobody talks about it?" Katie gave a short, disbelieving laugh. "From what I've seen so far, this town talks about everything, from homemade grits to porn stars. I can't believe the story behind their bad history hasn't been bandied about."

"I agree. It's weird. But truthfully, even if everyone had heard the tale, there's no way the truth wouldn't be exaggerated and distorted. I wouldn't trust what I heard." A sly smile tilted Bertie's full lips. "I bet *you* could get Vance to talk."

A loud snort escaped her lips. "Hardly." Grope, yes. Kiss, most definitely, but *not* talk.

"From my vantage point Saturday night, all you have to do is crook your finger, and Vance will come crawling with his tail wagging and his tongue hanging out."

"Clearly, you're delusional. I'm the one with the tongue hanging out, chasing after those kids."

"Trust me. Vance is not only interested, but he's got it bad. Otherwise, he wouldn't have been so angry when Brogan brought up all his past girlfriends, or whatever." Bertie flipped a hank of hair over her shoulder. "If you'd been one of those floozies sitting there, he wouldn't have given two door knockers over conversation about his love life."

Instead of feeling elated, Katie's breakfast weighed heavily in her stomach. She felt the same connection to Vance, but what difference did it make? They were from two different worlds. And she needed to get back to hers and continue to live according to her parents' edicts *or* make a clean break…forever. *Easier said than done, people*. Weak and wimpy didn't begin to describe her inner turmoil. When the patriarch of the family was domineering, demanding, and belittling your entire life—unknowingly, of course—you acquired things like twitches and huge vats of doubt that you carried daily.

Walter McKnight had no idea his delivery was tough. Katie never doubted his love for her, but his expectations were too high. And trying to reach them, well, Katie found it to be…exhausting.

"If you won't use your influence with Vance to get the story, maybe you should try the general. He's really taken with you."

Fiddling with her napkin, Katie said, "Oh, I don't believe—"

"You've struck a chord with the general. He barely engages with anyone in town, and today he actually sat and ate breakfast with us. That's progress, and I think you had a hand in it."

"He's really very nice. I'm sure if anyone took the time to visit with him, they'd get the same results."

Bertie shook her head. "You've managed to do what the people of Harmony haven't been able to do for years." Bertie stopped speaking and gave Katie a dicey look.

"I'm almost afraid to ask," Katie said warily.

"You've managed to snag the elusive but oh-so-dreamy Vance Kerner, and you've encouraged the general out of his hardened shell."

Flattered, she laughed nervously. "Don't be silly. I haven't snagged anything in my life except a fingernail, and the general came out of his shell on his own."

"We'll see." Bertie leaned back, folding her arms

across her emerald-green knit top. "Tell me, were you getting a weird vibe between Dottie and the general?"

"Like running for cover from incoming missiles? That kind of vibe?"

Bertie's shiny mahogany hair bounced as she shook her head. "There was an undercurrent not based on their dislike for each other. Quite the opposite, if you ask me."

"You think they're…attracted to each other?"

"There have been weirder couplings around here—"

"Bert, what are you gossiping about?" A good-looking guy with an apron tied around his waist started gathering their dirty dishes. "Don't you have a family to take care of? Dogs to walk? Walls to paper?"

"Bite me," Bertie snapped. "Katie, meet my brother, Cal. One of the weird couplings I'm referring to. Cal happens to be married to my least favorite person from high school. Liza Palmer and I are now frenemies, aren't we, my sweet bro?"

"You're so nutty," Cal said to Bertie. "Nice to meet you, Katie from California. Word travels fast." A killer smile flashed, and Katie wondered how so many good-looking men ended up in this small town. "Liza's home taking care of Allison, your adorable niece and goddaughter. You might want to stop by and keep her company."

Alert, Bertie shot forward in her seat. "What's wrong with Allison?"

"Just a cold and cough. Liza didn't want to send her to preschool."

"My poor baby. Okay, I'm off." Bertie reached for her handbag. Katie scrambled from the booth, chasing after Bertie.

"Cal, it was nice meeting you," Katie called over her shoulder. Cal nodded and hoisted the tray of stacked dishes.

Outside, Katie said to Bertie, "Thanks for breakfast. Can you point me in the direction of the nearest grocery store?" She needed to stock up for the week. An empty box of Cap'n Crunch had almost caused a toddler revolution this morning.

"If you want healthy, hit BetterBites right down Main Street. For everything else, Piggly Wiggly is a little farther out toward the highway."

"Got it."

Patting Katie's arm, Bertie said, "I'll call you later… I think I'm on the verge of being brilliant," she said with a gleam in her bright green eyes.

"What?"

"Let me mull it over first. Then I'll fill you in."

"You've piqued my curiosity. Am I involved?" Katie gave a nervous chuckle.

"Only if you're a romantic at heart." Bertie waved and disappeared inside her car.

Chapter 10

VANCE CHECKED HIS WORD COUNT FOR THE UMPTEENTH time in the last hour, scowling at the stagnant number on his computer screen. He shuffled the stacks of notes on top of his desk and muted the war video playing on the DVD. He'd been up since five a.m., having slept only four hours the night before. Even with two days of quiet and uninterrupted writing time, he'd barely managed to finish six scenes. This time he couldn't blame the kids.

He blamed Katie.

Sweet, sumptuous, voluptuous Katie. His Achilles' heel. Why now? Ever since she'd stood inside his kitchen with her fresh face and wide eyes, he'd felt like a damned fool. He considered himself normal and intelligent, but since Saturday, all he could think of was Katie and her bright smile and pretty widow's peak, and he felt like a complete moron.

He'd tried hiring a starchy nanny with tight bun and hawk nose to help with the three whirling dervishes. Someone he could easily ignore, but he ended up with a California cupcake who scrambled his brains and had him thinking about sleeping arrangements. Not war strategies and hidden explosives. If he had an ounce of sense, he'd escort her finely shaped ass out his door and into her classic Mercedes. Old Mrs. Cornwaddle with her walker would have been a better babysitter for his peace of mind. Hell, Colonel, their half-blind retriever, would have been a better babysitter. If he was smart, he'd say the hell with turning his books into movies and send Katie back to the land of fruit and nuts. But he knew, like he knew his own autograph, he wouldn't be sending her away. Because he was hooked...captivated. Not exactly sure why now or why her, but the minute those contracts got shoved under his nose, he'd sign whatever she wanted. Anything to make her happy. And didn't that suck green donkey balls?

He glanced at the computer clock...9:15 a.m. Katie had left around eight to drop off the kids and then texted him to say she'd be having breakfast with Bertie. Vance gritted his teeth, knowing Bertie would be filling her head with more stories about his sordid sexual past. Nothing about his past cast him in a good light. Sure, he'd sowed his wild oats like any red-blooded, healthy male. Right? Right. He'd probably sowed more than most...a lot more, but for the last three months, he hadn't been "sowing" anything, unless you counted buttons on Dana Sue's overalls.

He set his mouth in a tight line and stared at the dreck he'd spent the last two hours writing. As he highlighted three passages for deletion, his phone buzzed.

"Yeah," he growled at his agent on the other line.

"You know I wouldn't disturb you unless it's very important. You sitting down?"

"All day and into the night." Maybe getting off his butt and shooting some hoops would open the door to his creative juices.

"Our agents are brokering a deal with Walter McKnight. He's in for all three books."

Vance scrubbed his hand across his unshaven face. "How much of my soul do I have to sell?"

"Spoken like a true tortured writer. No *wow* or *fantastic* or *thank you, Mike, you're a fucking genius*."

"Thank you, Mike, you're a fucking genius."

"You wait. You'll be thanking me and calling me the greatest literary agent ever to walk God's green earth."

"I say that already. Didn't I dedicate my last book to you? It was so touching you said it brought tears to your eyes."

"Wrong. I said the money I'll be making off your sales brought tears to my eyes."

"Same diff. So, what's next?"

"Ball's in his court. We wait. How's Katie? You making her happy? Because it's important she stay happy. If Katie's happy, then Daddy's happy." Vance would like to make both Katie and himself happy between the sheets…multiple times.

Vance leaned back in his chair and fiddled with a notebook on his desk. "She seems happy. Or at least she doesn't seem unhappy. The kids haven't pushed her down any wells or locked her in the storage shed…yet. I haven't signed her damn contract, but that's only a minor detail at this point." Because he'd resigned himself to the fact that whatever she wanted, he'd make sure she got.

"Do whatever it takes to keep her happy until we hear back from Walter's team, okay?"

"Yes, Master. Anything else, Master?"

"Don't forget you have a book signing this week in Raleigh." Vance thunked his head against his desktop. "Remind Shannon to email your updated calendar."

Shannon Nichols, Vance's assistant, helped keep him organized and stayed on top of his social media platforms.

"Got it," Vance mumbled into the phone.

"And…finish that third book."

Right.

———

Around noon, Vance stood and stretched. He'd managed another scene he thought might make the cut. Katie had texted, saying she'd be picking up groceries, then Danny from preschool before heading home.

Home.

Vance liked the idea of Katie coming home…to him. Permanently. Crazy thinking. Katie belonged in California with Tad Pole, who probably sat around gnawing on a silver spoon and clipping coupons with all his spare time. Not holed up for days, weeks, months, bleeding the written word. Who'd want to live with a half-deranged writer who drank too much coffee before five in the morning and too much bourbon before noon, who slept very few hours and swore enough to make lifers behind bars cringe?

Vance chuckled aloud as he filed some research folders away. The story would've taken a different turn if Katie had shown up on his doorstep covered in designer labels from the top of her bleached blond hair, to sprayed-on tan, past collagen-injected lips, and over fake tits. First, he would've gotten some, and second, he would've kicked her designer-clad ass out the door, never to be seen or heard from again. Because he wouldn't have cared. Just another lay. Nothing more or less.

But Katie's presence had the same effect on him as a belt of Jim Beam on an empty stomach…like a burning inferno. And the only way to put the fire out was to have her, body and soul. He let out a shaky breath. He was lost, and Katie was the only person who could find him. He hadn't even been inside her, and he already knew his world would tip and never be the same.

Through the loft's windows, Vance spied his black truck rolling down the driveway. He hurried to the bathroom, splashed cold water on his face, brushed his hair with his fingers, and hit his teeth with a toothbrush. He replaced his rumpled T-shirt with a clean, white button-down and bolted down the steps. He tried telling himself his hungry stomach needed lunch, but what he really needed was…Katie.

———

Katie watched Vance jog from the back of the house as if he'd been expecting her. Technically, he had been, since she'd texted, announcing her arrival. The sun cast a bright glow around his head, giving the dark angel a golden halo. Katie smiled as he slowed to a nonchalant stroll, shoving his hands in his jeans pockets and wearing an adorable crooked grin.

"I want Uncle Pance," Danny called from the backseat.

"He's coming to get you, little ladybug."

"I no ladybug. I a boy," Danny declared in a loud voice. Katie heaved a sigh. She needed to find some little girl playmates for Miss Dana Sue before she grew up wondering why she had boobies and not a ding-a-ling like her brothers.

"I'm starved. What's for lunch?" Vance asked, holding Katie's door open. She held his offered hand and managed to jump to the ground without stumbling.

"Thanks. I'll grab the groceries if you get Danny. She's been asking for her *Uncle Pance*."

"That's because she knows a good-looking guy when she sees one." Katie caught Vance leering. The bounder. She checked the top buttons in the front of her tunic.

"I'm not showing an ounce of skin except from my knees down." She gestured to her exposed legs below her Bermuda shorts. "What are you ogling, Pirate Man?"

"If I'm ogling when you dress like a sixty-year-old woman, then you know there's something good underneath."

Katie blinked at him in surprise. "I know what's underneath, but you certainly don't, unless you've resorted to peeping through bedroom windows."

"Uncle Pance…get me out," Danny yelled, kicking her legs.

"No, but maybe we can change that." He warmed her with another leer as he unbuckled Danny from her car seat.

Katie huffed. "And I don't dress like a sixty-year-old woman." Oh God…yes, she did. She swallowed her groan, pulling shoppers from the back of the cab.

"Yeah, you kinda do. The burning question is: Why?"

"I wanna ride horsey… Horsey. Now." Danny wiggled in Vance's arms.

"Okay, wild thang, hold on." Vance lifted Danny up and over his shoulders, hooking his arms over her legs to hold her in place.

"Fast. Go fast, Uncle Pance." Danny clapped her

hands, and Vance jogged up the front walk and steps, jostling her on his back. Katie gasped at Danny's bobbing head as she laughed hysterically.

"Careful. Don't give her whiplash." Katie climbed the front steps, carrying two shoppers filled with lunch food and staples for the kids. Vance held the door open, pretending to smash Danny's back against the door as she squealed with laughter.

Katie shook her head. "No wonder she thinks she's a boy," she muttered under her breath.

"Boys are the best. Aren't they, Danny?" Vance said in a loud voice.

"Yep. Imma boy."

"That's right. What are girls?"

"Girls are dummies!"

Katie rolled her eyes and started unloading the groceries in the kitchen. "You better keep writing bestsellers, because I suspect you might have to pony up for a sex change operation when she gets older."

Vance stopped jostling Danny and allowed her to slide down his back to the floor. "You think?"

Katie snuck a peek at his confused face. She shrugged, trying not to laugh. "What do I know? She's a beautiful little girl, but she's never going to appreciate her God-given assets with you guys telling her all the time she's a boy. What does her mother say about all this?"

Vance cleared his throat. "Dana Sue, go wash your hands and get ready for lunch." He gave her a gentle shove out of the kitchen. "And don't put the cat in the toilet," he called after her. Katie paused at the open refrigerator and watched big, bad Vance Kerner shuffle his Nike sneakers against the clean tile floor. "Gloria doesn't know. I guess she'll be pretty mad, huh?"

"All I know is a girl puts up with enough crap about her image. *Don't wear this; don't wear that. Dress sexy; don't dress provocative. Show some cleavage; cover up. Get a nose job. Don't eat that. Watch your weight. Nobody wants a fat girl—*" Katie clamped her mouth shut. She'd probably heard versions of those phrases a million times. Oh boy...TMI. "Anyway, mixed signals can be confusing. That's all I'm trying to say."

Ducking her head, she got busy digging inside the next shopper. Holding two boxes of cereal, she turned right into Vance's broad chest.

He caught her by the upper arms and held her immobile, his hands burning brands into her arms. "Is that why you dress...the way you do? Because of all those messages?"

Yes. No. Probably. Absolutely. She shook the boxes of cereal. "Need to put these away. I bought Cap'n Crunch *and* Lucky Charms...no more cereal wars. Yay." Vance didn't budge. He continued to study her with his dark, inky eyes as if he could see inside straight to her soul. As if he could hear the harsh words and the demeaning comments her oblivious parents made. Who truly believed they were helping with their constant harping and endless lectures. Hot, unwanted tears began to prick the backs of her eyes. Mortified, she wrenched free of his grasp and bolted past him.

"Katie—"

"I can't find Pixie. Where's Pixie?" Danny entered the kitchen with Lollipop cradled in her arms.

Katie swiped at the damning tears on her face and

opened the pantry door to put away the cereal. She could still feel Vance's steely gaze boring into the back of her head.

After a few beats, she heard him say, "In her cage. You can let her out now."

Danny scurried to free Pixie inside the laundry room. "I want lunch. Can I have lunch now, Kay-tee?"

"S-sure, honey. What would—" Vance pulled Katie in for a tight hug and kissed the top of her head, murmuring words she didn't understand. But that simple gesture was all it took for the floodgates to open. Katie gulped back a sob, trying to gain her release from his strong, comforting arms, knowing she couldn't stay there and bawl like a baby, no matter how wonderful it felt. "Please...let me go." She sniffed, and Vance slowly dropped his arms.

He cupped her chin and rubbed his thumb across her wet cheek. Concern etched across his face. "Go. I'll get Danny's lunch. Take a break until you need to pick up the boys. We'll talk later," he said in a low, gentle voice.

Embarrassed by her weakness, Katie gave a wobbly nod and fled from the kitchen...away from the cruel memories and away from Vance's understanding pity.

~~~

Inside her bedroom, she kicked her flats aside and pulled off her tunic top that suddenly felt heavy and unattractive. Without warning, the room felt oppressive, as if the walls were folding in on her. She pushed open the French doors to let the outside in and inhaled huge gulps of clean, country air. Breathe. In and out.

What in all *Hollywood Squares* had gotten into

her? Only moments ago she'd been having a pleasant, somewhat bizarre new day, when…*poof*! All her emotions had welled up and practically choked her to death. Emotions she'd learned at an early age to tamp down and not let them get the best of her. One look from Vance, and she'd made a blubbering mess of his crisp cotton shirt—which, by the way, smelled like spicy decadence—in lieu of Kleenex.

Eyebrow twitching, she stared at her pale face in the mirror and got to work on tidying up her internal emotions, because when Vance said, *"We'll talk…"* he meant he wanted an explanation for all those stupid things she'd said. How could she explain her twisted relationship with her parents? Her parents found fault with everything she did. And through the years, she'd become this huge wimp, always taking the path of least resistance. She'd learned it was futile to argue with their views, and if she'd nod and acquiesce, they'd finish up sooner rather than later. But being that cowardly wimp ate at Katie, tying her stomach in knots. She hated that she never stood up for herself, and allowed their words to continue to hurt her. When would she start living her own life? In another twenty-eight years?

Disgusted, Katie yanked a thin yellow T-shirt off a hanger in the closet. Slipping it over her head, she dug for her phone in her back pocket and called Inslee.

"Do I dress like a sixty-year-old woman?"

"Uh, yeah, in a boring, church-lady way."

"Great. Just great. I'm twenty-eight and I look sixty. What do I do now?" she wailed.

"Change your wardrobe?" Inslee said, confused.

Along with her attitude. One major change at a time.

"How? I'm stuck in the middle of small town USA, and the closest store with clothing is The Kitchen Sink. It sells everything from toenail clippers to bib overalls, but it doesn't sell kitchen sinks…I asked. No way I'm shopping there."

"First of all, calm down, Kim Kardashian. Why this sudden urge to buy new clothes? *Not* that I'm discouraging you. I've been waiting years for you to improve your wardrobe."

"I don't know. I guess…well, Vance said I dressed like a sixty-year-old woman."

"I love that man. Have I told you that lately?" Katie growled in Inslee's ear. "Relax. You've got credit cards and money in your account, don't you?"

Katie nodded. She made decent money with McKnight Studios, and prior to that, she'd saved a good portion of her teaching salary. She'd never been a big spender. She still lived at home…God help her. This called for an intervention!

Her mother had handed down her Mercedes; Katie didn't take extravagant trips or buy expensive jewelry. Which left her only weakness: photography. Recently she'd splurged on her new Nikon digital camera, but other than that…she didn't spend her money.

Katie flopped back on the king-size bed and groaned. When had she become so boring? Not only did she dress like a sixty-year-old woman, but she lived like one too. "Yes, I have money, and I want to spend it. I need a change, and I need one yesterday. Tell me what to do." Her determination renewed. Inslee had been right. Katie deserved some fun and should enjoy being away from home and the criticizing eyes of her parents…and Tad.

"You got Internet in that one-stoplight town?"

"Sure."

"That's all you need. Online shopping is the bomb, doll face! Free shipping, free return shipping. It's addicting. It's time for a real mean Hollywood-style shopping spree," Inslee said, glee coloring her voice.

Two hours later and several thousand dollars poorer, Katie had a new wardrobe that would be shipping from Bloomies, Nordstrom, and Saks. Inslee forced Katie into uncharted territory with her choices and had given her opinion whether Katie wanted it or not. Inslee even convinced her to splurge on new bras and panties.

"My bras are perfectly fine," Katie had argued.

"Yeah, but do they push up the goods? You need at least one or ten sexy bras in your repertoire. Sam loves it when I wear—"

"Oh no!" Katie interrupted. "I don't want to hear about you and my brother. Baby sister may never recover."

Inslee snorted. "You are so repressed. All I'm suggesting is when you get around to mattress surfing with Mr. Fifty Shades of Gorgeous, you might want to rethink what's under your new clothes. White cotton undies with green turtles parading across your butt are not sexy."

Clearly Inslee didn't appreciate the comfort of Fruit of the Loom. "*If* I get around to mattress surfing. He's not a sure thing."

"Oh ho, he's a sure thing, doll. I'm betting from his pictures he doesn't go without for long." No doubt. And didn't that make Katie a crabby crabster.

Katie checked the time on her computer. Close to two. "Back to babysitting. Need to pick up the boys. Thanks for all your help."

"Take selfies when your new clothes arrive so I can critique."

"Don't you think you've critiqued your best friend enough? My fragile self-esteem can't take much more."

"Let me rephrase. Take selfies so I can compliment you," Inslee said.

Katie smiled. "You got it. Thanks again. Love you—"

"Katie!"

Katie jumped at the thunder in Vance's voice. "Er, better go. Pirate Man is yelling, and it doesn't sound good."

Chapter 11

VANCE STOOD ON THE FRONT PORCH WITH HANDS SPLAYED on his hips, glaring at his front lawn. Various cars and trucks had parked in his driveway with people from town spilling out. By the looks of their "costumes," he had a sneaking suspicion why they were here.

Auditions.

Exactly what he hadn't wanted to happen. Exactly why he should've placed Katie's perfect ass in her Mercedes and on the road back to the land of grapefruit and avocados. Top two foods he detested the most. The peace and quiet he craved had disappeared faster than beer at a frat party as the misinformed citizens of Harmony crowded his front lawn. In truth, he was surprised it had taken them this long.

The Harmony Huggers piled out of a light blue minivan, wearing ridiculous straw hats tied under their necks, matching Hawaiian shirts, and goofy lipstick-smiles plastered across their wrinkled faces. They played the banjo and guitar, and their leader, Irene Appleton, played the accordion. Yep. Accordion. Overall consensus: more painful to watch than hear. But they were considered a staple at any and every Harmony event, from the Miss Pickle and Peanut Parade to the Square Dancing Jamboree. Next came the Happy Hookers, a group of old ladies who sat around crocheting toilet seat covers and stuffed monkeys for the children's wing at the hospital.

"Hey there, Vance. Brought the girls with me today. Don't want to miss the show." Mrs. Cornwaddle, a founding member of the Happy Hookers, waved as she rocked across his lawn with her walker, smashing his green-and-white hostas along the way.

"Shit," Vance said under his breath. Clancy and Clinton Perry jumped out of their rusted-out truck with *Lawn Wrestlers* painted in green on the side. More cars and trucks parked willy-nilly over his front yard. Vance released a tortured groan. He had more important things to do than watch the town of Harmony roll all over his property and break out into song. Dammit. He had important things to do, like finish his next scene or his bottle of bourbon…or wrap his fingers around a certain California fruitcake's neck.

He spun around and yelled again, "*Katie—*" Danny came running out the front door, chasing Lollipop, and beautiful, tempting Katie, with wide eyes and creased brow, followed on her heels.

She froze at the festival of people destroying his ground cover with their folding chairs and coolers. Before the day was over, they'd be roasting a pig and grilling burgers.

"What's going on?" Her gaze darted around the yard. "Are you having a party?" she asked, blinking serious brown eyes at him.

"*Me?*" Fiery anger pierced his chest like a hot poker. "Oh no. I'm not the attraction here, sweet cheeks. That would be *you* and your Hollywood movie crew, which is nowhere in sight, but that won't stop the fine citizens of Harmony from camping out," he ground out between clenched teeth. Wise Katie backed up a few steps from the rage she must've witnessed building on his face.

"But…they're…we…" She gestured loosely.

"Uh-huh. There are *no words*." Vance took a threatening step toward Katie, who had managed to create more havoc in his life in the last three days than Scooby-Doo, Shaggy, and Velma had in three weeks. "I knew this would happen. I don't need this shit right now. Got any great Hollyweird ideas on how to get rid of the town rubberneckers and performers?" Katie's pretty mouth worked, but no sounds came out. And as angry as he was, he still couldn't stop thinking about kissing her silly. "Something wrong with your eyebrow?" he asked, examining her more closely.

She slapped a hand over half her face, covering her twitching brow. "No. Everything's fine—"

"Vance Kerner, what is going on around here?" Vance turned at the sound of his name. Sweet major fucktard. If he'd had his gun, he would've put a bullet in his head. Swishing up the walkway, wearing a skintight, zebra-striped dress, hot-pink hooker shoes, and a come-do-me smile was Jo Ellen Huggins, Harmony's most famous bachelorette—not by choice. Jo Ellen wanted marriage in a bad, bad way. However, since Brogan had married Lucy, Cal had married Liza, and Keith had scattered broken hearts like bread crumbs by snatching up Bertie, that left Vance and a few other single guys prime for the picking.

Vance snagged a surprised Katie and pulled her into his side, where he covered her shoulders with his arm. "Play along, or you won't be able to sit for a week," he growled low for her ears only. "Hey, Jo Ellen. Have

you met Katie McKnight, my *girlfriend*?" The sounds
of Irene Appleton warming up her accordion masked
Katie's gasp.

Jo Ellen's big, pink-lipped smile dimmed. "Why no,
sugah. Haven't had the pleasure," she said, extending
her hand to Katie. "Hey. Jo Ellen Huggins, Mary Kay
consultant and *special* friend of Vance's." Bullshit. By
special she meant they'd peed in the same kiddie pool
as toddlers.

As handshakes went, Jo Ellen's wasn't very friendly.
She didn't bother disguising the once-over she gave
Katie, from the top of her dark hair to the bottom of
her shoes, landing back on Katie's face, where Jo Ellen
feigned horror.

"Sakes alive. Let me give you my card." Jo Ellen
rummaged through her matching pink handbag and
whipped out a business card. "I'm no miracle worker,
but I might be able to eliminate those dark bags under
your eyes and your blotchy skin tone." Vance bit back a
laugh. He had to hand it to Jo Ellen…she knew how to
come out swinging.

Katie plucked the card from her hand. "Nothing a
full night's sleep won't cure." She leaned forward, confiding in a conspiratorial stage whisper loud enough for
half the front lawn to hear. "If only Vance would leave
me alone." She waggled her eyebrows. "He's a tiger in
the sack."

Two jaws hit the front porch with a thud: his and
Jo Ellen's. And then Katie growled like a jungle cat,
clawing the air with her hand in front of Jo Ellen's
shocked face. Backing up, Jo Ellen caught herself before
tumbling down the front steps.

"My, my. Aren't you a live one?" Flashing Vance a syrupy sweet smile, she purred, "Call me, sugah, when you've dumped—when Katie returns to Hollywood," Jo Ellen amended with a smug look. "Katie, honey, flag me down any time. Just look for the pink pickup truck. Might want to take care of those crow's-feet while we're at it." She waggled her fingers and sauntered down the walkway. "Bye, y'all."

"Ahhh! Shit!" Vance jumped back in pain. Katie had ground the heel of her shoe into his instep.

"You...you arrogant, self-centered...slug nugget." Tossing her head, ponytail swishing, Katie stomped down the front steps.

"Wait...what did you call me? A *slug nugget?*" he said around a chuckle he couldn't contain, wiggling his injured foot.

"Watch Dana Sue. I'm going to pick up the boys." But she didn't get very far. The yahoo Perry brothers blocked her path.

"Hey, we heard you was shooting porn, and we want in on it," Clancy the nutsack said.

"Yeah. We watch porn all the time. We're experts," Clinton, dumber than a furball, added.

"Well, here's the deal, guys...McKnight Studios does *not* shoot porn. However, I understand Vance is quite the star with Slimeballs R Us. Why don't you get in on his next movie?"

"Huh? We ain't seen him in no movies."

"Hey, Kerner, which pornos you been in?"

Hellfire. The piercing pain in his chest was turning into a full-blown heart attack. His career was spiraling downward right before his very eyes. The smirk playing around Katie's ripe mouth was like a shot in the arm. She had just messed with the wrong guy.

Game on, sweet cheeks.

Vance shot Katie his most evil smile when she ducked her head and hurried through the throngs of people. "That's right, run away. But remember, you can't stay gone forever," he yelled at her retreating back.

"Kerner, you in *Amy Does Aberdeen*?"

"Shut up, Clancy, and get the hell off my property."

———

Smart Katie stayed as far away from Vance as humanly possible for the remainder of the afternoon. Vance escaped to his loft and watched through his window as Katie got stuck dealing with all of Harmony's movie-star-wannabes and their lack of talent. The afternoon had turned into a colossal nightmare. Vance laughed out loud when the Harmony Huggers made Katie sit in one of the folding chairs and listen to their medley of songs, asking for suggestions and critiques. The Ardbuckle twins performed with their twirling batons. And jumpy Katie kept throwing glances over her shoulder. Vance reveled in knowing he made her nervous. Very nervous. Good. She deserved it for pulling that porno shit.

By six o'clock, Katie interrupted his writing and texted him: U coming down 4 dinner?

Vance picked up his phone and responded. Nope. But I'll put kids to bed. And then deal w/u. U can't hide 4ever.

Look who's hiding! The only deal is u signing contract. 2nite! No more excuses...Or else.

Vance chuckled, reading her text. U threatening me, California Cupcake?

Call it what u want. I have ways to make u sign.

God, did she ever. But Vance didn't want to make it too easy for her. He glanced at his Twitter page on his computer screen, and his jaw locked. His followers were going nuts, speculating on whether he'd filmed porn. *Porn*. He watched porn. Not as much as the dipshit Perry brothers, who probably had it on constant feed. And yeah, once in a while, he'd reenact a scene or two with one of his hookups. But not in a million years *did* he or *would* he ever star in a porn film.

These off-the-chart rumors smacked of Miss California Cupcake running her sweet mouth. Shannon Nichols, his assistant, worked overtime on damage control, dispelling the stories and repairing his tattered reputation through his social media platforms. Vance had also called Mike, and after unleashing his frustration and anger, Mike gave Vance the pat industry line about any publicity—even bad publicity—being good and selling books. It didn't make swallowing the bitter pill any easier. Vance prided himself on his reputation. He wrote war thrillers to honor soldiers…real soldiers like Adam Reynolds and his brother. He wrote to honor his dad. Now his name was being linked to Hugh Hefner's and the Bambi Twins.

Around nine o'clock, Vance saved his manuscript and prepared to head over to the house. He had promised to Skype Gloria so she could chat with the kids before bed-time. His cell rang, and an unfamiliar number showed up on the screen.

"Yeah." Vance barked into the phone.

"Vance Kerner? This is Walter McKnight with McKnight Studios."

He'd be damned. Katie's dad.

"What can I do for you, Mr. McKnight?" Vance dropped back down into his desk chair.

"Call me Walter." Walter had a fast, gruff business-man's voice, as if he gave a lot of orders and expected them to be obeyed. "I'm sure you're aware that we're in negotiations about acquiring the rights to your Honor series."

"Y-yeah. I'm aware," Vance said slowly.

"This looks to be an interesting proposition for the both of us. But before we let our agents and brokers get too bogged down with paperwork, I thought you and I could come to an agreement first." The little hairs on the back of Vance's neck stood up. Already the vibe from this phone call was off.

"What kind of agreement?"

"The kind where you agree to my terms…which will allow me to make movies based on your books. The kind where we both make money."

Jim Beam started screaming his name. Vance lifted the half-empty bottle of bourbon, poured a hefty shot in his glass, and knocked it back. The burn to his throat went a long way in calming his nerves. Slamming the glass down on his desktop, he said, "You have my attention."

"Good. I thought so. Now, regarding my daughter, Katie…"

Crapshitdamn. Walter had probably seen Vance's Twitter account and wondered what his precious daughter was doing with an alleged porn star. Vance closed his eyes and massaged his forehead, which had started to pound.

"…I understand she thinks your home and property would be perfect for the new miniseries we're going to be producing. I've seen the pictures Katie emailed, and—"

"I was planning to sign that contract tonight, sir. Just been a little busy—"

"That's exactly what I *don't* want you to do."

"Excuse me?"

"Vance, I'm a big fan of your writing. Big fan. As are my two sons. I want to turn your books into blockbusters, but I'm going to need a little cooperation on your part in order for this deal to happen." Vance couldn't see Walter, but he imagined him relaxing in a huge, black leather executive chair with a cigar clamped between his lips, stroking his cuddly pet Burmese python curled on his desk.

Vance hesitated. "Uh, okay?"

"You're an intelligent man, and I'm confident I won't need to spell this out…"

Vance had never been trapped in a foxhole with artillery blasting around his head, but he'd watched plenty of videos and listened to hundreds of war stories, and right now he'd take a war-torn foxhole over this conversation with Walter McKnight any day of the week.

"…*do not* sign the contract. Your property doesn't interest me. I've already placed a top-notch scout in Wilmington, and he's found the right kind of home for this show."

"But Katie—"

"Katie's inexperienced and clueless. Just between you and me, she's all wrong for this job. Truth of the matter…she hasn't been right for any job I've given her the last two years. What Katie needs…"

What Katie needed was to get out from under Daddy's protective wing. After two years of job bouncing, shouldn't she be looking for another place to work?

"…stall, ask questions, demand amendments, but don't sign anything. String Katie along as if you're going to sign it," Walter ordered.

"I'm sorry. Could you repeat that?"

"Katie's no longer working on this project. She's been replaced, but she doesn't know it, and I'd like to keep it that way for now."

What the hell? "For how long?"

"However long it takes for me to sew this deal up in Wilmington and create something else for Katie to do. Unfortunately, Katie's not qualified for much. Education major… Jesus." Walter snorted. "She didn't listen to me when I told her what to study in college, and she refuses to go back to graduate school. She flounders with no direction and no talent."

The exasperation Vance detected from Walter's voice was suddenly beginning to piss him off. Outrage percolated inside him over Walter's dismissal of Katie, as if she meant nothing and her work meant nothing. The same feeling of rage he used to get when his own dad treated him with disapproval and an iron fist. As a young teenager, Vance had no interest in the military, and his father had no interest in him. Vance was getting that same sick vibe from Walter McKnight regarding his daughter. It seemed Walter had no faith in Katie. He wanted to throw her under the bus, and he wanted Vance to help push her. One giant step into hell.

"Let me see if I understand…you want me to keep your daughter busy with a job and a location she no longer has for however long you tell me, and if I don't, we don't make movies together. Does that about sum it up?"

"Fine, intelligent mind you got there," Walter said.

The irony of all this was not lost on Vance. Walter was handing him precisely what he wanted. A babysitter for the kids. His home and grounds undisturbed.

And…Katie.

He felt like he'd won the lottery. Except these winnings came with a steep price: deceiving and hurting someone Vance cared about…a lot. Yeah, he barely knew her, and yet it felt like he'd known her all his life. He could probably use a good shrink. But his gut and heart both weighed in on this one…he'd be wise to listen. And if Walter McKnight wanted Vance's help in selling out his daughter, then Vance wanted to be compensated…on his terms. Because this could potentially blow up in his face like a hand-tossed grenade, and Vance would lose Katie forever.

"I'm glad you think so. Now, I have a condition of my own."

"Sure you do." Walter gave a gruff chuckle. "You want Gerard Butler to play the leading man."

"More important than that—"

"Don't underestimate the importance of the right leading man," Walter informed him.

"I'll leave that up to you and the casting experts." Vance paused. "I want approval rights on the screenplay." He could hear Walter suck in a surprised breath.

Coughing and clearing his throat, Walter said, "That's

not the way we roll around here, Kerner. I've got a talented team that will be working on your screenplay...*if* we come to terms."

At this point, Vance didn't give two shits if his books ever saw the inside of a Hollywood studio. Hollywood could kiss his ass. "Them's my terms. You want me to keep your daughter busy by pretending I'm going along with this location, keep quiet about your other deal, and not let on she's getting fired. For an undetermined amount of time." Vance gave a harsh laugh. "That's a lot. You don't even know if I have the acting skills to pull it off. All I'm asking is to read over a few lines. We both know damn well that I can read and I can write."

"You know, Kerner, I don't have to agree to anything, including signing a deal for your books," Walter growled through the phone.

"That would be fine too. I'll make sure Katie hits the road tonight, heading west." During the awkward silence, Vance could practically hear the wheels turning inside Walter McKnight's calculating head.

"She is *not* to know we spoke." His voice was harsh. "I don't want her finding out I've gone behind her back. Do you understand?"

That you're a prick? You bet. "Perfectly. Do we have a deal?"

After several beats, Walter exhaled. "Yes, Kerner. We have a deal."

"Good. May I ask a question?"

"What now? You want to be the new host of the *Tonight Show*?"

"Nah, Jimmy Fallon can have it. Why all the subterfuge? Why don't you tell Katie the truth? She seems pretty levelheaded to me." Except when spreading rumors about him and porn.

"Look, Katie begged for this position. She has no qualifications and no experience"—Vance wondered how hard could it be? You drove around and looked for houses—"so she needs to be guided. Katie's a wanderer. Her mother and I will come up with something to keep her busy."

Vance didn't like the sound of their plan any better than the one he'd just sold his soul for. Or any better than when his dad would give him an ultimatum. And the idea of hurting Katie ate the lining of his stomach worse than Mr. Beam sitting next to his computer.

"I'm sure you're right," Vance lied.

"Now, I'm going to leave the contract details to our brokers. And, Kerner…you better pray you can act."

"I've made you a plate," Katie said, pouring a second glass of wine with a shaky hand. On the kitchen table, a plate of pasta and side salad waited for Vance, right next to the McKnight Studios' folder with the contract tucked inside. It was after nine, and Vance had come down from putting the kids to bed, wearing a black look that promised revenge. She got it…and hugged the kitchen sink.

She took a drink with an unsteady hand. She didn't fear him. Well, maybe a little. His bark was bigger than his bite—she hoped. Inslee had texted pithy comments earlier to boost her courage. Besides, technically, Katie hadn't started the porn rumor. She may have fanned the flames with those brothers, who could star on the next

Duck Dynasty, but it hadn't taken much—one word in this town could spark a blazing California wildfire.

"What's this?" he asked, dropping into a seat and picking up his fork.

"Homemade spaghetti and salad."

"I meant the folder." He forked spaghetti into his mouth and chewed. "Quit cowering like a frightened squirrel. Come sit down. I'm not going to bite you." His evil smile said otherwise.

Katie bolstered her courage and pulled the chair out opposite him. "It's the contract from McKnight Studios, waiting for your signature. The one you promised to sign," she said to his impassive face. Vance flipped the folder open and read the first page. "There're probably a few things you'll want to change—"

He flipped the folder closed. "I'm meeting with my attorneys tomorrow. They'll take a look. Probably more than a few things will need to be changed," he said to his dinner plate, never meeting her eyes.

On alert, Katie sat forward. "Really? You're going to meet with your attorneys? You're not swooping me…or trying to get back at me for, you know…today?"

Vance finished another bite and leaned back in his chair. He twirled his glass of wine between his long fingers, and Katie's insides twirled right along with the wine. She feared the unknown more than the punishment itself. "Whatever you're going to do to me, do it. I can't take the suspense anymore. I know you're plotting something."

Vance's eyebrows rose. "Why, K-K-Katie, whatever are you referring to?"

"Okay, okay, I'm sorry. I shouldn't have mentioned,

you know, the whole porn thing." His eyes got scary dark, and Katie hurried to explain. "But I swear I didn't start the rumor. Somehow porn came up in conversation at the Dog and then...*zing*! It took off like a greyhound at the races. I've never seen anything like it before."

"Uh-huh."

"I'm not kidding. I think Dottie Duncan started it, and then the whole conversation got twisted around. People in this town sure take an interest in your life. And I've never seen so many people with different, er, talents?" she said, referring to the myriad entertainers she'd suffered through that afternoon.

"*Talent* might be a stretch. Folks from Harmony are more suited for never-seen-before reality TV. Some of them make that Honey Boo Boo show look downright civilized. Just when you think you've reached the bottom of their craziness, there's an entire crazy underground garage." Katie's wine went down the wrong pipe as she half choked/half laughed. Vance continued, "You could have a whole show about who's got chiggers or who's your daddy, or in the Clancy brothers' case, 'Name Them Droppings.'"

Eyes watering, Katie laughed, and Vance joined along. After what she'd witnessed today, she couldn't agree more. Katie had watched some old guy in bib overalls and a John Deere cap play the spoons, and the Happy Hookers even performed a geriatric rendition of "YMCA" with walkers and all.

"You think they'll be back tomorrow?" she asked, fearing the answer.

"No doubt. We've been a little slow on entertainment this spring. The Downtown Get Down festival is coming up this summer, but nothing will beat a TV show about vampires and zombies filmed in their own backyard."

Katie nodded, thinking she wouldn't be here to see Harmony in full festival mode. She imagined colorful tents, local music, and festival food, and even some country baking or homegrown veggie contests. She smiled, knowing it wouldn't be overproduced or overbudgeted. And there wouldn't be a red carpet for miles. Or starlets wearing skintight, overpriced designer dresses or borrowed jewelry that came with matching armed guards, like so many events in Hollywood.

"It was entertaining, I have to admit, and the kids loved it. Donald and Dover played football with a painting crew that showed up this afternoon. And Danny squealed and clapped every time some old man played the spoons." Katie had gotten some great candid shots of the kids and the townspeople of Harmony. She couldn't wait to play around with the images on her computer. She planned to make prints for the kids to take back to their mom. "Speaking of the kids, I had to bathe Pixie again, because they found a bucket of paint in the shed and decided she'd looked better in yellow."

"I thought I'd locked the shed door."

"You did. Apparently Donald has become quite the locksmith."

"Did you put them in boot camp?" Vance smiled around another bite.

"I did indeed. Those boys are going to have muscles by the time I'm finished with them. And poor Dana Sue is going to lose all her hair if I have to wash it three times a day." Katie remembered her ruined pair of shorts and figured she'd have to stop by The Kitchen Sink for some work clothes and shoes. At this rate, the new, exciting, younger wardrobe she'd ordered would be destroyed.

Vance pushed his plate away and refilled his glass of wine. Katie waved off his offer to refill hers. "I'm good. Still need to call my dad. He likes the pictures I've sent so far, but he wants to see more. I took pictures of the interiors today and will email those tonight."

Vance carried his dishes to the sink. Rinsing and putting them in the dishwasher, he asked, "How long have you worked for your dad as a location scout?"

"One month. This was my first real assignment. Before that, I worked as Production Runner, Production Assistant, and Boom Operator. Stunk at all of them, but I'm much better at Location Scout." Not really. But Katie loved being on the road and away from home. Away from the watchful, judgmental eyes of her parents. Away from the 24-7 surveillance.

Vance crossed his legs at the ankles and leaned against the kitchen counter, arms folded over his chest. "What do you like about it? Besides the obvious...babysitting rug rats and living with...me." His gaze flared, turning hot.

Wicked. The man was perfectly wicked. Heart thumping, Katie gulped the remainder of her wine, allowing the rustic, earthy tones to coat her throat. She didn't trust him. He wore that dangerous look that could either melt the most arctic heart or scare the pants right off you. With him...probably both. She knew her punishment still hung in the balance.

"What excites you about this particular job?" he asked again in his deep, honey-coated drawl.

Escaping. Being on her own. "Traveling to different

places and meeting new people. Before working for my dad, I taught for five years in the public school system. It was challenging, but eventually my dad convinced me to give it up."

By the end of the day, Katie's brain would be fried from teaching fifth graders who couldn't read or write. And her dad would seize every opportunity to point out how rough she had it, always badgering her to come work for him.

Katie squirmed under Vance's scrutiny, feeling he saw way more than he revealed. "Actually, I love photographing the places I've been. Some people write in journals. I take pictures." She tried putting a positive spin on what had become her dull life.

"Show me."

Katie blinked. No one had ever shown an interest in her photos. Wait, that wasn't fair. Inslee loved her photos and encouraged her photography.

"It's just a hobby. I'm no professional." She skirted around him to put away her wineglass. "You have more important things to do besides look at photos...like finish your book and sign my contract." She chewed her lower lip at his unreadable expression.

Vance pointed at her face. "Your eyebrow's twitching." Katie slapped a hand over her left brow. "What's the deal with that? Do I make you nervous, cupcake?"

Uh-oh. That look coupled with that voice—Katie backed up, and Vance stalked her.

One hand covering her brow and the other outstretched to ward him off, she said, "Just because I'm around doesn't mean I'm available. Go visit one of your girlfriends, like your *special* friend who insulted me and wanted to make me over. What was her name? Carolina Cougar?"

Vance lunged and snagged her wrist, pulling her against his chest, his arm banded around her waist. "You jealous, Kat?" he murmured near her ear.

She scoffed. "Hardly. I was surprised by her lack of Southern manners, that's all." Vance's breathing tickled her neck. Her brain scrambled, and her heart flipped. His mere breath had her shuddering, and she already knew his potent kisses could enslave her. "Come on, cupcake. Tell me how much you want me," he whispered against her heated flesh.

Katie's eyes rolled back into her head as Vance nibbled on her throat and along her jaw. His five-o'clock shadow rasped against her sensitive skin. Her head tilted on its own accord to allow him better access.

"Katie love, tell me…tell me what you want." He breathed against her hot throat.

You. In the bed. On the table—"Stop." Katie pushed away her dangerous thoughts. Vance's arms dropped, and his head lifted. "Nothing's changed. You're still a rake, chasing anything in a skirt."

He lifted one brow. "Rake? Is that word still current?"

Katie shrugged. "Sometimes. Or if you prefer *man-ho, man-whore, man-slut*—"

Vance drew back as if she'd slapped him. "Got the message. Now, I'm insulted. You don't know anything about my past except what you've heard around town. Didn't you learn a valuable lesson today on how unreliable those stories can be?" Vance leveled her with a pirate's glare and splayed his hands on his hips. "I'm not denying who I am or what I want. Right now, I want you.

I've wanted you since the minute I laid eyes on you. The question is…what are *you* going to do about it?"

Katie sputtered, at a loss for words. She'd angered him, which had never been her intent. Confused and insecure, she couldn't come right out and tell him she wanted him back. She'd never been that bold. The very thought scared her senseless. She'd always second-guessed what she wanted in life, letting her nerves rule and her parents' voices in her head beat her down. She'd always been a coward. Always.

Face hot, Katie confronted Vance and her inner turmoil. "It's not that easy for me. I can't… come out and say…my boyfriend, er…he'll be back, and then what'll I do? Don't I owe—"

Vance rubbed his fingers across his forehead as if in pain. "For the love of Pete, the shit that comes out of your mouth—Katie, you have to talk to me."

He was asking too much. She looked up and away from his exasperated face, feeling raw and exposed.

"Earlier today, you made some pretty telling comments about appearances and how criticism affects you…and girls. I want to know what's going on. I want to know why you dress like you're hiding something." Vance put both hands on the wall near her head, caging her in, his voice low and urgent. "Katie, my love, I want to know who has done a number on you."

Katie's insides shriveled. She hated her story. It painted her in a really bad light. A take-charge, strong, smart guy like Vance would have difficulty understanding her hang-ups and neuroses. He lived on his own terms and answered only to himself. In typical guy fashion, he'd want to fix her, and that wasn't possible.

Because only Katie could fix Katie. Even she knew that much.

She searched his intense face and drew strength from his compelling gaze. Within that strength, she made a snap decision. She'd give him what he wanted and take what she needed. She'd be with him for the next few weeks if he'd have her. She deserved that much. And then she'd leave. A much stronger, more independent person than when she came. More complete. A better Katie. She could do this. This would be her test.

Before she lost her nerve and changed her mind, Katie looped her arms around his neck and pulled him down. Desire lit his dark eyes. His breath accelerated, and she could feel the thudding of his heart against her chest. And then she kissed him. Surrounded by his warmth and strength and delicious woodsy scent. Vance had gone still, but not for long. He crushed her to his chest, swooping in and taking over. He aligned his body with hers, letting her feel every inch of his hard frame. He settled in for a nice long, lust-filled kiss, and Katie reveled in every weak-kneed minute. In him, his taste, and the ripening sensations throughout her body.

He slid his hands up her waist until his thumbs touched her breasts and drifted across her pebbled nipples. A whimper escaped her lips. A buzzing noise hummed around her head when Vance stopped and dropped his arms. Katie stumbled back; the buzzing continued.

Blam…hit with what she'd done, she wondered if her first bold move had been maybe…a little too bold.

"Shit." Vance pulled his cell from his jeans pocket, staring at his phone, and an odd look crossed his features. What? Katie tried reading the lit screen, but he thumbed it off.

She fumbled for something to say. "Sorry…that got a little out of hand—" And then, maybe not. Katie swallowed hard at his signs of arousal: glittering eyes, heightened color in his cheekbones, rigid stance—speaking of rigid, her gaze slid down the length of his body and settled on the impressive bulge beneath his fly. Knees wobbled. "Um, wow."

"Staring only makes it grow," he said with a wry smile.

Vance's sexy grin turned into a laugh at her mortified expression. "Come here." He cupped his hand behind her neck and kissed her hard and way too fast. "Need to return that call. Gotta get back to work," he said.

"Right. Work. Gotcha."

Katie stopped breathing at his possessive gaze. His finger left a light trail down her neck as he stepped back. "Good night, oh Kat of mine. See you in the morning." He flashed a hungry grin and then vanished behind the back door. Katie's knees gave out as she slid down the wall and landed on her butt. The victim had fallen for her captor.

Chapter 12

THE NEXT MORNING, AFTER DROPPING THE KIDS AT SCHOOL, Katie grabbed a cup of coffee at the Daily Grind. Instead of returning to the house for another day of talent show auditions, she looked forward to exploring the area. Vance had not come down for breakfast, and she felt nothing but relief. In the light of day, her POA—plan of action...Inslee's term, not hers—looked like a thin piece of Swiss cheese: full of holes. In other words, chicken-wing Katie had an attack of second thoughts. All last night as she'd tossed and turned and relived her moment of boldness, she'd convinced herself this new daring Katie would never survive in a pirate's world. She lacked the guts and that damn backbone.

After passing the shops on Main Street, Katie drove through the neighborhood streets and stopped to take pictures of blooming azalea gardens, bungalow-style houses with stone and wood columns, and pretty, refurbished Victorians. People waved as she cruised by in Vance's truck. This fanciful place could easily play a quaint small town on television or in the movies. The farther she drove, the more the land became farm-like. She shot pictures of weathered wood fences, grazing horses, and even a rare, old, abandoned tobacco barn sitting in a field of wildflowers. Winding her way back, she drove toward the entrance of a huge lake with homes nestled along the shoreline and various-sized boats quietly floating at their docks. Katie jumped out and strolled toward the clearing. The damp smell of lake water and pine trees all meshed together and formed a fresh, outdoor balance. Pine straw cushioned her sneakers as she followed the trail leading to the lake.

At the entrance of the clearing, picnic tables, Adirondack chairs, and built-in barbecue grills dotted the straw-covered sand. Katie stopped and breathed. Birds singing and small animals rustling enhanced the quiet. The lake water lapped the shore, and the sound of a slapping screen door could be heard in the distance. Allowing the peace of the outdoors to wash over her, she closed her eyes and soaked it all in.

"Going for a swim?"

Katie jumped and whirled around. She clutched at her heart to keep it from pounding out of her chest. "You scared me!" she said to a smiling, shirtless, sweaty but kinda gorgeous Brogan Reese.

"Sorry." But his sneaky grin said he wasn't. "You been exercising? Or are you joining the Harmony Huggers?" He gave a nod to her outfit. Katie looked down at her faded, stretchy pants and tattered Nikes. She wasn't wearing a Hawaiian shirt, so how could he ask that? *Because you dress like you hate your body*, Inslee's voice said in her head.

Tugging on her T-shirt, she said, "No. I have no excuse except these clothes are kid-proof, and since two outfits have been ruined already…" She shrugged her shoulders.

Brogan cupped her elbow and turned her back to the lake as he pulled her along next to him. Katie would have been blind not to notice his incredible six-pack abs and muscled arms. Hollywood really should broaden its horizons. The men of Harmony could sell lots of tickets.

"I get it, because there's no way you'd be wearing this disguise to put Vance off the scent. Hmm?"

"That's right." Katie's new wardrobe couldn't arrive soon enough. Her sagging image could use a huge boost among these all-too-knowing, blunt-speaking Southerners. "Vance is busy writing his book. He doesn't notice what the babysitter is wearing." She performed her lines like a three-time Oscar-winning actress.

They'd stopped by the lake's edge, and Brogan gave a bark of laughter that carried across the water into the next state. Katie folded her arms and pretended to be bored. Being around movie stars paid off after all. "California Katie, you don't know Vance like I do. You could wear army fatigues, smear mud on your face, and blend in with the trees, and he'd notice you." Brogan bent down and unlaced his jogging shoes. "But I applaud your effort. Make him work for it. It would be a first." *And* didn't that make Katie want to run to the nearest trophy store for her reward. The scourge of Harmony never worked for a woman. Shocking.

Brogan rolled his broad shoulders. "Wanna join me for a swim?"

Katie gave him the universal get-real look. "Um, hell no."

"You and Lucy must've spoken. She said the exact same thing, wearing that same expression."

"Lucy struck me as a very smart woman."

Brogan shot her a disbelieving glance. "She said that too about you...verbatim. Are you two secretly texting?"

Katie chuckled. "No. Not since the other night when we met. But I could tell right off the bat that she was a kindred spirit."

Brogan backed up a step. "Okay, now you're freaking me out."

"What?"

"Same thing, about kindred spirits."

Katie's grin grew broader. She was delighted that Lucy felt that way about her. Between Bertie and Lucy, she could claim strong reinforcements. She never knew when they might come in handy.

Brogan pointed at her camera. "Taking pictures for your TV show?"

"No. For me. It's kind of a hobby of mine. And your town is very picturesque."

He held out his hand. "Mind if I take a look?"

Katie hesitated only a moment before handing over her camera. Brogan clicked the button as he scanned through her pictures. "That's the Whipshaws' farm with the horses. And you got a nice shot of Bertie's house." Katie leaned in to see which one he was referring to. The beautiful old Victorian with the wraparound porch. "Bertie renovated that house from top to bottom before she and Keith were married. If those walls could talk, you'd hear some pretty colorful stories...no pun intended." Brogan gave her a sly look. "Keith was a newcomer like you, and it took a long time before Harmony felt like home to him. Bertie helped in a big way." Brogan continued to scroll through her shots, chuckling at pictures of the kids. He stopped on one she'd taken of Vance without his knowledge, leaning against his porch column with arms crossed, slight smile tugging his lips as he stared into the distance at something the kids were doing. "Vance will do the same for you," he murmured.

"What?"

Brogan leveled a steady gaze at her. Gone were the laughing green eyes and teasing smirk. "Home. Vance will make Harmony feel like home to you. You only have to provide an open mind...and heart."

Katie licked her suddenly dry lips, going for a casualness she didn't feel. "All you Southerners know how to make a girl feel at home. You're born with the ability."

Brogan appeared as if he wanted to say more but turned his attention back to her photos. "Wait. That's General Kerner's place. Where'd you get that picture?" His tone was accusing.

When she'd been snooping around his property before he almost scared her into an early grave. "The other day when I walked around the grounds."

"Did you meet him?"

Katie gave a hesitant nod, knowing he'd find out anyhow. "We met. He was very nice." Once he was no longer aiming his rifle at her head. "And he had breakfast with Bertie and me yesterday morning at the Dog."

Brogan lowered the camera and raised his brows in disbelief. "You trespassed on the general's property? I'm surprised he didn't eat *you* for breakfast."

"Well, he scared me at first, but then when he found out I was babysitting his grandkids, he seemed to relax after that."

"Shee-it. This is unbelievable. Does Vance know about this?"

"Maybe. I didn't tell him, but he might've heard about the breakfast. The Dog was packed."

Brogan studied her as if she were a superpower figure. "California Katie, do you believe in fate? Karma? Destiny?"

"No." She believed in doubt, weakness, and fear.

"I believe in fate, and I believe in you." Brogan's eyes glowed. "There's been bad blood between Vance and his dad for…well, a really long time. But I get this feeling a California girl might bring those two stubborn, hard-headed lug nuts together."

Yeah, right. Katie laughed. "I like you, Brogan. You're a funny guy. But don't get your hopes up too high. I'm leaving in less than four weeks—"

"A lot can happen in four weeks."

"Look, I have more than I can say grace over." Like quitting her job and finding a new life. Yeah, that thought alone kept her up nights. Katie reached for the camera and threw the strap over her shoulder. "What exactly happened between the two of them?"

Something flashed across Brogan's face before he scrubbed his hand over it. "Angry words. Spoken in the heat of the moment. And after all these years, neither one of them has taken them back."

The spoken word could damage more than a piercing sword to the heart or a bullet to the abdomen or a tire iron to the skull. The spoken word stayed with you, killing you slowly. A tightness squeezed her chest. "I'm sorry. I sincerely hope they work it out." But from what she could tell, both men were stubborn and proud. Dangerous combination.

"Yeah, me too." Brogan moved toward the dock in his athletic shorts and bare feet.

"You need a ride home? I can wait," she offered.

"Nah. I'm good. My house is just beyond those trees." He gestured over his shoulder with his thumb. "Listen, we're all getting together on Friday night for a cookout right here at the lake. Why don't you come with Vance?"

"Uh, you're forgetting…I'm only the babysitter." Besides, Vance had never said anything about a cookout. He hadn't mentioned anything, including taking the kids to see their mom this weekend. All they had managed to do was lunge at each other and fog up the appliances and defrost the freezer in the kitchen. Their steamy encounters floated through her mind, causing a heat wave to flame her cheeks.

Brogan laughed. "Yeah, keep telling yourself that. We'll be setting up around six thirty." He waved and then dove off the end of the dock. Katie watched until he emerged eight feet farther out and started stroking the frigid lake water. *F-schizzle*. She shivered at the thought of a cold lake swim. With determination, she marched from the lake. Her new clothes had better arrive soon, because she wasn't wearing The Kitchen Sink's bib overalls on Friday night. Even if it was an old, countri-fied cookout. Oh, hell no.

Back at the house, Katie escaped inside without having to judge the tryouts taking place on the front lawn. Vance still hadn't made an appearance, and Katie hoped he'd left for the meeting he'd mentioned with his attorneys to go over the contract.

Using the antique table desk in the master bedroom,

Katie downloaded her pictures onto her computer and played around with the images in Photoshop. She tagged ones of the kids to be printed, and emailed Inslee her album. Inslee immediately zeroed in on the photo of Vance, which Katie had tweaked and cropped. *Hot chipotle beefy burrito*, Inslee aptly described Vance. And then Inslee emailed pictures back of the kids in puzzle form, including the program that made it happen, suggesting the kids play with their pictures online as a jigsaw puzzle. Katie clapped her hands, loving the idea. A great project where the kids could have fun and learn at the same time.

At the sound of her chirping phone, Katie rolled her eyes. "What now?"

R u avoiding me? Tad texted.

Been busy with kids & trying 2 nail down location. Aren't we on a break? Katie didn't want thoughts of Tad clouding her newfound decisions. She didn't want thoughts of Tad at all. Once she quit her job, he wouldn't want her anyhow. Her chest ached. The disappointed looks, coupled with lectures and recriminations, would be unending, and the seed of doubt that lived inside her would take root and start to grow.

What kids???

Long story.

I'm calling. We need 2 talk.

NO! Don't. Can't talk now. Later. Katie placed her phone down in disgust. Maybe if Tad had worried less about his job and more about her before the "break," they wouldn't be in this mess. Katie folded her arms and grumbled to herself. Her left eyebrow picked up a new tempo.

"Stop it." She rubbed her fingers over her brow. She still had an hour to kill before picking up Danny. She glanced out her bedroom window at the entertainers unwrapping sandwiches and passing canned drinks. Her stomach rumbled in protest. Did she dare join the crazies on the front lawn for lunch? Her phone chirped again.

"Dammit, Tad. Stop bothering me," she said, snatching it up. "Oh!"

Lunch at my house? Sweet tea & barbecue.

Luv 2! B there in 5. Katie threw on clean jeans and a long-sleeve purple T-shirt, snatched her iPad, camera, and handbag, and snuck out the back door, heading straight for the general's home.

———⁓———

Barbecue? Katie chewed and tried swallowing the shredded meat swelling like a fuzzy ball in her mouth. What kind of barbecue looked stringy and gray and tasted like vinegar? She gulped more tea.

"You ever tried Eastern Carolina barbecue before?" Chuck asked as he heaped some on a bun and made a mountain of a sandwich for himself.

"No sir," she said, swallowing, dreading her next bite.

"It's not for everyone. Here we shred the pork and then season it with vinegar and spices. Western barbecue is probably what you're more familiar with. Meat on the bone and slathered in red sauce. Beef or pork."

Katie nodded, remembering a tasty Texas-style barbecue restaurant outside of Santa Monica. A rack of ribs with sweet barbecue sauce. Not stringy, rubbery meat that tasted bitter. "It's…very different," she said, reaching for her glass of tea again.

The general smiled as he chewed. He got up from the table and opened the refrigerator. Katie pushed the barbecue around on her plate to make it appear as if she'd eaten more. She forked some coleslaw into her mouth and swallowed. Maybe if she ate all the coleslaw, he wouldn't notice. A small plate appeared by her place with a pimento cheese sandwich sliced on the diagonal. Katie looked up, lips twitching.

"Told you it's not for everyone. Eat the sandwich instead." Chuck smiled and took his seat.

"Thank you. I guess it's an acquired taste."

He grunted, making headway with his own sandwich. They ate in silence, and Katie admired his cozy interiors. Her gaze traveled over his family room, with the matching red-plaid sofa and chairs, to the stone fireplace, and up to the open loft with the rustic bannister and knotty pine spindles. She could imagine how excited his grandkids would be to sleep high up in the loft. Like camping out.

"General—"

"Call me Chuck. Not much use for titles around here."

"Maybe not. But from what I've heard, you served our country long and hard. The title is well deserved."

He gave a dismissive shrug of his broad shoulders. "What were you going to say?"

"Would you like to see pictures of your grandkids? I have some great ones on my iPad." Katie held her breath, afraid she'd overstepped and he'd reach for the shotgun leaning in the corner. He finished his barbecue sandwich and brushed his hands over his plate. Katie played with the napkin in her lap, waiting.

Finally, he nodded. "That'd be real nice. Let's sit where it's more comfortable."

Settled on his plaid sofa, Katie opened her iPad and scrolled through the images she'd taken of Harmony and landed on the ones of his kids. "That's Dover. He's a handful, says whatever comes to mind. But he loves to read."

Chuck leaned forward and stared as if fascinated. "What grade is he in now?"

"Kinder. And that's Donald, and he's in second. Smart, and likes to take charge. You can't turn your back on those two rascals for a second. Not only are they bright, but they're fast. They wear me out. But this one"—she tapped the screen—"this little angel thinks she's a boy. She's going to tie her brothers up in knots when she gets bigger." Katie laughed at a picture of Dana Sue, with yellow paint smeared on her face and in her hair, squeezing the life out of Lollipop.

Chuck laughed and reached for the iPad, holding it close as he studied the pictures of Danny and her brothers, shaking his head. "They've gotten so big. I remember when Donald was born. I was afraid to hold him. Thought I might crush him or drop him."

"You don't seem clumsy to me. I bet you did just fine. Didn't you hold your own boys when they were babies?"

His mouth formed a grim line as he continued to scroll through the pictures. "Wasn't around. I was stationed in the Middle East for the first years of the boys' lives." He stopped scrolling when he landed on the picture of Vance leaning against the column. Chuck's dark eyes went cold and flat.

"Here…let me show you something clever." Katie

took the iPad and scrolled to the jigsaw puzzles of the kids, hoping to lighten his mood. "Look, you can make puzzles of the pictures and then try and put the pieces back together. Isn't that neat?"

"How did you do that?" he asked and seemed genuinely interested.

"A friend of mine in California sent me the program. Try it. Play with this one of all three kids." Chuck tapped the screen with his index finger, but the image kept jumping and changing in size. "It's more fun on a laptop. Sometimes iPads can get wonky. I can bring my laptop next time, and you'll have more control."

"I have a laptop. Can you send me the puzzles?"

"Sure. I can make them hard or easy. I've made a few easy ones for the kids, but I think you might like more of a challenge."

Chuck leaned back and fixed Katie with his military stare, precise and knowing. Straightening her shoulders, she squashed the desire to salute. She'd been on the grill more times than she'd like to remember, but she'd never received a dressing-down from a general, and she didn't want one now.

"You're full of surprises and hidden talents, aren't you?"

"I'm not sure I know what you mean," Katie said, sounding scared and unsure to her own ears.

"What does my son Vance think of you?"

Beach blanket bingo. Besides the physical lust…she had no idea. "I wouldn't know. But relieved is one word that comes to mind. He's glad to have someone help with the kids so he can get back to his writing."

A dark scowl ruled Chuck's features at the mention

of Vance's books. She wished she could do or say something to bridge the mammoth gap between the two men. But not knowing their full history put her at a huge disadvantage. "General…I know it's none of my business, but what happened between you and your son?" At his fierce frown, Katie inched as far away as the sofa arm would allow. And yet her mouth kept babbling. "It just seems you're only punishing yourself by not spending time with your grandkids. Before you know it, they'll be grown and gone."

Chuck abruptly stood and moved toward…*not the shotgun*! Katie's breath released in a whoosh when he stopped in front of the stone fireplace and stared into its black opening. "You been spending too much time with that nosy, meddling, smart aleck Dottie Duncan. Don't let her fill your head with a bunch of nonsense."

"Dottie's not filling my head with anything. I'm basing this on pure observation. You're holding a grudge and hurting yourself and your grandkids. Don't you think it's time to let it go?" Katie stood and gathered up her personal items. The fact that Chuck hadn't reached for his shotgun made her bold and careless. "The war's over, General. Time to lay down your arms and make peace."

A harsh, cracking sound split the air. Startled, Katie looked up at his attempt to laugh. "Don't tell me you've been reading my illustrious son's books."

She shook her head slowly. "No, but I hear they're quite good. I don't know if they're based on fact or fiction. But I do know you've retired from the military, and it looks like you've retired from life along with it."

Katie clutched her iPad to her chest at the narrowing

of his eyes. She'd been bold enough for one day, and her heart was starting to race straight up her throat. "I need to be going," she managed to croak as she sidestepped her way toward the door, keeping him in her sights. "Thanks for lunch…"

"We'll do it again tomorrow." Katie gripped the cold, bronze doorknob and glanced over her shoulder. "And, Katie…bring a copy of my son's latest books when you come. That's an order."

Chapter 13

SO HERE'S THE THING…IF YOU'RE GOING TO BE BOLD AND speak your mind, you need to be able to do it without breaking out in a cold sweat while your heart tries to hammer its way through your chest and your throat closes up so tight you can't swallow. Still shaking from her conversation with General Kerner, Katie fished through layers of tissue paper. Her new clothes had arrived. She wound and rewound the conversation in her head, adding lines and deleting others, berating herself for bringing up the taboo topic. What had she been thinking? She couldn't fix her own screwed up life—what made her think she could fix Vance and his dad's?

Katie stole a few precious moments to try on her new wardrobe while the kids watched a movie before bedtime. Vance still hadn't returned home. She couldn't imagine an appointment with an attorney taking this long, but maybe she'd have a signed contract, or at least a revised one, to present to her dad later tonight.

She wiggled a short, tight, smoky-blue dress over her head and down her hips, adjusting the draped neckline over her breasts. Katie wasn't too sure about the fit, pressing her palms to her stomach. She couldn't remember the last time she'd worn anything quite this tight. But Inslee assured her the gathered ruching around the middle was flattering for any figure. Katie twisted left and then right in front of the massive, silver-framed mirror leaning against the bathroom wall, trying to picture an occasion where she'd wear this dress.

"Katie, Danny's gluing pennies on Lollipop with a glue stick," Dover said, standing inside her bathroom door.

Katie touched her hand to her chest. "Goodness. You startled me." She hoped he hadn't been standing there watching her wiggle her full hips into this seam-splitting dress.

Dover tilted his head, wearing a goofy smile. "Wow. You're pretty...for a girl."

Katie swallowed her laugh. "Awww, thanks, buddy. That's very sweet of you. Come help me rescue Lollipop." Katie extended her hand and hustled him from the room as quickly as her high-heeled shoes would allow. Danny had indeed managed to stick pennies on Lollipop, who was screeching and hissing. Not good. Only a matter of seconds before Danny would be sporting red kitty scratches on her tender skin. Katie loosened Danny's grip, and Lollipop quickly disappeared under the sofa. If Katie had been that cat, she'd stay hidden until these kids turned eighteen and moved away from home.

"Dana Sue, Lollipop doesn't like to be decorated with pennies, peanut butter, paint, or anything else you decide to put on her fur. Okay?" Danny nodded her head, avoiding eye contact, which only meant Katie would be delivering this same lecture again and again.

Checking the time on her watch, Katie said, "Bedtime. Pick up your toys and march upstairs and start brushing your teeth." The kids grumbled, dragging their feet. "Teamwork. And if you do a good job, I'll read each

of you your favorite story." Katie clapped her hands.
"Look alive!" All three kids scrambled to pick up toys
and shove them in the toy baskets. Katie watched them
scurry past her and up the stairs to prepare for bed. "I'll
be up in five minutes," she called after them.

Katie headed back toward her room to change into
something more comfortable—and kid-appropriate—
when she heard pounding on the front door. She sighed.
Probably another Harmony resident wanting to try out
for the miniseries.

"Coming. Auditions are over for today," she said and
pulled the front door open.

"Auditions? What the *hell* is going on around here?"

Katie's mouth gaped open. There on the other side
of the door stood Tad Poole…all five foot ten and one-
hundred and sixty pounds of him. A jolt went through
Katie…but not in a good way. Seeing Tad in person
after several weeks apart made Katie feel…er…nothing.
No tingle of excitement. No wobbly knees or curling
toes. Not the way she felt every time Vance came within
a mile of her. Instead, she felt a surge of irritation that
was starting to make her blood boil.

"How did you find me? Did my dad send you?" She
narrowed her eyes, but Tad ignored the warning.

He pushed his way into the foyer. "Something is not
adding up, and I demand to know what's going on. You
won't answer my calls, and you keep texting about kids
and—dogs—and what are you *wearing*?" Katie had the
pleasure of watching Tad's pale blue eyes bug out of his
head. "I've never seen…how…who…what—"

"What's the matter? You don't like it?" Katie twisted
her hips side to side, showcasing the snug fit of the dress.

Tad visibly gulped. "I like it, but it's just not you. You look…you look *ridiculous*." Tad waved his hand at her. "You're turning into someone I don't know." Katie's shoulders slumped, and the inner feminine power she'd felt only moments earlier leaked from her body. Playing dress up was never going to change anything.

"And what are you doing in this house? I know for a fact that Vance Kerner lives here, and he has a reputation. With the ladies," Tad sneered, as if telling Katie something she didn't already know. "They even say he's starred in some really bad porn."

Oh God. She groaned. Katie didn't appreciate Tad spreading rumors about the porn, even though a twinge of guilt reminded her how they'd started. "False. There's no truth to the porn rumors. And why are you here grilling me? Are you spying on me? Last time I checked, you were casting recruiter, recruiting agents looking for talent." *And kissing my dad's butt along the way.*

"I've been promoted…to location manager…"

Alarm bells went off inside Katie's head. Location manager meant only one thing…Katie would be working directly under Tad as location scout. There might've been a time in the not so distant past when she would've welcomed this situation. But not now. Not today. And not here.

Planting her fists on her hips, she said, "How convenient. What did you promise my dad this time? Part ownership in your thoroughbred running in the next California Cup Derby?" Walter McKnight had held a fascination with horse racing for as long as she could remember, and the fact that Tad's family owned several racehorses had certainly enhanced Tad's standing with McKnight Studios.

"Don't be ridiculous," he said, not quite meeting her eyes. Splotches of red showed on his cheeks. Tad buying his way into McKnight Studios gave Katie a sick, twisted feeling. Working there may not be right for her, but she didn't trust this alliance forging between her dad and Tad. Katie made a mental note to speak with her brothers.

"And that's not the point. You still haven't told me what you're doing here…in this house. I have a right to know," Tad pushed.

"What she's doing here is none of your damn business. In fact, you need to leave so she can continue to do it."

Katie whirled around at the sound of Vance's deep voice. He'd come through the kitchen and stood in the middle of the dining room, looking a lot like a dark avenging angel. A jolt went through Katie. This time her breath caught, and her heart skipped several beats.

"Where have you been? We've been waiting all day," she blurted before she could stop and think.

"Katie! This is an outrage. I demand you leave with me right now." Tad tugged on her elbow. "If you come with me, I won't breathe a word of this to your father."

Suddenly Katie was being yanked in the opposite direction, straight into Vance's rock-hard chest. Unable to control herself, she took a long whiff. His smell was intoxicating. Like outdoors and clean cotton.

"Look, slick, Katie's not going anywhere…especially with you," Vance growled in his don't-mess-with-me-or-I'll-kick-your-ass voice. Vance wrapped his heavy arm in a protective way around her shoulder, and Katie couldn't help but snuggle into him before moving away.

Only Vance wouldn't let her go. His hold tightened, and Katie secretly reveled in his macho protective act.

"You stay out of this, Kerner." Tad made an aggressive step but stopped short. Vance's expression was about as welcoming as a pit of rattlesnakes.

"Um…guys?" Katie wiggled out from under Vance's arm. "This is not the time or place—"

"Kay-tee, I want story," Danny interrupted as she hurried down the stairs in her fuzzy pink kitten pj's.

"You promised," Dover added right behind her. The boys held several books in their hands. At the sight of their squeaky-clean faces, her heart squeezed…in a good way. And it dawned on her that she would miss these kids something fierce when she finally pulled out of Harmony and headed for the West Coast.

For the second time that evening, Tad's eyes bugged out over the kids, and he started to sputter. "What the…? Your new family, I presume?" His voice took on that supercilious tone she'd always hated.

Suddenly Katie felt very tired…and used. "It's not what you think, Tad." Although she kind of wished it was. Vance gave her hand a reassuring squeeze, lending her his strength and support. She blinked at him in surprise, wanting nothing more than to let him handle everything.

"Go on up and start reading to the kids. I'll be there in just a minute. Need to clean up a few things first." And by clean up, Katie knew he didn't mean the kitty litter box. Unless he planned to use Tad as the scooper.

"Katie, don't you dare leave…we are not finished, and I deserve—"

"What you think you deserve and what you're gonna get are two different things, pal," Vance warned in his scary pirate voice. Katie hesitated for a second, but Vance gave her an encouraging nod. That was all she needed to get away from her irrational ex-boyfriend and the man she was becoming attached to like bark on a tree.

Vance watched Katie hustle the kids up the stairs. The backside view she presented in the amazing, sexy dress almost had him following her up and forgetting the petulant dickhead who still stood in his foyer as if he owned the place. Ungluing his eyes from Katie's wonderfully curvaceous bottom, he gave Tad *Pole* his meanest badass stare. The one he'd learned from hours of watching war films.

"Outside. Now," he ordered in his best military voice.

"Just a minute. I'm Katie's fiancé, and I have a right—" Vance herded Tad out front before he could finish his rant, closing the door behind them.

"Bullshit. There's no ring on her finger. Who are you, anyway?"

Tad Puff straightened his scrawny shoulders and lifted his nonexistent chin. "I'm Tad Poole the Third. My father is—"

"I don't give a rat's ass who your father is. What I want to know is what you're really doing here." The fine hairs on the back of Vance's neck prickled. This smacked of underhanded maneuvering by Walter McKnight. Vance had spent the better half of the day talking to Katie's father, reassuring him that he would hold up his end of the bargain. The one where he purposely lied to Katie about using his house and about her daddy wanting her off the job after only a few short

weeks. But Vance got the sense Walter never left anything to chance, and Tad Poodle must be his minion,
here to do his bidding.

"Look, Kerner, you want the truth? I was sent by
Walter McKnight to secure the location he wanted in
Wilmington. Katie blew it. But Katie doesn't know that,
and you're not going to tell her. I know all about the deal
between you and Walter."

Bingo. Vance struck an easy pose, arms crossed over
his chest, but he was feeling anything but relaxed. He
didn't need this shit today of all days. His defenses were
down, and his emotions were bubbling near the surface.
After convincing Walter he would stick to the shitty
bargain, Vance had spent the other half of his day sitting with Adam Reynolds, in Starbucks, watching Adam
swig black coffee with a shaky hand, and listening to
him relive a particularly haunting memory. When he'd
first met Adam, Vance had listened to his stories for the
sake of research, but as Vance grew to know the vet he
started listening for another reason altogether. In some
small way, Vance thought by listening and showing support, maybe he could ease Adam's pain. Something he
was never able to do for his own dad.

"You're not exactly in a great position either, bud.
I'd watch those threats you like to throw around," Vance
said. He wasn't above using his height and size to tower
over Tad Puny. "It's obvious you don't exactly have her
back." Neither did he, but he couldn't think about that
right now. She was here, and he planned to keep her as
long as possible.

Tad lifted his aristocratic nose even higher. "I've
always had Katie's best interests at heart. We have

history together. And I know for a fact that Walter thinks Katie's staying at the Lazy Oak Inn…not shacking up with the next American gigolo. Sure would hate for that to get back to him, wouldn't you?" Tad had the nerve to laugh. "By the way, your Twitter fans want to know when your next porn flick is releasing." Vance gave Tad points for the edge he detected in his voice. He guessed Tad hadn't weaseled his way into Walter's good graces without playing dirty on the side. But Vance hadn't grown up in a military family without learning a thing or two about dirty warfare.

Grabbing Tad by the shirt collar and lifting him onto his toes, Vance witnessed the fear in Tad's eyes. "I'd be very careful if I were you. You don't know who you're messin' with. Now get off my property." Vance shoved Tad Pimp off his front porch.

"This isn't over, Kerner," Tad sneered, yanking on his wrinkled shirt and running his fingers through his already receding hairline. "Katie's a wanderer…she won't play house for long. She'll lose interest, like she does with everything."

"Just like she did with you?" Vance said in a dry tone, satisfied at the doubt skittering across Tad's pale face.

"You'll be hearing from Walter…I'll make sure of it," Tad warned before he strode to his car in the driveway.

"Shit a brick," Vance said to no one in particular. Could he add any more stress on top of the pile he'd already amassed? Not only did he have Walter McKnight making threats and breathing down his neck, and a deadline looming over his head, but he had to worry about Tad Pimple showing up and upsetting Katie. And that disturbed him most of all. He didn't want anyone upsetting Katie. And he felt certain Katie had been upset…a lot. She'd been manipulated and dismissed, and Vance's twisted gut told him it went even deeper. And since he couldn't claim to be taking the high road, because he'd sold his soul to deceive her too, that put him in the same cesspool with Walter and Tad Puke.

Vance grabbed a bottle of cold water from the refrigerator and guzzled it, hoping to dissolve the burning lump in his throat. More subterfuge to add to what already swirled inside his head as he tried plotting his last book in the Honor series. Fighting, hatred, evasion, anguish…Vance wasn't sure he was up for another round. He wanted calm, and he wanted peace. He blew out a heavy breath. Katie with her bright eyes, wide smile, and luscious curves was anything but peaceful for his state of mind.

"Katie?" Vance knocked on the cracked bedroom door, allowing it to swing farther open. "You in here?"

Katie sat cross-legged in the middle of the king-size bed, chin resting in her palm, wearing ratty gray sweats and a defeated expression on her pretty face. Gone was the confident woman in the sexy come-and-get-it dress.

Vance hesitated. Shipping boxes littered the floor and looked to have been unpacked and then repacked with their contents. The sexy blue dress lay folded neatly on top of one of the boxes. "You wanna talk about it?" he asked.

A rattling sigh escaped her lips. "I wouldn't know where to begin." She looked up, and Vance's lungs seized at the tracks of tears staining her cheeks. "Sorry about all that drama. Don't worry. I'm not running. I won't renege on babysitting…even if you don't sign the contract," she added in a resigned voice. He should've been thrilled to know his job of deceiving her would require no effort on his part, since she planned to stay regardless, but instead, the vise around his heart only tightened. "But I need to get home as soon as this gig is up. It's obvious I've displeased my dad and Tad again." Katie sounded as dejected as she appeared.

Vance didn't like seeing this side of her. The crushed side beaten down too many times. He knew the feeling. Being dressed down by his dad had left deep scars. And he especially didn't like seeing her upset over Tad Prick. Katie couldn't pick her family, but she certainly had a choice in whom she dated. It didn't take a degree in couples therapy to know this guy was wrong for her. Vance needed to hear the story inside her head. He needed to know what kind of hold Tad had on her, and why.

Vance toed off his loafers, strode to the bed, and flopped back against the pillows. "Come here." He pulled a startled Katie into his chest, wrapping his arm around her stiff shoulders. The smell of her clean hair made him light-headed. Her fragrance of orange blossoms with a hint of sadness curled through his nose. "Relax. Let me…hold you." His body wanted to do a lot more than hold delicious, sad Katie. He wanted to consume her inside and out. But he clamped down his raging desires in order to help her. Katie needed his understanding and a strong shoulder to cry on. And he could provide both. Even if it killed him. Vance picked up the end of her braid and tickled the side of her face, trying to ease her tension. "I'm not here solely to get you naked, although I wouldn't be opposed if you so desire…" She lifted her head and narrowed her gaze at him. "I'm here if you want to talk. I'm a good listener. Maybe I can help." He nestled her against his chest and kissed the top of her head. "But you have to open up to me."

"I don't know if I can," she whispered. "I'm not proud of my history. It doesn't show me in a very good light."

Speaking of light, Vance twisted and flicked the bedside lamp off, casting the room in shadowy darkness. "Better?" Light from the moon filtered in from the French doors. "I'm not here to judge, Kat," he murmured against her silky hair.

Katie snuggled against him, curling her arm across his waist. Torture. Vance sucked in a huge breath, channeling his more noble instincts. He could do this. For Katie.

Chapter 14

KATIE KNEW WHAT VANCE WANTED. A STORY SHE HATED reliving. Saying it out loud made her sound worthless and weak. And she didn't want anyone latching onto her vulnerability. Inslee knew the whole story. She always sided with Katie, like a true best friend. Tad sensed the truth, but he had crossed over to the dark side and agreed with her parents. Her brothers remained neutral, but being successful, high-powered attorneys, they struggled with Katie's lack of direction. But with Vance, she didn't feel the censure or the prejudgment. He'd been open and honest with her from the beginning—except when it came to the contract. She knew he was stalling, only because he really didn't want strangers roaming all over his property. She got it. Now he was asking her to expose her soul and let him in, to trust he wouldn't crush her like a bug beneath his boot.

She heaved a thick sigh and took a leap of faith. In Vance. "The truth is my parents see me as a huge disappointment. I don't live up to their expectations. Never have." She twisted and stared at the moonlit ceiling, the back of her shoulder resting against his. "When I was younger, I remember overhearing a conversation where my dad said he couldn't believe McKnight blood ran through my veins. And that I disgusted him." Katie felt the tension emanating from Vance even as he gently ran his rough palm up and down her arm. His quiet support encouraged her to go on.

"It was the year I hadn't signed up for any academic or social clubs at school. Instead, I chose to stay home and play around with my photography."

"How old were you?"

"Fourteen. First year of high school. I didn't have the drive or grades like my brothers. And I was never class president or a member of the Honor Society. My mom kept pushing me to try out for cheerleader." Katie gave a soft snort. "As if. My whole life…it's been like they never knew me. Or I just wasn't significant enough. They've always been super busy with the studio and my mom's charitable organizations. Somehow, they always seemed to forget about me."

"Christ," Vance muttered.

Glad for the darkness that hid her face, she swallowed around the lump forming in her throat. It wasn't an easy story to tell, because to most people, Katie lived a charmed, privileged life, wanting for nothing. Her dad ran a successful studio, allowing Katie access to all kinds of stars. What did she have to complain about? Most people would trade places with her in a skinny minute. She should be counting her blessings, not complaining about her parents' lack of attention. But Katie had never cared about the trappings surrounding her, or the Hollywood stars who came and went. She had always craved her parents' attention. She wanted to belong to something. To feel connected to her family. After years of trying to please her parents, she realized her efforts were never good enough. Somewhere along the way, her parents stopped believing in her. They focused on her brothers' accomplishments, and Katie felt ignored. Invisible. Even as an adult, she couldn't shake it.

"But that wasn't the worst thing," she heard herself saying. Katie shouldn't be telling Vance these stories about her family. It wasn't like she'd been physically abused or starved or left in foster care.

"Take your time. I'm still listening," Vance said in a low, rough voice, tightening his hold as if to shield her from her past.

She drew a shuddery breath. "Once, when I was twelve, we went camping as a family. Camping in the sense that we stayed in a well-equipped cabin out in the middle of the woods. Otherwise, my mom would not have come. My dad and brothers would go on these long hikes and leave me behind because I couldn't keep up. I wandered around the campsite with my camera and took pictures." Vance shifted, pulling her closer. "On the third day, my dad and brothers were off fishing and my mom was napping inside the cabin, and I wandered farther than usual to take pictures of some wildflowers. When I returned to the campsite a couple of hours later, they were gone."

"What do you mean?"

The steady beat of Vance's heart gave her courage. "They had packed up and left. Without me. The cabin was locked, and the site had been swept clean. It was beginning to get dark, and I was terrified. You know how suddenly you hear things like coyotes howling, snakes rattling, bears rustling? I'm sure none of things actually happened, but when you're alone and scared to death…that was all I could think about."

Vance suddenly turned and pinned Katie beneath his ferocious gaze. "They left you? How long?"

Four hours. Katie had waited, huddled on the porch of the cabin with her back against the wall, crying. Terrified. The memory came back to her in sharp detail; her body shook despite Vance's heavy weight.

"They eventually remembered…m-my mom had had a hair appointment, and she hadn't wanted to be late. My dad dropped her off first before coming back to pick me up." And then proceeded to lecture Katie the entire way home about being irresponsible for wandering off.

"How long?" Vance gritted between his teeth, giving Katie an insistent shake.

"F-four hours." Katie lowered her eyes, mortified at her admission.

"Those heartless assholes." Fury vibrated through his big, solid body, furious on her behalf. No one, with the exception of Inslee, had ever completely taken her side.

Vance shook, and Katie heard the emotion in his voice. "It's okay, honey. You're safe with me," he said in a husky voice. "Don't cry." He gently wiped her cheeks with the pads of his thumbs. Katie swallowed a sob, along with the memories threatening to engulf her. She didn't want to turn into a puddling mess of salty tears. Baring her weaknesses and vulnerability in front of this hulking, scary, but mostly lovable pirate had been a huge risk. He now held all the power in his strong, capable hands, along with her heart. And he could destroy her.

Vance didn't know how long he held Katie in his arms, but eventually her breathing evened out and she fell asleep. It would be a long time before he could do the same. Her camping story reached out and grabbed him by the throat. Who did that to a twelve-year-old child? The terror and fear she must've felt made Vance want to smash heads…starting with Walter McKnight's and ending with Katie's selfish mom. His mind filled in the gaps of the stories she hadn't told him.

Vance pulled the covers up and settled Katie more comfortably against his side. In the quiet darkness, he examined his own life with more clarity. His family wasn't perfect, but he knew he had people who loved him and he could rely on. His mom had always been supportive, and his older brother, Eric, had looked out for Vance when they were younger. Vance had always felt secure. In that respect, he'd had it way better than Katie.

But the similarities they shared with disapproving parents put Vance on edge. The chasm between him and his dad had expanded over the years. Vance hadn't figured a way to close the gap. He thought by honoring war heroes in his books his dad would accept his apology, but his dad hadn't acknowledged Vance as a writer, much less read his books. Where did he go from here? If only his dad would meet him halfway.

Vance hated that Katie wallowed in uncertainty, trying to make her parents happy. And he hated the machinations of her manipulating dad.

His gut split in two over the part he'd played in deceiving her. He'd made a deal with the devil, and it was a living hell. Vance kissed the top of Katie's head. A fierce impulse to protect her swarmed over him. He would make damn sure Katie never found out what he and Walter had cooked up. It would destroy her.

Vance had sensed strength in Katie from the first day. Fighting her own insecurities, she allowed the world to see her big heart and capacity for love. Vance wanted to care for her and give her the security she craved. He wanted to give her a family she could call her own. He would move mountains with a thimble to give the woman he loved—

Loved.

His thoughts froze on that one word. For months, he hadn't looked at another woman, much less hooked up with one. In only four short days, California Katie had disrupted his life like an earthquake measuring ten on the Richter scale.

Katie mumbled something in her sleep, burrowing closer and entwining her leg with his. Vance swallowed a groan, loving the feel of her soft curves draped over him. His heart took a tumble. He'd never felt this kind of connection. In the interior of the dark room, what he wanted became crystal clear. His spine prickled. Vance wanted to give Katie everything she desired and deserved. He wanted to be her family. Her rock. Her home. If that wasn't love, he didn't know what was.

—⁓—

Katie stretched and moaned at the same time. Why was her pillow so hard and uncomfortable? Her eyes popped open. The dawn's gray light illuminated the shadowy bedroom. Katie's hard pillow was none other than Pirate Man's chest. She stopped breathing. How long had she slept? In this bed. With Vance Kerner. Without moving, Katie tried to determine if she was still clothed. She didn't feel naked. In fact, she felt hot and uncomfortable from sleeping in her clothes. Yes! She still wore clothes. A gasp of relief escaped her lips.

"You awake, cupcake?" Vance rumbled near her ear. Thankful for the gray light so he couldn't witness her morning-after shame or the raccoon eyes she had to be sporting from sleeping in her make-up, Katie surreptitiously moved her hand where her mouth had been resting to check for drool. His shirt was dry. Thank the Lord.

"Yeah," she croaked. "Sorry for using you as my pillow. You must've been uncomfortable." She scooted away from his warm, mind-robbing heat and swiped beneath her eyes with her hands, hoping to rub away yesterday's mascara.

Vance stretched like a big black panther. "My pleasure. You doing okay?"

Everything from the night before came flooding back, and a new flush burned her cheeks. "Yeah, about that...I shouldn't have unloaded on you. And sorry about Tad. I'll make sure he doesn't disturb you again. He can be a bit...pushy." Along with arrogant and annoying.

"I can handle that dirtbag. Don't worry about me." Vance swung his legs off the bed. "Stay put. I'll brew some coffee, and then we can talk before the Three Musketeers come charging in." He strode from the room in his rumpled, heavenly glory. Katie flopped back against the pillows and groaned. *Talk about what?* She'd told him more than he needed to know, and didn't that make her look like a spineless loser? A grown woman struggling for her parents' approval and still hung up on some slights from her past. She should be over all this by now.

Katie hustled to the bathroom and stifled a cry at the sight of her tear-streaked, make-up-melted face. She quickly washed up and threw on a fresh pair of jeans and clean knit long-sleeved shirt. She found her ballet flats next to the boxes of clothes she planned to ship back. She reached out and touched the soft fabric on the pretty blue dress, wishing she could get away with wearing it, but Tad's blunt words had had a crushing effect...like getting hit in the face with a cream pie. Katie knew her limitations. Pretending to be someone new was a recipe for disaster.

"I hope you're not planning to send those clothes back." Startled, she straightened with a jerk. "Because that little blue number was a total knockout." Vance handed her a piping-hot mug of coffee, and Katie's fingers brushed his, reaching for the cup. The jolt of electricity hadn't dimmed...she shivered with anticipation. And the fiery light behind Vance's dark eyes told her he felt the same.

Katie focused on her coffee, breathing in the dark-roasted aroma and allowing the hot liquid to wake up her foggy brain. "Um, they're really not my style. I'm more of a plain—"

"Stop. Don't say another word." Vance pushed her down on the leather bench at the foot of the bed. Playing with her fingers, he said. "Kat, there's nothing plain about you. But you dress like you're trying to blend in with the senior set." Katie winced at his accurate description. Vance put aside his coffee and pried open one of the boxes, pulling out tops and skirts and slacks.

"Vance...please. Put it all back. I'm not keeping the clothes because..." Katie almost choked on her coffee at the sight of a pink push-up bra with matching skimpy panties, dangling from Vance's fingers. Lingerie Inslee had insisted she buy.

"Oh ho. You are most definitely wearing these. With this." In his other hand he held a deep coral crocheted dress with scalloped hem and illusion sleeves. The scoop neckline revealed more than Katie felt comfortable with. "This one is a winner." Vance's smile was pure sin wrapped in desire, and Katie felt a pang of longing squeeze her heart. After all she'd revealed to him... he saw her as someone vital and attractive, who would actually wear a sexy outfit to catch a man's eye. But Katie didn't want just any man. She wanted Pirate Man.

"Vance." She sighed. "You're the best thing to happen to me and my ego in a very long, long time, but—"

"No buts. Let's stick with *I'm the best thing*. It works for me." A smile twitched around her lips. Vance dropped the clothes in a heap on the carpet and crowded next to her on the bench. "Thursday night there's a book signing in Raleigh. I want you to come. We'll have dinner afterwards. A real date." The color of doubt must've clouded her eyes, because he cupped her chin in his big hand. "No more hiding. It's time you started living your life...for you. No one else. Not me. Not your dad, and certainly not Tad Pole."

If only. An unwanted tear slid down her cheek. "I don't have a life," she whispered.

"Well, honey, that's all about to change." Vance leaned down, careful not to spill the coffee she held, and gave her a heart-warming, body-humming kiss. Full of promise and hope. She melted into him. Her free hand clutched his shoulder, never wanting to let go.

"Sealed with a kiss," he murmured against her lips. "Thursday night. You, me, and that kick-ass dress."

Katie arched a brow. "Now you're pushing it. The jury's still out on the dress—"

"The jury has rendered a verdict. The defendant will wear the dress as ordered." He kissed her again. This one hard and insistent. Katie brushed his cheek, loving the feel of his morning stubble against her palm. If he asked her to wear nothing but a thong and two pasties she'd do it. Suddenly, his tongue no longer tangled with hers, and Vance pulled back. Katie blinked. "Kids are up."

Something crashed down the stairs, and her eyes widened. "What could that be?" she asked.

Vance stood. "I'll check it out. Finish your coffee, and then meet me in the kitchen."

Katie relaxed, knowing he could handle the kids with no problem. Besides, she had a lot of thinking to do, along with heavy sighing and swooning. She was going on her first real date in a very long time.

Vance reached the door and turned back. "And, Kat…wear the sexy bra and panties under the dress…or nothing at all. I'm flexible." He winked.

Katie swallowed a groan and maybe part of her tongue. Make that her first date with a very dangerous pirate.

Chapter 15

KATIE WAS GLAD FOR THE FEW MOMENTS OF PEACE THAT morning to enjoy her coffee, because the bedlam that followed with making lunches, hunting for lost tennis shoes, cleaning up spilled yogurt, and dressing three kids for school chased the calm right off the property and into another county.

After rushing Danny inside her preschool classroom before the ringing of the bell, Katie heaved herself up behind the wheel of Vance's truck and caught her breath. Her cell chirped, and she hesitated, not wanting to go another round with Tad. Curiosity won out, and she picked up her phone.

Meet us @ Daily Grind 4 coffee. Lucy & Bertie.

A small thrill coursed through her. Ok. C u in 5.

Katie smiled and put the truck in gear. She could use some "girl time," and more important, time away from Vance. He needed to write, and she needed to think. He made chucking responsibilities seem as easy as stumbling upon celebrity handprints on the Hollywood Walk of Fame.

Lucy and Bertie had already ordered their coffees when Katie pushed through the entrance.

"Hey there. What would you like?" Lucy asked, standing next to the order counter.

"Skinny latte would be perfect. Thanks for inviting me."

"Earl, meet Katie from California," Lucy said to the guy behind the counter, who wore a brown-and-white-striped apron and goofy grin.

"How you doing, Katie? How 'bout a muffin or bagel to go with your coffee?" At the mention of food, Katie's stomach rumbled.

"Muffin, please." Katie reached for her wallet, but Bertie tugged on her arm, stopping her.

"Come. Sit here. Coffee's on Lucy and me."

Katie sat at a round bistro table in front of the window and next to the chip rack. "You Southerners make it hard for someone to pay their own way."

Bertie sipped her coffee and smiled. "Only if we like you…if not, then watch out for a good ol' Southern butt-whupping."

Lucy laughed, handing Katie her coffee and blueberry muffin, and sat in the vacant chair next to her. "We're also known for our good ol' cookouts. You're coming with Vance Friday night, right?"

"Sure! You'll meet a few more of our close friends; it'll be fun," Bertie said, green eyes sparkling.

Katie straightened in her seat, trying to swallow the bite of muffin swelling in her mouth. She'd almost forgotten about the cookout, because Vance had never mentioned it. Maybe he didn't want her going. These were his friends, and she was merely…what? His kissing buddy? His little fling on the side? Another piece of a— Katie didn't finish the thought. She stopped her mind from wandering down the well-worn path of self-doubt.

"Brogan's supplying organic Angus beef for the burgers, and I'm making brownies for dessert." Lucy watched Katie with her intense gray eyes.

"The guys will provide the keg and other drinks. I'm bringing homemade rolls and baked beans from the Dog. We'll have plenty of food and drinks to go around," Bertie added.

Sounded delicious, and Katie didn't want to show up empty-handed. "I'll make a salad…if I go, that is," she said, not wanting to appear presumptuous.

"Wonderful. Of course you're going. Vance wouldn't dare come without you." Bertie scooted her chair back.

"Yeah. Brogan's already told him not to bother showing up unless he brings you."

Great. Nothing like being the pity date. Third wheeling it. Awkward wallflower. Katie gave a jerk with her head. Pushing those thoughts away, she replaced them with Vance's intense eyes, strong arms, talented lips, and the date he'd made with her for Thursday night. Suddenly, she didn't feel like an afterthought. Vance Kerner had been protective, supportive, and understanding. And he'd not only told her he desired her, but he'd showed her as well. By removing ugly, unwanted thoughts from her mind and focusing on Vance, she started to feel unburdened. Free. Baby steps. But they were steps in the right direction.

"You okay?" Lucy asked, giving her another strange look.

Katie smiled, lifting her chin. "Never been better."

Bertie clapped her hands. "It's a beautiful morning. Let's take a walk."

Katie nodded, her head buzzing. "I'd like that."

They gathered their coffees, said good-bye to Earl, and stepped out onto Main Street. Lucy gave a quick wave to some women entering BetterBites across the street. Katie followed Bertie as she wandered off the sidewalk toward the white Victorian gazebo at the center of the town commons. Pots of colorful flowers decorated the steps, and park benches surrounded the green space. A separate building off to the right served as the community center, and a smaller building flanked it on the left. If Katie hadn't known better, she'd think she was on one of the McKnight Studios sets.

"This is so picturesque. Who maintains the flowers?" Katie asked, wishing she'd brought her Nikon along.

Bertie climbed the stairs to the gazebo and leaned against a column. "The Harmony Huggers maintain all the potted flowers. We hold lots of events and festivals on the grounds. As Keith used to say, it's a regular Mayberry around here."

"What is that building used for?" Katie gestured to the low structure next to the community center.

"Used to be an art park for kids, but the family who ran it moved away a couple of years ago, and it's been sitting empty since," Lucy said, skipping up the gazebo steps.

"Yeah, Keith's been pushing to find another business to lease the space. He thinks it'll become an eyesore if it sits vacant for too long."

"Is Keith into real estate now?" Katie asked. She knew he didn't play professional tennis anymore, but she thought he was still involved with his tennis academy.

"Not really. But he's been a big proponent of revitalizing Harmony."

"He's the one who convinced Brogan to open BetterBites here."

"According to Keith, a vital downtown is the sign of a healthy economy. And in order for his tennis academy to survive, Harmony and the surrounding areas need to thrive," Bertie said.

"It would be great if we had something for kids again. I'd love a place to bring Charlotte after preschool, where she could play and tumble or create something." Lucy finished her coffee and tossed the cup in one of the camouflaged recycle bins.

"Don't you have programs at your library?" Katie asked, dumping her empty cup after Lucy's.

"Yes. But the space is very limited. There needs to be some place more hands-on, where the kids can make noise and burn energy. The Jaycee community park is great, but they cater more to older kids, and the nearest Gymboree is twenty minutes away in Raleigh."

Katie wandered over and pressed her face to the glass front, cupping her hands to the sides of her face to block the sun's glare. The space was empty, with the exception of a few built-in bookcases lining one wall. Leftover plastic kiddie chairs and stranded balls sat in the middle of the room. But Katie saw way more than that. She saw potential. With a little bit of paint, creative design from the set department, and the right equipment, it could be a thriving space for a great after-school program. She could picture Donald, Dover, and Danny going from station to station, learning different skills and having fun. There was room for tumbling and hands-on activities.

Bertie and Lucy stood behind her. "Kids could ride bikes and scooters around the commons and make creative art projects. It's a great location for something like that," Lucy said.

"We need to encourage a franchise, like Gymboree, to consider this space. Luce, this calls for a campaign," Bertie said. "Lucy is a marketing genius. She single-handedly turned BetterBites around in less than two weeks and has been instrumental in helping Keith with the tennis academy. Katie, if you need a good marketer, she's the one to call." Bertie hugged Lucy around the neck.

Katie gave a slow nod, her mind reeling with possibilities. "Before you launch a massive campaign, check with me first. I might be interested in the space."

"What?" they chorused together, exchanging looks of shock.

Bertie hooked her arm through Katie's and pulled her to one of the park benches. "Miss California Girl, what is going on behind those pretty brown eyes of yours? Are you seriously thinking about staying in Harmony?"

Lucy and Bertie crowded next to Katie on the bench, looking like eager puppies waiting for their ration of Kibbles 'n Bits. Katie gave a small laugh. "If you could see your faces. Your tongues are hanging out. You two are dying for the latest gossip."

"Damn straight." Lucy rubbed her hands together. "Spill it. Or we have ways of making you talk."

"Does this involve a certain tortured but oh-so-gorgeous author we all know and love?" Bertie batted her eyelashes at Katie.

Katie laughed. "Now your true colors are showing. Here I'm thinking you're the sweetest Southern belles, when you're really ruthless piranhas."

"You ever see the movie *Steel Magnolias*?" Katie nodded at Bertie's question. "That movie could've been made right here in Harmony. Don't be messing with us, girlfriend."

"We want details. Juicy details," Lucy added, nudging Katie's side.

Katie shook her head. "You're going to be sorely disappointed. I've got no juicy tidbits to share."

"Liar. Your face is beet-red. Just tell us if he kisses as smokin' hot as he looks."

Katie's lips twitched, trying to hide her smile. "You're both as bad as my friend Inslee back home. She's been hounding me with the same questions."

"I like her already. Hope we meet someday," Lucy added. "Now quit stalling, because we aren't letting you go until we know how Mr. Badass Vance kisses."

Katie threw up her hands in surrender. "Like you would expect. Amazing. He takes kissing to a whole new level—"

"I knew it!"

"Of course. We all did. It's not like he hasn't had tons of experience. Sorry," Bertie said, patting Katie's arm. "But that's all in the past, because Vance has been pierced by Cupid's arrow, and it appears he's convincing you to stay. Am I right?"

Flustered by Bertie's assessment, Katie didn't want them to get the wrong idea, or heaven forbid, start spreading more false rumors. "Not exactly. I mean, Vance is wonderful, but please, there's nothing going on between us except…" Uncontrollable lust? How should she put this?

"Sex?" Lucy said matter-of-factly.

"No. No. We haven't…it's complicated."

Bertie and Lucy exchanged knowing looks, which only added to Katie's uncertainty. "What?"

Bertie smoothed her hand over her designer jeans. "Katie, if Vance only saw you as his next fling or one-night stand…you would've had sex by now. From what I've heard…he's *that* persuasive. But since you two haven't…you know…that proves he's fallen hard. This is new territory for him, I assure you."

Katie gulped. Could she and Vance be feeling exactly the same? Katie didn't know who or what to believe. "The thing is…I've been doing a lot of thinking lately. Not to bore you with the details, but I might be making some changes with my career, and—"

"And you and Vance are getting married and will live happily ever after," Lucy practically shouted.

"No! Please." Katie pressed her fingers to her temples and rubbed. If Vance got wind of this conversation…Katie cringed. A guy spent some quality time with her, stole a few kisses, and she announced to the world they're getting married. This would be more harmful than the porn rumors. This called for serious damage control. "Vance has been kind and supportive, but there's nothing more to it. He's grateful I'm helping out with the kids…"

"Stop worrying. We won't force it out of you…yet. But don't kid yourself. We know Vance Kerner, and it's not his pending deadline that's driving him mad." Bertie raised one delicately arched brow. "A certain California gal has managed to wrangle that wild country boy to the ground, and he's got to come to terms with it."

Katie's heartbeat kicked up a notch. Yes, Vance

SWEET SOUTHERN BAD BOY

wanted her…but only in the sack. Not in his life…like in forever. And Katie wanted that too. Not the forever part—that would be emotional suicide. She wanted to be with someone who wanted *her*. Not because her father ran a successful studio, and not because she was some charity case. Two consenting adults sharing a mutual lust. Right? Right. Then why did it feel like so much more?

At the sound of her chirping cell, Katie dug for it inside the pocket of her sensible khaki skirt. She still hadn't worked up the nerve to wear a new outfit. Yep. Chicken. She couldn't stop the tiny smile that curled her lips when she read the screen.

"Ooo, is Vance sexting you?" Lucy leaned in to peek at her phone.

Katie giggled. "Even better. His dad is reminding me about having lunch with him today."

Lucy's gray eyes widened in surprise. "No way! You did *not* say what I think you said."

"Listen, this doesn't need to be bantered about. General Kerner made me promise *not* to tell Vance I spend time with him, and I'd like to keep that promise, because quite frankly, he scares the devil out of me."

"He scares the devil outta everyone," Lucy added. "That's why I'm shocked he's texting you about lunch. You sure it's not an invitation to hogtie and boil you for lunch?"

"Luce, he actually had breakfast at the Dog the other day. He's really taken with Katie," Bertie said, flashing Katie a warm smile.

Holy Justin Bieber. Katie hurried to explain, to keep the Harmony crazies from making up their own false story. "General Kerner has no interest in me. We're friends. He treats me like a daughter. There's nothing more to it." She couldn't have Bertie and Lucy thinking she and Chuck had a "thang" going on. Wouldn't that be a train wreck? "We've shared a couple of lunches, and today he wants me to bring him copies of Vance's latest series. I get the impression he's never read them."

"Your impression would be spot-on. He's never read any of Vance's books. This has to be a good thing for Vance and his dad." Bertie tossed a hank of hair over her shoulder. "You're a true ray of California sunshine to those lost Kerner men. Fate has played a hand. There's a reason your car stopped in Harmony." Bertie and Lucy both nodded.

"You're a miracle worker. Brogan says those two could stand touching noses for months and never see eye to eye. If you get them to stop feuding after all these years, we'll erect a monument in your honor right here in the center of the town commons." Lucy spread her arms wide.

"And we'll name our next festival after you," Bertie said.

Katie's gaze darted from Bertie to Lucy. A twinge of panic tap-danced inside her chest. "Let's not get excited. No monuments or festival namings. But I could use some help finding copies of Vance's books. I haven't seen any extra ones lying around the house."

"They're probably up in his loft. But don't worry. The Kitchen Sink will have them. They sell everything—"

"Except the kitchen sink," Katie and Lucy chorused together and then burst out laughing.

Chapter 16

KATIE BOUGHT COPIES OF VANCE'S HONOR SERIES AT The Kitchen Sink, along with Lego Bionicles for the boys and a stuffed pink kitty for Danny. Lucy and Bertie had kept her company while shopping and promised to come by Friday afternoon before the cookout to help her get ready. Katie questioned their motives but secretly looked forward to the visit. Maybe some of their backbone and gumption would rub off on her. She could benefit from these two Southern steel magnolias.

That afternoon, Danny stayed after in the preschool's play program, which gave Katie more time for lunch with Chuck. She snuck out the back of the house, avoiding the Hollywood star wannabes crowding the front yard. By the number of people who showed up every day, you'd think Katie was Jennifer Lopez, holding auditions for American Idol.

Sneaking a glance at the loft windows, she wondered if Vance was holed up inside working. She hadn't seen him since the morning's chaotic breakfast. It was better this way. She needed time to think, and her mind turned to guacamole when bold and beautiful Vance entered the scene. Katie needed a clear head to figure things out. And Pirate Man, with the dangerous eyes, honeyed words, and devastating lips only complicated things.

Katie knocked on Chuck's door ten minutes later,

clutching Vance's books and her iPad loaded with more pictures and puzzles to share with him.

"Right on time," Chuck said by way of greeting. "I picked up some fried chicken and biscuits from the Rolling Pin. I think you'll find it more to your liking than the Eastern barbecue." Katie followed him to the kitchen bar where he had laid out lunch.

"Smells and looks delicious. Next time I'll treat and bring you lunch."

Chuck pulled out her chair and gave her a genuine smile. "I'd like that."

Katie placed Vance's books down between their place settings. "As you requested," she said to his sudden closed-off, hardened expression. "Word is they're quite good. I plan to read them." Chuck fingered the paperback cover of *Honor Bound* but didn't open it. "You might want to take a glance at the dedication," she said before focusing her attention on the crispy chicken on her plate. Chuck grunted and pushed the books farther down the bar and out of his reach. She gave a shrug. The ball was in his court now. Vance had dedicated both his books to his dad and his brother. The real heroes in his life. Katie couldn't think of a more permanent way to express one's feelings than having them appear in print for millions to read. At some point, General Kerner would have to acknowledge the olive branch being extended by his son. Katie sensed he had the desire but was mired in so much muck from the past, he couldn't take the first step.

"Dottie tells me you were sniffing around the town commons this morning, checking out the vacant space with Bertie Morgan and Brogan's wife...her name escapes me. Lori, Laney…" Chuck snapped his fingers in search of a name.

Katie almost choked on her fattening bite of buttermilk biscuit slathered with honey. She didn't recall seeing Dottie Duncan, and she would be a hard person to miss. But even more surprising than the speed in which Dottie gathered her gossip was the fact that she and the general spoke…to each other.

Katie gulped her iced tea and cleared her throat. "Lucy," she said, supplying Lucy's name.

"That's right. Lucy. Lucy Doolan. She was a funny kid…got herself in a bit of trouble back in high school if my memory serves me correctly."

"Excuse me. But was this a civil conversation with Dottie, or were you two drawing battle lines for your next war?"

Chuck leveled a look at Katie, as if staring down the scope of an MK11 rifle or something equally devastating. Katie's mouth snapped shut. Note to self: Avoid angering man who knows how to use weapons of mass destruction. She remained quiet until Chuck pushed his empty plate away and faced her.

"Are you thinking about putting down roots here in Harmony?"

Yes. No. Maybe. Probably not. Katie had barely formed her own thoughts, when it seemed Harmony had already held a town meeting and decided her future for her. She wiped the corners of her mouth with her napkin, searching for a plausible answer.

"I'm not sure of anything right now. I still have a job to do for my dad, and that's my number-one priority." Or at least it should've been. Katie's priorities seemed to have taken a careening detour down a fast, slippery slope, gaining momentum and heading straight for disaster land.

Chuck crossed his arms over his chambray shirt. "That's commendable. Do you enjoy working for your dad?"

No. Sometimes. Hardly ever. "It can be challenging, but I think once I get the hang of this scouting business, I could be pretty good at it," she hedged.

"Is it something you've always wanted to do?"

Uh, hell to the no. "Not really, but I enjoy scouting the country and taking in the sights, and I love the photography."

"Ever consider doing something with your photography? Seems to me you have a passion for it." Chuck reached for Katie's iPad and tapped the photos icon. The first picture to pop up was of his grandkids, and his granitelike jaw softened. "You seem to have a knack for taking children's photos. I bet people would pay good money for you to photograph their kids."

Funny he should be so observant after knowing her only a few short days. Her own parents had never tapped into her real desires…ever. Photography and working with kids had always brought her pleasure, but she'd never put the two together until she'd spied that empty space on the town commons. There had to be a market for an interactive after-school program for young kids. Something involving computers, photography, creativity, and physical activity. Katie had emailed Inslee earlier, throwing out ideas to get her take on it. Inslee immediately shot back great suggestions on interactive, challenging computer games, including the puzzle program using photography. Excited, Katie couldn't wait to hear what else her best friend came up with.

"Doing something with photography intrigues me. I'd like to figure a way to seamlessly combine creative computer learning with physical activity. Before we raise an entire generation of glowing, green-face couch potatoes. It's not original, I know. I'm sure somebody is doing exactly that all over the country, but from what I can tell, no one is doing it here."

"And how would you go about this…if you decided to take it on?"

"I'm not really sure. My girlfriend in California designs computer games and has offered to help. But first, I'll need a solid business plan. My brothers could handle the legal aspects. And then I'd tap into the set designers and crew at my dad's studio to create a feel or brand. Maybe Keith Morgan could help me with the physical part of it. He's bound to know some great coaches or trainers who could work with young kids."

"How do you plan to pay for all this start-up?"

Good question. She wouldn't have her parents' blessing or backing. *Not* that she would want it. This would be something she did entirely on her own. "Small business loan. If I qualify. That's what the business plan will tell me. If the numbers don't add up…well, it won't be worth pursuing."

"Maybe you need a partner. Somebody who could invest and split the responsibilities with you."

Katie nodded. That would be awesome. But who? Inslee might consider being a silent partner. But hooking up with someone local would be better. Only one problem: Katie didn't know the people of Harmony well enough to start forming partnerships. She shook her head and gulped more tea. How had she gotten started on this topic? Another one of her crazy ideas that would never amount to anything. In a town twenty-five hundred miles from her real home. Her parents would never go for it. They'd make her life a living hell if she even hinted about moving away. Settling down in a small Southern town had never crossed her mind until…until she'd laid eyes on the mysterious dark pirate who invaded her daily thoughts and dreams. She couldn't make a life-altering decision based on the attentions of one shady, sneaky, sexy man. Everyone would call her crazy. She'd be the biggest fool. She'd never live it down.

She'd never be happier.

Chuck watched her with keen eyes, as if waiting for her to come to some conclusion. "You bring up some valid points, General. I have a lot to weigh and think about. I'll let you know what I finally decide."

"I hope so. I'd like to see you putting all your talents and smarts to good use. I believe you can do anything you set your mind to, Katie McKnight. But it doesn't matter what I believe." He tapped a blunt finger to her temple. "It only matters what you believe. And the first order of business is…you need to believe in yourself."

Katie's heart hammered so hard she pressed her palm to her chest. Chuck spoke to her as if she was his own daughter, someone he cared deeply about. He believed in her, and he barely knew her. His words became a small gold nugget to cherish. Words to live by.

She nodded. "Th-thanks. I'll keep that in mind." Before she started blubbering like a sappy girl, she changed the subject. "Would you like to see the new puzzles I made with your grandkids' pictures? They're more challenging, and you can alter the images."

"Can you email them to me? I'd like to play around with them later."

"Absolutely. I'll do it right now." She tapped on her iPad and sent the email with the attached link. "That should do it." She gathered her things. "I better be going. Need to pick the kids up from school."

"You think about what I said." Chuck walked her to the door with his big hand resting on the small of her back. "You have a lot of potential. You just need to decide how to put it to good use."

Right. Potential. In other words…go for it. Whatever "it" was.

"I'll be in touch." He checked his stainless steel watch. "Right now, I have some reading to do." Shock followed by sheer delight at the thought of him reading Vance's books must've skated across her face, because the general delivered one of his scary military expressions designed to make the most highly trained soldier quake in his boots. "This stays between you and me, understood?" he bit out between clenched teeth.

"Yes sir!" And without thinking, Katie saluted just as he closed the door in her face…but not before she heard him laugh.

Chapter 17

VANCE GLANCED AT HIS WATCH. IT WAS THURSDAY EVENING, and he'd been waiting over twenty minutes. What was taking Katie so long? Emma and Opal Ardbuckle had agreed to babysit the kids and were already in the kitchen getting supper on the table.

"Katie! Today, while I'm young!" he called down the hall toward the closed-off master bedroom. Vance had purposely stayed away from Katie these last two days in order to write, because her presence made him lose focus. Just knowing she was puttering around his house broke his concentration. It took an iron will and a few carefully worded emails from his editor, wondering where he stood, that kept his butt in his chair and fingers on the keyboard. But now he was anxious to get this book signing behind him so he could enjoy his date… the captivating and delightful Katie McKnight. He wished they were staying in…preferably in his bed, but dinner out in a nice restaurant beat checking homework, running baths, and playing dunk the kitty with his niece and nephews.

"We're gonna be late—" Vance froze, his tongue glued to the roof of his mouth. There in the doorway to the family room stood Katie. At least he thought it was Katie. He blinked and gave his head a vicious shake. His gaze swept from her high-heel-clad feet up the length of her long, killer legs to the scalloped hem of the coral crocheted dress. The dress he'd pulled from her boxes of clothes only yesterday morning. The dress that fit her like a glove. A glove he wanted to slip his hand up under to see if she wore anything underneath. Vance pressed his itchy palms against his navy dress slacks. Dark, wavy hair fell in layers over her perfectly rounded breasts. Stunning. At a loss for words, Vance noticed the glossy lips she worried with her teeth and the uncertain expression clouding her face, and he managed to unglue his tongue.

"You look amazing." He stepped forward, capturing her cold hand in his. "Better than amazing." He leaned down to press his lips against hers.

She skirted back, avoiding his kiss, and gave a husky laugh. Her soft brown eyes, luminous with appreciation, bored into his. "Come on, Pirate Man. I wanna see you in action." Tugging on his hand, she threw a saucy glance over her shoulder and pulled him toward the front door. "Your fans are waiting."

What fans? Shit. The book signing. How the hell was he supposed to concentrate and field questions when Katie would be there, looking like an angel and pure depravity all wrapped in one tight, enticing package? Vance needed a stiff drink and a bucket of ice…poured down his pants. Because for the next few hours, he'd be living in purgatory.

———◦◦◦———

Fans packed the Barnes & Noble in Raleigh, eagerly waiting to have their books signed by the infamous Vance Kerner. When they entered the store, Vance was immediately hustled to the roped-off area, where a table had been set up with his books on display. People were already filling the folding chairs provided for the event. Katie noticed quite a few veterans in attendance, which had to be a pretty impressive testament to his writing. Katie hung back against the stack of self-help books. Her heart swelled over Vance's accomplishments. She'd had no hand in his success but still felt a sense of pride. She knew enough about writing screenplays and the hard work and perseverance it took to get one made into a movie. Very few made it that far. The publishing industry wasn't much different. But Vance had managed to produce a number of bestsellers, with another on the way. No easy feat.

Katie slipped into an empty chair in the back row, waiting for the program to begin. Vance had his back to the crowd, and was holding a conversation with the store manager. When someone entered her row to take the next seat, Katie glanced up and almost fell out of her chair. Dottie Duncan gave an impatient shooing motion with her hands for Katie to move down so she and General Kerner could sit.

Uh-huh. *General Kerner*.

"Good. They haven't started yet. You gonna catch flies if you keep your mouth hanging open like that. Move over," Dottie said in a stage whisper, loud enough for everyone in the shopping mall to hear.

Katie scrambled into the next seat. "Did Vance know you were coming?" Because he hadn't mentioned it to her on the ride over, or any time for that matter.

"Thought we'd surprise him," Dottie said with a cackle. Hoo boy. You either loved surprises or you hated them, and from what Katie knew of Vance, she thought he fell into the latter category. "Almost didn't get here in time. Had to practically bomb old General Stubborn out of his bunker."

"You made up for it, driving like a crazy bat out of hell," Chuck said in a low, strained voice.

Katie leaned around Dottie, who was dressed in a purple knit pantsuit with sequin belt, and greeted Chuck. "Glad you made it safe and sound. I'm sure Vance will be thrilled," she whispered. She had no clue how Vance would feel, but she hoped he'd be happy to see his dad. At least his dad had made an effort. Chuck squeezed her hand and gave her a tight smile. Katie straightened in her seat and faced the front, only to be hit with Vance's dark eyes, chiseled jaw, and glowering face. She shrugged one shoulder to convey she'd had nothing to do with who had shown up. More people gathered in the store, and Katie noticed Jo Ellen Huggins squeezing into a seat in the second row, along with other Harmony residents. Jo Ellen stood out in her lime-green, skintight leggings and black top with cutouts, showcasing her hot-pink bra. She made a big production of waving at Vance and blowing him kisses. Vance tugged at the collar of his crisp white dress shirt, appearing uncomfortable or embarrassed or both. His gaze kept darting from Jo Ellen to his dad, and Katie couldn't decide which one disturbed him more.

Dottie elbowed Katie in the side. "That boy needs to get married. You better stake your claim before someone else beats you to it."

"Married? This is only our first date." And from the looks of things...could easily be their last.

"Woman, stop meddling and let them be," Chuck said to Dottie.

"I'm simply pointing out the obvious—" Interrupted by the store manager introducing Vance, everyone quieted down. Katie sat riveted in her seat while Vance settled himself in front of the crowd and began talking about his books and writing experience. The more he talked, the more animated and engaged he became, and the more it showed.

He loved what he did.

A little green pea of envy tumbled around inside her. Katie wanted to harness that same emotion. She wanted to be passionate about her work.

When Vance started to read a moving excerpt where the hero survives an enemy ambush but his best friend does not, Katie slipped a guarded glance at the general. He held a rigid pose, with his arms crossed and a faraway look on his tired face as if reliving painful war memories. Katie's heart ached, wondering how he coped with all that. At the end of the passage, Dottie pressed her hand to Chuck's thigh, giving him a reassuring pat. Chuck unfolded his stiff arms and started to applaud with the rest of the audience. The tension seemed to seep from his body in small increments. Katie only hoped the détente held when father and son came face-to-face.

Vance probably signed over one hundred copies of his books with a black Sharpie until his hand began to cramp. A few female fans would've preferred he'd sign something else...like exposed cleavage. Jo Ellen Huggins exposed her right shoulder as she pulled the sleeve of her top down. Fortunately for Vance, a mob of eager senior citizens accidently bumped her out of the way.

The line of fans snaked around the folding chairs, blocking his view. Every now and then he caught a glimpse of Katie's sexy coral dress, standing next to Dottie Duncan and his dad...*his dad*. Vance had waited years for this day, and now that it was here, his heart kicked into overdrive and his palms sweated. All through his talk, he'd tried to get a read on his dad's reaction. The driving force behind his books had been the stories he'd heard from his dad and brother. And then when he started attending meetings for Helping Comrades and got to know the veterans suffering from PTSD and other ravages of war, their stories compelled him even further. But the real barometer had always been what his dad thought about his books. And until today, he hadn't thought his dad gave a shit. And he certainly hadn't expected to see him with Dottie Duncan, or chatting it up with Katie. The Harmony rumor mill had kept him abreast of Katie meeting his dad at the Dog for breakfast, but Katie, being the wise woman and peacemaker she was, had never brought it up. And Vance hadn't had the energy to deal with the latest sightings of his reclusive father. The last time he and his dad had been in the same room, Eric had been home on leave. Still, they'd managed only to nod, and barely exchanged three words.

The crowd had cleared, and Vance signed the last customer's copy. He stopped to stare at his dad. Not much had changed, with the exception of a few more gray hairs and a few lines of age around his eyes and on his forehead. He still stood as tall and strong as an oak tree, leaving no doubt he'd served in the military.

Vance's cell beeped with a text from Mike. Hope

book signing went well. Still negotiating with McKnight.
We need to talk. He's worried about Katie finding
out...??? Vance cursed under his breath. He hated
lying to Katie and keeping her in the dark while Walter
McKnight played games. After what she'd revealed to
him about her family and how she'd been treated, the
guilt churned into burning acid in his gut. Vance didn't
want to contribute to her insecurities. He didn't want to
hurt Katie...ever.

"Nice job. You really know how to weave a story,"
Dottie said, standing in front of his table. "Now come on
over and speak with your daddy. It took an order from
the Pentagon to get him out of that shack he hunkers
down in."

"I was wondering how you managed," Vance
mumbled.

"We aren't gonna stay long. I know how he likes to
be in bed by nine...the ol' coot." Dottie snorted. Vance
wouldn't know. But he didn't plan on hanging around
much longer either. A warm, beautiful woman waited for
him, and he wanted to enjoy every last minute with her.
He fixed his gaze on Katie's fresh face as he crossed the
store to where she stood. Better than looking at the man
who watched him with a closed-off, guarded expression.

Vance nodded. "Dad." Something flickered behind
his dad's eyes. Something Vance hadn't seen in years.
Hope, maybe. Pride? Could be his imagination. For
someone who made his living with words, Vance's
tongue was tied. He couldn't form a single coherent
sentence. A soft hand curled around his. He turned,
and Katie's reassuring smile gave him all the courage
he needed.

"Glad you were able to make it. It really means, er…a lot to me," he choked out, as if facing the principal back in elementary school.

Everyone seemed to hold their collective breaths, and before his dad could respond, Adam Reynolds shuffled forward in his faded army fatigues. Adam had apparently ventured out to hear Vance speak. His effort touched Vance, knowing what it cost him to listen to war stories—real or imagined.

Adam shook Vance's hand. "The guys and I wanted to let you know you've made a big difference, and we thank you." Vance heard the slur in his voice and felt the tremor in his grip.

Vance gripped Adam's upper arm. "You guys are the ones who've made the real difference. I appreciate all the information and stories you've been willing to share." Dottie gave a loud clearing of her throat. "Adam," Vance said, "I'd like you to meet my father, General Chuck Kerner. He served twenty-seven years."

Adam extended his hand. "It's an honor, General, sir."

"The honor is all mine, soldier," Chuck said.

"And this is a good friend of the family, Dottie Duncan, and er…Katie McKnight." Vance pressed his hand to the small of Katie's back, not knowing quite how to classify her. Except to beat his chest like a caveman and yell "mine" for the entire male population to hear.

"Nice to meet you folks. I won't keep you. Just wanted to stop by and thank Vance again for the generous donations he's made to Helping Comrades. And I understand you're donating a portion of the sale of your books as well."

Shit. That kernel of information had been safely under wraps, and Vance had hoped to keep it that way. He hadn't wanted it bantered about Harmony or exploding all over social media. Not because he was ashamed, but because he wanted his books to stand on their own merit. He was donating to Helping Comrades because it was the right thing to do…for him.

"How much has he donated?" Dottie asked Adam. Vance tensed. *Motherfuh…*none of Dottie's damn business. When Adam revealed the number, Dottie's eyes widened, Katie's breath caught, and the brackets of tension around Chuck's mouth deepened.

"That's quite a sum," Dottie said, "and I'd like to match it." *What?* Vance hadn't seen that one coming. Dottie started digging around in her silver fringed handbag, searching for her checkbook. "How do I make it out?" she asked, checkbook and pen in hand.

"Just like that?" Adam's faded eyes brightened as he glanced from Vance to Dottie. "I don't know what to say." That made two of them. Frozen, speechless, and stunned, Dottie's generosity humbled him.

"You could start by giving me a name." Dottie chuckled. Adam told Dottie who to make the check out to, and when she handed it over, he thanked her profusely and shoved it in his front shirt pocket with a shaky hand.

After Adam said his good-byes, Dottie gave Chuck a nudge. "What do you have to say about that? I'm mighty proud of your son. Aren't you?"

The moment of truth.

Katie stiffened next to him. They both stood like two steel beams. Rigid and poured to the spot.

Waiting.

Chuck cleared his throat. Twice. "I talked to Gloria today. Asked her if it would be okay if I brought the kids home to visit her this weekend." Vance swallowed the lump of emotion clogging his throat. Katie pressed closer to his side. Dottie narrowed her eyes and pursed her lips. "Gloria said it'd be fine and would give you a break," his dad said, not quite meeting his eyes.

"Don't worry. He ain't going alone. We'll be driving my Escalade," Dottie announced.

Chuck jerked back and glared at Dottie. "Woman, no one said anything about you riding along. I'd rather be captured and tortured by the Taliban than ride four hours with you inside a car."

"Who said you'd be riding *inside* the car? I planned to tie your old carcass on the roof rack like a dead deer."

Katie started to shake, and Vance thought she might be upset until her snickers reached his ears. She covered her mouth in an attempt to hold back the laughter while Chuck and Dottie kept bickering. So much for a poignant reunion. The best thing he could say about the encounter was at least his dad and he weren't fighting. Katie's sparkling gaze captured his.

"You hungry?" he whispered close to her ear. The scent of orange blossoms made him dizzy.

"Starved. Do you think it's okay to leave?" she said, indicating the dueling odd couple.

"Absolutely. Not sure about my dad, but I'd bet fifty bucks Dottie's packin' some heat in that fringed bag of hers. We better get out of firing range." Vance pulled a giggling Katie toward the exit.

————

Katie checked on the sleeping kids while Vance walked the Ardbuckle twins to their car. After barely escaping the escalating battle between Dottie Duncan and General Kerner, Vance had driven Katie to a small café in downtown Raleigh for a quiet meal. The tension rolled off his stiff shoulders and dissipated as he relaxed and enjoyed a glass of red wine. He kept the conversation light, regaling her with stories of being rejected, chasing publishers, getting "the call," and missing deadlines. Katie laughed, enjoying the sound of his honeyed deep voice and the animation in his expression. But when she'd tried to mention his dad or ask him about the motivation behind his donations to Helping Comrades, the spark would disappear, and he'd clam up. She wondered if his dad knew this side of him. The man who supported a worthy cause but sought no accolades for his efforts. The man who'd held her and offered comfort as she bared her soul, reliving painful childhood memories. Katie wanted this man to be a part of her life, but deep down knew they lived worlds apart...literally. Katie kept a lid on her thoughts while Vance continued to charm and be attentive all evening, and she couldn't remember having a better date. Ever.

She descended the stairs and checked the front room and kitchen, searching for Vance. No sign of him anywhere. A soft sigh escaped her lips. She wanted to thank him for a wonderful evening. She wanted to reassure him everything would work out with his dad. Dammit. She wanted a good night kiss, at the very least.

Disappointed, Katie turned out the lights and headed for her bedroom. She stepped inside, and the man of her dreams stood by the open French doors. Her legs turned spongy at his sexy smile and glittering gaze. He held a single yellow rose between his strong fingers, and her heart locked up.

"I'd thought you'd gone...up to your loft."

He moved silently across the carpeted floor, closing the distance between them, and extended the rose. "Without saying good night? Not likely."

Katie touched the velvety petals to her nose and breathed in the sweet smell. "Where did you get this? It's lovely."

"Seems I have a blooming bush in my yard." Vance tucked a tendril of hair behind her ear, and his magical fingers lingered along her neck and jawline. "Kat, this is your call. I don't want to start anything you're uncomfortable with." His voice, raw and thrilling, jump-started her lungs again.

"A pirate with a conscience. Who knew?" Katie pressed her hand to the side of his face. His skin was warm and scratchy from his stubble. Vance turned into her touch and kissed her palm. Her girly parts—rusty from lack of use—started to squeak.

"This pirate is making a noble effort, but his desire is to ravage a certain California cupcake." He treated her to a naughty grin. "He wants nothing more than to throw you down on that bed and kiss every inch of your delectable body—"

Katie touched her fingers to his firm lips. A part of her—the part sizzling beneath her clothes—wanted to take this growing attraction...infatuation...lust to its natural conclusion with this man. But Katie had wised up and didn't dive headfirst anymore without knowing the water's depth. "There's nothing I'd like more"—his dark eyes flared—"because there's obviously a spark between us."

"More like a fiery inferno." He wrapped his arms around her waist and pulled her close until nothing separated the front of her dress from his shirt. "I'm feeling a 'but' coming on."

Katie let out a shaky breath. "Call me old-fashioned, but it's weird being with you in this room with the kids sleeping upstairs." Vance's eyebrows rose, along with the heat flaming her cheeks.

"Have to say…not what I was expecting to hear."

"I mean, what if they wake up? I'm not kidding!" she cried when Vance started to laugh. "I'd be scarred for life, not to mention what it would do to them."

"I've got the perfect solution. We go to the loft," he whispered close to her ear.

"And what if they're crying and come looking for me? I can't do that."

Vance heaved a huge sigh of frustration. The effort had to be killing him if the stiff rod poking her in the belly was any indication.

"Oh, there's going to be crying…just not from the three monkeys. So…are you only taking sex off the table, or does that include heavy necking and feeling you up?"

Katie rocked her hips against his erection, and the groan he emitted curled her toes. "I think a good night kiss could be in order," she said in a sultry voice.

"So, kissing is allowed?"

She nodded. "Most definitely."

Vance swiftly backed Katie against the closed bathroom door. Dropping to his knees, he shoved her dress above her hips. The yellow rose slipped from her shaky fingers, and Katie shivered at his lips pressed to her belly. The pressure from his big hands held her in place. Her mind reeled with anticipation and excitement.

"Wh-what are you doing?" Katie felt a jolt of desire at the fingers between her legs.

"Kissing is allowed. I'm choosing where," he growled against her sensitive skin. Then he proceeded to kiss and suck and lick his way around her quivering belly until his hot breath practically melted her pink panties. Katie's head hit the back of the door in pleasure, and her eyes fluttered close. Pirate Man deftly removed the triangle of silk between her legs, and his tongue plundered and pillaged until Katie started to see stars. Her knees shook, and she grabbed his shirt covering his shoulders. "V-Vance…please." A loud moan escaped her lips as she arched her back and strained forward. Katie's eyes flew open. This was nothing like…like…what was his name? No one came to mind. This was something else. Something erotic and primal and wicked. She wanted to be taken by *this* man and be reborn a new woman.

Vance struck a chord between her legs, stroking and tormenting, driving the sensations higher. His name fell from her lips, and she flew apart as her orgasm slammed into her and ricocheted throughout her body until it exploded from the top of her head.

Dazed, Katie slumped against the door, only half-aware of Vance's hands moving up her trembling body, until his grinning face appeared before her.

"What was that?" She managed to breathe. "I've never, you know…come like that…ever." She locked her knees before she dissolved into a puddle of liquid goo.

"There's more where that came from," Vance whispered, nibbling her neck where her pulse beat an erratic rhythm. Katie swallowed hard. She didn't know if she'd survive. "You sure you don't want to continue this discussion naked...on your back...in my bed...with your legs wrapped around my waist?"

She couldn't think of any place she'd rather be. "You don't make this easy." He shoved his hand in her hair and possessed her with another fierce kiss. The man was a master, hot and forceful, and her lips, along with the rest of her chorusing body, fell under his powerful spell. She felt a kind of intimacy with him she'd never felt before.

Vance's fingers traced the line of her dress dipping beneath the neckline, causing her to moan. Her breasts grew heavy, nipples tightening. "Not gonna pressure you, sweetheart...unless it's working—"

Katie gathered what little strength she possessed and pushed away from his addicting allure. "Sh-h-h. Did you hear that?" she whispered, her eyes wide.

Vance looked up. "What?" And then his forehead thunked against the door at the sound of Danny's cry.

"Kay-tee...I wet."

"Fuh...*effin' A*. Did you plan this?" he accused as his eyes narrowed.

"You're kidding, right?" Katie scrambled to lower her dress before she embarrassed herself and traumatized Danny. Frantically, she scanned the floor. "My underwear...has disappeared."

"Kay-tee!"

"Coming, Danny!" Katie called out.

Vance grabbed Katie by the shoulders and planted a

hard kiss on her mouth. "Tomorrow night, you're *mine*," he growled in her face.

"Katie, I'm thirsty." Katie's heart tripped over Vance's declaration, but there was no time to respond. She was too busy being shocked at the sound of Dover's voice coming closer.

"Jesus." Vance threw his hands in the air and stormed for the open French doors.

"Wait. Where are you going? And where's my underwear?" Katie hissed, trying to contain the laugh bubbling forth. The night had the makings of a skit for Comedy Central.

"To take another ice-cold shower," he said over his shoulder. "And if you want these…you'll have to come get 'em." Vance pulled a sliver of pink lace from his back pocket, and twirled her panties around his forefinger.

━━━━

The next morning, Katie packed for the kids' weekend away to visit their mom. Dottie Duncan and Chuck would be picking them up as soon as the kids got home from school. Vance was locked in his loft, working on his book, allowing Katie time to process or brood or second-guess. The powerful flames of desire he fanned soared beyond sexual for her. She felt different with him. And it scared her. The idea of having sex with no strings attached looked good on paper but made her uneasy. She didn't know if she had the nerve to carry it out. The truth: She wanted more than sex. She wanted something meaningful…special. By already exposing her scars to him, she feared she appeared desperate and needy.

In the light of day, the desire to flee made Katie twitch

to jump in her car and hit the road. But there was still the business of the unsigned contract. In order for Katie to move on with her life on her terms, she needed to finish this job for her dad. She would not quit, or worse, be fired over failing to score this location for McKnight Studios. And she would not allow Mr. Too Hot for His Own Good, with his incredible, over-the-moon orgasms, to distract her. Yeah, right.

Katie stopped shoving clean socks and underwear in Dover's duffel bag. She fanned her overheated face. Once the kids were gone, there'd be no excuses. No human shield. She'd be completely at his mercy. He'd already threatened as much. For a magical night of heart-stopping sex and…and she deserved exactly that. Dammit. She yanked the overnight bag's zipper closed. She was right back where she'd started.

Vance stood on his front porch with his arms crossed, watching Katie hustle the kids into the back of Dottie Duncan's Escalade. Part of him was sad to see them go. Yeah, they were a pain in the ass, but he loved them and would miss all the noise and commotion they made. The other part of him couldn't wait for everyone to get off his property, including the Harmony Huggers playing a medley of their greatest hits. He wanted everyone to disappear so he could concentrate on his book…and Katie's body. Yeah, he was a guy out for one thing… so sue him. But deep down, he knew it was more than that. Ever since Katie had walked through his door a week ago, his reaction to her had been beyond physical. From the moment he'd seen her that first day, standing in his kitchen wide-eyed and shocked, the urge to help her had swamped him. And when she'd opened up about her family and her insecurities, he'd wanted to serve and protect her, to shield her from a world of hurt. He wanted to own her. After last night, tasting her and having the power to make her come...went straight to both his heads. Whenever he looked at Katie, everything inside him stirred. Desire, lust, and a burning need to be connected both mentally and physically. Vance glanced at his dad, rearranging the bags in the back of Dottie's SUV, and that need to feel connected burned even hotter. He'd been living with a huge void for years. Since the day his mother had died and his dad had decided to treat him as number one unlawful combatant.

The knotted rope around his heart loosened an inch. He gave his dad credit for showing up today and taking an interest in his grandkids. Maybe he would do for them what he'd never done for Vance. They still hadn't spared each other more than a few words, and Vance realized progress came in all forms. Theirs happened to be at the speed of a slow-moving glacier. Seeing his dad at the book signing the night before had been a shock. Overcoming Adam Reynolds's innocent blunder when he'd exposed the one thing Vance had hoped to keep quiet hadn't been as difficult as calming his racing heart over the sight of his dad. His reason for donating anonymously to Helping Comrades was to keep the attention away from him and on the cause. He wanted all the focus to be on the needs of the veterans. But as his agent, Mike, reminded him, his celebrity status brought attention to the cause...and didn't hurt in selling books either. Standing next to his dad last night, Vance hadn't felt his usual regret for what might've been, because Katie had been there. She soothed all his rough edges. Moving past the hurt and forgiving himself seemed possible with Katie curled into his side. The conversations and ease with his dad would come with time…he hoped.

Vance loped down the front steps. Yellow trumpet-shaped daffodils dotted his front lawn. Dogwoods blossomed, and petals floated in the cool April breeze, dusting the footpaths. He shook his head, wondering how anyone could see zombies and vampires on this picturesque property. Katie's desperate attempts to please her dad had obviously clouded her vision. Maybe he could put a different spin on it and convince her this location was all wrong, without revealing the deal he'd cut with her dad. The more time that passed, the more Katie would be hurt by their deception, and hurting Katie was not an option for him.

"Bye, Kay-tee. Bye, Uncle Pance." Danny waved from the backseat of the car, clutching Lollipop with her other hand. Poor Lollipop had that resigned, I'm-doomed look about her as she posed with all four paws in the air.

Katie blew kisses. "Good-bye. Have fun with your mom."

"Bye, sweetie. You guys behave for your granddad and Mrs. Duncan, ya hear?" Vance leaned inside the back window and ruffled Dover's hair and reached over, fist-bumping Donald.

"We will," Donald said, wearing a serious look on his young face.

"You're in charge, bud. Okay?" Vance said to his oldest nephew. Donald and Dover had been hesitant when they realized their granddad would be accompanying them on their road trip. Vance couldn't blame them. They barely knew the guy. But after a long conversation with Gloria, she'd convinced him it was the right thing to do, giving everyone time to get to know each other.

"They're gonna be just fine. I've got everything under control. As long as they call me Dottie and not Miz Duncan. Reminds me of my mother-in-law, that clattering bag of bones."

"Oh! Wait. I forgot Pixie's dog food." Katie rushed toward the house, her short blue skirt flying around her legs.

"Praise the Lord and pass the ammunition." Dottie heaved a sigh. "It's bad enough I've got to babysit General Sourpuss here. Good thing I didn't bring Sweet Tea along," she said, referring to her mongrel of a dog.

Vance's dad leveled a military stare at Dottie that would've broken the worst enemy under intense interrogation. It had zero effect on Dottie.

"I'd be more than happy to leave you behind, rattling around in that God-awful mausoleum you call a home," his dad said between clenched teeth.

Dottie gave a loud snort, as if what the general had suggested was preposterous, and adjusted her skintight T-shirt with Toot-N-Tell spelled across her chest in silver sequins.

Katie returned with the bag of dog food and bowls in her arms. "I think that's everything," she said, slightly out of breath. Vance reached for the items and placed them in the rear of the car. "General Kerner," Katie continued, "I took the liberty of downloading some picture puzzles on your laptop for the kids to play with. I hope you don't mind." His dad and Katie exchanged a look. The suspicious hairs on the back of Vance's neck stood up. He hoped Katie, in her big-hearted, misguided way, wasn't trying to mend broken fences behind his back. Vance didn't want anyone running interference, and he'd bet his last royalty check his dad wouldn't appreciate it either.

"That's fine. I'm sure the kids will enjoy them," Chuck said in a gruff voice.

"We all set? That dog secure in her crate?" Dottie asked.

"Yes, ma'am," Donald said.

"Let's hit it." Dottie put the SUV in gear. "You two have a nice weekend, and don't do anything I wouldn't do." Dottie waggled her painted-on eyebrows. Katie's cheeks pinkened, and she cast her eyes to the ground. And Vance mentally blocked images of Dottie Duncan…doing anything. At. All.

Chapter 18

DUN, DUN, DUN, DUUUUNNNN. YOU KNOW THAT SCARY music that played in your head when something really bad was going to happen? Yeah…that. Katie felt Vance's sizzling gaze as soon as Dottie had exited the driveway with her merry band of kids and animals. And the general. What a road trip. Relief washed over Katie at not being invited. Until she glanced at Pirate Man. The promise of what was to come in his smoldering look rattled the California grapefruits from Katie's tree. The urge to give chase after Dottie's car suddenly washed over her. She needed more time. She needed to process. She needed at least a week to groom…shave, bleach, pluck, powder, perfume…lose weight.

"Oh no you don't." Vance tipped her chin up with his finger. "No second-guessing and no running. Got it?" Katie gulped. Her face must've read like a Sunset Strip billboard. Next time her mother insisted she take acting classes, Katie was signing up. Because she sucked at hiding her emotions.

Katie jerked her chin from his mind-scrambling touch. "I hope you don't think we're going to start something right here. Right now. While the Harmony Huggers are performing 'I've Been Working on the Railroad.'" She slid a glance at the ladies harmonizing the old folk song.

Pirate Man bared his teeth in a piratey smile designed to make pathetic-girl-desperately-seeking-validation freeze with fear…anticipation…excitement? "Give me a couple of hours to finish a scene. I'll meet you under the outdoor space. I'll be the one with the chilled champagne. You be the one wearing a come-and-get-me smile and nothing else." He winked.

As if. A nervous laugh burst forth at what he suggested. Scandalous. Vance had a knack for taking a tense situation and lightening the mood with humor. She loved that about him. Errk…there it was again…the *L* word. And it felt right, and that made Katie want to run screaming for the Hollywood Hills. Certified hot mess. No other way to describe herself.

Vance's phone chimed. His jaw tightened, and all signs of humor disappeared as he read his text. "Son of a—"

"What? Are the kids okay?" Visions of faces covered in blue paint, peanut butter topped with cat hair, and Dottie swerving off the highway blindfolded flashed through her mind. "Maybe I should've gone with them," she murmured, squeezing her hands together.

"Relax. It's only Brogan, reminding me about the cookout tonight. We don't have to go, if you don't want to," Vance said, hope coloring his tone.

"Funny, but this is the first I'm hearing about it… from *you* anyway. You never invited me."

"Sure I did"—Katie shook her head—"didn't I?" A flash of guilt skittered across his face.

Oh, Vance, all six feet two inches of solid muscle, arrogance, and badass confidence. Got her every time. Her phone chimed next, and she pulled it from her skirt pocket to read the text. "Bertie and Lucy are reminding me of the same thing."

"You wanna go, don't you?" He didn't bother hiding his disappointment.

She shrugged. "Well, sure. Sounds fun."

"You know there'll be poking and prodding and trying to wring out every juicy detail the entire evening."

Yeah, kinda. The town was famous for that very thing. Katie went for polite. "Bertie and Lucy have been very nice to me and supportive of you—"

"I'm talking about Brogan. He's worse than a middle-school girl when it comes to gossip."

"You're an easy mark."

He arched a brow. "How do you figure?"

"Exotic dancers, Russian spies…Jo Ellen and her ruby-red lips and pink pickup truck…need I go on?" She batted her eyelashes.

Vance's naughty grin did nothing to Katie except make her rusty uterus contract. "That's all old news. *You'll* be the hot topic tonight, cupcake. Hope you can take the heat." And by heat, Katie had a feeling he was referring to what he generated every time he leveled his wicked gaze at her. He tapped a response into his phone. "We'll meet them by the lake at seven. Does that work for you?"

Plenty of time to work up a good case of cold feet. "Yes. That works." She nodded, shoving her hands in her pockets. "I'm going to the store. You need anything?" She planned to make a classic California salad to contribute to the cookout.

"I'm good, unless you want to stop by the Scanty Panty and pick up some edible undies," said the pirate with too much swagger.

"Nah. No need," she tossed over her shoulder.

"Pity."

"Last time I was there, I bought a pack…strawberry flavor. Hope you're hungry."

"Starved." Vance's bold laugh carried across the lawn, broadcasting things to come.

—⁓—

Vance stretched his arms over his head, rolled his shoulders, and loosened his cramped muscles. He'd saved his work, having finished the scene he'd been working on. The war stories Adam Reynolds had shared after finally opening up to Vance fueled the motivation behind his hero and gave his scenes an authenticity and rawness he'd been searching for, but they also left Vance on edge. He could only imagine Adam's nightmares.

Vance moved to the open window. The cool spring air carrying the scent of new cherry blossoms brushed past his heated skin. He shoved his fingers through his hair. Getting inside his characters' heads took a toll. For the emotion to appear on the page, Vance became one with his protagonist, much the way an actor did studying for a part. He massaged his temples and emptied his mind. Tonight he wouldn't be fighting demons. Tonight, stories of snipers, ambushes, and gathering military intel would be shut down, along with his computer. Tonight he'd be spending time with the enticing and delightful Katie, and all his thoughts would be centered on her. Katie's husky laugh played in his ears as he remembered her teasing about edible panties. Her laugh. It was the first thing he wanted to hear in the morning and the last thing he wanted to hear at night. He wanted to spend his days and nights getting to know everything about her.

He wanted to erase the vulnerabilities that held her back and made her doubt. He wanted to scoop her up in his arms and never let her go.

He checked his watch. But first they'd have to endure the teasing and bullshitting his close friends felt compelled to heave his way. Vance had thick skin…he could take it. But Katie had smooth, soft skin, and he hated to see it bruised or marred by the careless things his friends might say or imply.

Reaching for his ringing phone, he groaned in disgust. "Great," he muttered. "What can I do for you, Walter?" he said, pressing the phone to his ear.

"Vance, good to hear your voice." Yeah, it was becoming a daily unwanted occurrence. "Things are progressing right along on my end. Almost have the details ironed out on the Wilmington location. You won't need to detain Katie much longer." Vance didn't like the sound of that. Detaining Katie had been the highlight of his days—and soon to be nights—and he wanted to keep it that way.

"What's your time frame?" Vance asked.

"Few more days. Five tops. My location manager will have an update for me later today." By location manager, Walter meant Tad Pole, the dickless wonder. Vance eyed the half-empty bottle of bourbon sitting next to his computer. He hadn't been drinking, but maybe now would be a good time to start. "You're doing a good job of keeping Katie in the dark, and I appreciate it."

And didn't that make Vance feel as low as Tad Pondscum. "About Katie. How am I supposed to break the news?"

Vance could've sworn the sound of Walter's chuckle

was evil and sinister. "You're a clever man. I'm sure you'll think of something."

"Assuming I do, then what happens to Katie? Where does she go from here?" Not back to California, if he had anything to say about it.

"Home. I've enrolled her in the community college, where she'll be taking accounting classes. She needs a useful skill, and accounting will be good for her. Keep her grounded. Good, solid profession."

Accounting? What the hell? Forcing bright and vivacious Katie into accounting would be a terrible fit. Vance couldn't imagine a duller career choice for someone with Katie's spirit. "Does she know about this? Have you discussed accounting with her?" *Like ever, you controlling puppeteer.*

"Katie never knows what she wants. She has to be told. Otherwise, she tends to wander from place to place and job to job. Never sticking. Katie needs to stick."

"And accounting will make her stick?" He couldn't keep the sarcasm from his tone.

"Accounting is a noble and useful profession," Walter said on the defensive. "There will always be jobs for accountants. She'll have a career she can be proud of." Whose pride were they concerned about? Katie's or Walter's?

"From what I know about Katie…I'm not sure accounting is the right path for her. She seems more creative—"

Walter's voice grew stern. "You let me worry about Katie. I know what's best for my own daughter." The hell he did. Vance almost snorted. Walter McKnight didn't know the first thing about his daughter. "You just keep stalling until I give you the green light. Got it?"

Vance gripped his cell phone to keep from hurling it out the window. "I'll keep stalling until I hear from my agent regarding *my* contract. You still haven't satisfied my end of the bargain. Where do we stand on that, Walter?" Vance struggled not to sound disrespectful. After all, this was Katie's father.

"My boys are working on it. I'm sure we'll find some common ground we can both agree on."

"Sure. As long as the common ground is my getting approval rights to the screenplay, we shouldn't have a problem."

Vance recognized the sound of back molars being ground to the nub. "Like I said, my boys are working on it," Walter said between clenched teeth.

"Good. Because I wouldn't want to hurt Katie with the truth about her fake job. And how everyone lied to her."

"No. That would put us *both* in a really bad light. And from what I gather…hurting Katie would not be in your best interests." Shit fire and call him Sally. How much did Walter know? He'd bet he had Tad Poke to thank for playing squirrelly informant and blabbing about all the porn rumors. It still didn't change their agreement. Vance prayed like hell Katie wouldn't get caught in the crossfire, but he had no intention of surrendering his balls to Walter either. Business was business. It wasn't personal.

———

"This looks delicious." Bertie and Lucy stood in Vance's kitchen, watching Katie throw together her favorite salad: romaine lettuce, red onion, sliced avocados, sectioned grapefruit, and homemade poppy seed dressing.

"Not the first thing that comes to mind for a cookout, but I thought it'd be refreshing." Katie laughed, enjoying the female companionship. Bertie and Lucy had stopped by for a visit…and to snoop. Just as Katie had suspected and Vance had warned. But they dug for dirt in such clever ways that Katie didn't mind. It made her feel part of the group. As if she belonged. She ignored the small voice in her head telling her it was only temporary.

"Brogan's bringing healthy stuff from BetterBites. Half of which I won't touch," Lucy said, dipping her pinky finger in the dressing for a taste. "Yum. This is good."

"And Lucy will be supplying the Cheetos and ranch-flavored Doritos. She's our resident junk food ho. And it never shows." Bertie swiped a section of grapefruit and popped it in her mouth. "I have to count every morsel, but Lucy can eat anything and never gain weight." Katie understood Bertie's plight…all she had to do was look at food, and the pounds appeared by the bushel.

"My poor eating habits drive Brogan crazy. I have gotten better. But every now and then a girl needs to spend time with her two best friends…Ben *and* Jerry."

Katie sighed. She missed those two guys. She couldn't remember the last time they'd shared a pint of Chunky Monkey. "You both look amazing. You must be doing something right." Katie covered the large salad in the wooden bowl with tin foil and screwed the lid on the Mason jar holding the dressing.

Bertie glanced at her gold watch. "We've got an hour to kill before heading to the lake. Let's grab our wine, and while we drink, you can model what you're wearing tonight."

Whoa. Katie didn't mind modeling for Inslee, but in front of Bertie and Lucy? Hmm. She had a sneaking suspicion they were up to something.

"Wouldn't you prefer to sit on the porch? We could ask the Happy Hookers to perform their rendition of 'Mama Mia.' It's surprisingly entertaining." Katie tried to steer Bertie and Lucy toward the front door.

"We've heard it. Dozens of times. Nope. You're just going to have to trust us," Lucy said, locking her arm through Katie's. She and Bertie physically turned Katie in the opposite direction. Straight to Vance's bedroom. "Be grateful my friend Wanda isn't here. She'd have you dressed up like the pit lizards at NASCAR before you could say Richard Petty," Lucy said.

"What's a pit lizard?" Katie asked, fearing the answer.

"Groupies. Some people call them waffle bellies, helmet chasers, box climbers…whatever. You don't need to be quite that obvious to catch Vance's eye." Lucy pushed open the bedroom door and dragged Katie inside. "Here. Drink. You look a little shocked." Lucy nudged Katie's arm. Only too happy to oblige, Katie lifted the glass to her lips and practically inhaled her wine.

Bertie flopped down on the off-white overstuffed lounge chair and propped her feet on top of the gray leather ottoman. "Lucy, give Katie a minute. You can be quite terrifying and pushy."

"Yeah, right. Don't be pretending to be good cop to my bad cop. You're the one who suggested helping Katie with her wardrobe." Lucy crawled to the middle of Vance's bed and sat cross-legged. Embarrassed, Katie glanced down at her old blue cotton skirt with the bleach stain on the pocket and then at Bertie's stylish silk tunic over crisp orange linen slacks. And Lucy's curve-hugging jeans and trendy, layered tank tops. Katie was easily the least put-together.

Bertie waved her hand in Katie's general direction. "Don't pay us any mind. We don't mean anything by it." Bertie shot Lucy a warning glare.

Katie moved to the closet where she'd stored most of the new clothes she'd purchased. "Listen, I appreciate all you're trying to do, but really, Vance and I are friends only." Maybe friends with benefits. *Maybe*. "Besides, I'm only going to be here a few more weeks. As soon as Vance signs the contract for the series and he no longer needs a babysitter, I'm taking off for another assignment." A slight chill crawled up her spineless back. Leaving Harmony and Vance in a few weeks would feel weird because... Katie's thoughts came to a screeching halt. No deviating from the plan. Learn to live in the moment. Take advantage of what Vance was so gallantly offering...a night with him...in bed. *Zing* went her rusty girly parts. No dwelling on the rest. She'd get back to her life in California eventually, and maybe by then she'd have developed a backbone.

Bertie followed Katie into the walk-in closet. "Until that day comes, which we hope is later rather than sooner, let's have some fun." She pulled a Caribbean-blue knit top with cap sleeves, and palazzo pants with a geometric pattern from the hangers. "Here. Try this on. It looks comfortable, sexy, and cookout-appropriate."

"I like the way the top wraps in the front. The V-neck is very flattering, and those pants are to die for," Lucy added, coming up behind her. "Where'd you get them?"

"Bloomingdale's, I think." Katie couldn't remember.

Inslee had her shopping every store online. Katie hesitated as Bertie shoved the outfit in her hands. "You sure? Wouldn't I be better off wearing some jean shorts and a T-shirt? Won't we be sitting on the ground surrounded by sand and dirt?" Katie remembered the clearing at the lake the morning she'd run into Brogan.

Bertie chuckled. "Not exactly. There are picnic tables and chairs. And we bring blankets."

Lucy flipped through Katie's wardrobe. "You haven't worn any of these. Price tags are still on them." She shot Katie a surprised look.

"Er…they just arrived, and I haven't—" Katie heaved a sigh of resignation. "What can I say? I'm trying to turn over a new leaf, but when it comes to wearing new clothes…I don't have the nerve."

Bertie clapped her hands. "I love it! Katie, you have more courage than you give yourself credit for. I don't know many women who'd drive across the country to convince an irritable, sometimes scary, bestselling author to let you commandeer his house for a freaky teenage TV series. Vance can be really intimidating. You are beyond brave, girlfriend." Brave or crazy… depended on how you looked at it. "And making yourself over at the same time? That takes gumption. Trust me; these clothes are going to look fabulous on you. Vance will be sniffing around you like a hound dog." Bertie hustled Lucy out of the closet. "Come out when you've changed. Oh, and wear those great silver wedges," Bertie ordered, closing the closet door.

Here went nothing. Katie emerged from the closet in her new outfit, and Bertie's and Lucy's faces beamed. "Told you! You look wonderful. I wish I had your legs and glossy hair." Bertie circled Katie as if inspecting a thoroughbred for purchase. "This is a great look on you."

"Oh yeah. Vance is a goner." Lucy smiled, sipping her wine.

"Come on. You need to see yourself." Katie and Lucy followed Bertie into the master bath, where the full-length, framed mirror leaned against the wall. "What do you think?" Bertie asked.

Katie stared at her image in the mirror. What did she think? "Um…it's very comfortable. And that's important because—"

"Forget comfortable! You look hot! Nice cleavage… just shy of slutty. And those palazzos do wonders for your butt." Lucy nodded.

Katie twisted to see the butt in question. "Are you sure this isn't…you know, too much for a casual picnic? What are you guys wearing?" She didn't want to stand out like an outsider trying too hard to fit in.

"This outfit has inspired me," Bertie said, cocking her head to one side and examining Katie through the mirror. "I have a great pair of palazzos too, but I won't look half as good as you, because I'm so short."

"I'm wearing a sundress." Lucy picked up one of Katie's lipsticks. "Nice color. Do you mind if I try it?"

Katie smiled. "Help yourself. It's a great line of make-up made only in California. All the movie stars swear by it." Bertie's eyes widened as she moved toward the vanity. "I've hardly touched it, so feel free."

Bertie opened the gold compacts with eye shadow, and Lucy played with the lipstick and blush. "Wow. This is really beautiful make-up. You might need to hook me up. But don't tell Jo Ellen. The competition will kill her," Bertie said.

Lucy nodded in agreement. "She's throwing another Mary Kay party next week, and BetterBites is catering. She's insisting Brogan deliver and serve the food." Lucy gave a big eye roll. "We've got to find someone for that woman. I'm tired of sharing my Bro-man."

"Oh, I think she might've moved on." Katie gave a sly smile and ran a brush through her hair.

"What do you mean?" Bertie dabbed some hand cream into her palm.

"She's made it perfectly clear to me that she and Vance are involved." Katie bit her bottom lip to keep from laughing. Not that it wasn't possible, but she still found humor in the way Jo Ellen had immediately seen her as a threat.

"You've got be joking. Vance has no romantic interest in Jo Ellen. They've known each other since kindergarten. We've got to do something about this," Lucy said, pressing her fists into her hips.

"We'll figure something out. Don't worry about Jo Ellen. She's no competition, believe me." Bertie squeezed Katie's hand.

"Oh, I'm not worried. It's really none of my business. Like I said, I'll be leaving—"

"Leaving, schmeaving. You're not going anywhere. Now, come on. We've got juicy burgers to eat, alcohol to drink, and good-looking men waiting for us. Doesn't get much better than that." Lucy danced a little jig out of the bathroom.

"Lucy's right. It's Friday night. Time for the weekend to begin." Bertie followed Katie into the bedroom.

Katie gathered her small wristlet that held her cell phone and grabbed her camera.

"Katie!" All three froze at the sound of Vance's roar. "Where the hell are you? We need to get going." Vance appeared at the bedroom door in all his dark, hunky, badass magnificence. Surprise lit his features as his gaze darted from Bertie to Lucy. "Aw, geeze. Don't tell me. You've come over to plot my demise."

"You should be so lucky." Bertie waggled her fingers and winked at Katie.

"Hey, Vancy Pancy. Glad you decided to emerge from your cave. Clean shirt *and* combed hair. Must have a hot date." Lucy hip-checked Vance as she scooted out the door.

Vance tugged on Lucy's arm, stopping her. "Tell Brogan he better not serve any of that grass-fed tofutey crap he tried to dump on us last time."

"Don't worry. He knows I hate that stuff. He's learned his lesson. My Bro-man doesn't like to go without…if you know what I mean." Lucy nudged Vance with her elbow.

Vance shook his head as if pained. "Ever since he married you, he's a changed man. Oh, how the mighty do fall."

"You'll be eating those exact words, big guy. Just you wait." Katie blanched at Lucy's knowing look and watched as she slipped down the hallway.

Chapter 19

"WHAT'S IN THE BOWL?"

"Salad." Katie stood awkwardly next to Vance and his truck, scanning the group of his friends gathered around the tables and chairs. She'd met most of them before, but Vance understood her shyness. She'd be the newbie in the crowd, and they'd descend on her like vultures on road kill, picking and pecking until nothing but dried bones remained. Most of his friends were good-natured when it came to slinging dirt. They treated it as a casual sport designed to entertain, not hurt. They never turned against anyone. But he could sympathize with a newcomer's hesitation.

"Come on. This will be fun," he said, hoping to erase the worry line appearing below her widow's peak. "Have I told you how beautiful you look?" He smiled. Vance liked this look on Katie. Confident, stylish, and sexy.

Katie blushed. "Only about eighteen times. But I don't get tired of hearing it. Thank you, again."

Katie started to move past him, when he wrapped his hand around the back of her neck, rubbing his thumb against her thudding pulse. "You're gonna be fine. Stop worrying." Then he kissed her glossy lips and tasted berries and Katie...by far his favorite flavor. "You sure you wanna stay?" he murmured. "We can jump back in the truck and go home right now. No one will miss us."

Vance wanted nothing more than to cart Katie home and straight to his bed. Hell, he'd throw her in the bed of his truck, if he thought she'd go for it.

"Hey! No PDA until it gets dark. Come on, you two." Katie jerked back at Wanda Pattershaw Upton's startling interruption. Wanda pushed on Vance's chest to get closer to Katie. "I'm Wanda, and you must be California Katie. I've heard so much about you." Wanda looped her arm through Katie's as if they were old pals. "I understand you're filming a movie at Vance's place. Need any extras? Like a sexy femme fatale? I don't mind a little frontal nudity, if it's done tastefully, of course. Not like those porn flicks Vance stars in," she tossed over her shoulder and gave Vance a saucy smile.

Jesus. "Wanda, cut the crap. Don't start with that porn shit. It practically shut down my Twitter account. My assistant, Nicole, threatened to quit on me." Vance rolled his eyes at Wanda adjusting her cleavage for better ogling. "And put your boobs back in their holster. You're scaring Katie."

Wanda sniffed. "My, my, honey. Seems you've tamed the mighty Vance Kerner. Not many gals can make that claim. He never had a problem with my fabulous ta-tas before." She shot Katie a sly wink.

"Oh. Well, yes. I could see how he wouldn't have a problem with your"—Katie waved in the vicinity of Wanda's chest—"but Vance and I are just friends and—"

Wanda stopped abruptly next to the picnic table holding the containers of food, and Vance almost plowed into her back. "Friends with benefits, I hope," she said loud enough to carry across the lake and grab everyone's attention.

Vance plopped the salad bowl he'd been carrying on the table and wrapped his arm around Katie's waist. "Wanda, not everyone is as comfortable discussing their sex life in public as you seem to be." He leveled his famous outlaw stare at her. It had no effect. Nada. Zip.

"Vance, darling, are we going down that road? If memory serves—"

"Russell," Vance shouted over Wanda's head. "Come get your woman before I throw her in the lake." He didn't need Wanda dragging up any more of his past sexual exploits. Katie had plenty of stories to condemn him with.

Russell Upton laughed as he ambled over, carrying two beers. "Come on, honey-pie. Remember last time? Vance doesn't make idle threats."

"Russell, if you allow this Cro-Magnon man to throw me in the lake again, you will not live to see another day. And your son will grow up fatherless." Wanda pressed her voluptuous figure into Russell's side with a warning glare.

"Come on, Kat. Let me introduce you to the others. Russell, God bless you man. I don't know how you do it every day." Vance clapped Russell on the shoulder and sent Wanda a quelling look.

"Happy wife…happy life. Right, Pookie Bear?" Wanda cooed in Russell's ear. "Something you're gonna have to learn, Mr. Clueless." She smirked at Vance. "Katie, nice meeting you, and good luck…you're gonna need it."

—◆◇◆—

Katie lounged in one of the Adirondack chairs surrounding the fire pit next to the lake. The sun had dipped completely behind the horizon, taking the purplish sky with it, until the blanket above them turned a deep midnight blue. The pine trees rustled from the evening breeze. And the smell of smoke and grilled meat lingered in the air.

"What a beautiful night, and I'm so full I could pop," Bertie said, easing down into the chair next to Katie. "Are you having fun?" she asked.

"Great time. The food was amazing, and it's been nice relaxing and listening to all the funny stories."

Bertie chuckled. "Yeah? Well, don't believe everything you hear. Some stories have been way over-embellished."

"Who wants another brownie?" Lucy asked, waving a plate in the air. Liza, Bertie's sister-in-law, and Wanda both groaned.

"Not another bite," Liza said, leaning back in her chair and digging her toes into the sandy ground cover.

"Katie, your salad was delicious. Be sure to give Brogan the recipe," Lucy said, plopping down on one of the blankets.

Katie cringed at the mention of her salad. "You're being kind. The salad was no hit, but thank you all for trying it."

"Just because Vance hates avocados and grapefruit doesn't mean it wasn't a hit. I had two helpings, and Keith loved it," Bertie said.

"Don't go by Russell. He grew up eating soggy canned peas. I'm slowly working fresh veggies and fruit into his diet." Wanda crossed her legs and jiggled her bare foot.

"At least Vance tried it. Give him credit for not hurling. Unlike Brogan." Lucy laughed. "Y'all remember when I fed him that hotdog smothered with everything at the bowling alley? I thought he was gonna barf for sure."

"Poor Brogan. Lucy tortured him with her disgusting eating habits before they were married. Talk about opposites attract." Wanda snorted.

"Vance turned almost as green as the avocados," Katie muttered. She'd had no idea she'd made a dish with his two least favorite foods on the planet. She did give him credit for trying. The gagging and chugging his beer notwithstanding.

"Look, if I can learn to eat the healthy food Brogan sells, then Vance will learn to love your salad." Lucy gave Katie a reassuring smile. "Because that man wants to make you happy." Yeah. In bed. Katie felt a tingly buzz in her girly parts. *Go back to sleep.*

"Would you look at them?" Wanda said, referring to the guys playing football. "I don't know where they find the energy. They ate twice as much as we did."

Everyone's gazes locked on all the men playing ball. A spectacular sight. Vance, Brogan, and Keith had removed their shirts, and the play of muscles across their shoulders and down their arms could make a weaker woman giddy with lust. Katie suddenly experienced quivering legs. She pressed her hands to her thighs. Each of the guys had a fluid way of moving, their bodies shifting with loose-limbed grace and power. Their athletic ability and fierce competitiveness made for some heavy breathing...on the side of the women.

Intent on watching the guys—well, okay, watching Vance—Katie felt someone's stare boring into her. She glanced to her right, and her gaze snagged Liza's.

A sly smile tipped Liza's lips. "So how serious is this thing between you and Vance?"

Shiz. These Southerners did not mess around when it came to hunting their prey. Katie gave her pat answer. "Vance and I are merely friends, and I'm going to be leaving in a few short—"

"Uh-huh. You keep telling yourself that. I'll check back when those three weeks are up." Liza rested her head against the back of the Adirondack chair.

"That's right. Vance is not going to let you go without a fight. Mark my words." Wanda wagged a finger at Katie. "Rumor has it you're looking into that empty space on the town commons. Something about opening an after-school program for kids."

What the— This time she glowered at Bertie and then Lucy, who both had the unmitigated gall to look innocent. The whole town had diarrhea of the mouth. Reining in her patience on a deep breath, she said, "Don't believe everything you hear. No plans have been made. My priority is to complete this job for my dad and then..." And then what? Katie stood at a crossroads. Going home weighed heavily on her mind. Staying in Harmony had potential. Because of Vance. No. Yes. Maybe. Katie swallowed a sigh, along with a lot of anxiety. In his beautiful, warm farmhouse surrounded by his beautiful land with this beautiful man. Ridiculous. A hook-up, maybe. A few laughs, hopefully. But no future. You'd need a relationship to secure a future. Katie's brain kept knocking on her forehead, reminding her they lived on opposite ends of the country.

He hated avocados and grapefruit.

And she was no fan of Eastern Carolina barbecue.

"Listen, Miss California, Vance is a pretty great guy. You might want to take advantage of what he's offering. There isn't a gal among us who hasn't dreamed about that stud at one time or another. Am I right, ladies?" Liza said.

Wanda burst out laughing, and Lucy covered her mouth, trying to hold back the giggles.

Bertie squeezed Katie's hand and glared at her sister-in-law. "Liza, I hope my brother doesn't mind your overactive fantasy life. Try not to frighten Katie away before she's gotten to know us." Liza shrugged her shoulders and remained silent. "Katie, if you decide to stick around, which we all hope you do"—everyone gave an enthusiastic nod—"then we'd love to brainstorm with you about that empty space. I think it has real potential."

"And with your fresh face and cool ideas, you'd have the whole town backing you," Lucy added.

"But even if you change your mind about the space, we'd still love it if you stayed," Wanda said sincerely.

"You're good for those stubborn Kerner men. They need someone like you to help bring them together." Bertie gave her a warm smile.

"Yeah, if Vance loves you, then you're all right. Because we love Vance."

Katie's heart swelled at the outpouring of kind words. These women she'd only just met made her feel a part of something. They made her feel wanted, and if she left Harmony, she knew she'd be missed. A heady emotion. But Vance *loving* her…she almost snorted aloud. Katie was no fool. She lived in Hollywood and knew how lust looked and acted firsthand. Vance wasn't looking for a relationship. He was looking for a distraction, and Katie was available.

At the sound of loud shouts and teeth-jarring grunts, Katie and her new girlfriends stopped talking and looked up in time to see Vance block and Brogan launch the football for a long pass.

And then Vance's gaze snagged hers, and time stood still, as if the world was holding its collective breath. His face was all dark angles and shadows, his eyes hot with desire and laced with mischief. Katie hid a grin behind her hand and then gasped when Vance got tackled from the side by Russell and hit the ground hard.

"Holy motherfuh—" Vance groaned, rolling on the ground. "Upton, Jesus, you hit like a Mack truck."

"Thatta boy! You go, Pookie Bear," Wanda cheered for Russell. "You are so getting lucky tonight."

"I hope Vance's okay," Katie said, trying not to sound worried or race over to check him for injuries.

"He's fine. Tough as nails." Russell winked at Katie and gave Vance a hand up.

Vance brushed the sand off his board shorts and shook it from his hair. "I need a beer. I'm getting too old for this shit."

"I'm buying." Keith trotted over to the keg, along with Cal and Russell.

Brogan clapped Vance on the shoulder. "You still suck. But you take a hit like a man."

"If you'd release the ball a little quicker, maybe I wouldn't have to take so many hits," Vance grumbled, scooping his shirt up off the ground, pulling it over his head, and covering his chest. And wasn't that a darn shame?

With beers in hand, Cal planted a kiss on Liza's lips

and dropped down beside her on an empty chair. Russell sat next to Wanda, Brogan flopped down next to Lucy on her blanket, and Bertie joined Keith by the keg, wrapping her arms around his waist.

And that left Vance.

Watching Katie with hooded eyes. Katie drew a ragged breath. Sauntering toward her—yes, sauntering, you know…walking with attitude—Vance stopped in front of her and held out his hand. "Hop up, cupcake," he said in his lazy drawl, pulling her from the chair. Vance dropped down in Katie's vacant seat and lowered her onto his lap. Hoo boy. Katie remained stiff, her back ramrod straight. Unsure of what to do with her hands. The last time she'd sat in a man's lap, she'd been five, and he wore a red suit with a fake white beard. "Relax. I'm not going to cop a feel…until later," he murmured close to her ear, wrapping both arms around her waist and causing her to shiver against his hard chest. "Better?" Katie could only nod due to the swallowing of her own tongue.

After the guys finished their beers, Brogan piped up, "Who's up for some volleyball?"

"You're kidding," Liza muttered.

"Come on. When was the last time you played volleyball?" Cal hooked his arm around Liza's neck, kissing her on the temple.

"High school. It was required for gym."

"You any good?" Cal asked.

"I could've been, if I'd cared."

"What about you, Wanda? You play volleyball in high school?" Russell said.

"With these bad boys?" Wanda hefted her breasts with her hands.

Lucy laughed. "She would've knocked someone out for sure. Bertie and I played in gym class. We both stank. Being short didn't help."

"If Bertie played volleyball like she plays tennis…" Keith shook his head. "Not good. Not good at all."

Bertie sniffed. "Not all of us can claim to be professional athletes. Besides, I think it's a hand-eye coordination thing."

"Ya think?" Keith teased.

"This is beach volleyball. Come on, it'll be fun." Brogan jumped up from the blanket, yanking Lucy up by her hand.

"Okay, Mr. Triathlete. I'm game."

Liza joined Cal, grumbling about being too old for any kind of volleyball, and Keith pecked Bertie on the lips and told her she could sit this one out. Wanda blew Russell a kiss and settled more comfortably in her chair to watch the game.

And that left Vance.

With Katie still wrapped in his arms.

He cocked his head, peering down at her. "What do you say? You up for a game?"

Katie reached down and removed her shoes. "Sure. I'll give it a try."

---~~~---

"Whoa! Where'd that shot come from? Hey, Kerner, you know she could play like that?" Brogan said, grinning at Katie from the opposite side of the net.

Teams had been decided, with Brogan, Lucy, Keith, and Cal on one side and Liza, Russell, Katie, and Vance on the other. Lucy hadn't been kidding when she'd said she sucked, and Liza ran a close second. But Katie… holy hell. She'd already executed a perfect bump arm pass, a couple of digs, diving to her knees in the sand to save the ball, and a dink over the net to end a point. All while wearing those crazy flowing pants that clung to her great butt and the blue, curve-hugging shirt that exposed soft skin around her middle every time she went for a shot.

"Yay, Katie! You are so saving my butt. Y'all don't mind if I sit the next one out," Liza said, brushing sand from her knees.

"One more set, and we'll call it quits. I wanna see more Katie-action," Cal said, tossing the volleyball in the air.

With twinkling eyes, Katie flashed a devious smile. Vance would like to see more Katie-action too. A different kind of action. A contact sport involving skin on skin with Katie under him, long legs wrapped around his waist. Vance balled his fists in an extreme effort not to go all hillbilly and haul Katie over his shoulder and into the bed of his truck.

Liza rolled her eyes at Cal. "Whatever. But I need a drink."

"Five minute water break." Brogan clapped his hands. "Come on, babe. Hop on." Brogan bent down, and Lucy wrapped herself around his back for a piggyback ride.

Vance watched Katie brush sand from the knees of her dirty pants. "I've got a few more points left in me. How about you guys?" she asked him and Russell.

"Absolutely! We're kickin' ass and takin' names." Russell rubbed his hands together in glee.

"You never told me you could play volleyball,

cupcake." Vance dropped his arm over her shoulder, peering into her upturned, flushed face.

"You never asked. As everyone in this town loves to point out…I *am* from California. One thing I know how to play is beach volleyball." The satisfaction and pride on her beaming face looked damn fine on her. His Kat had game whether she knew it or not, and with the right encouragement, it could be a real confidence booster. "I don't play like Bambi when it comes to volleyball," she said.

Bambi? He'd dated a Bambi once, but Kat couldn't be referring to her…God help him, could she? "What are you talking about?" Hoping she didn't pick up on his nervous tone.

"Bambi…it's slang for a player who tenses up and doesn't play aggressively."

Vance laughed with relief. "Uh, no. I wouldn't call you Bambi."

"Break's over. Lucy, honey, we need some points… sing something and distract them," Brogan teased. Everyone in Harmony knew Lucy couldn't carry a tune in a bucket. The joke around town was that anytime there was a fender bender, Lucy's singing voice must've been the cause. It was *that* bad.

Lucy dug her toes in the sand in the ready position. "What do y'all wanna hear?"

"Doesn't matter. It all sounds like nails against a chalkboard." Keith hugged Lucy around the neck.

"Ready to take 'em down, Beach Bunny?" Vance growled next to Katie's ear.

Katie shot him a cocky grin. "Serve it up!"

Vance glanced at his watch for the umpteenth time. Eleven o'clock. He wanted to end this party so he could start one of his own. A party for two. With Katie. All night long and into the early morning. No cell phones. No computers. No blinking cursor. No plot holes. And no rug rats.

Vance did double time, cleaning up and loading chairs and coolers in the backs of all the cars. Dark clouds had started to roll in, threatening rain. Katie stood next to Keith's SUV, chatting and laughing with Bertie and all the women as if they hadn't just spent the last four hours together. What more could they have to say? The conversation over the course of the evening had spanned baby food to nail polish to toilet bowl cleaners to bikini waxes. Katie had observed more than participated, taking pictures with her professional camera at the group laughing and joking. She appeared to be enjoying herself, and Vance didn't want to rob her of any fun by whisking her home early. But enough was enough.

"You and Katie want to come by the house for a drink?" Brogan asked, closing the hatch to his car.

Heck no. "Nah, man. I need to get home. It's been a long day—" Lightning flashed across the sky, followed by a huge clap of thunder.

"Whoa. That storm is rolling in fast." Brogan glanced at the dark sky. "Luce, come on before the skies open up." Brogan motioned to Lucy. "Sure you don't want to stop by? Oh, I forgot, you have the kids."

"Actually, I don't. My dad and Dottie Duncan drove them to visit Gloria this weekend."

Brogan's look of worry over the impending storm turned to surprise. "Your dad and Dottie? Don't you find that a little strange?"

Vance shook his head. "So strange that no publisher would touch the story if I decided to pitch it." Dottie had texted earlier, announcing their arrival, and Gloria had confirmed that everyone was alive. No missing eyes or limbs…in other words, his dad was in one piece.

"Shee-it. Think your dad can hold it together and not kill Dottie?"

"I'm more worried about her killing him. He's a stick in the mud, and Dottie's a real pain in the neck."

Brogan grinned. "A match made in heaven."

Vance grunted. "God, I hope not."

"How did the book signing go?" Brogan asked, referring to the night before. "I hear your dad showed up. That's pretty awesome. Think he's read your books?"

Vance still hadn't figured out what had prompted his dad to appear at his book signing. But from the stern expression and lack of words exchanged, Vance hadn't seen it as much improvement. He shrugged one shoulder. "Who knows? The man won't talk to me. But he seems to be coming out of his shell a little more. He met Katie and took an instant liking to her. And now this road trip with Dottie and spending time with his grandkids. We've made progress."

"Kinda hard not to like Katie. What's the deal with you two? She's not your usual type." Vance narrowed his eyes in warning, which Brogan ignored. "News flash. Like I'm telling you something you don't know. But you better hear this…she's forged strong bonds with our wives, and if you break her heart, I'd hate to imagine what they'd do to you. Liza's downright scary," Brogan warned.

Vance wished for once everyone would mind their own business. "No one is breaking anyone's heart." Unless Katie found out he'd made a deal with her dad and lied to her. But he'd make sure that never happened. Vance shoved his hands in his back pockets. "Look, we're just…" Friends? It was more than that. And from the skeptical look on Brogan's face, he knew it too. But to admit that Katie meant the world to him and he couldn't live without her after only a short week would be ludicrous. Who fell in love in such a short span of time? Not him. No way. Hell no. Katie's husky laugh caught his attention, her bright smile lighting her face. Vance almost whimpered at the sight.

Crapshitdamn. His single-carefree-horndoggin' days were gone…never to be seen again.

Brogan clapped him on the shoulder in sympathy. "Join the club, man. You're fucked."

And with that, the clouds opened up, and it poured cats and dogs.

Chapter 20

"Run for it!" Vance yanked Katie out of the truck and hauled her across the lawn toward his barn through the drenching rain. The storm had hit hard and fast at the lake and soaked them before they'd made it inside the cab of the truck. "You okay, cupcake?" he asked, shaking water from his head, droplets splashing her.

Snickering, Katie glanced at her sopping wet clothes and ruined shoes. "I'm okay, but I look like a drowned rat." Smiling, she peered up at Vance and froze. His T-shirt plastered to his chest and stretched across his broad shoulders seized her lungs. If you liked sculpted chests and rock-hard muscles, you'd be in heaven over this dark angel. Katie shivered, not from the chilled rain soaking her clothes, but from the man in front of her warming her heart.

"You're freezing." Vance wrapped his hands around Katie's arms and pulled her close. Touching his wet chest lit an inferno inside her and sparked heat behind his eyes. All of a sudden he was kissing her, and Katie found her arms wrapped around his neck and her back against the door. She was no longer cold but burning from his raging heat. Firm and insistent, his mouth demanded entry as he slipped his tongue past her lips. He tasted of beer and spicy male and pure decadence. Katie ran her fingers through his wet hair. Vance pulled back and nipped at her lower lip with his teeth. The solid hammering of his heart beating through his chest smashed against hers. "Please stay with me tonight," he said in a fevered whisper. Katie's knees threatened to buckle, and her head wobbled. "Is that a yes?" Vance fiddled with the barn door behind her, sliding it open while still holding her tight. Clever man.

"Y-yes."

"Thank God." And before Katie could take another breath, he scooped her up in his arms and bounded for the stairs. The interior of the barn whirled past her in a complete blur.

"Vance, put me down. You might hurt yourself. I'm not exactly a lightweight." The fact that he took the stairs two at time without labored breathing or wheezing didn't go unnoticed and scored huge points in her book.

He smiled down at her. "I'm getting you in my bed as fast as I can...but first...a hot shower." She laughed at his eager persistence.

At the top of the landing, Katie caught quick glimpses of an open loft bathed in white, covered in floor to ceiling built-ins crammed with books. Vance whisked her inside the bathroom and lowered her slowly to the grey marble floor, making sure every inch of her body stroked his along the way down. Desire surged inside her to a flash point, and Katie bit back a groan. Vance gripped the back of her neck and took her mouth in a bruising kiss. And the melting began.

Releasing her mouth much too soon, his voice rough, he said, "As much as I'd love to act out my fantasy of peeling your clothes off inch by inch, we need to hurry and warm up." Vance reached around her and turned the water on inside the glassed-in shower built for two.

"Take those wet things off, cupcake, before you catch cold." Ripping his wet T-shirt over his head in one motion, he toed off his Topsiders, kicking them to the side, and his shorts and boxers followed. Katie's skin went tight, and her mouth dried up. The temperature in the room suddenly surged from the steam curling from the shower and the Greek Adonis standing before her. Katie trembled not from soggy, cold clothes but from being in the presence of such perfection. She sucked in a breath; the exhale stuttered out with the impact of how gorgeous he truly was. Fascinated by the ripple of every muscle, Katie stared, unable to take her eyes away.

"Your lips match your shirt." He reached for the hem of her blue top and peeled it up and over her torso, exposing her wet bra and pebbled nipples. *Plop*. It landed on the pile of wet clothes. Vance laid his hands on the bare skin of her shoulders, stroking with his fingers and sliding her bra straps down. His light touch woke up all the nerve endings under her skin. Desperate to move, she reached behind and unhooked her bra, letting it fall to the floor. His hands stilled at her waist, and his eyes flared with smoky desire.

"You're killing me," he said in a husky voice. His hands pushed at the waist of her pants, and she wiggled out of them, kicking them to the side along with her shoes. "Nice." Vance fingered the pale blue bow at the top of her lacy underwear. Something about the way he looked at her body told her he didn't mind her slightly rounded belly or hips. "Real nice…but it's coming off." His fingers dipped below the elastic, and he ripped her panties down and away. Then his hands circled her waist, and he lifted her into the steaming shower, standing them both under the rain-bath showerhead as warm water poured down over their bodies.

Torture. Pure torture of the warm-water-hot-guy-all-knowing-roving-hands type. Katie didn't know where her body began and Vance's ended. Somehow, he'd lathered them both in suds, igniting every inch of her body with his touch, leaving her gasping. And then he massaged musky, Vance-smelling shampoo in her hair. His strong fingers dug in her scalp, and Katie almost orgasmed on the spot. A groan slipped from her lips. "Whatever you do, don't stop," she moaned and lowered her head to give him full access.

"You don't know your cues." His fingers pressed into the base of her scalp, causing her to grip the slick shower wall to keep from falling.

"Huh?" Katie couldn't understand a word he was saying; her brain had evaporated.

Vance tilted her head up and seared her with his intense gaze. "You're supposed to say 'don't stop' when I'm deep inside you…thrusting in and out—"

Grabbing his head, she covered his mouth with her lips, delivering her version of a spellbinding kiss. His hand slid down her body in deliberate slowness, causing her legs to clench together. Undeterred, his finger worked its way between her thighs and dipped inside, parting her flesh. Katie gave a long moan. His hard cock pressed against her belly, and his muscles strained beneath her hands as he held himself back.

Vance hauled his mouth off hers. "Let me love you. I want to make you come right here, and then I need to be inside you and make you come again." She was trapped by his feverish eyes as he worked his finger in and out.

He found the magic sweet spot that connected directly to the fireworks going off in her head. "You okay with that, my love?" The heat in his voice poured over her like a trail of hot wax. Katie's head swayed. Her eyes squeezed shut as stars burst behind her eyelids, and she came apart, clutching his shoulders for dear life.

Vance watched Katie climax in his arms. All slick and wet and warm. She latched on to him, her full breasts pressed against his chest. The half-moons her nails dug into his bare shoulders still stung. And her swollen-kissed lips and luminous face almost brought him to his knees. It took every ounce of willpower not to shove her up against the shower wall and drive into her wet heat. His body craved hers like it craved air. But this was no wham-bam-thank-you-ma'am. This was no casual hook-up. This was not someone he could walk away from. Katie had carved a hole in his heart with a fierceness that made it hard to believe it still beat. This was someone to cherish and love for the rest of his life.

This *was* the rest of his life.

"V-Vance, you…that was…don't let go, or I might collapse," Katie murmured against his chest. Too late. He held her collapsed form close, wondering how a miserable bastard like himself got so lucky. Vance turned off the shower, and Katie lifted her head. "Are we done?" She blinked wet, spiky lashes at him, sounding disappointed.

The irregular beat to his heart confirmed what he already knew. He smiled. "Not even close, darlin'. But we're done turning into prunes." Vance helped her around the glass shower wall and wrapped her in one of his thick gray bath sheets. He took a second towel and dried his hair and body before wrapping it around his waist. Katie bit into her lower lip as her gaze landed everywhere but on him. This may be a tactical error on his part, but he needed to tell her how he felt *before* making love to her. He needed her to believe him before sex fried their brains and they were incapable of coherent thought. Because one thing he was absolutely certain of…the minute he made Katie his own, he'd never be able to think of anything else.

"Come here." He reached for Katie's hand and led her from the bathroom through the open loft and behind the interior sliding barn doors to his bedroom. He stopped next to the king-size bed. "You warm enough?" he asked, pressing his hands against her cool upper arms.

"Y-yes. Is everything okay?" Vance kissed the crease marring her brow below her widow's peak.

Pulling back, he cupped her face with his hands. "Everything is perfect." He swallowed hard. "Kat, my love…I want you more than I've ever wanted anything or anyone in my whole life." She opened her mouth to speak. "Don't. Not yet. I need to say this." Vance drank in the perfection of her face. Her dark eyes sliced through him. "I know it sounds crazy and we've only known each other seven days and I don't believe in fairy tales and I'm no frickin' Prince Charming." He stopped. He had to get this right. His future happiness depended on it. "In fact, I'm the polar opposite of charming, which you've already discovered. But something happened to me when I met you. It's impossible to explain. Nothing has been the same since you arrived, and nothing will be right if you—" He couldn't voice that thought. He couldn't think of her leaving. "Everything has changed. I've changed. And I don't want to change back."

"Vance, I—"

He pressed his fingers to her lips. "Shh." Vance kissed her soft mouth and breathed in her essence, hoping it would calm his racing heart. A wave of nerves clogged his throat. What if she didn't share his feelings? What if she didn't feel the same way? Katie's dark brown eyes stared into his, and he had his answer. "What I'm trying to say is…I love you." She gasped. He smoothed his palm down her slender throat, resting his thumb against her thudding pulse. "And I didn't want to make love to you until I'd told you. Because this is not a one-night stand or roll in the hay or sleazy hook-up. This…this is the rest of my life…with you. If you'll have me."

He waited for what felt like ten minutes…under water. Until Katie slipped her arms around his waist and a smile tipped the corner of her mouth. "I'm sorry, but I wasn't paying attention…do you mind repeating that?"

Vance's stomach dropped two feet. "What? The whole thing?"

She gave his neck a hot, open-mouth kiss. He went rock hard and ached all over. "Hmmm, just the part about loving me," she murmured against his tight skin, taking nips with her teeth.

Vance wove his fingers through her wet curls, wrapping several strands in his grip and tugging her head backward. He groaned at the sight of her heaving chest and flushed cheeks. "I love you, Katie McKnight. The girl who wants to hustle my house from me and turn my front yard into a freak show. The same girl who spreads rumors about me and porn all over the Internet. And yet, for some inexplicable reason…I love you. How's your hearing now? Did you get all that?"

"Every last word." Katie pushed on his chest until he bumped the side of the bed with the backs of his legs. "So…you think you love me, Pirate Man?"

Vance flashed his best pirate grin. "I don't think… I know." He toyed with the tail of the towel tucked between her breasts. "You on board with it? Think you might be able to love me back? One day in the very near future? Like right now?"

Katie gave him a final shove. He fell back on the bed, and she followed him down, laughing. "Why don't I show you how I feel?" she said, raining kisses on his face and down his chest. Vance's heart leapt at her words. He shifted his weight, inserting his body between her legs. The towel loosened, and he slid his hands under and over the smooth skin of the backs of her thighs until he cupped her spectacular ass. He rotated his hips, and his hard-on found a home between her legs. Katie shimmied against him until he thought his eyes would cross. Grabbing his head between her hands, she covered his mouth, and Vance let her control the mesh of tongue, lips, and teeth for about ten seconds. Then he rolled until she lay trapped beneath him. He reclaimed her mouth with a kiss full of the pent-up sexual heat that had simmered between them since day one and the love they felt for each other. Ravenous to consume her, he untied the towel and pushed it aside. Katie gasped when he pulled away, gazing down at her heaving breasts.

"God, you're gorgeous. How did I get so lucky?" He lowered his head and sucked a tight nipple into his mouth. Katie groaned and squirmed beneath him, and Vance thought he might lose it right there. He raised his head, panting. "I want you. I want to do things to you that might be illegal in several states. I want you in my bed, but mostly I want you in my heart, my home, and in my soul," he said, his voice sounding rough and edgy.

"You've got me. I'm not going anywhere. Please make love to me…now," she breathed.

———

Katie's body hummed—more like belted the Hallelujah Chorus. Somehow, some way, in her screwed-up, wretched life, she'd done something right. Because the most gorgeous man with the most talented hands and lips had declared his love for her, setting off a marching band with crashing cymbals, making her rusty girly parts high kick like the Rockettes in celebration. Vance loved *her*. Cue swelling heart.

All was right in the world.

Vance jumped up, throwing his towel aside, and reached for a condom in his nightstand drawer. Katie watched in fascination as he rolled it over his impressive erection. *Holy Queen Latifah*. She scooted until hitting the wood headboard to make room for her man. Vance crawled toward her, wearing only a condom and a sexy smile. Life didn't get much sweeter.

"Kat." His voice was husky. His gaze raked over her and seared her flesh. "Feels like I've waited my whole life for this." And by this he meant his hard erection nudging the notch between her legs. "I love you."

Astonished by his admission, she knew she'd never tire of hearing it. Overtaken by the sensation of him invading her body one slow, agonizing inch at a time, she gasped at the delicious perfection. She arched into him, drawing him deeper until they became one. "I love you too," she said to his dark, intense face. In his eyes, she saw the same thing she felt; a love so deep she thought her heart might burst from the ferocity of it. This night was about two damaged souls finding a home in each other. Katie had yearned for this life, where she abandoned all rules and became a new woman. Living the life she was meant to live. Where she was accepted, valued, appreciated…loved.

"Oh, Vance," she sighed. He captured her lips in a long, hard kiss.

"You're so damned beautiful."

"No. You make me feel beautiful." She smoothed her hands over his shoulders and around his neck.

"I'm about to make you feel more than that." Rising up on his arms, he started to move inside her with long, deliberate strokes. She lifted her legs and wrapped them around his waist, drawing him closer. Vance closed his eyes and threw his head back, tendons tight in his throat. Low, tortured moans escaped them both with every thrust. Katie dug her fingers into his side and arched her back. "So tight," Vance grunted. "Damn, you're amazing. This is killing me."

The hard planes of his abdomen stroked against her pelvis as he moved. Katie panted, not knowing if she could take much more. "I'm going to explode," she said between clenched teeth. Her gaze shot up to meet his. He continued thrusting into her, long and hard. He was hers, a vibrant blend of heart and soul and flesh. Katie climaxed, shattering like a zillion tiny shards of glass.

Vance covered her lips, his tongue invading her mouth as his hips slammed against her one last time. She swallowed his moan. His entire body went rigid, the muscles on his back like iron under the sweaty silk of his skin.

. Vance collapsed against her, his breathing labored. A sheen of perspiration covered both their bodies, gluing them together. Forever. Katie stroked his back. "Thank you," she whispered.

He lifted his head and placed soft kisses on her nose, cheeks, and lips. "Thank you for allowing me to love you." Hair tousled around his shoulders, he resembled a fallen angel. "How do you feel?" he murmured, trailing his fingers along her jawline.

"Alive." She sighed in a sea of contentment. "More than I've ever been."

"Me too." He rolled to the side, sliding out of her. His heavy leg remained draped over hers, pinning her down.

Katie's heart tripped, and she beamed at the man of her dreams. "Is it always that good?"

A grin stole over his face, and he wrapped his arm around her. "Hmmm, could've been a fluke."

"Really? You think?"

"Absolutely. Maybe we should do it again to make sure."

Katie pressed her lips to his. "Maybe we should."

Chapter 21

KATIE AWOKE TO THE SOUND OF RAIN HITTING THE TIN roof of the barn and the tapping of a keyboard. She lifted her head from the pillow and realized she was alone. The bed linens still held Vance's musky, masculine scent, but they no longer held him. Katie sniffed and picked up the heavenly fragrance of freshly brewed coffee. Sitting up, she gathered the top sheet around her and listened to the rapid tap, tap, tap of the keyboard for a full minute before it stopped. Leaning forward, she hoped to see past the sliding barn doors into the adjoining sitting room where the night before she'd spied a desk piled high with books, papers, and a computer.

"Good morning, cupcake. Did I wake you?"

Her very own gorgeous pirate appeared at the opening, wearing scandalously low-riding sweatpants and a sinful smile. His prime physique was designed for ogling and uncontrollable drooling. In his large hand he held a mug of coffee.

"Is that for me?" she croaked while clearing her throat.

"Freshly brewed." Vance's weight dipped the mattress, making Katie roll in his direction—okay, so she might've leaned on purpose. She reached for the mug and slipped him a shy smile before taking her first sip. Her mind scrambled as she tried to remember everything they'd done and said last night. If her memory served correctly, the night had been a fairy tale come true. A very naughty fairy tale, with Vance starring as the depraved Prince Charming. Katie felt a flush heating her skin as she recalled all the inventive ways Vance had made love to her. She'd been meaning to start a new exercise program, but if she continued the mattress aerobics with insatiable Pirate Man, she'd be thoroughly worked out and wrung out.

Vance tucked a curl of hair behind her ear. "How'd you sleep, cupcake?" His tone said he already knew the answer to his question.

"The little sleep I got was amazing. How long have you been awake?"

"Couple of hours. I needed to get some writing done."

Worried, she said, "You've got to be exhausted. Will you be able to work today?"

Vance chuckled. "I don't plan to work all day. I have better activities in mind." His suggestive leer sizzled inside her belly.

"What time is it, anyway?" The early morning gray light gave nothing away, due to the steady rain.

"Around eight." He tugged on her wrist, careful not to spill her coffee. "You look good in my bed." The delicious heat from his body caused more sizzling.

"I'm naked. Of course I look good to you." Typical man.

"Naked is always a good thing." His smile went lopsided. He toyed with a strand of her hair. "Your hair's all curly."

Her hand flew to the mess of knots and curls from going to bed with wet hair. Great. It must resemble a rat's nest after a tornado. Not him. His disheveled locks made him all the more mysterious and handsome. Katie hated to imagine what the rest of her looked like. She'd never been the sexy starlet type, with perfect tousled hair, pouty lips, and dewy appearance. Instead, she was sporting telling beard burns in some very sensitive spots on her body. And she was sore in places she'd never known existed.

"I'm sure I look a wreck. Things look different in the light of day." His inscrutable expression gave nothing away. Nervous laughter bubbled forth. "You change your mind since last night?" It took a Herculean effort not to yank the covers over her head. Katie's attempts at making light of the situation were feeble at best. She felt a little unsure and a lot insecure.

"What the hell are you talking about?" His gaze dropped from her eyes to her lips. He kissed her with a fierceness that calmed her fears. Katie fell in love all over again. Pirate Man excelled at kissing the way Van Gogh excelled at painting. He was a master. Katie could lose herself in his kisses alone.

"No second guessing and no going back. Got it?" he said, his words hot against her mouth. His muscles tensed beneath her hand as he waited for her response.

"I love you, and I'm not going anywhere."

He breathed as if relieved. "Good. That's more like it. You hungry?" he asked, nibbling at her lips.

"You offering…?" Kiss, kiss, nibble, nibble.

"I'm yours," he murmured. "All day."

Katie pulled back, slightly dazed. It would be so easy to do nothing but Vance all day…but she knew he had the pressure of a deadline, and she didn't want to be the reason he couldn't make it. Besides…she had her own agenda, like figuring the best way to disappoint her parents—again—with her change of plans. "As tempting as you are"—she slid him her best sultry gaze—"I don't want to get in the way of your work. Why don't I rustle up some breakfast, and I'll call you when it's ready."

"Oh no. You're not getting away from me that easily. I've waited all week to have you, and now that I do…I'm not letting you out of my sight." Vance placed her coffee mug on the nightstand and followed Katie down onto the fluffy pillows. "The only thing I'm hungry for right now…is you."

—∿∿—

Katie glanced up from behind the lens of her camera and paused. She'd been taking candid shots of Vance while he worked. Curled in the overstuffed chair in the corner of his office, wearing one of his soft green Army T-shirts, she listened to the sudden quiet. The rain had finally stopped. She hadn't left the loft the entire day. Vance sat at his desk, typing away on his book, and Katie sighed in contentment. Being in love and great sex had a mellowing effect, and it felt wonderful.

After another adventurous shower, this time with pulsating showerheads, Vance had brought food up from the main house to make sure Katie didn't starve, but mainly to keep up her strength for more physical activity of the horizontal type. Katie had never been a big fan of wrestling until she'd discovered Vance's version…now it was her new favorite sport.

Katie's hand trembled as she fiddled with the lens on her camera. Her complicated, messy life had taken a sudden detour, and it felt weird and exhilarating, knowing she wouldn't have to go it alone, because Vance would be with her. By her side. Her rock. He didn't say those exact words, but he did declare his love for her—numerous times—and she was thinking maybe that meant he wasn't going anywhere.

The tapping from the keyboard stopped. "What's with the Mona Lisa smile?" he asked.

"Hmmm? Just happy, I guess." Vance wore a clean pair of jeans and T-shirt, making her shiver, knowing she had an intimate knowledge of what lay beneath his everyday clothes.

"Glad to hear it. I'm done here." He closed his laptop. "You want to catch a movie? Bowl? Hit the bars?"

"You bored with me already?"

"If it were up to me, I'd keep you under lock and key and never let you leave my room. But since it's my fault you haven't gotten out much…" He shrugged his strong shoulders.

"Well, I could use some fresh air. How about we take a walk and then grill some steaks? We can eat in your beautiful outdoor space, and you can build a fire in the fireplace," she said, excitement coursing through her.

A slow smile curved his firm lips. "So, you don't want to be seen in public with me, is that it?"

Katie sprang from her seat and wrapped her arms around the back of his shoulders, nipping his ear with her teeth. "No. I don't want to share you with anybody. Like all your adoring fans. I want you all to myself for one more night," she purred.

Stroking her arms, he said, "You got it…and me for as long as you want."

—∿—

Katie enjoyed a glass of red wine while Vance cleared
their trays from dinner. He had expertly grilled steaks
and fresh corn on the cob, and she had thrown together
another salad…without avocados or grapefruit. The
clouds had cleared, and a few faint stars were starting to
appear. Vance had lit a fire to stave off the cool night air.
Earlier, they had walked the perimeter of his property,
which had taken a little over an hour. The pungent smell
of damp earth and fresh new blooms had permeated the
air after the cleansing rain. Vance had pointed out the
various tenant properties his family owned, and he even
showed her where his dad lived. Katie still banked on
a reconciliation to bring the two back together, but in
order for that to come about, Vance would need to open
up to her. Maybe by talking about it, he'd find answers,
along with some peace.

"You get enough to eat?" Vance asked, topping off
her wine.

"Plenty. Thank you. You grilled the steaks to perfection. So multitalented."

"Thank *you*…for not putting avocados or grapefruit
in the salad. Not sure I could've kept it down tonight."

Katie squinted at him. "Such a baby. How can you not
like avocados and grapefruit? Do you eat guacamole?"

"Nope. And I don't drink grapefruit juice."

"Anything else I need to be aware of?"

"Yeah…I do eat California cupcakes," he growled,
wrapping his hand around her neck and pulling her in
for one of his hot, demanding kisses, his body's heat
warming her against the cool night. Her palm cupped the
razor stubble covering his jaw. A flare of rightness filled
her chest. A perfect ending to their perfect day.

Sucking in a breath, she pulled back. Her heart swelled, growing tighter against her chest until it pained her rib cage. The evening breeze rustled her hair, and Vance gently brushed a few strands from her face. Katie took a moment to revel in his loving gaze. Then her stomach flipped, full of nerves. She might be detonating a bomb by bringing up the topic of his dad and the bad blood between them. The idea of opening old wounds that might cause him any pain made her uneasy. But if any hope remained of building a bridge to close the gap, she needed to know what had triggered the animosity. Loving him the way she did, it felt only natural to want to help mend those fences.

"You're thinking again," he said, appearing wary.

She nodded. "I want to know something."

He hesitated, his eyes narrowing. "Okay. What?"

"What caused the rift between you and your dad?"

Several beats passed, and Vance's face clouded with memories as he scrubbed the nape of his neck with his hand. "It's confession time, huh?"

"It won't change the way I feel about you. Besides, you witnessed the pathetic baring of my soul."

His expression turned militant in her favor. "That's different. You did nothing wrong. You didn't deserve the way your parents treated you."

He didn't know the half of it. The way they *still* treated her. Tonight was not about her. Tonight she wanted to be *his* support.

"What is it you think you've done that is so wrong… or bad?" she asked in a quiet voice.

He paused and then released a breath that seemed to rattle inside him. The strain and sadness behind his dark eyes broke her heart. Whatever his crime, he'd paid a steep price.

"I was a disrespectful, angry teenager, carrying a huge chip on my shoulder. And my dad was...being my dad in his tough, military way. After my mom died, he came down hard on me. Eric had already expressed his interest in joining the military, and my dad couldn't have been more proud. Thinking I would never measure up, I decided to be the complete opposite, acting like I didn't give a shit about life. I didn't want anything to do with the Army, Navy, or Marines. I hated the military and let my dad know every chance I got."

"What do you mean?"

He briefly closed his eyes as if closing off the pain. "Every day a new argument would escalate between us. I could never please him. Not that I tried very hard. But my dad only knew hard discipline as a way of communicating." He must've noticed her wary expression. "Don't look so shocked. He didn't physically hurt me. But he'd make me clean the bathroom with a toothbrush if I left my dirty towels or clothes on the floor. One time he made me stand at attention for a full eight hours because I'd missed curfew. He'd waited up for me, and since I'd kept him awake, he decided to keep me awake." Vance gave a self-deprecating smirk. "I never missed curfew again."

A shiver ran down her spine, imagining the tough scenes between Vance and his dad. "I'm sorry you two were at such odds. Your dad tried to control you the only way he knew how."

"Yeah, and then I retaliated."

Katie's heart seized. Her breath caught, waiting

for him to continue but not wanting to cause him any more anguish.

Vance slouched against the sofa cushions, propped his feet on the teak coffee table, crossed his long legs, and closed his eyes. Despite his lazy position, his body tensed like a taut wire. Katie waited so long, she didn't think he'd answer.

His words were low and measured. "I told my dad I hated him and that I could never respect a man who killed innocent children for the sake of democracy." Katie gasped. His jaw tight, he slid her a sideways glance. "Yeah, it was that ugly. And I've regretted it ever since."

"But your dad didn't kill innocent children, did he?" she asked, not allowing the horror of those pictures to form in her mind.

"Darlin', war is hell. Don't kid yourself. Innocent children die every day. No, he didn't deliberately kill innocent people, but it happens. It's happening today with air strikes, night raids, and drone attacks." Tucking her legs beneath her on the seat cushions, she leaned toward him. She rested her hand on his hard chest, and he stiffened beneath her touch. "What I said had nothing to do with the way I felt about war and everything to do with hurting my dad. I wanted to cut him off at the knees. He took his responsibilities to his men very seriously and believed their missions were necessary in reaching peace." He paused, his lips twisted in a smirk. "So, I said the most hateful thing a rebellious, angry teenager fighting against strict rules and regulations could come up with."

"You were young. Lashing out. You didn't mean what you said. Surely the general knows that now."

Vance covered her hand, lacing his fingers with hers. A look of pain flashed across his face as he stared off into the distance. The dwindling sunlight colored the darkening sky a dusty purple rose. "I called him a murderer." He cleared his throat as if he'd swallowed a lump of coal. "If you could've seen his face…" Katie gulped hard and tried to blink back the tears threatening to spill. She hated seeing him in this much pain. And she hated thinking how his words had hurt his father. Two hotheads saying hurtful things neither one meant. Words that pierced like a bayonet straight through the heart. Katie had firsthand knowledge of that pain.

"When I went off to UNC, I knew I wanted to become a writer, because I thought I had something to say. To impart my viewpoint to the world. A lot of bottled up anger. But the more I wrote, the more I realized my words were hollow and baseless. Until I wrote a letter to my dad, apologizing."

"How did he respond?"

Vance raised his shoulders as if he held the weight of the world. "I never gave it to him. Instead, I started writing stories about war and heroes."

"And twelve books later, you're still trying to apologize."

"Something like that." His sad smile touched a nerve.

Katie had personal experience with trying to please a taskmaster of a father. She understood Vance's pain, which made her sorry for him and his dad. Never measuring up to a parent's standard played a real number on the psyche. And Katie hated seeing her tough pirate hurting.

"Maybe it's time you spoke the words. I'd imagine

your dad has mellowed over the years, and maybe he's struggling with how to broach the subject."

Vance rolled his head and faced her. "Maybe." Suddenly, Katie was flat on her back, and sad, introspective Vance had disappeared and her lusty pirate had taken his place. He hovered over her. "Now, I'm thinking why the hell am I reliving depressing stories from the past when I could be making love to you outside in the open spring air, under the stars," he growled, covering her mouth with his. He kissed her with an urgency and poignancy that hadn't been present before. Katie understood. He needed reaffirming. She understood his desire to forget and lose himself. And she was more than happy to provide the comfort he sought.

"What do you need?" she asked. She would give him anything. Anything to erase the sadness, grief, and regret he'd revealed to her.

He stared down at her. Desire mixed with love poured from his expression. "I need you. Only you. When I look at you, everything else fades away, and my head clears. Does that make sense?" She nodded, and he stroked the side of her face with his finger. "You make everything bad in me disappear," he whispered.

Katie wrapped her arms around him in a fierce hug. "You're not bad. You're wonderful and kind and loving. And you make me whole. Just be with me. Stay with me." She would do everything in her power to protect him and soothe him.

The love swirling in his eyes caused her breath to catch. "You're so beautiful inside and out, and you've worked your way into my heart. You're all I want, Kat."

He kissed her with possessive hunger, and Katie

returned the kiss, elated to know they shared the same feelings. She shifted beneath him and he trailed hot kisses down her throat, unbuttoning her pink linen blouse with his clever fingers. "So soft," he murmured against the lacy edge of her bra before he flicked the front clasp open, the cool night air a direct contrast against his hot breath. A moan escaped her lips as he latched on to her nipple, causing her to squirm in pleasure beneath his hold. Weaving her fingers through his thick hair, she held him in place. She welcomed his hand as he unsnapped her jeans and started pushing them down past her hips.

"Here, let me…" Katie lifted her hips to help remove her jeans. "Wait. I need to kick off my shoes—"

"*Kathyrn Ann McKnight!* Wh-what are you doing? With *him*?"

Katie shrieked, grappling for her loose top, and Vance's head jerked in the direction of Tad Poole's voice.

Chapter 22

DAMMIT TO HELL IN TARNATION AND BACK. WHAT WAS TAD Putz doing on his property...again? Vance pulled Katie's pants up, blocking Tad's view with his back. Katie frantically buttoned her blouse with a look of pure panic on her face.

"*Well?*" Tad Patsy had the nerve to say.

"You okay, darlin'?" Vance murmured for Katie's ears only. Her face had turned as red as the homegrown tomatoes they'd eaten with their salad earlier. Vance pecked her lips for reassurance. "It's gonna be okay." He pushed up and faced the turd who stood there with his scrawny chest puffed out, emphasizing his outrage. Tad gripped an official-looking folder in one of his hands. Vance narrowed his eyes. Tad returning when Vance had clearly warned him off was not a good sign, no matter how you dissected it.

"I thought I made myself clear the last time you showed up uninvited. What part of 'get off my land' did you not understand?" Vance growled low.

"Katie wasn't answering her phone. Naturally, I was concerned about her welfare. And rightly so, from what I just witnessed." What a dickless wonder. A sound of distress or maybe rage came from Katie's direction. Vance threw a glance over his shoulder, and Katie stood with arms crossed and lips pressed into a thin, angry line. Her expression did not look promising for Tad Pissant.

Only too glad it wasn't directed at him, Vance had a good mind to step aside and let Katie open up a can of whup-ass. He had no doubt she could take him down. But something about that folder he kept tapping against his thigh put him on alert. Tad was here to cause trouble. Vance would bet his priceless autographed basketball from UNC's 2009 NCAA Championship team on it.

"What are you doing here?" Katie asked, stepping forward with purpose. "I don't want you checking on me. I've got everything under control."

"Is that what you're calling it these days?" The jerk smirked.

Katie huffed. "Look, I'm sorry. Maybe this isn't the best time, but I think it's safe to say…we're over." She slashed the air with her hand. Vance watched as Tad bristled. He directed a burning glare first at Katie and then at him. "It's not like I'm telling you anything new. You wanted the break for a reason, and you were right. We aren't compatible. Let's move on, shall we? Because…uh, I already have."

"Man, he's really done a number on you, hasn't he?" Tad snarled, jerking his head in Vance's direction.

"No. Vance and I are in love…but I don't need to ex—"

"In *love*?" Tad gave a bark of laughter. "That's rich. The only thing he's in love with is himself and his career."

Vance's head buzzed with fury, and a cold anger tensed his shoulders. He could see this going south real fast, and he needed this asshole to shut his effin' trap. Vance advanced on Tad, effectively blocking Katie's view. "Look, slick. Katie has made her wants known. Why don't you let it go and get on back in your car while you still can…on your own two legs."

"You don't scare me, Kerner. You want to know why?" Vance's gaze flicked to the folder in Tad's hand. "Yeah, that's right. It's all here in black and white. You want to tell your *girlfriend*, or should I?"

"Tell me what?" Katie pushed past Vance and glowered at Tad. Vance's chest tightened, and queasiness scaled the walls of his esophagus. All the guilt and regret he'd been feeling since his first conversation with Walter McKnight was about to come crashing down on his head. Tad had revenge written all over his snotty, pasty face. And Vance would've liked nothing better than to coldcock him to shut him up.

"Tad, I don't think this is the time or the place to bring—"

"Will someone please tell me what's going on here? What is Tad talking about?" At the sight of the confusion in Katie's eyes, Vance felt a surge of desperation low in his belly. He didn't want to hurt Katie, and telling her about her dad and their deal would do that... or more.

"Look, Kat, I'll tell you all about it inside. But first let me walk our guest to his car." Except Vance said the word *guest* like he would've said *serial killer*.

"I don't see the need for any more secrets," Tad said. Katie's head swiveled from Vance to Tad. "Looks like lover boy has gone behind your back and struck a deal with your dad...at *your* expense."

"What do you mean? What deal?"

"Kerner here wants final approval of the screenplays, and he willingly agreed to Walter's conditions to get it. And apparently, you were part of the negotiations. Am I explaining this clearly?" Tad wore a smug smile.

Vance shot daggers at him, hoping they would pierce his insignificant heart.

"I don't understand. Tad, what does any of this have to do with me?" Katie pressed a palm to her now-twitching eyebrow. A sure sign of stress. Anxious dread started to numb Vance's limbs.

"Only everything. Walter told Vance you were off the job. He had no intention of using this property for the show. He ordered Kerner *not* to sign the contract and to keep you here and string you along any way he could. Kerner agreed in order to gain full approval of the screenplays. Looks like he figured a way to keep you occupied." The only thing stopping Vance from plowing his fist in Tad's face was Katie's stricken expression.

She folded her arms across her middle as if to hug herself. "Vance, is this true?" Her voice quavered, and Vance jammed his fists in his pockets to keep from grabbing her up and running as far away as he could get.

"Look, your dad decided he didn't like this site for the show, but he didn't want to hurt your feelings, so—"

"So, he fired you and hired me to do the job right," Tad interjected like an asshole, rocking back on his loafered heels.

Katie's look of shock sent a cramping pain to Vance's stomach. "He *fired* me? My dad wouldn't fire me. I mean…yeah, he's moved me around some, but…"

Vance reached for Katie, but she backed up even farther, shaking her head. The horror and dismay skating across her features put him in panic mode. Vance inhaled a huge breath. He needed to remain calm. But how? He pinched the bridge of his nose. This was turning into a real goat screw. "Katie, it's not what you think. Please, come inside with me, and I'll explain everything," he practically begged.

"Enough. Out with it. Both of you." The finger she pointed at Tad Potatohead shook. "Finish what you started." For the first time since turning their evening into a shitfest, Tad appeared uncertain. "Now!" Katie ordered.

"Uh, I was just following orders, Katie. You know how your dad can get. He told me you were fired and sent me to Wilmington to secure the right location. I had nothing to do with the deal Kerner cooked up." Tad shot Vance a look of utter disgust. As if his underhanded dealings were aboveboard and acceptable.

"But you knew I was fired from this job, and you didn't say anything," Katie accused.

"It wasn't my place to tell you," Tad said. "Besides, I didn't want to hurt—"

"Baloney! You could care less about hurting me. It's never been about me. It's always about you and sucking up to my dad."

"Katie, let me explain—" And the whining portion of the evening had begun.

Katie stopped him with her raised hand. "No. You've said enough. We're not dating anymore, and for that I'm eternally grateful. I never have to listen to anything you say ever again. What a relief." Vance couldn't help the small smile curling his lips.

"You don't mean that. What about all the times—"

"Oh, but I do. Tad, we're through. Over. Kaput. I'll no longer settle for second best. I deserve better."

Yes. Fire sparked from the depths of Katie's dark eyes. And Vance barely refrained from pumping the air with his fist. He didn't think he could love her any

more than in that moment. Vance suppressed the urge
to pull her into his arms and hold her forever. But then
Katie slowly turned her attention to him, and his little
warrior's shoulders slumped, and the bite she gave her
lower lip had Vance checking for blood. His heart plum-
meted to the ground at the anguished look of disillusion-
ment clouding her face.

"You were never going to sign my contract." The lack
of emotion in her voice and the hurt brimming in her eyes
punched him right in the throat. "I mean, I'm not an idiot.
I knew you were stalling, but I had no idea you'd been
scheming with my dad. I've already taken steps toward
leaving McKnight Studios, but I wanted to finish this last
assignment on *my* terms." She stabbed her chest with her
thumb. "Not be a pawn in a game of wills between you
and my dad. Did you think I'd never find out? Were you
ever going to tell me?" Anguish and disappointment fell
across her face, draining it of all its vibrant life and color.

Vance's stomach plunged to the ground to join his
already sputtering heart. "Kat, I know you're upset, and
it's understandable, but if you'd give me a moment, I
can explain."

"I understand everything," she said in a harsh whisper.

"Kathryn, honey, why don't you let me take you
home? Away from Kerner. It's for the best," Tad said in
a placating voice. Vance balled his fists as a roar erupted
from his chest. He'd see Tad facedown in the dirt before
he'd let him take her away. Both Katie and Tad stared
at him in alarm.

"Why don't you leave? *Now*. Before this gets any
uglier." Vance made a threatening move, and Tad
jumped back.

With palms pressed to her chest, Katie said, "Tad, you need to go. Please. This is between me and Vance. I'm fine." Tears pooling in her eyes said otherwise. Shame overwhelmed Vance like a surging wave. He'd crawl on his hands and knees through fifty yards of sewage to erase the look of disbelief and distrust from her face.

Tad straightened his shoulders and gave a curt nod. "I'm staying at the Lazy Oak Inn, if you need me. I'm only a phone call away—"

"Leave! *Please*," Katie begged.

Moments that felt like years ticked by as Tad finally made his way to his car. Vance could only stand by helplessly and watch Katie as she lifted her chin along with her resolve, blinking back tears. He felt lower than the ten-year grime ground into the floorboards of his truck. Whatever she threw at him he deserved and worse. He'd known this debacle would blow up like a grenade in his face. Damn Walter McKnight. And damn his stupid, idiotic self for getting sucked in. Vance spread his arms, palms open. "Go ahead. Let me have it. I deserve your anger and anything else you want to hit me with."

Katie exhaled a shaky breath. "It's not that simple. If I could smack you and make it all disappear, I would. I'm having a hard time picturing you in complicity with my dad. I thought you were tougher than that." She rubbed her temples. "But he's a hard man to say no to. I should know."

"Kat, I'm so sorry. I'm not proud of what I did, and believe me, if I could go back in time, we wouldn't be having this conversation." Vance took a tentative step toward her. "But I can make it right. Please, don't allow this to ruin what we have. I love you, and I never wanted

to hurt you. You have to believe that. Let me fix this."
It would take one phone call to terminate the whole
thing. Making movies be damned. Mike could earn his
fifteen percent and work damage control. Vance didn't
care. She meant everything to him. He knew she had
issues standing up to her dad, but he sure as hell didn't.
He'd fight her battle and never let Walter hurt her again.
Setting this right with Katie and gaining back her trust
was the only thing that mattered.

She shook her head. Vance couldn't tell from the
faraway look in her eyes if she'd even heard him.
"This is my moment of truth. I can continue to let other
people rule my life, pushing me around, making decisions for me. Treating me like dirt." Vance cringed,
hating himself even more. "*Or* I can take charge of my
own life."

"Babe, that's what I want for you too—"

"This is something I have to do for myself. I can't
allow you to take over where my father left off."

The hairs on the back of his neck stood up. "What are
you saying?"

Katie stepped forward and cupped him around the
neck. Pulling his head down, she gave him a fleeting
but sad kiss. "I have some things to settle that are long
overdue. I can't say I'm not hurt by what you did, but I
kinda understand. My dad has a way of grabbing people
by the jugular. Where they're the most vulnerable." She
shrugged her shoulders. "It's complicated, and by getting involved, we've complicated it even further."

Vance gripped her wrist, not allowing her to pull
away. "It doesn't have to be complicated. This will
never happen again...I swear." He didn't care that he

sounded desperate or afraid. He didn't like the resigned look she wore.

"Nevertheless…I have to do what I have to do."

"Are you going to share it with me?"

"No. Not now. Finish writing your book. Don't miss your deadline. I'd never forgive myself if something happened to your career because of me. And don't worry about my dad. I'll take care of him," she said as if something bitter lingered in her mouth. Slipping her wrists from his grasp, she straightened her spine. "I'm staying in the main house tonight. Um…I'll see you in the morning." She ducked her head and started for the house.

"Katie, don't go!" He grabbed her by the elbow, wheeling her around. A thousand needles pierced his chest, making breathing difficult. "Babe, listen…I can't…don't leave…I'm begging you. Don't leave me like this." Vance had never begged for anything in his life. Never exposed his vulnerability, even at the lowest points with his dad. But Katie had changed everything. He'd beg, borrow, and steal if it meant he got to keep her.

Katie shrugged out of his grip. "I need to be alone. Please don't make this harder than it already is."

"Can you ever forgive me? Please tell me you forgive me." His voice shook with the fear of losing her.

"I can't. Not now. I will one day, but not today." Katie lowered her head and moved toward the house.

"Katie, I love you." *Turn around. Please don't leave me.*

"I know. Good night," she called over her shoulder.

Vance stood alone in his backyard while the sounds of his world came crashing down around his ears.

Katie sat cross-legged in the middle of the king-size bed, with her head resting in her palm. The only light in the room sifted through the French doors from the starry sky. She'd been sitting for the past two hours, plotting the remainder of her life. She knew if Tad hadn't come waltzing over tonight she'd be making love with Vance right now, blithely ignorant of all the shady deals taking place behind her back. Damn Tad and his sneaky, conniving, ratty self. She'd gotten only one full night with the man she loved, and she wanted more…like a lifetime more. But more than Tad, who was no more than a slimy worm to be smashed beneath her shoe, Katie couldn't stop picturing her dad controlling all his minions from behind his executive desk, barking orders and signing deals, not caring whom he trampled in the process. Including his own daughter. And yeah, Vance, the big dope, shouldn't have agreed to anything with her dad, but he was only looking out for himself and his career. And her dad had ways of convincing people. He dangled just enough reward to get exactly what he wanted. Katie had witnessed the routine a thousand times.

"Not this time. You will no longer be my lord and master, Daddy dear." Katie swiped at the hot tears on her cheeks. This day had been long overdue. She knew confronting her dad wouldn't be easy. She felt as stable as a jellyfish. But if she ever wanted to hold her head high and become the woman she was meant to be, she needed to reclaim her life on her terms.

"Katie?" Lifting her head, she stopped at the sound of Vance's voice. "Are you okay?" She scrambled off the bed and hurried to the closed bedroom door, pressing her hand to the cold doorknob, making sure it was locked. "Can you hear me?"

"Y-yes," she croaked. "I'm okay." Katie closed her eyes and pressed her ear to the solid wood door. Her heart splintered into a million pieces at Vance's labored breathing on the other side. She wished she could fling the door wide and throw herself in his arms. But it would only muddy up what was already a volatile situation.

"That's good. Um…okay. You don't have to open the door or anything, just listen." Katie nodded, even though Vance couldn't see her. "I know I hurt you, and I'll never forgive myself for the pain I've caused you. Please believe me, I'd rather cut off my right arm than ever hurt you again."

"Don't say that," she whispered.

"Look, I don't want to overwhelm you. I never meant to steal your freedom, and I certainly don't want to ruin your life. I just…I just want to be with you." Katie placed her palm against the door as if she could touch him. She could hear him shifting his weight on the other side. "I don't know how to make you love me. All I know is I want to be with you. You have the power to knock me off my feet, and I wouldn't have it any other way." Katie stifled a sob with her fist pressed to her mouth. "This is the reality…at the end of the day, when all this other bullshit fades away…I'll still be loving only you."

"I love you too," she mouthed. But the cold hard truth: Katie had to fix herself before she could be free to be with Vance. She had to regain her self-respect. Without relying on Vance as her crutch. She loved him, and he loved her, but they were both going to have to hang tight and not give up. Katie drew in a deep breath, hoping and praying her stance wouldn't derail their love. She had to believe in their strength and love combined to ride out the storm.

Vance tapped the door lightly with his knuckles. "Anyway…I wanted you to know that. I won't bother you anymore. Um, if you need anything…anything at all…I'm here." He paused, and her breath caught. "G-good night."

"Good night." She listened to his footsteps as they faded away. She plunked her forehead against the door, and her rib cage crushed her heart. Katie pushed away and straightened her shoulders, and drew several shallow breaths. No more doubting. Time to put her plan in action and make darn sure nothing went wrong. Not on her watch.

Chapter 23

THE NEXT MORNING, KATIE STUMBLED TO THE EMPTY kitchen, half-asleep, to find coffee and freshly squeezed orange juice already made, her favorite yogurt waiting in a bowl, and a beautiful yellow rose next to her place. But the gorgeous man responsible for all this loveliness was conspicuously absent. Even as Katie's heart skipped a beat, she knew this was for the best. After talking with Inslee for over an hour the night before, she'd put her plan in motion and didn't want the sight of Vance to cause her to lose focus, or worse, crawl back into his welcoming arms and never leave. Once she let him take charge, she'd never learn to stand up for herself. Operation Grow a Backbone had commenced, and Katie needed to stay the course.

She pressed the velvety rose to her nose and inhaled its sweet scent, when she noticed the notecard next to her place. Vance had scrawled in his barely discernable handwriting: *I'm sorry. Whatever I can do, just tell me. Love you. Vance.* Katie held her breath. He wasn't making this easy. Pulling her phone from her pants pocket, she texted: Thanks 4 breakfast. Running errands today. Will talk 2 u later. She hated not telling him about her plans, but she knew he'd try everything in his power to stop her. And his arsenal of tricks could make a woman made of steel collapse like a house of cards. Katie wouldn't stand a chance. She had to believe that as long as Vance had patience, they would be just fine.

She hoped…and prayed.

The night before, she had spoken with Inslee and her brothers, informing them of her plan to quit McKnight Studios and start her own business right here in Harmony. It would be called Imagination Station—she and Inslee had brainstormed over the name—and she'd be teaching kids again. Buoyed by her brothers' encouragement, Sam had told her it was about time she stopped being a doormat—but in a nice, big brother way—and Doug had started crunching numbers before Katie had given him all the facts and figures. With their help, she'd have enough information to make an informed decision. Her next call was to Bertie and Lucy, giving them a rundown of her plan. Of course, they peppered her with all kinds of nosy questions about Vance. Katie and Vance. Friday night after the cookout…with Vance. Saturday. Saturday night…with Vance. Katie managed to cut them off without spilling too many juicy details and got them to focus on what she really needed: help procuring the location on the town commons and garnering local support. Both were eager and willing to assist in any way possible. Team Katie was in place and hard at work.

Katie paced the length of the master bedroom, tapping her hands against her thighs. Yeah, now for the hard part. She'd love the luxury of a month to rehearse exactly what she planned to say to her parents. She knew from experience they would not listen rationally and allow her to make her own decision. Being supreme control freaks, they'd hit her with everything they had. Something resembling heartburn seared her breastbone.

She stopped and pressed a fist to her chest, trying to alleviate the burning sensation. Then she felt the twitching of her spasmodic eyebrow. *Holy Lady Gaga*. The anxiety alone might kill her. With her dismal record of caving in, she prayed for the strength of all the feisty, confident Harmony women she'd met and for that elusive backbone she'd lacked since birth.

Katie got busy and put in another call to the Ardbuckle twins. Reinforcements were in place for the kids so Vance could concentrate on finishing his novel. A text from Dottie Duncan said they were only an hour from home. Katie would miss welcoming them, but she couldn't afford a messy exit. Things could get loud and ugly…with her uncontrollable crying. She hoped the kids had had a great time with their mom and granddad. Any amount of time Chuck spent with his grandkids was a positive sign. Now to get him to spend time with his son…

Katie exited the house from the front, carrying her packed bags. Since it was Sunday morning, the church-going Harmony residents hadn't swarmed the yard for tryouts, making her escape that much easier. She shoved her bags in the trunk of her old Mercedes and wound her way down Vance's driveway, refusing to glance in the rearview mirror. She didn't trust herself not to turn the car around and abort her mission.

Around noon, Vance stopped typing. He'd received a text from Dottie, saying they were almost home. He heard the loud blare of a horn, and a car rolling down the driveway. Closing his laptop, he rolled his stiff shoulders. He'd manage to write nothing but dreck all morning. And he blamed it all on Katie…who still refused to speak with him. A few lame texts did not constitute speaking and confronting their issues. Vance was in hell. He couldn't stand not being with her. Wondering what was going through her head created a firestorm in his belly. Respecting her wishes was the hardest thing he'd ever done. She'd asked for time to sort things out, and he'd give it to her. But if she didn't come around soon, he'd storm her space any way he knew how and get her back.

Vance came down in time to see Donald and Dover tumbling from the car, followed by Danny clutching Lollipop to her chest in a death grip.

"Uncle Pance! Look what Granddaddy got me." Danny held up a Barbie doll wearing a froufrou pink princess outfit. The doll's blond hair looked to have been chewed by the dog, or Danny…he didn't know which.

"Wow. What a pretty Barbie." Vance held out his arms, and Danny ran to him, keeping poor Lollipop in a chokehold. Vance's jaw clenched. Chuck must've embraced the role of granddad. He caught a glimpse of his dad rounding the hood of the car. It seemed the general would give to his grandkids what he'd failed to give to Vance. A chance at a real relationship.

"Granddaddy showed me how to shoot a BB gun, and I hit a tin can!" Donald said, snagging his attention.

"And Granddaddy told me I'm gonna make a great field marshal. That's higher than even a general," Dover said, blinking up at him.

Vance's heart tripped in relief over the enthusiasm they had for their grandfather. His dad wore a faint smile as he watched the kids climb all over Vance. Working his lower jaw, Vance loosened the tension. Progress. This was a good thing, and it made him happy. Vance hefted Danny in his arms and ruffled Dover's hair. "Sounds like an awesome time. How's your mom doing?"

"She was happy to see us. We Skyped Dad too, and all of us got to talk to him. Even Miz Dottie," Donald said.

At the mention of Dottie, Vance watched as she climbed out of the car, looking reasonably unscathed considering the road trip she'd endured.

"Well, we made it back. What'd we miss? Where's Katie?" Dottie said in a voice a shade too loud.

"Where's Kay-tee? I want Kay-tee." Danny squirmed to get down.

After giving his property a cursory glance, Dottie shot him a suspicious look, as if she knew exactly what had transpired between Katie and him…along with how many times and how many positions.

Vance cleared his throat and lowered Danny to the ground. "Kids, grab your stuff from the car and head inside. Dottie, Dad, come on in for some iced tea. I'll unload the bags." Vance purposely skirted around Dottie and her questioning arched brow only to bring himself in direct line with Chuck's glinty stare. Katie's obvious absence did not sit well with anyone…especially Vance.

In the kitchen, Dottie handed the kids snacks and shoved them out the back door, ordering them not to kill each other. With fists planted on her generous hips covered in paisley denim, and casting her dagger eyes at Vance, she boomed, "What in the Sam Hill is going on around here?" She stomped forward in powder-blue cowboy clogs, standing toe-to-toe with him. "You gonna start talkin'? Because something has happened, and from the looks of things…it ain't good."

———

"Go ahead…say it. I know you're dying to." Thirty minutes later, Vance gave his dad, still sitting in his kitchen, a defeated I-don't-give-a-shit look. Dottie had left to round up the kids, tsking and shaking her head. Vance had spilled the beans about what had transpired the night before. When he told them about Tad showing up, and his involvement with McKnight Studios without Katie's knowledge, Dottie's face turned purple under her thick mask of make-up, and his dad grew military quiet. Scary military quiet.

Once he'd finished speaking, Dottie had poked his chest with one of her terrifying long blue nails and basically told him he was dumber than a pet rock. A fact Vance already knew. She then stormed from the kitchen in high dudgeon, shaking her head and mumbling under her breath something about stubborn Kerner men with corncobs up their asses and cow manure for brains. Which summed things up perfectly.

So that left Vance alone in the kitchen.

With his dad.

He couldn't remember the last time they'd been together like this. Even though he'd yearned for a relationship with his dad beyond the curt nod and grunted hello, he hadn't known where to begin. His dad looked way more comfortable than Vance felt, despite the drumming of his war-worn fingers on the table. He appeared to be weighing his next words. A definite first in their volatile history. Neither had excelled at holding back…or thinking before they spoke. A Kerner curse, for sure.

Vance couldn't stand the suspense any longer. He shot up from his chair. "Well? Come on, you can say it. I screwed up. It's not like I haven't already said it to myself hundreds of times already."

Chuck appeared nonplussed. "You made a tactical error. It happens."

Vance stopped pacing the black-and-white tile floor. "That's it? No dressing down for being a selfish ass? For only thinking of myself and my career? Not caring about anyone else?"

Chuck leveled him with a steady gaze. "You're a grown man. It's not my place to dress you down. Besides, I did enough of that when you were young. And I was wrong. Instead of building you up, all I managed to do was tear us apart. And that was never my intent. But I was too stubborn and set in my military ways to realize what I was doing." His face was a mask of regret.

The tense air in the room seemed to shift. Vance's chest ached as if a burning stone lodged there. His old man must be getting really old, because he'd never expected to hear those words from his lips. "I deserved it…most of the time. I made your life at home a living hell."

"No. I managed that with no help from you. When your mother died, something…everything in me died along with her. Nothing felt right after that. I'd served too long in the military and seen more death and destruction than any one man should endure. It only made sense I'd go before her. I couldn't understand how my life had been spared all those years at war and hers was snuffed out. You boys needed her. She always had the answers. She had great patience, and she loved you with all her heart." Chuck shook his head in confusion. "I can't help but believe God got it wrong that time."

"Dad…"

In a much stronger voice, his dad said, "I should've been the one to die first. Things would've been a lot… easier if I had." An icy chill ran through Vance's veins. Losing his mother had been hard on all of them, but his dad had always been a rock, holding their family together. Vance couldn't imagine his world without him, even if they lived like virtual strangers.

"Don't say that. Dad, some men are put on this earth to do all the dirty work, and you're one of those men. You and Eric. And guys like Adam Reynolds. You make the world a better place for the rest of us… whether we deserve it or not. And you do it all without expecting rewards or medals or ribbons." Vance raked his fingers through his hair. "You guys put your lives on the line and carry out orders, even when you disagree or don't believe in the cause. So we can continue to enjoy our freedoms. Mom was proud of you and Eric. She always said she couldn't wait for you to get home, because her boys needed their father. If she said it once, she said it a thousand times." Vance tried to keep his voice from cracking.

Chuck stood and clamped his hand on Vance's shoulder. They stood eye to eye, and yet Vance felt two feet tall. Memories came crashing back of all the years they'd faced off in this very kitchen, fighting and yelling. Neither giving an inch. And the day Vance had spewed those hateful words, he'd destroyed any chance at a relationship. It was the worst day of his life…until yesterday. Terrified, he stood rooted to the floor like that teenage boy so many years ago. Lack of communication was rearing its ugly head and biting him in the ass again. He'd made a horrible mistake by not confiding in Katie. Now he was afraid he'd lost the only woman he'd ever loved, besides his mom, with his stupidity and lack of foresight.

His dad squeezed his shoulder, bringing him back to the present. In a quiet voice, he said, "Your mother was proud of you too, Son. She recognized your talents before anyone else did." He chuckled, and a twinkle flashed behind his eyes. "She always told me you'd be famous one day. I didn't believe her."

Vance stared down at his black snakeskin cowboy boots and his dad's polished work boots. Yeah, no kidding. His dad had pictured a different kind of fame altogether…as Harmony's most wanted delinquent.

"And now look at you… You managed to surprise the hell out of Eric and me. And your mother is smiling down on us right now, saying I told you so."

Vance raised his head. "You think?"

"Yes. You can do whatever you set your mind to. And if you want that pretty little California Katie…well then, you're going to have to make it up to her. Make things right."

Vance shoved his fists in the pockets of his jeans. "I don't know if I can."

"Do you love her?"

Vance nodded slowly. "So much it hurts."

His dad smiled with a faraway look on his face. "It was the same way with your mother. I knew the minute

I spied her at the state fair, selling hot apple pies to support the USO." He chuckled. "She never stood a chance against my blitzkrieg."

"I knew the minute Katie stood in this kitchen and whistled."

"She's got spunk. And a good head on her shoulders. I like her style. She'll keep you on your toes. All she needs is a little confidence." His dad had nailed Katie's character to a T.

"Any suggestions? I could use some advice."

Surprise lit Chuck's dark eyes. The giving and taking of advice had not been a common exchange in their past. A small smile curled his lips. "Apologize from the bottom of your heart. Appeal to her sweet nature. And if that doesn't work...beg."

Vance released an unsteady breath. "Yeah, I think I'm at the begging stage."

His dad clapped him on the back with a few hearty strokes. The closest they'd come to a hug in eons. Vance didn't dare look him in the eye for fear of tearing up.

"Nothing wrong with humbling yourself. Remember, no one ever choked swallowing his pride."

Maybe not, but as he swallowed hard around the clump of sawdust in his mouth, Vance felt like choking. All pride had managed to do was keep him and his dad worlds apart.

Vance pressed his sweaty palms to his thighs. "Dad... about what I said...years ago. I never meant... I didn't think... I'm so sorry." Shame weighed heavily on his shoulders. "I was wrong. My harsh, careless words hurt you. I've regretted it ever since."

His dad didn't blink. A shattered world passed

behind his eyes but didn't linger. So much wasted time and emotion. "We hurt each other. I'm sorry too. For not having more patience and for pushing you so hard. It's time to let it go, Son. Don't let the past cloud your future. Life is for the living… Make the most of it." The shame shifted. Still there, but a slight ease of the burden.

Chuck clapped him on the back again. This time, a satisfied grin widened across his face. "Now get moving. You've got a filly from California to wrangle. Dottie and I will settle the kids down." He jerked his head toward the back door.

Determination settled deep inside him, overriding his fear and insecurities. "Thanks, Dad," Vance said, reaching for the doorknob.

Before he could make a clean exit, his dad's next words stopped him in his tracks. "My pleasure. And, Son…I'm proud of you."

———

Vance swiped at the moisture around his eyes as he crossed the yard to the barn. Pollen was a bitch this season. He gave a loud snort. *Who you kidding?* He was on the verge of blubbering like Dover when teased mercilessly by Donald.

His dad was proud of him.

He'd waited years to hear those very words. Half a dozen books later, where he'd left his heart and soul and blood and guts on the page. Years of always wondering if he'd ever measure up. It took only three rug rats, a nosy gossip, and everyone's favorite California cupcake to bring his dad around. They'd had a breakthrough. Vance didn't know what he'd done right to deserve this second chance, but he'd take any fallen crumb on his path. His dad had gotten one thing right: Life was too short not to savor every moment. And Vance wanted his life to start right now. With Katie. The woman he loved. He'd be a colossal fool not to grab hold of her and never let her go. Katie had changed everything. She'd melted the ice surrounding his bitter heart and brought sunshine back into his life. Sounded like corny song lyrics, but he didn't care. Now to convince her he'd changed and was worthy of her love. Vance knew what he had to do.

Inside his loft, Vance stared at his closed computer and scattered notes littering his desktop and painted wood floor. He'd be pulling all-nighters, compensating for lost writing time, but the phone call he was about to make took precedence. He palmed his cell and tapped in a number. "Walter? We need to talk."

Chapter 24

LATER THAT SAME DAY, AFTER LEAVING VANCE'S HOUSE, Katie found herself shifting uncomfortably on Chuck's plaid sofa. His military stare bore down on her, seeing more than she wanted to reveal.

"You sure this is what you want to do?" he asked, reaching for his iced tea.

She shook her head. "General, I'm not sure of anything anymore. But if I'm ever going to be my own person, I need to make a clean break."

He nodded. "If you change your mind, no one will hold it against you. This is a big step."

By big step he was referring to her decision to stay in Harmony and rent her own place. Confronting her parents over the phone *instead* of in person. Yeah, she was taking the easy way out on that one, but if she wanted to call Harmony her home, she needed to be here to make it happen. On her own terms, with a new partner. Yep. Katie and General Chuck Kerner were joining forces. Along with investing some start-up money, Chuck would be in charge of devising and implementing a kid-friendly boot camp for Imagination Station. Obviously, he was way overqualified for the job, but he'd offered, and Katie was thrilled to have him on her team. She sensed a new peace in him and signs of happiness in his sparkling black eyes that had been absent before.

Katie glanced at her watch. "Now or never. I'm meeting the realtor to sign the lease." She'd spent half the morning looking at rental properties for a place to live. She'd settled on a two bedroom, totally furnished bungalow on the other side of Main Street, not far from her new place of business. The other half of the morning she'd gone over her business plan with Bertie and Lucy. Lucy had come up with a superaggressive marketing strategy, and Bertie had started preliminary sketches on revamping the interior for Imagination Station. Her brothers were busy drafting a professional proposal and ironclad contract, and Inslee had already sent outlines for new computer learning games, including an advance version of Katie's favorite picture puzzles.

"Have you told Vance your plans?" Chuck asked in a low voice.

Katie fidgeted with the hem of her T-shirt and tried not to scratch the backs of her legs from the itchy cotton upholstery. "No. I want to be sure everything falls into place. I mean, what if I don't qualify for the loan, or the numbers don't add up? I'd be a failure before I'd even started." Or what if she changed her mind? Or got cold feet? Not about loving Vance...that would never change, but she wanted to be worthy of his love. Katie wanted to pull her weight as an equal partner, not be an albatross around his neck. She wanted to pull her weight with the strength of her own backbone.

"That's understandable. Maybe it's best to play your cards close to your chest. He'll be upset enough at you living across town and not with him. Adding me as your business partner might send him straight to the therapist's couch."

His argument was valid. Why upset Vance about her new business when it may never come to fruition?

"Okay, but if I get a green light, he's going to be the first person I tell."

"Agreed. But make it clear my role is very minor. The bulk of the work will fall on your shoulders."

"Don't sell yourself short. Your advice and help are immeasurable," Katie said.

"Nevertheless. This is your brainchild. Own it and make it happen. How do you plan to tell him of your sudden move and new plans?"

Butterflies stirred up in her stomach. Katie was kind of hoping Vance would drown himself in work and not notice her absence. *Yeah, right*. What a chicken. Always her default mode. Vance hadn't been far from her thoughts all day. He'd left her alone like she'd asked, but from the tone of his last text, she could tell he was not happy and had begun to worry. An aching sadness tore through her. She already missed him and didn't know how she'd survive living apart from him in the same town.

She had only one choice. "Confront him, I guess." Katie's eyebrow twitched at the thought. "You wanna come along…for moral support?"

He chuckled. "You don't need me. You hold all the power. Believe in yourself."

Right. Believe. "The very reason I'm doing this…to make a clean break and to start believing in myself." She couldn't afford to lose her courage now. "And while I'm busy working on Imagination Station, he'll have time to finish his book…without any further distractions from me." Katie averted her eyes from the steely hard stare the general shot her way. "We both need this time apart to work things out," she said, hoping her words would convince herself.

"That boy loves you something fierce. A feeling I know you return."

Katie looked at her feet, unwilling to let him see the emotion in her eyes. She hated hurting Vance. But she hated being a pushover even more and not controlling her own life.

"Don't break his heart." It sounded like an order. "Keep him guessing, and don't let him have his way all the time, but don't break his heart."

Katie's head popped up. "Huh?"

Chuck laughed like a man enjoying life. "You've got him tied up in knots. Something he's never felt before, I'm sure. Arguing and disagreeing are just as important as making love and keeping peace. You've got to strike the right balance, and true love will prevail."

Katie's skin grew hot. "That must've been some talk you and Vance had."

"It was a start. A good start. And we have you to thank for it."

"Me? Really?"

"Don't sell yourself short, young lady. You've managed to soften some pretty hardened hearts with your smiling face and generous nature." Katie's heart skipped in pleasure, knowing Vance and his dad had finally had a normal conversation. Chuck held out his hand and pulled her up. "Come on, soldier. Day's half-gone. Time for you to face your challenges. Call me once you've settled in, and I'll bring dinner over," he said as he escorted her to the door.

Encouraged by his faith in her, she managed to squash the dread of confronting Vance *and* her parents. "Thanks. For everything." Katie went up on her toes and kissed him on the cheek, when the front door blew open. There on the threshold stood her favorite pirate, blocking her exit and gnashing his teeth.

"What the hell is going on around here?" Vance practically growled.

"Katie stopped by for a glass of iced tea and a visit," Chuck said in a matter-of-fact tone, as if this was an everyday occurrence. Okay, yeah, it had been kinda every day.

"I've been looking all over for you. Are you leaving?" He pierced her with a fierce gaze.

Her nod was unsteady. "Y-yes, but it's not what you're thinking—"

"Good. Because your room has been packed up, you're not answering my texts, and the Ardbuckle twins have shown up and informed me they'll be helping out for the next three weeks. Which makes me think you're leaving. What am I missing?"

"Um, I'm moving out—"

"Because of last night. Instead of talking to me. Why?" His eyes narrowed dangerously, and she knew that expression from the hours she'd spent mooning over his handsome face. He would not be happy with her answer.

"Partly. Last night made me realize what I've been putting off for far too long. It's time I confront my dad and quit my job—"

Vance took an aggressive step forward. "I'm going with you. You're not going home and facing your parents alone."

The very fact that he had no faith in her ability to handle the situation strengthened her resolve. "*No*. I don't want your help. And I'm not going home."

His brow furrowed in confusion. "I don't understand."

Her take-charge pirate wanted to jump in headfirst and fix things. Katie couldn't allow him to run her over. "I'm moving into a rental property…right here in Harmony, and I'll be dealing with my family over the phone."

Surprise snapped his head back. "Rental property? Don't be ridiculous. Look, if you need your space…fine. You can have the whole damn house. I'll stay in the loft. You won't see me unless you want to. I'll keep the Ardbuckle twins around to manage the kids. Whatever you want, it's yours."

Katie knew this would be hard for him to understand, since he never suffered from low self-esteem or questioned his purpose in life. "Tempting, but I can't accept. I need…no, I *want* to be on my own, to figure things out."

"Why? Being on your own is overrated. Believe me, I know. Kat, I want to help you. You shouldn't have to confront your parents alone. I don't want them hurting you. I should be there—"

"No. This is my war. My job. You…you concentrate on finishing this book and turning all of them into blockbusters." A flicker of something she couldn't quite define flashed across his face.

"I don't give a damn about the book. The book is not important. The only thing important to me is you."

Her stomach hollowed out at the expression of frustration on his face. Katie scoffed to hide her own churning emotions. "Don't be ridiculous. Your book and career are important, and you can't stop because of me. I'd never forgive myself. Besides, I'm going to be busy—" Katie stopped midsentence as she spied Chuck's subtle head shake from the corner of her eye.

Alert, Vance caught the same exchange. "What's going on here? What are you two plotting?" As if it suddenly dawned on him, he crossed his arms and widened his stance, becoming a human blockade. "When did you two become so friendly? Last I checked, you barely knew each other."

"Katie and I have been well-acquainted since she first arrived," Chuck said in a calm tone.

"Really?" Vance's sarcasm was not lost on her.

She hastened to explain. "We met by accident the day I went for a walk, and your dad invited me—"

"And you never told me? Why the hell not?" His voice escalated.

"Because I asked her not to."

Vance went from angry to hurt as his rigid shoulders slumped. Katie's gaze darted nervously between the two men, grasping for something to say to make this right. She came up empty.

"I made her promise. I was being cautious and paranoid." Chuck gave an apologetic shrug. "Old habits die hard. So sue me."

Several beats passed, and Katie feared the recent goodwill created between father and son would blow up like a powder keg touched with a lit match by Chuck's challenge.

Vance drew a deep breath. "Okay. I guess I deserve that."

Chuck seemed satisfied, grunted, and then excused

himself, allowing them some privacy, which Katie appreciated.

Then Vance turned his intense scrutiny on her. "Why are you doing this? You have a home. My home. It's yours, and everything in it is yours...including me. Especially me. Don't do this. Don't run away from us."

Guilt, ugly and raw, riddled her insides. "Give me time. Don't you see? This is my fight I need to win all by myself."

Vance plowed all ten fingers through his tousled hair. "No. No, you don't. Ask my dad. It takes thousands of troops to win a war."

Despite her heart plummeting at the desperate tone in his voice, she stiffened her spine. No time like the present to build that backbone...one vertebra at a time. "My struggle to become happy with myself is a personal battle. Mine and mine alone. I appreciate your wanting to fight it for me, but if I'm ever going to be comfortable in my own skin, I need to take a stand." Vance reached for her, but Katie backed away. In a stronger voice, she added, "More important, I need to respect myself. And I need to handle my family. If I let you run interference for me, I'll regret it for the rest of my life. And you'll end up resenting me...for being weak and never taking charge."

The hurt in his gaze made her heartsick. Vance snagged her hand, capturing it within his strong, warm grasp. "I could never resent you. Ever." His thumb making small circles across her skin almost brought Katie to her knees. "I don't agree with you, but I'll respect your wishes. Will I ever get to see you?" He looked as if his world was shattering. Katie knew, because she felt the same way.

She shrugged her shoulder. "It's a small town. We're bound to see each other."

"When can I be with you?" His meaning was not lost on her.

Her tangled, mixed emotions unsettled her. Physical passion. A yearning to be one with this one man for the rest of her life. She heaved a huge breath. "You're making this as hard as possible."

His gaze snapped to hers. "I'm not the one moving out. You still haven't answered my question."

Katie moved in and wrapped herself around his solid body, pressing her cheek to his hard chest. Taking comfort in the beating of his steady heart. His warmth seared straight to her soul. "I can't give you an exact date." She had no idea how long this personal journey would take. A lot of broken pieces needed gluing back together. Vance had wrapped his arms around her and squeezed so tight that Katie didn't know where he ended and she began.

"Anything I can do to speed up the process?" he murmured, kissing the top of her head.

Katie smiled against his light blue cotton polo shirt, breathing in his clean, masculine scent. "Finish your book."

"Will you come home if I finish the book?"

"Finish the book, and then we'll talk."

"And in the meantime…what do we do about our relationship?"

Katie caught the taut line of his jaw and the grim set to his mouth. "We put it on hold," she whispered. Vance cursed under his breath. "Patience, my love. On both our parts."

Vance studied her for a few moments as if weighing his next argument. Cupping her face with his hands, he surprised her with a gentle kiss. A brush across her lips. An acceptance, so to speak. "Okay. We do this your way."

—◦◦◦—

"You did the right thing," Chuck said, standing next to Vance as he watched Katie drive away in her classic Mercedes. Away from him. Away from their home. Away from everything he believed in.

"Then why do I feel as though I've been shredded by a turboprop propeller, and my heart has been ripped from my chest?" Vance swallowed hard. Every fiber of his being rebelled against this plan of Katie's. He hated the thought of her dealing with her dad alone. Katie had been fighting her own battles her entire life. Vance should be there backing her up. But what choice did he have? Arguing her off the ledge would only make him look more like an ass than he already did.

"You'll survive. You both will." Chuck clapped a hand over Vance's shoulder. Grateful for the company, Vance still felt funny baring the secrets of his soul to his dad. They hadn't exchanged twenty words over the last five years until earlier today. But it felt good to confide in someone, and his dad would keep his trust, of that Vance had no doubt.

He stared down the now-empty dirt road and didn't know whether to congratulate himself for not kidnapping Katie and locking her away until she came to her senses or to shoot himself for agreeing to this asinine idea of hers. He shook his head. "Women…there's no understanding them."

Chuck gave a low chuckle. "Katie needs all the love she can get, and you're the right man for the job. Give her the time she needs to find herself, and I think she'll surprise you."

"I've got nothing but time," he muttered.

"I don't think so." Vance arched a brow at his dad. "Seems to me the sooner you finish your book…the sooner you get her back."

Vance scrubbed a hand over his face. The damn book. The deadline was eating him alive. He *had* to finish. Katie was right. Finding the time to focus was imperative. But he had so much more to tell her. Like how he'd told Walter everything about Tad and how Katie felt betrayed. And Vance wanted to reassure her he'd never hurt her again. And to prove it, he'd dumped the rights to selling his books to McKnight Studios. Katie meant more to him than some lousy, sappy Hollywood movie version of his stories. Last night, after hearing how Tad Pimp had sold him out in front of Katie, Walter had gotten real quiet on the other end of the line. Vance thought maybe he'd start putting his daughter first, before another shady business deal. Maybe. He didn't know for sure. They hadn't actually ended their conversation on a high note.

"I guess you're right." Vance dreaded heading home. Without Katie, everything felt out of whack.

His dad said, "If you need another place to get away, you can always come here. I'll be happy to clear out."

"Whoa." Vance choked out a disbelieving laugh. "Who are you? And what have you done with my dad?"

"Trying to help. That's all. You looked like someone shot your best huntin' dog." Chuck's cynical arched brow mirrored Vance's.

"I get it. Quit acting like a sap and grow a third nut. Right?"

"Your heart aches over not being able to help Katie. That's only natural. And I'm serious about offering up my place. Dottie and I can take over with the kids to help you out."

"You and Dottie, huh?" Chuck shifted, leaning his strong shoulder against the wood porch column. "Is there something you're not telling me?" For Chuck's sake, he hoped like hell Dottie Duncan would not become a permanent fixture in his life. No one deserved that. Vance cut his dad an assessing glance. The silence grew between them, and Vance recognized Chuck's unreadable military expression. He didn't make general by giving anything away.

"Okay. Minding my own business. Thanks. I might take you up on your offer." Vance inhaled deeply, catching the faint scent of the pine trees surrounding his dad's property. He started down the steps. "I better be shoving off. The kids are probably force-feeding the Ardbuckle twins cockroaches by now."

He was halfway across the front yard when his dad called out, "About your books…"

He stopped and listened…hard.

So hard he thought his brain might pour out of his ears.

Chuck regarded him with honest eyes. "You give an accurate, vivid account of heroes, renegades, and brothers. Very gripping tales of courage under fire. You're extremely talented."

His lungs seized. "You've read my series?"

"Yes. Thanks to Katie." Chuck smiled, brightening his entire face. "She sure has a way about her.

Anyway"—he motioned with his hand—"go on. Don't let me hold you up. You've got a book to finish. And I'm looking forward to reading it."

Slack-jawed, Vance watched his dad disappear into his house before he could say thank you. *His dad read his latest series and really liked it.* Despite standing there looking like the town fool, pride soared through Vance, making him want to pound his chest like Tarzan.

Chapter 25

KATIE CLOSED THE DOOR TO THE SMALL BUT ROOMY closet where she'd hung the last of her clothes. Her nose twitched at the pungent smell of cedar. Harmony wasn't exactly a hotbed of rental places. She'd been lucky to land this incredible old bungalow, beating out two other offers in a neighborhood on the other side of town, near Main Street. She squeezed her eyes shut, missing Vance's spacious master bedroom and luxurious bath. And the light and airy loft with its white-painted wood floors, king-size bed, and over-sized shower for two. But what she really missed was the hunky, sexy, and sometimes pushy guy crowding her space in bed and hogging all the hot water in the shower.

Chuck had stopped by earlier with take-out food from the Dog, so she was set for dinner.

Katie lifted her cell phone from the top of the antique wood dresser and drew in a deep breath. A bead of sweat trickled between her breasts. Her brother Sam had texted earlier, saying her parents would be home later. It was now later. The moment of truth. Pushing her heavy braid over her shoulder, she tapped the screen of her cell and listened to the phone ring.

"Hi, Dad," she said, easing down on the chintz-covered love seat.

"Katie? Where are you? I've been worried sick."

"Same place I was the last time we talked. Harmony, North Carolina."

"About that…it's time to come home. I don't think the location scout position is working out like we'd hoped. Your mother and I have something much better in mind for you."

Katie pressed her fingers to her forehead. "Um, I don't think so, Dad."

"What do you mean? Just a minute"—Katie heard some rustling on the other end of the line—"Crystal! Katie's on the phone"—more rustling—"I've put you on speaker so your mother can hear," Dad said.

"Katie, dear? It's your mother. When will you be home? There's a new exercise craze…Trapfit. Have you heard of it? You exercise on a trapeze. Like the circus. It really builds upper body strength, and you'll lose weight—"

"Mom, Dad…I need you to listen." Katie pressed two fingers into her twitching eyebrow.

"Crystal, hush up. What is it, Katie?" Dad had silenced Mom, and for once, Katie was grateful his command was obeyed.

"I'm not coming home any time soon."

"What?"

"I'm quitting McKnight Studios, and I'm staying in Harmony." Katie could feel the tension, even over the phone. It was like waiting for lightning to strike.

"I don't understand. Walter, did you hear what she said?" Katie could hear her dad's silence loud and clear. "Katie, why are you doing this? Are you sick? Do you need a doctor?" Mom asked.

"No, Mom. Listen…I'm doing this for me. I need time to think and to figure out who I am and what I want."

"You're Katie McKnight, and we can give you whatever you want. This is another one of those rash things you're always doing. Like taking all those pictures."

Katie rolled her eyes. "It's called photography, and it happens to be something I love."

"Walter, are you hearing any of this? What is she talking about? Our daughter is living in some crazy town—"

"Let me handle this," her dad said in a hushed tone. "Katie, your mother and I think it's best you come home and resume living here with us." Oh, hashtag *hell no*. "I've enrolled you in the accounting program at the community college. We think this would be a fine career choice for you."

Katie bolted out of her seat and started pacing the hardwood oak floors in the tiny living room. "Accounting?" Katie almost laughed at the absurdity of his suggestion. "I have a degree in education, in case it slipped your mind. Whatever gave you the idea that I'd be interested in accounting?"

"It's a respectable career. You can make a good living. There's no money in education—"

"No! No more. Dad, this is not up for discussion. I'm not some pawn or some lowly intern you can order around at your whim. And I'm no longer sitting quietly and allowing you to *handle* my life. I'm not becoming an accountant. If I want to start a bottle cap collection or weave placemats out of pine straw, it will be my choice and my career."

"Kathryn, you're distraught. Let me send you a plane ticket. It's better if we have this discussion in person." Yeah, so he could browbeat her into doing his bidding.

"Dad, there's nothing to discuss. I'm telling you, I plan to stay here in Harmony and—"

"Doing what? Have you taken leave of your senses?" Mom shrieked. "Your home is here in California. Not…not all the way across the country in some hillbilly *hick* town."

"Harmony is not a hillbilly town." Katie hoped her parents never met the Perry brothers, because she'd be eating her words. "It's quaint and charming, and the people are sweet and helpful." Along with nosy and opinionated. "I've found a home here, where I'm not only welcome, but appreciated."

Her dad gave a huge snort. "Does Kerner have anything to do with this? One good-looking guy pays you some attention, and you're ready to abandon your family." Katie jerked as if her dad had managed to slap her through the phone. Pulling the phone away from her ear, she stared at it in shock. How could her dad believe she made a habit of chasing after good-looking guys, like some wannabe starlet looking to get noticed? Like she'd been loose with her relationships in the past, with no concern for her family? He had no clue how truly repressed she'd been all these years.

"Vance loves me, and that's good enough for me." Okay, that sounded lame.

"Vance? What about Tad? I thought you sent Tad to keep an eye on her," Katie heard her mom say to her dad in the background.

"Really? I'm a grown woman, and you sent my *ex*-boyfriend out here to spy on me. And to do *my* job. Which you'd already fired me from but neglected to tell me. All while cooking up a deal with Vance to keep me busy so I wouldn't find out."

"Is that what Kerner told you?"

"No. Tad did. Who I'm no longer dating, by the way."

"Good. Because I fired the incompetent jackass," Dad muttered.

Well, at least they agreed on one thing: Tad was a jackass. "Look, I don't care about Tad. He's nothing but a tool. But Vance—"

"Kerner's a ticking time bomb. Don't be swayed by his cocky charm and—"

Katie cut her dad off before he said anything disparaging about Vance. "Vance came clean about the movie deal he made with you. You put him in a really tough position. After all that, you better approve the screenplays like you promised," Katie warned.

"I don't like your tone of voice. It's disrespectful," Mom said into the phone. "Where did she learn to speak to us like that?" *Ha!* Crystal McKnight better get used to the new and improved Katie.

"Katie, are you there?"

"Yes, Dad."

"There is no movie deal. Kerner backed out of the project."

She stopped midpace; her head snapped up. "What are you talking about?"

"He called me today. Said the deal was off. Told me he never wanted to hurt you again. I figured something was going on between you two, but I didn't know how serious it was until Vance bailed on the movie deal. Didn't give any details, but I don't trust the guy. Steer clear of him, you hear? He's an unreliable writer and doesn't have your best interests at heart. He's not family. Your mom and I will make sure…" Katie had stopped listening. Shaking her head, she blinked several times against the burning tears…*not* caused by her dad's concern but by what she'd learned of Vance. Her pirate had dumped a multimillion-dollar movie deal because he'd hurt her, and sworn he'd never do it again.

"…do you understand what I'm saying?" Dad finished speaking. Katie understood perfectly. The one person who truly believed in her and had her back was not on the other end of this phone line. No, he was probably sitting bleary-eyed in front of his computer, trying to finish a book so they could be together again. And she needed to get busy and hold up her end of the bargain.

"Dad, Mom, as a courtesy, because you're my parents and I love you, I want you to know I'm starting my own business. In Harmony." Deafening silence filled her ear.

Finally, her dad spoke. "What kind of business?" She detected the edge in his voice.

"An active-learning center for kids, where they can explore inventive computer applications and incorporate physical activity in fun, innovative ways."

"Fifty percent of all new businesses fail within the first year," Dad said, clearly not impressed with her business idea.

"I know. Which is why I've got the best lawyers in the country working on my business plan."

"Where'd you get the money to hire lawyers?"

"Seems I'm related to them. Sam and Doug are helping me."

"Your brothers know about this?"

"I know what I'm doing, Dad. I have a solid business

plan, a budget, and a team of talented people backing me," Katie said with a burst of confidence. Failing was no longer an option.

Katie had found a place to call home. Not the shabby-chic bungalow she presently stood in, but Harmony. Back at the farmhouse. In Vance's loving arms. Her transformation may never happen, but at least in Harmony, she stood a chance.

"This is another disaster in the making. You're wasting your time and money." The disapproval in her dad's voice rang loud and clear. Katie swallowed her frustration, along with her fear. Sink-or-swim time.

Ignoring the familiar feeling of guilt over disappointing her family, she said, "Mom, Dad, I love you both, and I know you care for me. But it's time for me to stand on my own. It's time I discovered what I'm made of. If I fail…it's nobody's fault but my own. I have to do this with or without your blessing." Katie closed her eyes and pictured Vance and his sexy grin he saved only for her. "And just so we're clear, I love Vance Kerner, and we're getting married." Katie held the phone away from her ear at her mother's earsplitting shriek and her dad's sputtering. Before they could catch their breaths and go another round, she hastily added, "Oh, and Dad, you'd be smart to sweeten that movie deal before another studio snatches him up. Um…okay. I guess that's all. Love you. Bye."

Katie shut her phone off, knowing her parents may never recover from the bomb she'd just dropped. In a restless state, she flung open the front door, welcoming the cool night air as it hit her heated skin. She pushed the screen door wide and stepped onto the front stoop.

Not to panic or anything, but, *oh God*. Did she really just tell her parents she was marrying Vance Kerner? Yes. She did indeed. The mere thought scared her senseless, but she didn't regret saying it. She'd handled her parents. Spineless Katie had stood up to her parents without caving. The rustling of leaves in the trees caught her attention as it began to rain. Katie stepped onto the sidewalk and lifted her face to the dark, cloudy sky. Raindrops pelted her face, and she laughed out loud. Sweet relief washed over her, and Katie stood there getting soaked, relishing her newfound freedom and sense of pride.

———

Katie had tried to sleep in this morning, but her body refused to relax. She had spent the last three weeks working nonstop on Imagination Station in order to be ready for its grand opening. The empty storefront on the town commons had proven to be the perfect spot. Chuck, Bertie, and Lucy had been real troopers, working right alongside her. And with the loan she'd been able to secure with her brothers' help, this crazy idea of hers was taking shape.

But as hard as she worked on Imagination Station, it was not what kept her awake at night. What kept her from sleeping was Vance.

True to his word, he had kept his distance these last three weeks. Katie had seen him twice picking up food at BetterBites, and three more times when she'd stopped by the house to visit the kids. It took everything in her power not to bury herself in his warm embrace, but Chuck kept her informed, and from the sound of things, Vance would be making his deadline…*today*.

Katie jumped at the sound of her phone. A combination of too much caffeine and lack of sleep. "Hello?"

"Did I wake you?" Bertie asked in a cheery voice.

"No. I've been up."

"Couldn't sleep, huh? Understandable. I don't know how you've lasted this long."

Katie chuckled. "I had some growing up to do, remember? Besides, I wanted him to finish his book. It's too important."

"And now it's time to celebrate. Need any help getting ready?" And by celebrate, Bertie was referring to the horizontal version in Vance's bed.

"Nope. I'm good," Katie said, glancing down at her tan legs and white linen shorts. "I think you'd approve of my outfit." Along with the shorts, she wore a form-fitting blue tank top and matching blue espadrilles. Rolling walls and laying new carpet at Imagination Station was hard, physical labor, but it had gotten Katie in shape. And she liked the results.

"Okay. Well…goodness, what does one say on an occasion such as this? Good luck? Congratulations?"

"All of the above." Katie smiled.

"You go, girl. And give Vance a big kiss for me." Katie planned to do that and a whole lot more.

No sooner had she hung up from Bertie when Lucy called with all the same questions.

Katie said good-bye to Lucy, thinking if she didn't get out of there soon, she'd be fielding calls all morning from the Harmony busybodies. Scooping up her handbag and the gifts she had for the kids, Katie raced from the house. Her packed bags were already in the trunk of her car. In the past few weeks, Katie had grown a lot from living on her own. She'd enjoyed the time to herself, working on her photography and creating lesson plans for her new business. She'd read and caught up on recent movies, texting and joking with Inslee as they both watched from different coastlines. And she'd continued to remain calm and not back down with each call her parents made, stating new reasons for her to return home. The gravel beneath her feet crunched with each step as she crossed the tight driveway next to her rental home. She opened her car door when her phone chimed again. "Good Lord and call me Sally." Katie giggled at her adopted country saying. "Morning, Dottie."

"Where in tarnation are you? It's almost nine o'clock on Saturday morning."

"Are the kids okay? Is something wrong?" The alarm in Dottie's voice made Katie freeze.

"Those rambunctious rascals are as wild as ever. Nothing wrong with them. It's their uncle I'm worried about." Vance? Her pounding heart dipped to her knees.

"Wh-what's wrong with Vance?" she whispered as her hand began to shake.

"He's as mean as a wet panther. Growling and snapping at anything that moves. If you don't get on over there and calm him down, I'm afraid his daddy's gonna do something awful, like enlist him in the Army for good."

"I'm on my way. What brought all this on?" Katie said, fumbling with her car key.

"Lack of nookie, I imagine. And pushing himself to make that darn deadline. I'll be so glad when this book is put to bed and we can all go back to normal living. Those kids have worn me out, and I'm gonna snatch their uncle bald if he doesn't watch his temper around me."

Katie drove as fast as she could without drawing the attention of Harmony's finest out strolling Main Street, sipping from Daily Grind coffee cups. Dottie had to be exaggerating about Vance's behavior, like she did about almost everything in this town. Katie turned down the rough road that made up Vance's driveway. Hard to believe it had been a little over a month when she'd first spied this perfect, picturesque location and wondered if the owner would agree to her terms. Now she wondered if the owner would agree to different terms altogether.

Winding her way down the driveway, she came to a complete stop in front of Vance's house. Off to the side, she spied Dottie's SUV, already packed for the kids' final trip home to be with their mom. Everything appeared still. No children running around and no homegrown talent cluttering up the front lawn. Birds chirped noisily, and Katie picked up the sweet scent of honeysuckle carried by the spring breeze. She reached for her packages on the passenger seat, when her head jerked up at the sound of the front door blowing open. Her eyes widened and her mouth dropped at Vance storming toward her, wearing threadbare jeans, wrinkled white button-down with most of its buttons missing, and carrying a thick packet of papers in his hand. At the sight of him intent on reaching her, Katie's remaining fears faded away into nothingness. The debilitating need to please her parents disappeared, replaced by the freedom to live her life and the burning love for this gorgeous, scowling man. Her heart filled until it nearly burst from aching.

Katie bolted from the car at a full run, desire clogging her throat. She didn't think. She simply hurled herself at

Vance and hoped to God he'd catch her. She slammed against his hard chest, and Vance wrapped her in his tight embrace. Choking back a sob, she buried her head in the crook of his neck. No one loved her the way he did. He expressed his love from the depths of his dark eyes and the strength of his arms binding her to him.

"Don't. Don't ever leave me again," he rasped against the tears burning a path down her cheek, sounding as desperate as she felt. Vance plowed his hand through her hair, pulling back her head until she stared into his bloodshot, tired eyes. "I won't survive it. Promise me," he practically begged.

Shaking from her own emotions, she whispered, "I'm here."

"Promise me," he urged, tightening his hold.

"I promise."

He made a noise of raw male hunger and covered her mouth with his. Katie whimpered at how much she'd missed this. No one kissed like her Pirate Man. No one. All her fears and problems floated away, until there was only Vance. He kissed her with bone-melting determination. Kissing her deeper than ever before, Vance lifted her off her feet, and Katie started to wrap her legs around his waist, when the front door banged open again, and three screaming children tumbled out.

"Kay-tee!"

"Hey!"

"Ignore them," Vance growled against her lips. "Maybe they'll go away." Katie gave a low chuckle and reluctantly moved back, adjusting her top, which had ridden halfway up her back. She poured all her love into the smile she gave Vance's exasperated face.

"I'm not going anywhere," she reassured him, push-ing his wild hair from his forehead.

Vance snorted. "Thank God they are. And not a minute too soon."

Katie gave him a playful smack on the arm and turned to the kids. "Good morning! You guys ready for your big trip?"

"Granddaddy and Miz Dottie are taking us home today. Our mom is all better now," Dover informed her.

"Kay-tee, you wanna play Barbie?" Danny held out a Barbie who'd seen better days, judging by the condi-tion of her torn pink tutu and whacked-off hair.

"Oh, honey, maybe another time. Hey, I've got something for you guys."

Squealing ensued as Katie pulled three kid computer tablets from her car, loaded with new puzzles and games for the long ride home.

"Cool!" Donald's eyes bugged out.

"Thanks. Can we play with it right now?"

"Yeah, whatever. Go back inside. All of you. Tell Granddad you're set to go." Vance made a shooing motion with his hands, still holding the thick packet of papers, when Donald, not looking, bumped Vance's arm and sent the papers flying just as the wind picked up. Katie gasped. Hundreds of papers flitted through the air, dipping and swaying and skipping over the ground.

Donald's mouth popped open, and he turned fright-ened eyes to Vance. Danny shrieked and started chasing the loose white sheets.

"Sorry, Uncle Vance," Donald said in a small voice.

The corner of Vance's lips lifted in a slow smile, and then he burst out laughing. "Don't worry about it. Go.

Run. Pick up as much as you can." Both boys scrambled after Danny. Vance turned his laughing eyes to her.

"W-was that your book?" Katie asked, gesturing to the scattered sheets.

"Doesn't matter. It's been saved and backed up. Besides, I still have the most important page." He held up his hand, still holding one piece of paper. He gripped her by the elbow and dragged her behind her car, away from spying eyes.

"What?" She blinked in confusion.

Vance planted a swift kiss on her lips. "I love you, Kat. These last three weeks have been pure hell, but my love for you never wavered. And it was the only thing that kept me sane." He lifted her hand and pressed soft kisses to her fingertips. "I love you so much I want the whole world to know." Katie's brain went fuzzy from his tingling kisses. It took a minute to comprehend his declaration. She looked down at the piece of paper he held out for her. "Take it." His raspy voice sent chills down her spine. His strong throat worked as he swallowed.

With shaky hands, Katie stared at the paper until the typed words came into focus:

> To Katie, the bravest woman I know. You gave me the gift of everlasting love at first sight. With you, anything is possible. Will you marry me?

Katie blinked and blinked again. Tears clouded her vision. When she looked up, Vance had slid down on one knee and held open a black velvet box with a stunning diamond ring cushioned inside.

"It was my mom's. We can have it changed, if you don't like it."

She shook her head as tears of joy trickled down her cheeks. "It's perfect," she whispered, gazing at the diamond nestled in its platinum filigree setting.

"Is that a yes?"

She nodded. "Yes. A definite yes."

In one fluid motion, he stood and placed the perfect ring on her finger and wrapped Katie in his perfect arms. "Just so we're clear...I love you and will love you forever. And we're getting married."

Katie laughed at the quiet but firm demand in his voice. "That's what an engagement ring usually implies."

"Yeah, they're good that way. So, how about next week? What do you say?"

Katie looped her arms around his neck and pulled him down for a kiss. Her toes curled inside her shoes, and her body sang with excitement.

"Is that a yes?" her impatient pirate growled against her lips.

She smiled. "I think I'm going to need longer than that—"

"How much longer? Don't say a year. I'll never survive a year," he groaned.

"But a girl needs to plan. These things take time."

Vance pressed his forehead against hers. "You're going to torture me, aren't you?"

"Maybe...just a little." Katie pressed her smiling lips to the thudding pulse on his neck, inhaling his essence. "But I promise you're gonna like it," she murmured, loving the sound of his groan.

"As long as I'm with you, I'll survive anything."

Lifting her head, she should've been warned by his wicked smile. She gasped as Vance bent and hauled her over his shoulder. She gripped his waist and squealed. "Where are you taking me?"

Vance ate up the ground with his long strides. "The loft. To have my way with you. Something I should've done weeks ago. It's past time I claimed my booty."

Upside down and bouncing, Katie laughed in delight, so full of love for the pirate of her heart.

Epilogue

KATIE BLINKED BACK HAPPY TEARS AS SHE GLANCED AT Vance next to her, wearing a custom-tailored black tux, a sexy smile on his face, and looking so handsome he stole her breath. Vance pressed a kiss to the back of her hand and shot her a teasing wink, making Katie's heart soar at the sheer magnitude of her luck. Yeah, getting lost seven months ago put an end to her crazy, crappy luck when she landed in Harmony. Her new home. With the love of her life.

"You okay?" he asked in a low voice.

Katie nodded, smiling. "Never been better."

"Because we can get out of here, if you want. No one will miss us." His expression bordered on wicked. Katie looked out over the crowded backyard filled with all their friends and most of the residents of Harmony. It had been a beautiful ceremony, and now everyone was milling around, drinking champagne and nibbling on stuffed mushrooms before the start of the sit-down dinner. The heavy scent of deep purple roses filled the cool November air.

"Of course we'll be missed. We can't ruin this perfect day. Now behave." Katie kissed her pirate's clean-shaven jaw.

Vance grumbled something not for public consumption under his breath as he tucked her hand in the crook of his arm.

Katie pressed her lips together to keep from laughing. Vance had been almost civilized the last seven months, all things considered. Imagination Station had opened on time with huge fanfare at the start of the summer with Bertie's help and Lucy's amazing ability at getting the word out. Katie's hard work and meticulous business plan had paid off. Kids loved her new and innovative computer games—thanks to her friend Inslee—and they eagerly rallied around Chuck and his kiddie boot camp, where workouts were disguised as games. Donald, Dover, and Danny had returned for a week so they could attend one of the summer camp sessions. Vance kept busy with edits on his book and developing his next series about a small-town cop caught in the middle of a big-time drug heist. He gladly left all the wedding plans and logistics to her.

"You ready with a toast?" Brogan Reese clapped Vance on the back. "It's not every day you get to witness your dad getting hitched."

"It was a beautiful wedding, and the general looked so proud in his uniform."

"What little you could see of it. He was practically drowning in the mountain of ruffles covering Dottie. Where in the hell did she get that dress?" Vance said out of the corner of his mouth.

Katie gave his ribs a hard nudge with her elbow. "Vance Kerner, *stop*. You know how much Dottie loves ruffles. She had that dress made to her specifications." Along with all the ruffled tablecloths and swags of fabric draping the tent covering her backyard. She even had a special ruffled bandana made for Sweet Tea. And poor Bertie had the honor of walking him down the aisle.

"All I'm saying is it's hard to see anything past all this…this…"—he gestured with his big hand in her direction—"…fabric. I almost couldn't find you." Vance's gaze raked her from the top of her purple ruffled headpiece to the bottom of her purple ruffled gown.

"Couldn't any of you talk her out of this theme?" Keith Morgan asked, smirking at the electric-blue version Bertie wore.

"We tried, but you know how she is when she gets an idea in her head," Bertie said on an exasperated sigh.

"Like a dog with a bone. At least you don't look like Kermit the Frog or the Incredible Hulk," Lucy said, looking down at her bright green number.

"I think you all look beautiful. So beautiful, that I'm thinking of asking you to wear them for my wedding." Five pairs of eyes swiveled in her direction and bugged out in shock.

"You can't be serious—"

"Wedding?"

"When is the wedding?"

"Yeah, when is the wedding?" Vance pierced her with his intense dark gaze.

Katie lifted her chin. "Don't look so surprised. You're acting as if I never planned to get married."

"It's been seven long months. Do not toy with me," Vance growled.

"Yeah, he's a desperate man," Brogan said.

Katie fiddled with the clasp to the matching ruffled clutch she carried. "Well, he's going to have to be patient a little longer." She pulled an engraved, off-white card threaded with charcoal satin ribbon at the top from her bag. "Everyone will be getting one of these in the mail."

Vance plucked the card from her fingers and quickly read the invitation. Both brows hiked up as he blinked in confusion at Katie. "There's a whole week of activities here."

"Yes. I'm aware of that. Be glad it's only a week. While you've been buried in your work, I've been battling my parents for months."

"Let me see that." Bertie snatched the card from Vance's loose fingers. "Sweet sassy molassy! We get to spend a night at the Pier in Santa Monica, with cocktails and dinner."

"We've hired a live band, and you'll have fun riding all the carnival rides. It's really beautiful at night," Katie added.

"And a tour of McKnight Studios—" Bertie gaped.

"Let me see that." Lucy reached for the invitation and started reading, with Brogan and Keith looking over her shoulder. "Spa day and shopping on Rodeo Drive *and* the bridesmaid luncheon at Spago!" Lucy and Bertie both squealed, gripping each other's hands.

"You haven't even gotten to the best part," Keith interjected, pointing at the card waving like a flag in Lucy's hand. "You're going down the red carpet at the Golden Globe awards."

"*What?*" Bertie and Lucy scanned the invitation until their eyes widened and their jaws dropped.

"Man, did you see the round of golf at the Los Angeles Country Club?" Brogan asked Keith.

"The *red carpet*?"

"I don't have a thing to wear—"

"Rodeo Drive, baby!"

Everyone talked excitedly at once, taking turns

reading the invitation. Katie pressed her hands together in a silent clap as the happiness she felt warmed her. She wanted her friends and anyone who could attend from Harmony to have a wonderful, star-filled, Hollywood experience. She would enjoy the festivities so much more through their eyes, knowing she never had to live there again.

"Excuse me." Vance cleared his throat. "But is there a wedding anywhere on that invitation?"

"Oh! Almost forgot..." Katie pulled another card from her bag, this one thick, ivory card stock with elegant charcoal engraving, displaying the McKnight family crest at the top. "Mr. and Mrs. Walter Douglas McKnight request the honor of your presence—" She read the first line and then stopped, looking up into Vance's expectant face. The face she never tired of. The last seven months had been the best of her life. She was working with children again, taking pictures, and becoming an active, respected citizen of a quirky, small Southern town. She'd carved a niche for herself and had grown a backbone. She loved everything. But most of all, she loved him. Katie wondered at the tremor she still felt in her belly as Vance stared at her. She pressed her hand against his warm cheek.

"Vance Kerner...will you marry me?" she whispered.

He turned into her hand, kissing her palm. "Absolutely. I'm yours, and you're mine...forever," he said without hesitation.

With misting eyes, she wrapped her arms around his waist, and he staggered her with his smile before his lips covered hers in one of his spectacular kisses.

"Hey, Kerner...looks like we're gonna be movie stars

after all." Vance slowly lifted his head and glowered at Clancy Perry standing at the edge of the patio, wearing creased jeans and red-and-white tuxedo T-shirt tucked in at the waist.

"What the hell are you talking about, Clancy?" Vance said between clenched teeth. Katie started to tremble, unable to control her laughter. Shaking his head, he turned to her. "Oh no, you didn't..." Vance scowled, and Katie clapped a hand over her mouth to stifle her unladylike snort.

Grinning like he'd just won the lottery, Clancy Perry waved one of Katie's invitations in the air. "Me and Clinton and heck, the whole dang town are showing up for your wedding in *Hooollly-woood*!" Clancy crowed.

"Oh my. Chuck and I will have to cut our three-month honeymoon short. 'Cause I'm not about to miss my favorite stepson's wedding." The newlywed, Dottie Duncan Kerner, rustled toward them, holding up wads of satin ruffles in her fists. Her lifted gown revealed dazzling white cowboy boots.

Brogan barked with laughter, and Vance slid him an evil look.

"Uncle Pance, I be the flower girl. Right, Kay-tee?" Danny barreled toward them, missing one shoe and the pink satin ribbon to her dress. Dover and Donald followed, their wedding outfits already sporting dirt and grass stains. Vance scooped Danny up in his arms, shifting her to his hip; he wrapped his other arm around Katie and pulled her in tight to his side.

Chuck smiled and reached for his granddaughter, freeing Vance's arm, and clasped Dottie's hand with his other. With half of Harmony laughing, toasting, and talking Hollywood, Vance tucked Katie behind a ruffled pink drape at the corner of the tent, blocking her view of the party. All she saw was him.

"You sure this is what you want?"

Throat tight, tears threatening, she nodded. "More than anything."

He held her gaze and then he grinned. "Me too."

Katie swallowed her laugh as Vance swept her off her feet and kissed her to the hoots and hollers of her new hometown.

Sweet *Southern* TROUBLE

Available Spring 2017 from
Sourcebooks Casablanca

MARABELLE DIDN'T SUCK AT EVERYTHING. SHE MADE A mouthwatering orange pound cake with chocolate ganache. She made the Wicked Witch come to life when she read aloud to her students. And she had a mean slice backhand that gave her opponents trouble on the tennis court. But when it came to biting her tongue and taking direction, she sucked.

"Marabelle, are you listening?"

Marabelle blinked several times to keep from dozing off as Mrs. Crow droned on and on at the tedious gala meeting. She forced her tired eyes to focus on the blue-and-gold-bound agenda in front of her. Marabelle's cell phone beeped, indicating a text.

"*Marabelle!*"

Marabelle straightened her posture, grappling to turn off her phone.

"Mrs. Evans is suggesting that you help with the auction as well as the coordination of the golf and tennis tournaments." Mrs. Crow enunciated as if Marabelle had comprehension problems.

Oh brother. Another project to add to her ever-growing list.

Marabelle shifted her attention to the bleached-blonde Mrs. Evans, head of the gala committee, and then to the other members seated around the conference table, all staring back as if a third eye had grown on her forehead.

"Why me?"

But Marabelle Fairchild already knew the answer to her own question. Brandon Aldridge. A five-year-old in her kindergarten class. Well, not him exactly, but rather his uncle, Nick Frasier, the famous NFL quarterback-turned-head-coach of the North Carolina Cherokees. Besides his impressive football career, Nick Frasier held the distinguished title of most eligible bachelor in the Raleigh-Durham area *and* the most smokin' hot and sexy. And Trinity Academy for Boys and Girls wanted this particular available hunk helping out with their fund-raiser. To be specific, the women across the polished mahogany conference table with undisguised lust in their eyes wanted him in ways that Marabelle did not care to contemplate.

"Marabelle, honey, you need to use your connections and…assets to convince Coach Frasier to participate." Carol Evans stumbled over the word "assets" as she clasped her yellow-diamond-encrusted fingers together.

Assets, my left toe. Compared to these perfectly coiffed women who looked as if they stepped out of the pages of *Vogue* on steroids, Marabelle felt like the poster child for unwanted orphans. Her wardrobe didn't help. She wore a navy-blue cardigan over a white button-down blouse, and could've passed for one of her kindergartners rather than a thirty-year-old with a master's degree in elementary education.

"We need to raise a considerable amount of money if we want to improve any of the playing facilities and add a permanent teaching position to the staff." Carol Evans spoke with a Yankeefied southern twang that grated on Marabelle's true-blue southern ears. It was a well-known fact that Carol Evans hailed from Trenton, New Jersey. But she'd married a native North Carolinian and had taken to her new identity faster than you could say, "Nothing could be finer than to be in Carolina."

At the mention of the teaching position, Marabelle's attention ratcheted up. She'd been barely eeking by on a teacher's assistant salary for the last three years, and she wanted nothing more than to be hired as a certified, permanent teacher.

Mrs. Crow said, "The board will seriously consider allocating monies we raise from the gala toward creating another teaching position if—"

"*If* I do what...exactly." Marabelle leaned forward in her chair and waited. She hated the age-old twisted plot of high society women out to one-up each other in the name of charity. She recognized the competitive gleam in their eyes and the tension around their mouths. Her own mother had worn that exact "game on" expression more times than Marabelle cared to remember. But she knew how the game was played and she was ready to deal.

"Clearly you don't understand what's at stake here," Mrs. Burrows, a native Tarheel, interjected as she played with a strand of perfect South Sea pearls around her neck.

She and Mrs. Evans gave each other "we're doomed" looks with the rise of their perfectly waxed eyebrows.

Marabelle definitely knew what was at stake…a significant increase in salary so she could continue to pay her mortgage without her mother bailing her out. A stand she took very seriously three years ago when she said no to her inheritance from her mother in order to be free. Marabelle put on her best schoolteacher face and said, "I know exactly what's at stake. You want to raise huge funds and you want Brandon Aldridge's famous uncle to participate by calling in a bunch of favors to all his celebrity friends and pro athletes who will donate sports memorabilia and money." This wasn't Marabelle's first rodeo.

"Well, yes, that's precisely what we want," Mrs. Evans said, sounding a bit startled at Marabelle's acumen. "Marabelle, honey, what we're all trying to say is you that don't exactly have the best track record. You remember last year's carnival?" Carol Evans sounded sympathetic while looking anything but.

Reaching for her water bottle, Marabelle took a huge gulp before addressing the committee. She needed to make a good impression. These women may have thought she had nothing in common with them, but they'd be dead wrong. Marabelle had lived in their world for years and had learned from the master. "Once again, I'm sorry about the mishaps at the carnival last year. But in my defense, the *minute* I noticed the clown was drunk, I had him escorted off the grounds. And the carny apologized for setting the Tilt-a-Whirl at warp speed." She omitted the part where he proceeded to proposition her.

"*Three* of our first graders were thrown into the holly bushes." Beak-Face Crow scowled. "Thanks to Mrs. Evans's husband, our school attorney"—she fluttered her hand in Carol's direction—"we avoided a costly law suit."

Marabelle had been thrust into taking over the volunteer job at the last minute, from a faculty member who'd suffered a broken foot. For the past three years, she'd been forced to "volunteer" a lot. Even though she hadn't booked the carnival company, her reputation had been on shaky ground ever since.

"So the committee, faculty, and I thought we would offer you another chance to…you know…shine, so to speak, *if* you acquire Coach Frasier's sponsorship…" Mrs. Crow's voice trailed off.

So, *that* was the catch. They planned to hold a teaching position hostage until she had hooked Coach Frasier for their cause. Brilliant! But her parents, Edna and Ed Fairchild, hadn't raised an idiot. Sarcastically, she blurted, "Why don't we raise some real money and have all the eligible bachelors auction themselves off to the highest bidder?"

The school conference room grew so quiet Marabelle could hear the sweep of the second hand on the oversized black-and-white clock hanging above the closed door. Mr. Turner, the only male member of the committee, stopped swiveling in his high-back leather chair. All eyes fixed on her. Marabelle twisted her hands in her lap to keep from clapping them over her mouth. She'd just catapulted herself from the frying pan into the fryer.

Beak-Face Crow cleared her throat, appearing very interested in the papers she shuffled between her bony fingers while the Blondie Twins, Mrs. Evans and Mrs. Burrows, grinned like the Grinch contemplating diabolical ways to steal Christmas.

Mrs. Cartwright, the eldest member of the committee, continued to needlepoint and without looking up from her stitches, said in her gravelly voice, "You've just come up with the only idea that might work. A live auction with the best-looking bachelors we can find."

Marabelle pitched forward, grasping the edge of the table until her knuckles turned white. "I was being facetious," she said through cold lips. "Nobody is going to agree to auction himself off to a room of drooling, miserable housewives with too much money. It's degrading."

"It's da bomb!" Carol Evans shouted in all her New Jersey glory. "A live bachelor auction! The perfect addition to this year's gala. I can see it now." Her eyes took on a dreamy quality while her hand floated in front of her face as if reading a marquee. "It will be a huge success. The mothers at St. Michael's are going to be *pea-green* with envy."

The image of besting her good friends, who gave of their time and money at St. Michael's, probably danced in Carol Evans's over-bleached head. Raleigh's high society had stringent requirements: children needed to attend either Trinity Academy or St. Michael's. The schools shared a long, bitter rivalry and just mentioning them in the same sentence was risky.

"I'm bidding on Coach Frasier. His abs make a great six pack," Mrs. Cartwright cackled as she snipped the end of a black thread.

Beak-Face Crow, the Blondie Twins, and even Mr.

Turner talked at once as their excitement escalated over the racy new element to be added to this fine Christian event.

Marabelle watched in horror. The tornado was heading her way and there was no stopping it.

―⁂―

Nick Frasier strolled into room B12, where his nephew attended kindergarten. He glanced around the empty classroom and then at his Rolex Submariner. Three minutes past four. The room appeared to have been swept clean of debris from a day of active kids. The small chairs pushed under the laminate desks looked like obedient little soldiers, and a hint of Lysol hung in the air as if the desktops had been wiped down. But no signs of life.

Until he heard grunting.

Nick's eyebrows rose as he caught sight of an attractive, heart-shaped ass poking out from under a wall of cabinets below the windows across the room. He spied hot-pink panties peeking from the bottom of a pleated skirt.

He double-checked his location.

This *was* where his nephew went to kindergarten. Hand-painted pictures tacked up willy-nilly, toys lining one wall, Play-Doh, paint smells. Yep.

So what kind of place were they running around here where young women showed their butts off to anyone who happened to walk by? Nick cleared his throat just as Miss Cute Ass yelled, "Gotcha!" and bumped her head scooting her way out from under the furniture.

"Shhhugar. That hurt."

A petite person struggled to stand with a very large

ball of caramel fur cradled in her arms. He remained unnoticed as she marched to the guinea pig cage on a nearby table and placed the furball on its wheel. She turned while brushing hair off her front, glanced up, and stopped short.

"Whoa, you're huge."

Miss Cute Ass gawked, but whether from fascination or fear, he couldn't tell. He figured she'd seen him on TV, of course, when the camera would pan the sidelines of a Cherokee game. He always wore a billed Cherokee cap like the one he had on today, but with a headset attached, and he usually paced up and down the sidelines, barking orders or reviewing plays on a beat-up clipboard. But against the other players, the Carolina blue skies, and evergreen pine trees, he imagined it could be hard to determine true size.

He smiled as she started babbling.

"I'm so sorry. I didn't mean to imply…it's just that you look much smaller on TV." She motioned with her hand. "Would you like some hand sanitizer?" She squirted some onto her palm from a huge commercial-size pump that sat on the edge of the teacher's desk. "You can never be too sanitary around here."

Nick couldn't agree more, but declined as she rubbed the clear goop over her palms and around the backs of her hands as if she were scrubbing up for surgery.

"Well, now we can shake hands without spreading germs." She thrust her small hand forward. "Hey, I'm Marabelle Fairchild, Brandon's teacher's assistant. Mrs. Harris is on maternity leave."

Brandon's *teacher*? She had to be kidding.

Nick masked his surprise as he engulfed her much

smaller hand in his, shaking it firmly but gently. "Nick Frasier, Brandon's uncle. I believe you wanted to meet with me about something?"

"Uh…Ms. Fairchild?" Coach Frasier gently shook her palm again. Marabelle stared at the end of her arm where her hand used to be, swallowed up within his warm grasp.

"Oh." Marabelle snatched her hand back as if she'd gotten too close to a burning flame. Her face blazed. God's nightgown, she needed to get herself back in the game.

Coach Frasier towered over her. He had to be about six four. *A fine specimen, indeed.* Chiseled from his jaw down to his toes, the perfect proportions created by his broad shoulders and a trim waist. Naturally sun-streaked, sandy-blond hair curled out from under his red cap. And golden-brown skin only highlighted his piercing blue eyes. The gods had kissed this guy but good. *No wonder all the women in this town want a piece of him.* Marabelle remembered the painful meeting the day before and what she had to do, and her stomach muscles tightened into a cramped ball.

"Take a seat, Coach Frasier, any seat," she said, dreading her next course of action. Coach Frasier arched a brow at the room full of miniature furniture.

"How 'bout I just prop myself up against your desk?"

Coach Frasier had a deceptively soft but husky voice. Marabelle had the strangest sensation of melting butter on top of a steaming bowl of homemade grits. Lord, this man was dangerous with a capital *D*!

Marabelle gave Coach Dangerous a covert glance from beneath her lashes as he rested one hip on the top of her desk. It wasn't so much what he wore as *how* he wore it. He made ordinary clothes look extraordinary. His off-white Nike fleece pullover with the Cherokee tomahawk logo hugged his mile-wide shoulders, and his well-worn jeans, snugly fit to showcase his muscled thighs, dropped comfortably over expensive brown ostrich-skin boots. *Why do all football players have to play cowboy?*

A large hand waved in front of her face. "Ms. Fairchild?"

"Sorry. I was having a moment." Marabelle erased the fantasy of playing cowgirl to his sexy Clint Eastwood and marched around her desk. "Um…just let me get my folder." She rustled through a stack of papers, hoping to get her mind out of the gutter and back on track.

"Is Brandon in some kind of trouble? Is he doing well in school?"

Marabelle's head popped up, the shuffled papers forgotten. "Oh no. Brandon is completely out of control and in danger of becoming much worse, but that's not why I called you here."

Coach Frasier's head jerked back. "Excuse me? Do you really teach here?" he asked.

Wishing she could shove her words back down her own throat, Marabelle gulped. Probably not the best time to bring up Brandon's awful behavior.

"Uh, yes, and I'm sorry if my comment offended you. But don't you think it would be better if you knew the truth? About your nephew, that is."

⌇⌇⌇⌇

Was this some kind of joke? Stumped, Nick openly studied this woman, not caring if she noticed.

No, make that half-woman, half-urchin with curly brown hair wrestled on top of her head in some claw-like device. She couldn't be more than five feet, if that. Nick's gaze tracked from her head to her feet. The extra-large gray Trinity Raiders sweatshirt she wore swallowed her entire upper body and fell somewhere midthigh, and a black-and-white-plaid pleated skirt peeked out as if gasping for air.

The only thing with any shape was her legs, and they were nicely formed. Slender ankles and muscled calves showed that she exercised regularly. Small, narrow feet sported a pair of Nike tennis shoes. No glamour in that footwear. Nick's gaze traveled back up her bulky form and landed on a faint blue paint smudge on her right cheek, which somehow seemed fitting. After sizing her up, he couldn't help but mentally question the credibility of the school. She should be *taking* the class, not teaching it.

Marabelle twisted her hands and gnawed her bottom lip. "Coach Frasier, may I be perfectly frank?"

"Have you ever been anything else?"

She hesitated before answering. "Well, no, but I think it's an admirable trait."

Nick bit the inside of his cheek to keep from smiling. "Then certainly don't change on my behalf."

Blinking huge chocolate-brown eyes, her expression grew more determined. Her face, sans the paint, was attractive. Faint freckles were scattered across her small, pert nose, but her mouth, by far the main attraction, had that bee-stung look that Hollywood stars coveted. For a moment, he wondered if her lips were as soft as they were full, if she tasted…

Where had those thoughts come from? *She's a kindergarten teacher, for chrissakes*. He punted those unwanted thoughts right out of the stadium, and got his head back in the game by focusing on her small hands, which seemed to talk even more than her sexy, full mouth.

Marabelle paced in front of the large dry-erase board. "Trinity Academy has a very important fund-raiser every spring that the whole community supports, and this year is going to be extra special, because they're raising money to improve the football field and add two more tennis courts. And—"

Nick had heard this pitch a million times. Same set-up, different location. "And you want me to contribute to the fund? Right?"

She stopped pacing. "Well, it's more than just your money. Don't get me wrong, your money is *huge*." Nick chuckled at her lack of tact, but she ignored him, intent on lining up dry-erase markers in alternating colors.

"We need your help in contacting your celebrity friends and asking them to participate in the golf and tennis tournaments," she said, leaning the markers against the board. "And we want you to ask the single, eligible men you know to sell themselves in our bachelor auction," she finished all in one breath and turned, knocking all the markers to the floor.

"Um, what?" Nick shook his head as he bent to help her gather the scattered markers. This had to be a joke. "Are you secretly filming me for YouTube or something? Is this some sort of practical joke?" He'd had enough of being secretly filmed to last a lifetime, and if this fairy-tale character thought she could pull a fast one on him, she had no idea who she was up against. His gaze darted around the classroom, searching for a hidden camera. The room looked clean. Then he smirked. "Did my offensive coordinator set this up?"

Kneeling on the floor, Marabelle's brows puckered. "Who?"

Nick handed over three reds and two blues. "Coach Prichard. We've been arguing about the draft, but I didn't think he was *this* upset."

Right on cue, she turned stern schoolteacher. Standing, she released the handful of markers on the metal tray, her back as straight as if fused with a goalpost. "Coach Frasier, this is not some reality TV show and I don't even know your offensive coordinator. But if he's upset, I suggest you make nice and maybe you guys will start winning some ballgames."

Splaying hands on his hips, he narrowed his eyes and delivered one of his fiercest stares. "You tetched in the head or something? Are *you* telling me how to coach a professional football team?"

Marabelle didn't flinch. A room full of five-year-olds must be tougher than he thought. Curling her fingers around a ruler in the metal tray as if she might rap his knuckles, she said in the same firm schoolteacher voice, "If there's dissension among your staff, it would be prudent to smooth things over. Arguing with your staff is bound to affect the players. It just goes to reason." *Tap, tap* went the ruler in her palm.

Nick swore under his breath. Many a rookie had backed down from his most intimidating stare. Its effect was legendary. But not on crazy Marabelle. "Ms. Fairchild,

you don't know jack shit about coaching football."
Nick rarely lost his temper off the field, but she'd
managed to push all his buttons. Nick knew his young
team had struggled last season. He certainly didn't need
reminding from little Miss Muffet. He had the team's
owner, general manager, and the press for that. But Nick
believed in his team. They had raw talent, and with good
coaching and proper discipline, they'd only get better.
Yet it still rankled when confronted with their less-than-
stellar record.

He didn't need this hassle. "I'm out of here," he
muttered, starting for the door.

"Coach Frasier, please wait!"

Nick whipped around to squash the crazy ruler-toting
fairy once and for all, when three high school boys
barged through the classroom door, carrying large tennis
bags over their shoulders.

"Hey, Coach, you comin' to practice today?"

"What?" The theme song from *The Twilight Zone* played
in his head. Why would he be coming to practice here?

"Whoa! You're Nick Frasier," said the tallest of the
boys as all three gazes landed on him.

Nick plastered on a smile, not wanting his scowl to be
reported all over social media. "Hey, guys. What's up?"
All three eagerly shook his hand, talking at once. "You
boys play for the tennis team?" Nick asked in between
introductions and hand pumping.

"Yeah. We're heading to practice and wondering if
Coach is coming."

"Coach?" Still confused, he searched their faces.

"Surprise, surprise," Marabelle chimed softly next
to him.

Chapter 2

"LISTEN, GUYS, START YOUR WARM-UP WITHOUT ME," Marabelle said.

After several more minutes of slobbering over Coach Frasier, the boys left for the courts. Marabelle pushed the heavy classroom door closed to the celebratory high fives, taking a moment to inhale much-needed air to calm her nerves. She turned, facing the man who stood between her and a successful auction…and her future.

"Um, could we start over?"

"You're a *coach*?"

Marabelle barely refrained from smacking her forehead with her open palm. She half chuckled, half smirked. "For the varsity tennis teams."

Surprise lit Coach Frasier's expression. "You actually play?"

"Since I was six." Time to steer the conversation back to her cause: approval from the board and a permanent teaching position. Marabelle clasped her hands together and in a steady voice, said, "Let's see if we can focus here. I'll start by apologizing for fouling this whole thing up—"

"You don't look like a tennis player. You barely look like you can ride a tricycle."

Marabelle stepped closer, ignoring her quivering belly, determined to say her piece and get back to the reason for this meeting. "There's an entire world of sports beyond football out there. You should give some of them a try. Besides, what I lack in stature, I make up for in guts. Now, can we get back to the business at hand?"

Coach Frasier peered down at her, his gaze zeroing in on her mouth. Heat crept up her face under his intense scrutiny. She nervously slicked her bottom lip with her tongue and could've sworn he groaned.

"Okay, Ms. Fairchild, start from the beginning."

The tension in her shoulders eased as she exhaled. She explained how she was responsible for the tournaments and securing eligible men for the auction, barely managing to omit that her independence, pride, and sense of worth were all at stake. Marabelle had thrown away a fortune…literally. She couldn't afford to screw this up.

"So will you do it?" She crossed her fingers behind her back.

Coach Frasier relaxed his hip against her desk again. He crossed his powerful arms and tilted his head, his mesmerizing blue eyes making a slow glide from her forehead down to her tennis shoes. Marabelle nervously shifted her weight from one foot to the other. If she'd been the kind of woman who fussed over her appearance, she would've been insulted by his blatant perusal. But she wasn't here to win a beauty contest. She had a job to do.

His scrutiny felt like hours instead of mere seconds. Finally, his gaze landed back on her face. "No offense, Ms. Fairchild, but are you the best this school has to offer?"

"None taken. And yes, compared to the rest of the staff, I actually look pretty good." She gave a nervous laugh. "Hard to believe, huh?"

Coach Frasier's gorgeous head fell back as he burst

out laughing, flashing straight white teeth. He had one of those warm, masculine laughs.

Marabelle liked it—a lot.

Smiling, she pushed up the sleeves to her sweatshirt. "Okay, okay, so I'm not in the big league." Damn, her small stature always put her at a disadvantage.

"Honey, you aren't even in the Pee Wee league," he said between hoots. "Has the committee ever conversed with you? I'm no expert or anything, but you kinda lack the finesse for winning friends and influencing people." Coach Frasier grinned.

Marabelle shot a grin right back, mimicking his body language by folding her arms. "I have zero tact. That particular gene skipped me. But I'm a damn good teacher and the students love me. Crazy as this sounds, I relate much better to children—"

"Now *that* I believe!"

"—and if I strike this deal with the sexiest, most famous guy Raleigh has ever seen, I will improve my status here at the school in a big way." Now there was the understatement of the century.

She bent to straighten a cup of crayons on one of the small desks when Coach Frasier entered her space. "You think I'm sexy?" he said in his smoky voice.

Marabelle straightened her shoulders. "Give me a break. Like I'm telling you something you haven't heard since coming out of the womb. You and I both know that every single woman and half the married ones would sing 'The Star Spangled Banner' *naked* on the fifty-yard line at the Super Bowl just to go out with you."

"Now that sounds promising. Would you?"

Coach Frasier moved so close, the glittery blue of his

eyes showed flecks of steel gray. An involuntary shiver ran up her spine. Marabelle knew what the feeling meant and didn't like it. At. All.

"Good God—no! You are not my type." She flapped her hands as if to brush him away, swaying back to regain her equilibrium.

"What do you mean, I'm not your type?" Coach Frasier boxed her in with the door to her back. "Are you gay?"

Of course he would think that was the only logical reason not to want him. This close, the intoxicating smell of spice and lemon filled her nose. Marabelle's mouth watered. If he'd been a dish, she would've eaten him on the spot.

She chose to refocus on his face instead of his edible broad chest, and almost groaned at the unfairness of it all. Swallowing her frustrated sigh, she said, "Why is it that every time a woman says she's not interested in a man, she's automatically assumed to be a lesbian?"

"Because she usually is." Amusement lifted the corner of his mouth.

"Hardly. Because your inflated ego cannot fathom that a woman might not be interested in you."

Coach Frasier moved back, allowing Marabelle to draw air into her deprived lungs, but her breath clogged her throat as he pulled keys from his pocket.

He can't leave now. He jiggled the keys in his hand. "Ms. Fairchild, as stimulating as this conversation has been, you haven't said anything compelling to convince me to sell my friends and myself for the cause. I'm afraid I need to be going, unless there's something important you have to tell me about Brandon."

Marabelle's hard-earned independence flashed before her eyes. If she didn't get his cooperation, her mother's prediction of failing would come true.

Unthinkable.

"No, wait," Marabelle said.

Nick peered down at her hand on his forearm, and she released him as if embarrassed. Man, he'd been working too hard if that innocent touch caused heat to shoot from his arm straight to his groin.

Marabelle reached for a folder on top of her desk. "I know I'm not the best salesperson for the job, but if you would take this packet and read it over, I think you'll change your mind." Hope shimmered in her huge brown eyes and Nick felt like crap crushing it.

What the hell. He gave a quick nod and took the glossy marketing packet, slapping it several times against his thigh.

Then Marabelle smiled. Really smiled, lighting her entire face, and Nick felt dizzy. A megawatt smile capable of making him forget about her abrupt personality, hideous outfit, and the fact that she was probably gay.

Spellbound, he said against his better judgment, "Okay, Tinker Bell. I'll read your packet." Her smile turned high beam, like the sun breaking over the horizon. "I'm not making any promises," he quickly amended, still unable to avert his gaze.

"Got it. So, when can we meet to discuss the prospects?"

Nick hesitated and then glanced at the keys he'd palmed. "Uh…I'll call you." The oldest line in history, and it failed miserably. Marabelle's megawatt smile faded like a lightbulb growing dim. He needed to get the hell out of here before he made promises he didn't want to keep.

Nick extended his hand. "Tinker Bell, it's been interesting, to say the least."

"Coach Frasier, I'm afraid I can't let you go."

"What?" Nick's hand hung in midair.

Suddenly, he watched in shock as Marabelle threw her back against the classroom door, spread-eagle, barring his exit. "You're going to have to agree to another meeting before I allow you to leave."

Nick's jaw dropped. *Allow me to leave?* "Or what? You threatening me?"

Marabelle's chin shot up a notch as she remained plastered to the door. "Y-yes. You gotta go through me if you want out this door. Or…we could be civilized about this and you can agree to another meeting."

Nick rubbed his hand over his face. "Did you forget to take your meds? Because I outweigh you by at least a hundred and ten pounds, and I don't want to hurt you."

Marabelle physically gulped. "Yeah, but I'm tenacious, not to mention desperate."

"Tinker Bell, I'm warning you. *Move away from the door.*"

Her stubborn chin quivered but she ignored his threat. "Promise to meet me next week."

Professional football players had more fear than this crazy fairy, or maybe they just had more sense, because Marabelle Fairchild shook in her little Nike shoes, but she was sticking.

At some point, Nick had made up his mind to meet

with her again because she'd been the most interesting weirdo he'd ever encountered and she made him laugh. And lately, there'd been a shortage on laughter in his life. But *no way* could he let her think she could take him.

Nick cursed low. "You can't say I didn't warn you." Dumping his keys back in his pocket and tossing the gala folder on top of a small desk, he wrapped his hands around her waist, lifting her away from the door. Marabelle flung her arms around his neck and coiled her legs around his hips, clinging to him as if he were a life raft in a turbulent sea.

"*What the—?*" Nick's jolt matched the utter shock written on Marabelle's face.

"Promise me and I'll let go!" she blurted.

Nick froze. This was no girl he held in his arms. Womanly curves teased his hands through her hideously bulky clothes. She was luscious and soft in all the right places. The urge to peel away the layers to see what lay beneath flexed his fingers. Flashes of hot-pink panties covering a heart-shaped ass replayed in his head.

Nick's entire body stiffened…including his cock. Marabelle's eyes flared even wider.

"*Marabelle.*" He tried disengaging her arms without hurting her, but she squeezed tighter.

"Please," she begged.

"Monday afternoon. My office. Same time," Nick gritted through his locked jaw. Anything to get her out of his arms before he did something really stupid.

Her stranglehold loosened and she slowly slid her legs down his rigid thighs.

The betrayal of his own body pissed him off. He

pushed away temptation a little more roughly than he intended. "Agreed?" The tic in his right jaw flared to life.

Unaware of his tenuous control, Marabelle nodded. "Thank you so much, Coach Frasier. Sorry about my strong-arm tactics, but I had to make you see reason. I *swear* you won't be sorry." Nick watched as her face morphed into an innocent cherub, making him instantly leery.

"I already am," he snapped. "Is it safe for me to leave now, or are you hiding a hand grenade in your desk drawer?"

"No. But I almost forgot." Marabelle lunged toward her desk and scooped up a manila folder sitting on top. "This is the progress report on your nephew. We can discuss it on Monday when we meet. Monday afternoon. Your office. Same time, right?" she confirmed.

With the folder in his hand, he reached for the door. "Until Monday, Ms. Fairchild." Then he touched the bill of his cap in a mock salute and walked out.

Acknowledgments

So many people to thank and so little space. As always, a team of people have helped, not only with this book, but with putting up with me in the process.

First and foremost, a million thanks to the many bloggers, reviewers, book lovers, and wonderful readers who have encouraged and supported me along this writing journey. You make me keep my fingers on the keyboard.

Thank you to the team at Sourcebooks, including Cat Clyne and Deb Werksman, for their editing skills, and for the staff's support in making sure Vance and Katie got their HEA.

To my agent, Nicole Resciniti, for being the calm voice of reason.

Paint Boss One and Two...by believing in my ability and sticking with me through my illness, you saved my family and me. I give thanks every day for you and my job.

And PFA, thanks for always talking me off the ledge and for sharing Lenny when the chores need to be done.

Thanks, Inz! For your name and inspiring your character!

And finally to my many friends, my husband, and family, especially my son and daughter...my love for you will never waver.

About the Author

Michele Summers writes about small-town life with a Southern flair. When not making up stories, she has her own interior design business in Raleigh, North Carolina, and Miami, Florida, where she lived for over twenty years. Both professions feed her creative appetite and provide a daily dose of humor. These days she also stays busy herding her two teenage kids. Michele's work has won recognition from the Beacon, Dixie First Chapter, Golden Palm, Fool For Love, Rebecca, and Fabulous Five contests. She is an active member of the Heart of Carolina and Florida Romance Writers chapters of RWA. You can contact Michele at her website, www.michelesummers.com, where you will also locate her other social media buttons.